THE RESENTMENT

ILLICIT LOVE
BOOK ONE

ASHLEE ROSE

OTHER BOOKS BY ASHLEE ROSE

Standalones:

Unwanted

Promise Me

Savage Love

Tortured Hero

Something Worth Stealing

Dear Heart, You Screwed Me

Signed, Sealed, Baby

Series:

Something New

Something To Lose

Something Everlasting

Before Her

Without Her

Forever Her

Duet:

Love Always, Peyton

Forever Always, Knight

Way Back When Duet

Novellas:

Welcome to Rosemont

Rekindle Us

Your Dirty Little Secret

A Savage Reunion

Risqué Read Novellas:

Seeking Hallow

Craving Hex

Seducing Willow

Wanting Knox

———————

All available on Amazon Kindle Unlimited

Only suitable for 18+ due to nature of the books.

Quietly, she fell apart – R.H. Sin

READERS NOTE:

This is a follow on from Dear Heart, You Screwed Me.

It is strongly recommended that you read Dear Heart, You Screwed Me before The Resentment so you have a better understanding of their background story as Connie is Killian's daughter.

Please be aware that Reese is British, so there may be words or phrases that may not be used in America, which is where this book is based. Kaleb and Connie are American. This is not a grammatical error but written in the correct form from her POV.

I always like my readers to go into one of my stories blind, but if you wish to check trigger warnings then please check the next page.

TRIGGER WARNING

Sexual Assault
Suicide
Depictions of Domestic Violence
Depictions of Rape

PROLOGUE

I SAT ON THE TOUR BUS A SHADOW OF MY FORMER SELF. HOW could I have been so stupid and naïve. Everything I thought I knew was a lie.

My moms both lied to me.

My dad lied to me.

And worst of all, I had that vile, hag of a woman who was my birth mom.

The hate that coursed through my veins at the thought made me feel sick.

I wasn't going back.

As soon as those words left my father's mouth, I ran until I couldn't run any more.

I confronted my moms, they didn't have to say anything; their faces said it all. They were full of guilt and deceit and that's what broke me the most. The fact that they couldn't even find the words to tell me what had happened. How it had happened.

Maybe I could have forgiven them all if they took the time out to tell me the truth, but by the time they were ready to actually sit me down and talk about it. It was too late.

I had already lost any sadness I had. I just wanted out.

I wanted to run away.

Away from New York.

Away from my moms.

Away from my dad and definitely away from the bitch of a dead-beat mom.

So, what do you do when you want to run away and escape reality for a little bit?

You become a groupie and tour with your rockstar boyfriend.

Maybe I will forgive, but I will never forget.

Ever.

The only one who didn't screw me over was Reese, aside from the fact that she was having a secret relationship with my dad. So yeah, she did screw me over thinking about it. But she is still my best friend so when I am ready, I'll call her.

I would meet up with her and explain everything. But for now, I want to numb out the pain with alcohol, sex, drugs and rock 'n' roll.

Goodbye to innocent Connie.

Hello reckless and scorned Connie.

You haven't seen nothing yet, and I can't wait for you to read my story.

I BET YOU THOUGHT I WOULD STILL BE ON TOUR AND BE WITH THE love of my life, Tryst. Right?

Well, wrong.

You thought wrong.

Life doesn't always go as planned, as my old best friend used to like reminding me. There is no white horse. There is no fairy-tale. There is no happily ever after.

Just when things had started to go to shit, I found Tryst balls deep with a groupie.

I didn't want to go back home, but right now, home seemed the best place for me.

But before we talk about that we have a lot to catch up on, so sit back and buckle up.

Love, Connie X

CHAPTER ONE

THREE MONTHS AGO

STUMBLING ONTO THE TOUR BUS, ALCOHOL SWAM THROUGH MY veins and drugs pumped through my blood stream. Before Tryst, I had never been one to dabble in anything other than alcohol, but since Tryst, getting high on whatever I can get my hands on is becoming a regular occurrence. Deep down I do it to numb everything; to numb the emotions that my *family* put me through. My stomach rolls with nausea, my calm mood beginning to be consumed by rage at what they have done. At how they treated me.

I kicked the floor with my heavy boots before falling down on the sofa, my head falls back off the edge, hitting the tour bus window. I inhale deeply before letting out a heavy sigh, the weight of the resentment crushing my lungs.

"Sugar," Tryst kneels next to me, his hand fisting my matted brown hair, pulling me up to look at him but I couldn't steady my gaze. "Come and ride me," he licks his lips before lowering his over mine, "then I promise, I'll get you the good stuff you want." He winks, his spare hand gripping my cheeks as he dips his tongue into my mouth and my body instantly relaxes.

Tryst was amazing at the beginning, promising me a free life of rock 'n' roll, but the promise soon fell short as *Chord* grew bigger and bigger, and to Tryst, I grew smaller and smaller. It was him, Callaghan and Rox. The members of Chord. They were his priority, not me. Now he only wants me when he needs his blue balls rectified. I'm happy to oblige, at least I feel something.

He got me addicted to things I should never be addicted to, and now he uses them as a bribe, and I lap up his demands like a child who'd been promised candy.

On some level I knew I had a problem; I knew I needed help. But help wasn't coming. No one was.

CHAPTER TWO

LYING IN BED, MY EYES WERE PINNED TO THE HOTEL CEILING. I was sick of living in the tour bus and after a very heated conversation, Tryst finally broke and booked us a hotel for when we got to London. This was our first night, and I'm glad I begged because it had paid off. The four of us were put up in *The Berkley*. Tugging the comforter up to my chin, I lay still as Tryst's loud snores filled the room. My head was pounding, my body aching and my mouth as dry as the desert. The not so nice reminder of my high last night. Every morning I vow to not get in that state again, but every night I do.

Turning my head slowly, I look over to where Tryst is laying on his front. His black, messy hair sticking up, his pale skin covered and dotted with random tattoos. He gets a new one in every country he tours in, sort of like a souvenir I suppose.

I would be lying if I said I didn't love Tryst, but I don't think I'm *in* love with him anymore. This is not the life I

7

wanted for myself. The private jets, the screaming fans and the paparazzi. Some may love this lifestyle, but not me.

It was so exciting at first, exhilarating even but, now, it was just *too* much.

I wanted so much more than this. So much more than I have.

I deserve better than this. I knew that and so did Tryst, but he also knew I wouldn't leave him.

He had the leash and collar bound tightly around my throat.

But that doesn't stop my thoughts from wondering that maybe, just maybe there is still a small slither of hope that I will be whisked away on a white horse with my prince.

Until then, I just get through the days.

Dressed in an oversized black *Palm Angel* tee and black cycling shorts, I slipped my feet into my Doc Marten boots and grabbed my bag, finishing the look with my NY hat. Running my fingers through the ends of my long, brown hair and detangling the knots from the wispy ends. Letting out a soft sigh as I rubbed lip balm into my dry and cracked lips, I was ready.

I needed to get out for a while. Tryst was still sleeping, and I was fed up waiting for him. Pushing out the main bedroom and into the large open planned lounge, I keep my head down, not wanting to catch anyone's attention.

We're staying in the Crescent Pavilion Penthouse. Only the best of the best for Tryst, but at least we weren't sleeping in that shitty tour bus every night.

"Hey, sweet stuff, where you off to?" I hear Rox shout behind me as I head for the front door.

"Out," I snap.

"Tryst won't be happy sweetness," he continues to call out as I grab a key card and open the door.

"Well, Tryst will get over it." I spin and smile, flipping Rox off before letting the door click closed behind me. Pressing the elevator button, I wait as I tap my boot to the floor. Slipping in and pressing the button for the ground floor I feel my anxiety begin to creep up my throat the longer I wait, worrying that Tryst will be hot on my heels because Rox, is a fucking snitch. I used to be so carefree, so breezy, but now? I was an anxiety filled train wreck, the drugs certainly didn't help with that and was one of the reasons I decided to get clean a month or so ago.

Breathing out a steady breath, I paced quickly across the lobby floor. The cream high glossed tiles shone brightly as my heavy boots thumped across them. Eyes were on me, the panic rose up my throat as my heart thrashed in my chest, the blood pumping in my ears that someone would recognise who I was. My eyes fell to my boots, counting my footsteps in my head and not looking up. It helped ease the nervousness that swam deep in my belly, if only slightly.

"Good morning, ma'am," the chirpy, impeccably dressed doorman greeted me as I got to the front of the hotel. I let my eyes flick up from the floor to see a few paparazzi outside, waiting like lions stalking their helpless prey. That was me. I was the helpless prey.

"Shit," I hiss, stopping in my tracks and moving to the side and out of sight.

"Is everything okay?" the polite, British doorman asks me. Squeezing my eyes shut, my head falls back against the wall as I gasp for air, willing my body to be able to breathe instead of suffocating.

"I need a minute," I pant, opening my eyes and focusing on the ceiling.

"Are the paparazzi here for you?" he steps towards me cautiously, concern lacing his voice as his head dips so his eyes can find mine. Turning to look at him, my heart slows slightly. His grey hair neatly trimmed under his hat, his kind, blue eyes on me as he watches my every expression, my every move. He calmed my erratic heart in seconds.

I was a socialite now, since being with Tryst and being there from the beginning of Chord's career. My social media blew up, the fans trying to see a little bit of Chord that they would never normally see. I was always pictured, followed and spoken too. I loved it at the beginning, but with that fame comes privacy discrimination. I never got a moment to myself.

I nod, swallowing the large lump down my tight throat. "And my boyfriend," I rasp as my eyes prick with tears, the familiar burn making itself known in my chest.

"Let me take you out the back way..." he ushers, his hand resting on my lower back as he walks me back across the lobby. "They're parasites; vermin," his voice is low, mumbling his words as we reach a fire exit.

"Go out that way, you should be able to escape them," he smiles softly at me then reaches into the inside of his tails suit jacket and pulls out a card, holding it out for me.

"When you're heading back, call this number and someone will let you in. Tell them that Ernest told you," he winks and tips his hat.

Tears prick behind my eyes at the kindness of this stranger, and I choke a laugh as I flip the card between my fingertips, watching it as I do. I want to thank him, but I cannot muster the words, my throat is tight and thick. I look up at him, scared to blink because as soon as I do the tears will fall and I don't want to cry anymore.

"I'll see you soon," he smiles then turns and walks back towards the main doors.

Swallowing the large lump down, I push out of the back exit and welcome the air that fills my lungs, a slight burn as I inhale sharply. This would be the time I would find my next hit, but I have been clean for just over a month.

One night me and Tryst were so intoxicated, things got heated and Tryst got more handsy with me than usual. He had never done anything like that to me before, but I couldn't stop him even if I wanted to. I was too *wasted* and I vowed to myself I would never let myself get in a situation like that again where I was completely helpless. Where I couldn't defend myself. Where I couldn't stop him if things went too far; so from the next morning, I've been clean.

Walking through *Harrods,* I aimlessly browse the aisles. There is nothing I want or need, but I can't help but look. My fingers run over the clothes, and I feel an ache in my chest as emotion swarms me. Rubbing my heart through my tee, my mind drifts back to when me and Reese used to go shopping. I hate that we don't talk, she still messages me but I'm not ready to message her back, not yet anyway. Days like today, all I want to do is click her name and speak to her, just so I could hear her voice. She always made everything better. But I had to do this on my own. I'm not ready to forgive the betrayal from any of them. They all betrayed me one way or another.

I scoff out loud, shaking my head as my fingers skim through the rails of hanging clothes. They're not my moms. My heart hurts, my chest aching at the realisation. Everything I knew was a lie and it wrecked my life. I feel like I don't belong. Everything I knew was fabricated, I lived in a fantasy world with two loving, kind moms. But then I woke up, and my life has been like a walking nightmare, filled with never ending darkness since; a nightmare I physically cannot wake up from.

Walking round in a daze, I find myself in the bag section, my eyes widen when I look at their stock. I don't need another bag, but I *want* another bag. They say you replace one addiction with another, and I guess this is my new addiction.

An hour later I walk out of *Harrods* with clothes, shoes and a pretty new *Chloé* bag. Slipping my sunglasses on, I burst out onto the busy streets of London as I continue my spending. Joys of having Tryst's card. The man has more money than sense since he was signed and is now part of one of the most known bands in the world.

Dropping my bags to the floor, I sit in a busy patisserie and let my eyes roam the room looking for a waitress before I realise it's a counter order. Puffing out my cheeks, I push away from the table, grabbing my bags as I do and join the queue.

"Good afternoon," the young lady smiles behind the counter, "what can I get you?"

"Umm," I stammer, looking in the glass counter, "I'll have an almond croissant and an oat milk latte please." Smiling, I tap my card then move to the end of the counter. Taking the tray that my food and coffee are on, I turn and head towards my table to see someone sitting in my seat. My brows furrow as I stand still, my eyes roaming over the older man that is sitting where I was. His hair is jet black and neatly styled. The sides are short with flecks of grey scattered through, but the top is long and tousled. His grey eyes met mine, they have flecks of blue and green imbedded into them. I watch as he holds his coffee in one hand, newspaper in the other. His jaw is angled and sharp and all I can think about in that moment is how it would feel to graze my lips against the edge of his chiselled jaw. His cheeks have a hint of red smudged into them, was he hot? Flustered? Or did he just have rosy, glowing skin? The rest of his skin tone had a light, golden, almost glowing feel to it. My eyes continue to roam over his beautiful face a little too long as I focus on his lips, my head tilting to the side ever so slightly. He has a pronounced cupid bow; his bottom lip thick and heavy set and I bet he would do a killer pout if you asked him. They're full and pink, his upper lip running a little thinner. I knew he would be a good kisser, the kind where he would linger a little longer than you, he would brush soft, gentle kisses just to get started before his lips would move with the rhythm of your heartbeat before widening them and letting his tongue dance with yours.

My heart skips a beat a little quicker in my chest as I try and control my thoughts. I would say he was around my dad's age, late forties maybe and when I hear him clear his throat, knowing full well I have been staring just a little too long at him, I snap out of it, placing my tray on the table then dropping my bags to the floor. My hands on my hips as I stand with a powerful stance, so he knew I wasn't going to let him push me over.

"You're in my seat," my tone is clipped and curt as I scowl, my brows digging into my skin.

"Am I?" he looks around the busy coffee shop, shrugging his shoulders up in a nonchalant way, before his eyes meet mine.

"Yes," I snap, irritation coursing through me.

"You must be confused," he gently chuckles, his American accent thick and I feel a little more at ease knowing he is from across the water like me. "No one was sitting here when I came in."

"Because I was queuing!" my voice a little louder now, "I was sat here before! But didn't want to leave my bags!"

His greying eyes move to my bags that are now sat on the floor before flicking those beautiful grey pools back to mine, "It doesn't work like that sweetheart."

Scrunching my nose up, my brows pinch. "Don't call me sweetheart." What is it with men and calling me sweetheart? *Ick.*

"You're more than welcome to sit down with me," he kicks the chair out that's opposite him.

"I suppose I don't have a choice do I," I groan, looking round at all the full tables.

Stropping and flopping down I cross my arms across my chest. My stubborn streak coursing through my veins and as much as I am happy to sit down and be in close proximity to this hand-crafted God, I still can't shake my mood.

"Are you always a sulking brat?" he groans, sitting back in his chair, his self-entitled ass reading The Financial Times as he sips his small, pathetic coffee.

"Only when entitled douche bags take my seat."

He clenches his jaw, causing it to tick, his eyes ablaze as he stares me down, "It wasn't your seat."

"Whatever, Gramps," I smirk, twisting my lips and sip my coffee.

"Gramps?!" he chokes, lurching forward and folding his newspaper and placing it on the table. My eyes sweep over his left hand and see no wedding band sitting on his finger, but that doesn't mean anything really, does it?

"Yup," I pout, tearing my croissant apart though suddenly I'm not even hungry. "You're very old," I nod.

"Whatever darling," he rolls his eyes, crossing his legs one over the other, shaking his head from side to side, then picking his newspaper up again and opening it with a little more gusto than needed.

"Finally," I let out a deep sigh, "I don't have to look at your ugly face anymore."

"So immature," he tuts, and somehow, I know he is smiling.

And I smirk, sitting quietly as I finish my coffee. Mr grumpy is actually very handsome, making this crappy day a little better.

CHAPTER THREE

Walking towards the hotel, my steps falter slightly when I see the group of paparazzi has grown considerably since I left this morning. Slipping Ernest's card out of my purse, I call the number that's noted down.

"Good afternoon, *The Berkley,* Robert speaking."

My heart drums in my chest, my palms begin to sweat as I step further back away from the hotel.

"Hi, hi…" I stammer, "my name is Connie Marsden; I spoke to Ernest this morning and he told me to call to get into the back of the hotel…" I sigh, "to be able to get into the hotel without the paparazzi seeing me," my voice lowers, changing to a whisper.

"Not a problem, ma'am. Walk around the side, I'll let you in."

"Thank you," cutting my phone off, I step back and turn down the side of the hotel without being seen. I did not need a run in with the paparazzi to ruin my mood. Plus, the more I am photographed, the more my dad can see, and I don't want him knowing my whereabouts. But, if I'm being honest with myself, I think he knows exactly where I am.

Reaching out to knock on the door, it swung open to a younger, well-dressed man smiling at me who looked like a younger version of Ernest.

"Connie?" he tipped his head before his eyes moved behind me to make sure the coast was clear.

I nodded, ducking my head and rushing past him. The heavy, metal door clunked closed behind us and I let out a sigh of relief.

"Thank you so much," I smiled as I let the bags drop to the floor, letting my fingers bend and straighten, stretching them.

"My pleasure, my dad, Ernie told me to keep a look out for you," he winked as he bent down to pick my bags up and began walking towards the lift.

"Oh, please, let me take them... honestly," my cheeks blazed red.

"It's fine, I'll take them up to your room for you." Rubbing my lips, anxiety swam through me. What if Tryst's possessiveness was out in force today and he caused a scene? What if he hurt Robert after he and his father had been so kind to me?

Swallowing the nerves down, I stepped into the elevator and waited for Robert to join me.

"Honestly, I really could just take them... it really is no bother."

"I know it's not, but it's also no bother for me taking them either," he smiles as a soft laugh leaves him. He pushes a key into the lift and presses for the penthouse we're staying in.

"How has your stay been so far?" he asks, making easy and light conversation.

"A little rushed, there is so much I want to see, I just don't think I'll squeeze it all in within our short stay." I shrug my shoulders up, rubbing my lips into a thin line as I focus on the lights indicating the floors we are passing.

"Well, I am off tomorrow so if you want a tour guide, East London born and bred, then please, let me know." Robert bends, grabbing my bags and standing tall.

"I would really like that," I stutter over my words quickly, falling silent. I shouldn't be doing this, Tryst would blow a gasket and the paps would have a field day with me being spotted with another man. My eyes widen slightly as I feel the sweat begin to prickle on the back of my neck, the nape of my hair beginning to feel slightly damp. "But I must politely decline," I give a half smile and let my eyes drop because I can't bring myself to look at him.

"That's a real shame," his voice is low and I instantly feel guilty. "I'll be around, so if you do change your mind... I'll be here somewhere," he chimes, as the lift pings. His British accent is thick, but not well-to-do like it is often portrayed. He has a slight twang to his accent, but I can't work out what it is.

"Okay, let's see then, shall we?" and for the first time, I give him a genuine smile. It's a smile that I haven't seen in a long while. Because truthfully... I haven't been happy in what seems like forever. Sighing heavily, I follow Robert out of the lift and pad down towards my room. Nerves swarm me, my stomach flipping as my skin prickles in perspiration. I hate that I get like this once I am near Tryst again. I hate that he makes me feel this way. But I can't leave. I have nowhere else to go. Am I stupid? Yes. Could I go back home to New York? Also yes. But I am too damn proud to walk back into my moms' home with my tail between my legs. Or my dad's for that matter.

Maybe I shouldn't be going out with Robert tomorrow,

Tryst will lose his cool. But do I have to tell him? Will he really care? He won't even notice that I have gone... will he?

Rubbing my sweaty palms down my thighs, I pinch my brows. Frustration courses through me but I soon push my feelings aside.

"Thank you, Robert," I smile, taking the bags from him quickly before he can stop me.

"I was going to take them in for you," he steps back, his brows furrowing as his lips twist.

"I am really grateful for all you have done, but honestly, I can take it from here..." A nervous laugh bubbles out of me as I step towards the door. "I'll see you soon?"

"I'll see you soon then," he smiles before turning on his heel and walking towards the elevator. I let out a sigh of relief and once he has disappeared, I pull my key card from my bag and swipe it through the door. As soon as my boot steps over the threshold, I hear him.

"Well, well, well... look who has finally returned," Tryst's cold and venomous tone fills the penthouse, and a shiver runs up my spine as dread fills me.

"Hey," I lace my voice with confidence and smile as I drop my bags.

"Out spending *my* money again, were you?" Tryst steps towards me and I see Rox and Callaghan exchange looks. They know what's coming.

"I'll take it all back, I'm sorry... I... I..." I stammer but soon stop once Tryst is towering over me. His eyes bug out of his head, redness filling the whites of his eyes, his pupils wide. That's when I realise he is high.

"Yeah, you will." He grits out, his stale breath on my face. I close my eyes for a moment. "I don't know who you think you are, what entitles you to go out and spend *my* money?" That's when I look at him, and my heart plummets. *What the hell happened between us.* Sadness suddenly fills me at the thoughts of how we used to be, but now, we're like this.

"I'm sorry," I mutter, and as much as I want to fight back, I know better. It's easier for me to stay mute. He isn't wrong. It is his money but I have never had to ask to spend before, I even had my own card but it seems that luxury is long gone. I let my head fall and brace myself for the abusive hurl that is due to come, but it doesn't. My head is lifted by Tryst's tight grip on my cheeks, his other hand pinching the skin on my exposed thigh.

"Maybe I need to teach you a lesson," he pants, ragged breaths leaving him.

"Tryst," I whisper, my eyes widening as I see the malice and spitefulness flash through his.

His fingers wrap around the waist band of my cycling shorts as he rips them down roughly.

"Tryst, please," I beg, panic lacing my voice, "please don't do this," I choke as a sob leaves me. My eyes move to Rox and Cal who quickly look away and that's when I realise that no one is going to stop him. One of the reasons I got clean was so I could defend myself, but it seems even sober I can't do it.

His fingers dig into my cheeks as the hot tears roll down them. "You're hurting me, I don't want this... please, please Tryst."

But he doesn't listen.

CHAPTER FOUR

I LAY CURLED UP IN THE FOETAL POSITION AS THE CASCADING water from the shower head falls over me. I locked myself away while Tryst slept. Everything was sore, I felt betrayed in the worst way. Humiliation flames my cheeks as my mind replays what happened and how Rox and Cal did nothing. They knew what was happening, yet they still let him do it. My throat burns as the tears continue to fall, not that you would know because the water is washing them away as quickly as they're coming. I have no idea how long I have been in here for, but my whole body begins to tremble as the uncontrollable sobs leave me.

After what seems like hours, I manage to pull myself from the shower and wrap myself in the warm, fluffy towel. I edge towards the door, anxiety riddling me as I stick my head round to see the empty bedroom. Relief washes over me as I cautiously tiptoe towards the room, and push the bedroom door closed, locking it behind me. I pace back towards the bed when I catch myself in the floor to ceiling mirror. Turning slowly, the girl staring back at me looks haunted. My eyes are puffy and red but have no life dancing inside of them, my skin is dry and pasty. Bruises are starting to form around my neck and the top of my arms where Tryst pinned me in place, pinching my skin as he did. Bite marks sit on the skin of my thighs, broken skin evident from where he got too rough. My hand presses to my mouth as I feel the overwhelming feeling of betrayal wash over me.

Rushing towards the wardrobe, I grab a comfy lounge suit and dress myself, keeping my eyes closed as I do. I couldn't look at myself. I felt disgusted that I had let it happen. Disgusted that he done that to me when he was meant to love me. Someone who loves you doesn't treat you that way. Do they?

He was high, maybe it was a bad batch of drugs. He has never laid a hand on me that way before, he has never forced himself onto me. It was just the drugs.

It won't happen again.

I tell myself that repeatedly.

It won't happen again.

SETTLED ON THE LARGE SOFA OF THE PENTHOUSE SUITE, I LOOK at the destruction Tryst has caused. My new clothes are cut up and lay scattered over the floor. My new bag is ruined from a substance I can't work out. I feel heavy, my head throbbing and every muscle in my body aches as well as feeling sore from Tryst's rough assault. *Friends* plays in the background, taking my mind away from the chaos around me and my heart aches. This used to be mine and Reese's go to show, our comfort show and now all I can think about is her. I would do anything to call her, to tell her everything that has happened, but I can't do it. She will tell my dad and then he will come for me and take me home. Not that I would go, or would I? Nothing has to change; the witch didn't want anything to do with me so why am I punishing myself and them at the same time?

They lied to you, Connie. Everyone and everything you thought you knew was a fabrication. It wasn't real.

My subconscious bites at me, reminding me of the pain and betrayal they put me through. I feel the heat of resentment slice through me, bitterness flowing through my veins and suddenly, I am wound up and angry again.

The penthouse suite door bangs open and Tryst rocks through the door, donning a low, V-neck white tee and black skinny jeans with rips at the knees. The front of his tee is tucked into his pants that show his studded belt. He finishes the look with all black *chuck star converse.* Everything about him screams *rockstar.*

His green eyes are heavily lined with black eyeliner, his dark hair is styled messy and his short, bitten nails are painted black. Both of his arms are scattered in random tattoos, but the one that always sticks out to me is the butterfly he got for me to prove that I was free from heartache; but I no longer felt free. I was caged, my freedom long, *long* gone.

I would be lying if I said he didn't look insanely hot, but anything I did feel for him is slowly seeping from me.

"There's my girl," he sung as he bounded over to the sofa, edging towards my lips to kiss me but I turn away last minute so his lips brush across my cheek. He falters back, his brows pinching. "What, you can't even give your boyfriend a kiss now?"

"I don't want to kiss you," I hiss, rage pumping through me as I push away from the sofa. He is hot on my tail, his fingers wrapping round my wrist as he drags me back towards him.

"What do you mean you don't want to kiss me," his tone is clipped, his eyes wide as they dance back and forth with mine. I am well aware of Rox and Cal being here, but I don't care. They watched him do what he did, they've seen *everything*. All dignity I once had is now gone.

"Look around Tryst!" I shout at the destruction that surrounds us. "Look what you've done!" The tears sting behind my eyes but I refuse to fucking cry in front of *him*.

"Baby…" his voice is soft and so is his expression.

"Don't baby me. You hurt me Tryst, what you did to me…" And I can't hold them back anymore as I choke on my sobs. He moves closer to me, reaching for me, and I flinch. I shake my head from side to side. "Don't." I snap, holding my hand up, "Don't come near me." My body begins to tremble as the uncontrollable sobs leave me.

"Con, come on," he scoffs, a smile creeping onto his lips as he turns his head to the side before his eyes fall back on me.

"No," I whisper as I palm my tears off my cheek.

"Tryst, mate…" Rox steps towards us cautiously, not sure if Tryst is about to implode at any moment. His temper can change quickly, like a slip of a finger on a grenade. That's all it'll take for Tryst to go from zero to ten.

It's *that* quick.

Rox's eyes volley between me and Tryst.

Tryst ignores my wish, stepping towards me and grabbing the top of my arms as he holds me tightly, causing me to jump in my own skin as fear courses through me.

"This isn't you, please let me go," I cry, sniffling as the tears fall. "Can you not see that? Can you not see what you have done and how wrong it is?"

Tryst breathes out hot, ragged breaths on my face and I can taste the alcohol on his tongue as he swipes it between my lips. He pushes me against the wall, pinning me there as the pain surges through me. I pull away, turning my head and scrunch my eyes shut.

One of his hands lets go of my arm as he grabs my cheeks and turns me back towards him.

"I act like this because of *you*," the venom in his voice is poignant, "your constant *why me* and you wanting to rebel against your parents. You're insufferable."

I don't know what comes over me, but I slap him. Hard. The sound of the contact from my hand on his skin echoes around the room and that's when Tryst loses it completely. He spits in my face and wraps his fingers round the base of my throat as he grins down at me looking scarily insane as his grip on my throat tightens, my eyes bugging as he slowly cuts off my air supply.

"You're going to pay for that," he grits, using his free hand to grab the root of my hair and dragging me towards the bedroom, not giving two shits that he is dragging me along the carpeted floor as my legs couldn't keep up with his long strides. I ignore the burning sensation that is currently spreading over my legs like wildfire.

"Tryst please," I cry out, begging for him to let me go.

"Rox!" I scream as he kicks open the bedroom door and throws me forward. "Cal!" I scream in one last desperate plea and the last thing I see is Rox and Cal's shocked and guilty expressions that they've let this happen before the door slams shut, making the door frame shake.

CHAPTER FIVE

I DIDN'T GO AND WATCH TRYST IN CONCERT. I DIDN'T LEAVE THE room all night and when I woke alone, I knew Tryst didn't come home either. Was I bothered? A little.

Rolling, I wince as parts of my body ache that I didn't even know was possible. Reaching for my phone, I saw it was already past nine. I debated staying here, the thought of bumping into Robert was making me nervous, but I really could do with getting out of this suite. I didn't want to be here when Tryst gets home, even though if he knows I've been round London with another man the consequences would be worse. I ignore my inner thoughts and push them deep down, burying them under the surface. I was allowed to have friends. Tryst didn't control me.

Throwing back the heavy comforter, I sit on the edge of the bed and let my eyes fall to the carpet that my feet are tapping on. Why was I still here?

Because you're an idiot with nowhere else to go. My subconscious so kindly reminds me.

"Fuck off," I groan to the empty room as I head for the wardrobe.

Standing in the elevator, I push my large black sunglasses onto my face to hide my puffy eyes. My NY cap is on my head, my ponytail sitting through the back and running down my spine. Kicking the toe of my sneaker into the floor, my nerves fill my tummy. I'm wearing black ripped skinny jeans and an oversized *Chord* tee. I was running out of clothes and seeing as Tryst had *out* all my new stuff up, I had to wear what I had and this was all that was left in the clean pile.

The lift doors pinged open and I was hesitant to walk out. Maybe I should just go back to the room. Maybe I should call my dad and ask to come home.

No.

No.

I shake my head as I argue with that voice. Finally looking up, I see Robert standing in the middle of the lobby, rocking up and down on the balls of his feet as he waits. Why did I come down here? Part of me thought he wouldn't be here yet… but alas, here he is.

Swallowing the thickness in my throat back down, I stride towards him and his smile widens when he sees me.

"I'm glad you decided to take me up on my offer," he smiles as he glances at his watch.

"So am I," I nibble on the inside of my lip, deep down nerves wrack me that I met him.

He looks smart, wearing a long crew neck top and slacks, finishing his look off with white sneakers.

"Ready?" he chimes, turning and facing the back of the hotel.

"I think so," I smile cautiously, my heart thumping in my chest.

"Then let's go."

I follow him to the back entrance, and he groans when he sees delivery lorries piled up.

"Crap," he sighs, "we're going to have to go out the front. I noticed some paps in the coffee shop opposite, I didn't think it was worth the risk."

"Oh," I whisper, turning to face the main entrance.

"I'm sorry, I just thought it was the better option," he looks between me and the doors.

"We have no other option," my tone a little snappier than I would have liked, and I instantly feel bad. "Sorry," I mutter.

"It's fine," he gives me a playful wink and my nerves calm, if only for a moment.

"I'll go out first, I'll start walking and I'll turn the first corner I see, then I'll wait for you there. If they see us go out together, they'll have a field day and then I will have some explaining to do to Tryst," the words rushing out as the panic begins to creep up my throat.

"Okay, that sounds like a solid plan," he nods firmly.

"Let's do this," I smile, strolling forward and heading for the main doors. The doorman who I've not seen before gives me a curt nod as I step into the sunshine and fear prickles over my skin when I see the group of paparazzi that Robert was concerned about.

Ducking my head, I walk quickly to the first corner and slip round it as I wait for Robert. Moments later he arrives, and my heartbeat slows quickly, helping me catch my breath.

"All clear," he smiles, linking his arm through mine, "so, I'm assuming you're with the band," he turns to look at me as we wait at the pedestrian crossing, wiggling his brows up and down as he eyes my tee.

"Yup," I breathe out, not wanting to elaborate. "But the paparazzi are here to see Chord members, I'm just like a bonus shot at the moment, but any picture they can get, they can sell..." I trail off as I watch the pedestrian crossing man icon flash from red to green indicating we're okay to cross.

"I see," he hums as we continue walking. "So, you must be with one of them."

"Maybe," I nudge into him and drop his arm suddenly when I see a camera man jump from an alley.

"Connie! Connie!" he calls but I ignore him, dropping my head and letting Robert lead me away and into a small, but busy coffee shop. My eyes widen as realisation sets in.

"They got photos of me... with you." Panic crawls up my throat as my chest tightens and I let my head drop forward as I blink away the tears.

"Hey, hey," Robert stands in front of me, reaching to cup my face but I flinch away, shaking my head from side to side. I voluntarily let my eyes lift to his. "You have nothing to worry about," he chimes, smiling at me.

"I have everything to worry about..." I gasp, "you don't know what Tryst is like..." trailing off my eyes volley back and forth between his.

"And I can vouch that we're nothing more than friends..." the sweetest smile crosses his lips. "Don't take this the wrong way, you're pretty and everything but you're not my type..." he winks before stepping back.

A nervous laugh bubbles out of me before he links his fingers through mine and drags me towards the counter at the back of the shop, there are bookcases filling one wall and my eyes widen with glee.

I stop and just stare in awe at the beauty and cosiness of this shop. The smell of fresh coffee and pastries fill my nose and my stomach groans, reminding me that I haven't eaten this morning. The dusty book pages warm my soul a little and I just want to take a moment to flick the pages slowly as I inhale the scent of the classic romance novels that I used to read.

"Wow," Robert whispers as we just stand in the middle of the shop. I hum in agreement, suddenly snapping back into the real world as I look for an empty table and find a table for two right at the back of the room.

I quickly step over there and sit my ass on the seat.

"What do you want?" Robert asks as he fists his hands into his back pockets.

"I'll have an oat milk cortado with caramel and a chocolate pastry swirl," I lick my lips just thinking about it. Robert gives me a curt nod and disappears towards the counter. I sit, drumming my fingertips on the table as I wait. Anxiety bubbles deep in my stomach as I try to keep my head down and myself to myself. I love to people watch, but the fear that is lodged inside of me unsettles me and pushes me to keep my eyes on my feet.

"Is this seat taken?" A low voice breezes over me, my skin covering in goosebumps as I instantly recognise the voice. I dart my head up, keeping my glasses on as I study him for a moment.

Absolutely delicious. All six foot four of him wrapped in the perfect navy suit. His grey eyes look sager today and I'm not sure if the sunnier days change the colour. I smirk, pushing my glasses down my nose to look through my lashes at him.

"Unfortunately for you, yes." I sit back, crossing my arms across my chest and put my feet on the cool, metal chair opposite me.

"What by your feet or?" he pops an eyebrow high and glares down at me.

"At the moment yes," I smile, "but my friend will be joining me any moment." I shrug and push my glasses back up my nose. Turning away, I would rather stare at the wall then let him see me watching him. My moment is soon ruined when my feet are moved and dropped to the floor.

"Hey!" I scowl, sitting forward in my chair and pulling my glasses off, "I told you my friend was sitting here."

"It doesn't work like that, does it sweetheart."

"You're horrid," I screw my face up, "and stop calling me sweetheart!"

"Mmhmm," he winks and unfolds his paper.

"And so boring," I yawn and turn to the side, focusing on Robert who has just got to the counter.

"Do you like being an immature brat?" I hear the clipped tone in his voice and my back is instantly up.

"I'm not immature, and I am certainly not a brat," I hiss, "I just can't stand stuffy, obnoxious assholes." I stick my middle finger up just as Robert walks back across with a tray in his hands filled with our coffees and pastries. He coughs, clearing his throat.

"Please, kind sir, would you move from my seat?" he says in the politest way, but his tone has a slight bite to it. I nibble my bottom lip.

"But this is my seat," Mr grumpy gramps turns slowly to look at Robert up and down.

"I'm here with Connie, this is our table. Move your handsome little arse."

I watch the handsome man's lips twitch as he tries to fight a smile. He thinks for a moment before pushing up.

"Okay kiddo, you take your seat." He offers Robert his

seat, his fingers wrapped around the back of Robert's chair as he holds it in place.

"Thank you, kind sir," Robert swipes his tongue across his bottom lip as sarcasm drips from his tone.

A low growl comes from behind Robert, and I see how quick the dark-haired stranger pulls his hand from the back of the chair, but he doesn't move.

"Bye then," I wave, not moving my eyes from Robert even though I still have my shades on.

The stranger didn't move. He just stood.

I slip my glasses off slowly and I stare at the six-foot god who hasn't lifted his eyes from me.

"Why are you still standing here?" I can't help my tone, but something about him puts me on edge and I don't know why. I watch as his eyes slowly slip from my face to my neck and I see his jaw tighten as I imagine he is grinding his molars together. I let my eyes move between his when suddenly it dawns on me what he is looking at.

My eyes widen and I place my hand on my neck, quickly covering the marks that Tryst left over the last couple of nights.

His large hand fists deep inside his suit pocket and Robert sits quietly sipping his tea, not lifting his eyes from his cup. I feel like shit for putting him in this awkward situation, but I am even more mad at this random guy who has shown up the last two days. Could it just be a coincidence or am I meant to be seeing this as some sort of sign?

"Is everything okay..." he lurches forward slightly but then stops himself a moment, stepping from foot to foot as I see a change in his mood. His stalling voice makes me wonder if he is making sure he is allowed to say my name and I nod. "Connie..."

I roll my lips, my throat burning because I want to say no, but I can't.

"I'm fine," I nod curtly.

Silence crackles between the three of us for a moment and I watch as my perfect stranger steps back. "Well, seeing as you now know my name, can I get yours?" I ask and I see Robert smile as he watches me.

"Kaleb." He nods before turning on his heel and walking away.

"Well, he is rather fucking handsome, isn't he?" Robert laughs and I laugh with him.

I sigh blissfully as I turn and watch the door slowly close, "Yes, yes he is."

I FLOPPED ON MY BED UTTERLY EXHAUSTED. ROBERT SHOWED ME everything and more, he was the best tour guide anyone could wish for. He invited me down for dinner tonight, but I politely declined. I had no idea what sort of mood Tryst was going to be in, and the way the last two nights have gone, I can't see him being any different. I'm even more worried because I went out with Robert and the paps found us. My heart thrums in my chest at the paparazzi pictures being printed tomorrow and I can just see the headlines now.

CHORD'S LEAD SINGER'S GIRLFRIEND SEEN WITH NEW MYSTERY MAN.

Nausea swims in my stomach which makes it coil and my skin pricks with cold beads of sweat. Even though Robert is just a friend, the vultures don't see it like that. To them it's a story, and a story that will sell.

Dressing in high waisted wet look shorts and a black bodysuit I finished with fishnet tights and doc martens. Running my fingers through my styled curled hair until I achieved the tousled look. I thought it was best to get dressed before Tryst returned home. I had no idea if I was going out to the show with him tonight, but I wanted to be prepared. Sliding my phone across the dresser I tap the screen and disappointment floods me.

They've given up on me. My moms, Reese, my dad. But then what did I expect. For the first six months it was constant, the texting, the phone calls... but then they just stopped. There is only so much effort they can put into someone, and I wasn't willing to even try.

CHAPTER SIX

KILLIAN

I PACE BACK AND FORTH, MY EYES FIXED AHEAD AS MY FINGERS wrap round my phone. I am angry and deflated.

"Baby," Reese's voice washes over me, calming me in an instant. I stop and turn to see her holding a sleepy Celeste, who is nuzzling into Reese's chest, her small fingers clutched around the soft fabric of Reese's tee. "Come to bed," she ushers, holding her hand out for me to take.

"I can't, I need to know she is okay," my eyes fall as my chest heaves.

"Kaleb will call you; he has kept you updated from the beginning. He has only just got eyes on her, he told you about the marks and now, we must wait." Her voice is full of sympathy, her eyes wide as they begin to glass over. "I know she's your daughter and you're worried sick, but I am worried too Killian, she's still my best friend and I miss her every single day, but we can't force her home," she whispers as she closes the gap between us, her small hand rubbing up my back and over my shoulder. I sigh, my breath shaky. She is right. I can't force her home. Turning my head to the left, I place a soft kiss on her fingers before straightening up and letting my head fall back.

"I just want her home," my voice cracks, my throat burns.

"I know baby, we all do," Reese whispers.

CHAPTER SEVEN

KALEB

Sitting in the living area of my suite, I sip my gin and tonic and let my mind wander. I have been staying in *The Berkley* since a few days before Connie arrived. I'm a couple of floors down, but close enough if needed. She has no idea who I am, to her, I am an annoyance and a complete stranger who steals her table in coffee shops. I shouldn't have given her my name, but I was wired so tight after seeing the marks on her that I forgot everything. My name was meant to be Tristan, but I was so consumed with rage and trying to keep my emotions in check that I didn't think.

Sighing, I take a sip of my ice-cold drink. I am pretty sure it wasn't her little friend that was with her today. My mind jumps the gun and assumes it's Tryst, but from what her dad said, Tryst loved her. He was a good kid. But he is just that, a kid. A kid who woke up to fame over night after one of his songs went viral on social media. Leaning across I pick up the file and flick through until I find everything I have on Chord. It's the same old story, young boy with a passion, gets famous quick, fame is his downfall. I hope my suspicions are wrong, but my gut tells me they're not. Killian is on me to get her back home but like I said to him, I can't just take her back home. I must wait for the perfect moment to swoop in and be there for her when she needs me.

Chord have two more shows before they go back to New York, then they finish their tour in Brooklyn, and I am hoping I can get her to stay here, in London, that way she is away from the band, away from all she knows, and maybe this is the fresh start she could use? Sure, her dad would be fucked off, but even if it was a few months just until I know she is away from Tryst. I just have no idea on how to do it.

My phone vibrates on the coffee table, reaching for it I see its Keaton, my brother. My brows knit as I answer.

"What do I owe the pleasure?" I smile, my eyes watching the ice swirling in my glass.

"Can't a brother call his other brother to see how his trip is?" I can hear the humor in his voice.

"Of course, a brother can, but we both know that you have an ulterior motive," I click my tongue at the top of my mouth and hear the rumble of Keaton's laugh down the earpiece.

"Ah, you got me."

"Fucker," I laugh and take a sip of my drink.

"How is it going? Have you found her yet?" he asks as he clambers around in the background.

"Yeah, it was easy to find her. It's like she doesn't want to be found but also doesn't do anything to change it." I shake my head.

"Cry for help?" Keaton asks as I hear the pop of the lid from his decanter bottle.

"Maybe, but then she won't go home," I shrug my

shoulders up, "I think she is having some domestic issues, I'm not sure but she has marks and bruises on her neck which she was quick to cover up when she realised, I had noticed them." I take another mouthful of my drink.

"Shit man," I hear him suck in a breath, "what's your plan?"

"Not quite sure yet, she is feisty and headstrong. I'm not used to going after young girls who run away with daddy issues... I don't even know why I took the fucking job," I roll my eyes and swallow the rest of my drink down.

"Because you're the best of the best." My brother so kindly reminds me.

"Or more like the bloke that hired me has more money than sense. It's nothing more than a spoiled brat running away with an up-and-coming band because the rock 'n' roll life seems far more appealing than the life she has come from."

"Do you know that or...?"

I sigh, running my hand round the back of my head and rub my hand back and forth over the short hair, gripping a little tighter at the nape of my neck, dragging my fingers across my skin. "Just an assumption," groaning when I hear the sound of him moving as the line muffles slightly and I hear a girl mewl in the background.

"Please tell me you haven't called me while you have a girl in your bed?" I groan.

He laughs and I put the phone down.

Idiot.

I push from the chair and look at my watch, time to get changed and go.

Wearing a black tee and black cargo pants I put a cap on and pull it lower over my eyes. Slipping my phone in my back pocket I head for the stairs; I don't want to risk her bumping into me in the elevator. Puffing as I push out the side exit of the hotel, my feet hit the ground as I head towards the *Shepherds Bush Empire* hoping that tonight is the night I witness something.

CHAPTER EIGHT

CONNIE

"Baby," Tryst calls as he walks through the penthouse door. I look up from my book to see him walking cautiously over to me. My heart begins to pump faster as he closes the gap between us. He leans forward and places a kiss on the top of my head. "How's your day been?" his voice is soft, his eyes alight with something but I just don't know what. I look behind him and focus on Rox and Cal and they both give me a small shrug.

"It's been okay," I keep my voice low as my anxiety has me in a chokehold.

"Yeah? What have you done?" his calmness is unsettling. I couldn't remember the last time Tryst was like this.

"Not much, got dressed and done some sight-seeing before grabbing some lunch and coming home."

"Sounds like a lovely, chilled day," he reaches across, and I flinch, and I see how his eyes widen. "Connie," he breathes before turning and looking at the boys then back to me. "I would never hurt you," his hand clasps my cheek as his thumb wipes a stray tear that rolls down my cheek. I am too scared and shocked to move. Too afraid to say anything in case it is the wrong thing.

"You know that don't you?" he edges closer to me, his other hand cupping my face as he holds me in place now.

I want to scream in his face, tell him I know he is lying but I am too scared, so I simply nod.

"Good," he pulls me into a hug and holds me tightly. "It's me and you till the end. Even in death I will find you, we're soulmates."

A chill dances up my spine as fear instils in me. I am never going to get away from him.

"Now, I'm going to get changed and then let's hit the road." He winks before jumping over the back of the sofa and slamming the bedroom door.

My eyes move to Rox and Cal before I begin to tremble, the tears falling. I could see how conflicted they felt. They were between a rock and hard place, but just this once I wanted them on my side. Cal stepped forward but Rox reached forward and grabbed his elbow, pulling him back and shaking his head from side to side. I needed out. I couldn't stay here.

Palming my tears away, I slam my book shut and throw it across the hotel room. Fear chokes me but anger consumes me whole. Pushing from the sofa, I storm across to the room that I share with Tryst and barge in.

"Con?" he asks as he pulls a fresh white tee over his head, his messy hair un-styled and flopped against his forehead. It was my favourite when it was like that.

"I don't get what's going on..." I whisper, panic clawing at my throat. Have I got this all wrong? Have I made a massive deal out of nothing? Have I let the thoughts in my head misconstrue what actually happened?

"Are you high?" he scoffs, as he rubs his hand over the

top of his head.

"No, Tryst! I haven't been high for three months!" Pushing my hands to my hips I stand. "How are you acting as if everything is okay?" I realise my voice is growing louder but I can't help it.

"Because everything is okay," Tryst walks towards me, pressing his hand to my head, "Are you running a fever?" his brows pinch.

"You assaulted me Tryst..." I nibble my bottom lip as the uneasiness swims through me, "twice."

His steps falter back, his eyes glued to mine as he turns his head to the side as if none of what I am saying is making sense, it's like he doesn't understand.

"I told you no, over and over and you still continued and in front of Rox and Cal," I choke as tears begin to fill my eyes. "You don't get to do stuff like that to me, just because we're in a relationship doesn't give you the right to do that when I don't want it."

Tryst says nothing, just rubs his hand under his chin and slowly licks his top lip before rolling his lips together.

"Are you going to say anything?" my eyes bug out and realisation finally hits me. He doesn't care. He steps forward, his fingers wrapping around my chin as he lifts my face up so I have no other option than to look at him.

"You belong to me Connie, I get to do whatever the fuck I want to you." He snarls, his grip tightening on my chin. I swallow the burning lump down in my throat. He shoves me back, giving me a look of pure disgust, "Now get out of my sight, we're leaving in ten," his tone is spiteful as he moves to the bathroom and closes the door behind him.

Trembling, I turn to leave the room when I see Cal standing outside the door. He nods his head back, asking me to follow him but presses his finger against his lips. I look over my shoulder to see the bathroom door still closed, then shut the bedroom door behind me. My eyes scan the room, but Rox is nowhere to be seen.

"Connie," he whispers, his own eyes flitting around the room as he fidgets, "he is out of control."

I keep quiet.

"He is constantly popping pills and smoking shit; I have no idea when he is sober or when he is high. All of his emotions are mixing, and his personalities are becoming harder and harder to work out. I'm sorry about what he done to you, me and Rox felt helpless, but we promise, if he ever lays a hand on you again, we will be there to stop him."

I nod as helpless tears roll down my cheeks, Cal is sweet to say that but we both know that Tryst will do what he wants, and he doesn't care what he has to do to do it.

"Thank you, Cal," I manage on a shaky whisper, reaching and giving the top of his arm a gentle squeeze. Cal and Rox are wonderful, but their loyalties lie with Tryst. I know that and I wouldn't expect any different.

Last year when things were good between us, I finally felt like I had found my family. They all looked out for me and made me happy. They were like the brothers I never had, until Tryst began to change, and fame seemed to surpass everything. Including me. Rox and Cal still chase the dream because it isn't just Tryst's dream. It's all of theirs and they're not going to want to give it all up for me. And as much as I believe that Cal and Rox will stop Tryst, I wouldn't want them to. Because Tryst will kick them to the kerb for betraying him. In Tryst's eyes, he is the lead singer and Cal and Rox are just the musicians, but what is a singer without his musicians?

He is nothing.

Cal hasn't changed much since school; he is tall and

lean but slim. His dirty blonde hair is styled in a side parting and neatly brushed over. His ocean blue eyes are big and wide and I feel like I could dive into them. He's cute, he was one of the most sought after boys in school but he was never interested in settling down. He didn't seem to follow the indie rock band look, he still had his prep schoolboy look and he suited it so well. Rox on the other hand was everything you would expect from an indie rock band. His mousy brown hair was dyed pillar box red and styled in spikes. He had nose rings and lip rings. Tattoos covered most of his skin but he pulled it off. He was every bit the rocker boy. They had girls throwing themselves at them, and at one point I was the only one they were interested in, but now, it seems that anything with a pulse is a good night. I always hoped that deep down Tryst wouldn't have been unfaithful to me, but then again, it wouldn't surprise me. Blocking it out and pretending like everything is perfect is much better then accepting the absolute shit show that I am currently living in.

I needed to get out. I needed a reason to leave. But where would I go? I knew for certain that I wasn't going back to New York. I couldn't. I have nothing left for me there. If I can get Tryst back to Brooklyn and out of London, I could stay here. I have enough in my savings to get a little rental and then I could find a job.

I couldn't stay in this circus anymore, to stand and watch the man I loved slowly lose himself to everything he said he wouldn't...

I need to do this for me.

It was time to be selfish and walk away from the monster that kept me chained.

I needed to break free.

I needed my wings back.

CHAPTER NINE

I stood in the side stage area and watched as Tryst, Rox and Cal owned the stage, like they did every night they've been here. The screaming girls were on form tonight which pushed the guys to perform even better than normal. My foot tapped along, but as the show was coming to an end, nerves unsettled me. We were heading back home tomorrow, back on familiar ground, but I didn't want to go back. I had already decided I was going to stay here. Build a new life and when I was ready, I would go back home. *Maybe.*

Tryst and the boys finished off with a fabulous finale for their end show. The screams filled the room, girls were crying as Tryst sat on the edge of the stage and took their hands, kissing them and making sure they remembered this night for the rest of their lives. I stalked back into the shadows and pushed into Chord's dressing room. My breathing fastened as I sat on the plush sofa, my eyes pinned to the wall. I could hear the heavy footsteps of the boys, my eyes fall to my lap as I pick the skin around my fingers, my anxiety rippling through me.

The door slams open, and I fight to look up. Tryst strolls over, cupping my face in his hands, his lips smashing into mine. His hot, sticky skin makes my own perspiration bead on my skin. Sweat runs off his forehead, running down his nose and dripping onto me.

"Baby, this was the best show ever," he smiles, stepping back and clapping his hands.

"Good," I smile, but it doesn't meet my eyes, but he doesn't notice. He doesn't notice anything like that anymore. He doesn't notice *me* anymore.

I hear cackling and giggles of drunk girls and my skin crawls, my stomach flips.

"Here they are," Tryst beams, holding his hand out to welcome the girls who give me the filthiest look. I scowl before rolling my eyes.

"Who is she?" The peroxide blonde snarls.

"She's mine," Tryst smiles proudly before turning to face the three girls. Pride swarms through me but uneasiness soon settles back in. I'm not wanted.

"I'm going to the bar," I swallow the lump down that bobs in my throat. I don't look back; tears sting my eyes, but I ignore them.

Ordering a gin and tonic, I look around the room at some of the girls that are still lingering. I don't know what they're waiting for, but if it is Tryst then he is long gone. Sipping my drink, it hits the spot. I feel eyes on me, a few knowing glances off those that know who I am to the band, but I ignore it. Turning my head, I see a figure standing in all black, his cap low so I can't see his face. Fear spikes through me and I turn, gripping onto my glass and heading back.

Walking through the narrow hallways, I slip into Rox's room, and I am grateful that it's empty.

47

I sit alone with my silence before the room goes black and sleep invades me.

———

BOARDING THE PRIVATE JET, MY WHOLE BODY ACHES. TRYST SAW me looking for hotels to stay in London and lost his shit. I got dragged into our room, thrown about and used in a punishing manner. My hands tremble as I grip onto the handrail and steady myself as I reach the top of the stairs, Tryst not moving from my side. The hostesses exchange looks but nothing is said or done.

I had to accept that I was trapped. He was never going to let me run. My freedom was slowly slipping through my fingers and it didn't matter how much I tried to claw it back, it was useless.

Cal and Rox pinned their eyes to me as I sat down but kept quiet, I couldn't even bring myself to look at them. I hid behind huge, black sunglasses and my NY cap. My long, brown hair framed my face as I used it as a veil to hide behind.

Tryst's hand glides between my thighs but not in a comforting or affectionate way, no it was in a controlling way. The way his long, skinny fingers dug into my flesh hurt. I didn't let him know that though. Turning my head, I looked out the window. I had seen a lot of the world on this tour, Sydney, Paris, Berlin, London, and now to New York before they finish up back home, in Brooklyn. Sure, I wanted to see the world and I was so excited when Tryst mentioned tour but I feel like I haven't seen any of it.

Not in the way I would have liked.

I didn't want this anymore.

But it looked like I didn't have a choice.

CHAPTER TEN
KALEB

I PUNCH MY STEERING WHEEL AS I WATCH THE PLANE TAKE OFF. I didn't get there in time.

"Fuck," I groan, punching it again as my temper rises.

I've chased this fucking brat around the world and yet I am now heading back to our starting point.

Is she even on the plane?

Shaking my head of the thoughts, I pull my phone out of my bag and check the next flight available to JFK, I need to be there before opening night tomorrow. Killian will be elated that she is back on home turf, but that doesn't mean she is going to waltz into his home and into his open arms. Scrolling the screen of my phone, I notice that a flight leaves in a few hours, that's perfect.

Turning the ignition on, I pull out and head towards the parking lot to hand the keys back to the hire company.

I had this, I'll be back home soon. Then I'll get her.

Even if it's the last thing I do.

CONNIE

Tryst is asleep, his grip loosening from my thigh, and I gently shuffle. I need the toilet, but I am too scared to move. My mind wanders to Kaleb, and I wonder why. He was a grumpy old asshole but he was so beautifully handsome. I have no idea why he came into my life, if even only a snippet but I feel he was there for a reason.

We were staying in The Plaza tonight, then moving because Tryst wanted to stay at The Four Seasons. Apparently, The Plaza wasn't good enough for him anymore. Anxiety swam through my veins. It felt as if I had come full circle. That's where my story began and now, I feel like I'm being catapulted back into a life I no longer want.

I am just grateful that I can tell my old work friends to keep my visit on the down low.

"Good afternoon, this is your captain speaking. We are due to land in JFK within the hour, so sit back, enjoy the rest of the flight and we will see you on the ground." The tanoy switches off and my heart races.

I shouldn't be here.

This wasn't part of the plan.

Tryst had kept me close the whole way back home. In the car, the airport, the plane, and now in the SUV that was waiting for us. I'm not silly, I know my dad will have been tracking the band's movements. He will know where I am and all I can do is hope and pray that he gives me the time I asked for. Clambering out the car, exhaustion hits me as I stand waiting to check in. I try not to look up at the staff as they check us in so I keep my head down and look at the marks on the floor. I still have my glasses on, my eye beginning to throb and bruise where Tryst hit me last night. I don't know what I was thinking getting on the plane, but the fear that seared through me when he lost it was enough to make me do whatever he asked. Anything for a quiet and easy day.

He knows I'm ready to run, that's why he has tightened the leash around my throat, keeping me at his side like a good little dog.

Tryst nodded curtly to the host and tugged me towards the lift whilst Cal and Rox followed like puppy dogs. Our bags were left with the concierge to bring to our suite. All I wanted was a bath and sleep.

I needed sleep.

I slept alone; Tryst went out drinking but made Rox stay home with me. He was worried I was going to run but honestly, I was too exhausted to run. I had no idea when Tryst returned home, but he was currently softly snoring next to me. Guilt swarms me that I never got a chance to thank Robert and his dad, Ernest. I look at the clock and count forward the time difference. Lifting to hotel phone, I dial the number for The Berkley. Whilst waiting, I wrap my finger through the wired cord of the phone.

"Good afternoon, The Berkley, Robert speaking."

I smile through the phone, albeit a small one.

"Robert," my voice is quiet as Tryst sleeps.

"Connie?!" His surprised voice breaks my heart.

"Yeah, it's me." I look over my shoulder at Tryst. He would go mad if he knew who I was on the phone to. He lost it when he saw the photo of me and Robert, but it didn't matter what I said. He didn't want to believe me.

"Is everything okay?" his own voice lower now.

"Yeah, yeah, it's fine," I nibble the inside of my lip, "I just didn't get a chance to say goodbye..." I trail off as I feel the lump grow, "and thank you," I sniff.

"Ah, mate," Robert chokes, "you don't have to say thank you or goodbye..."

"What?"

"This isn't goodbye Connie, it's just a see you later." He laughs and I stifle mine.

"Okay," I whisper.

"Okay," he repeats my words.

"I'll speak to you soon?"

"Sure thing, be careful, stay safe." I nod as the tears fall.

"You too," I just about manage before the phone goes dead. Swiping my tears away, I head to the bathroom.

The evening soon arrives and I'm not ready for tonight. All I want to do is stay home and order room service but of course I have to go. Whilst Tryst was getting ready, I left my number with the front desk for Robert, just in case he wanted to reach out in the future.

Standing at the side, hidden, I watch them own the stage with their last song to an even bigger audience than London. I let my steps falter when everything gets too much. Turning I head for one of the empty rooms. Everything feels heavy and for some reason I am finding it even harder to stand and watch him after the way he treated me. Each time he has assaulted me it's gotten worse and the night before we left was the first time he had really laid hands on me.

I was distraught and scared but I couldn't fear him for the rest of my life. I had to find a chance to get away, because if I don't take my chance and run, I will be trapped with him forever. And I won't do that to myself.

I don't want to be a victim.

The sounds of heavy footsteps echo through the backstage area and I stay put. I shouldn't. I should go.

But I don't.

He will find me.

He always does.

And that's the worst thing, how far can I run until he no longer finds me? Until he no longer looks, until he no longer cares.

CHAPTER ELEVEN

It's been half an hour.

He hasn't looked.

Curiosity spikes and I push from the sofa. Opening the heavy door my eyes scan up and down the darkened, narrow hallway. My brows pinch and I head for Tryst's room. My phone pings, my eyes fall when I see my dad's name with his demanding text.

DAD

You need to come home. Now.

I ignore it, like I always do, even though his text was a little more demanding than usual. I slip my phone into my back pocket.

Pushing the door open, my eyes widen, and I choke on my own breath. Tryst is knelt behind some little whore, slamming into the back of her. She doesn't give a shit, her fake ass moans fill the room and all I want to do is run but I can't, I am grounded to the floor; anchored.

Willing him to look at me, just so I can see the remorse in his eyes, but when they do finally find mine, there is nothing. No emotion, no love, nothing. He looks as if I am a stranger, all lustful as if he has an exhibitionist kink. I silently plea for something but all he does is smirk at me before winking. It takes everything in me to turn around and close the door, everything in me to swallow down the bile that is making its way up my throat and everything in me to ignore the tears that prick like a thousand needles behind my eyes. I've had my suspicions that he may have been unfaithful before, but to actually witness it with my own two eyes is a pain I will never get over. Because at the end of the day. I still felt something for him.

As soon as the door is closed, I let it all go. The tears roll down my cheeks, the twisting of my gut coiling making the nausea rip through me as my heart thumps hard against my chest. I slide down the door, my hands in my hair as I tug at the root. These are not just tears of sadness, they're also tears of happiness because he can't make me stay. I won't let him.

Cal rounds the corner and I see the panic on his face as he darts towards me, falling to his knees as his hands cup my face so I have no other choice than to look at him. My red rimmed glassy eyes land on his worried ones which causes another wave of tears to flow.

"Connie, what's happened? Did he hurt you again?" his voice is a whisper and I shake my head from side to side as much as I can in his restrictive grip.

"Not in the way you think," I choke out, "how long has he been fucking girls behind my back?" I ask, the tears suddenly stopping when realisation hits me.

Cal doesn't say anything. His eyes tell me everything I need to know. Sadness and relief suddenly turn to rage. I try to get Cal off me, but he won't let me go.

"It's okay, I've got you," he whispers, helping me to my

feet. His hands drop from my face but his fingers linger over a stray piece of hair that has fallen. Sweeping it away, he tucks it behind my ear. His eyes move slowly, following his finger before they roam over my face as if he is only just noticing every feature of mine.

"You deserve so much more," his voice is low and soft.

"I do," I agree, my throat thick. I feel his other hand move to the small of my back, edging me closer to him.

"Let me be the one to make you feel better," his lips edge closer to mine, "I promise, I will never hurt you the way he did."

"Cal?" I whisper, letting my head fall forward as I gently shake my head from side to side, but his fingers grip my chin as he lifts me to look at him.

"Baby, we can be together now. I know you feel it too," he whispers, his blue eyes moving back and forth between mine.

My brows pinch, my stomach sinking, and my eyes widen. Before I can protest, his lips are on mine, his hands dropping from my face as he gropes and pulls me flush with his body. I manage to push him away and shake my head.

"No, Cal..." I whisper but he ignores me, kissing me again as he tries to lift my leg around his waist, his growing erection edging closer.

"She said no," I hear a familiar growl and I freeze and all I see is Cal being pulled off me followed by a landing fist to his jaw.

"Oh my god," I whisper, my hands over my mouth as I step away slowly. Kaleb straightens and stands tall as Cal clambers to his feet after rolling on the floor. His dark and stormy, hooded eyes pin to me as he strides towards me. He stops outside Tryst's room, kicking the door open. Pulling his phone from his back pocket, he opens it up and snaps a picture.

"Hey, you old fucker, delete the fucking photo," Tryst grits, moving from behind the slut he's just had his dick buried in.

"Keep the fuck away from Connie; I swear you come after her, I'll kill you myself," Kaleb warns, turning away and grabbing my hand. Everything moved so fast, it was a blur until I was sitting in the back of a blacked-out SUV with no idea where I was going.

My body began to shake, and the tears started to fall again.

"You're safe now," Kaleb mumbles, his large hand over my small one and that one statement makes me sob.

CHAPTER TWELVE
CONNIE

WE PULL UP OUTSIDE THE PLAZA AND I STIFFEN. I WAS JUST grateful that Tryst had checked out before the show and was no longer here. I have had hundreds of questions circling my brain on the car ride here, but I've been unable to ask any of them. Kaleb makes me feel safe, I don't feel like he is a threat but then my judgement of character is questionable. I scowl as Kaleb's driver opens my door, Kaleb standing kerbside. He holds his hand out for me, but I decline and push out of the car myself. I catch Kaleb roll his eyes, but I ignore his childish behavior and storm into the hotel lobby. The shock is slowly seeping from me, and I am now very aware that this man is a complete stranger. *Stranger danger.* I knew I shouldn't have got in the car, but really, what other choice did I have?

"Where are you going, darling?" Kaleb is hot on my heels.

"Away from you," I fold my arms across my chest. I don't mean to act out, but my brain is trying to process what happened over the last hour. "I have no idea who you are, you're a stranger."

"Well, that isn't going to work now, is it?" he smirks, "and yes, you make a valid point but I assure you Connie, I'm not the one you should be worried about. Please, just trust me?" I roll my lips before letting my tongue dart out and run across my dry, chapped bottom lip. I give a soft nod, my subconscious screaming at me, but I know in my gut I can trust him... *I hope.*

"Thank you," his voice is low as he meets my nod with his own then pushes past me and over to the check in desk. My eyes move from his back before they land on the door. I could run but then again, it won't be long before someone finds me.

I have no idea why Kaleb was at the show, I am dying to ask but I stop myself. Instead, I stalk behind him as he checks us in.

"That's all done Mr Mills, enjoy your stay and of course, if you need anything please do not hesitate to call down," the young woman behind the counter bats her lashes as I glare at her, my upper lip lifting as my nose scrunches. She catches my facial expression before blushing and turning around. A stupid smirk graces my lips as I skip forward and next to Kaleb.

"Very mature," he scolds, and I shrug my shoulders up ending the conversation. I reach forward, pressing the button of the elevator. I can't help but put on a front in front of Kaleb. He doesn't know me. He has no idea of the hurt that is slicing through me from what happened tonight.

And even if I haven't told him, I am grateful he was there.

Whatever the reason was that made him turn up.

The elevator pinged as it reached our level, I stalled for a moment and looked up at Kaleb who was holding his hand out for me.

"After you, love," his voice was soft which made me give him a small smile.

"Thank you," I nod, my voice quiet as I step inside the lift and wait for him to join me. All worries that once filled me are beginning to ease, I have no idea why, but I feel safe with him.

As the doors close, I let out a deep sigh. My eyes fall to his duffel bag that he holds tight in his grasp before lifting them on the doors.

"I have no clothes," I whisper, my fingers knotted in front of me.

"I've already taken care of it."

"Okay," I lick my lips. The rest of the elevator ride was silent and once we reached our floor, this time, Kaleb stepped out before me. I followed, my eyes scanning the beautiful décor until we were outside our room. Swiping his key through the lock, the door swung open to show an impressive room.

"Not too bad," I try to make a joke in this awkwardness, but he doesn't reply. He heads straight for the bedroom and closes the door.

"Goodnight then!" I shout, frustrated suddenly. All my pushed down emotions slowly resurfacing.

I have no idea what to do, so I just pace back and forth. My phone has been constantly vibrating since Kaleb dragged me out of the show, but I haven't checked it. I don't want to. Lifting my cap off and tossing it across the room, I rub my hands over my face and wince as I rub a little too hard on my bruising eye.

"Shit," I curse, my hands dropping and my arms

hanging by my side, I felt so deflated and exasperated with it all. My soul was so fucking tired. So tired of running.

"Connie?" Kaleb's voice skims over me, my skin erupting in goosebumps as I turn to face him standing in the doorway of what I am assuming is his bedroom. His eyes widen and before I can do anything, his hand is cupping my cheek. "Did he do this to you?" he groans, skimming my hair out of my eyes with his fingertips to get a better look. I don't have to say anything. He knows. He isn't stupid. He has known since he saw me in the coffee shop with marks on my neck. "He will never get near you again; I promise you Connie. You're safe with me." His arms wrap around my shoulders, but I pull away, shaking my head from side to side. The tears choke me, but I don't want him touching me. I may feel safe with him, but he is still a stranger. A stranger I agreed to go home with and suddenly, doubt consumes me.

———

I CRIED MYSELF TO SLEEP LAST NIGHT. I SHOWERED, GOT CHANGED into one of the pyjama sets that Kaleb had bought then I sunk into bed and didn't leave it.

Stretching and groaning, realisation sinks in of what has happened over the last twenty-four hours. I reach for my phone and see the missed calls and messages from Cal. I quickly skim through them, but they all say the same thing.

CAL

I'm sorry.

Then there was some from Tryst.

TRYST

Where are you?

Get your ass back to the hotel NOW

Don't fucking test me Connie, I'll drag you back kicking and screaming

Tell your friend I am coming for him

Did you plan this you little whore? You're mine Connie. Keep one eye open because I am coming for you.

Fear creeps up my throat and I click to shut my phone off when it begins ringing with Tryst's name. I debate ignoring it, but I am petrified that he will find me if I don't answer. I click the button, swallowing the lump in my throat back down.

"Where the fuck are you, Connie?" he slurs. He is driving, I can hear the noise of his car engine.

I stay silent.

"Fucking answer me, you dirty little whore. I will find you Connie so why not save me the hassle and just fucking tell me." His breaths are ragged between his words. Fear claws at my throat.

"Please..." I whisper through burning, choked sobs.

"Please what?" he screams through the speaker, and I fall silent again. "FUCKING ANSWER ME!"

I choke. My eyes lift to the door to see Kaleb standing there. He walks calmly over to me, takes the phone from me and cuts Tryst off. He spends some time tapping the screen then tosses my now turned off phone back on the bed.

"He has been blocked. He won't find you; I won't let him." Then he turns on his heel, walks out the door and closes it behind him quietly. I can't cope. My anxiety is at an all-time high. I feel myself slowly slipping into a black hole and it doesn't matter how much I grab and claw around me, I still can't stop myself. This would be when I would get my hit, but I won't. I can't. I'm not being *that* girl again.

Tugging the comforter over my head, I squeeze my eyes shut until I fall back into a restless sleep.

CHAPTER THIRTEEN
KALEB

She hasn't come out of her room all day. I stare at the now cold dinner that sits on the table in the dining room. I look behind me at the closed door, I should check her but then I don't want to invade her privacy.

She hasn't asked me why I was at the show, she hasn't asked anything.

Tapping my fingers on the arm rest of the sofa, I feel uneasy. My mind starts ticking in overdrive, my heart drumming. *What if she has run?*

Moving from my seat, I rush across to her room and open the door. My eyes scan the room when I see a lump under the duvet on the bed.

"Connie?" I call softly, gripping onto the door handle and standing over this side of the threshold.

"Go away," she mumbles.

"I will, I just wanted to make sure you were okay," I edge a little closer, my foot over the door bar and into the room.

She sits bolt upright, her hands smacking the puffy comforter. I twist my lips before rubbing them together to stop my smile. Her long brown hair is wild, her eyes squinting from the light. Her skin is tanned, she is petite and slim. Her eyes are a deep, dark green and all I want to do is lose myself in them. Her lips are constantly pouted, whether she means for them to be or not. She has a button nose that has a small wrinkle formed into the bridge from where I'm assuming she scrunches it up. She has high, prominent cheek bones, her face slim.

"Do I look okay?" she asks sarcastically, the sarcasm is practically dripping off her tongue, her eyes pinned to mine and my rage flames in my chest at the bruising around her eye. It's worse today, the blue is bright, and the purple is prominent. "When can I go?" she falls back into the headboard and huffs.

"You can go when you want, I just didn't know if you *had* anywhere to go."

She stills, her eyes bugging, and she's just realised that unless she goes back home to daddy dearest, she has nowhere to go.

Her bottom lip trembles before her head goes into her hands. I cautiously walk over to her, sitting on the edge of the bed and just watch as she falls apart.

"You could always..." and I stop myself before I fuck up, back tracking I stumble over my words, "stay here, you know... until you find somewhere." I cough, clearing my throat.

"Would that be okay? I mean, it'll be a month tops..." she nibbles on her bottom lip and a bolt shoots through me making me shuffle. "Two weeks if a month is too much..." she squeaks out when I stay silent.

"No, no, a month is okay..." I nod. "Do you need any money or...?"

That's when it went south.

"I don't *need* your money. If you think I need your help, you're sadly mistaken Gramps." She scoffs, her defiance strong, her walls slowly building back up around me. "Oh my god, is that what this is? Are you some sort of sugar daddy and you're looking for someone to care for and spend your dead dollars on?"

My eyes widen and I stand up.

"No!" I scowl at her, "Jesus, no!" My hand pushes through my hair in frustration, "I was being kind, supportive... you *needed* my help so yes, I did think you needed my help but the sugar daddy thing," I shake my head, my voice rushed, "fuck, no."

"Not your type?" her brows pop into her head and she gives me a playful smile.

"You're young enough to be my daughter," I swallow hard, ignoring the blood that is thrashing so hard around my body, I can hear it in my ears.

"Ew," she scrunches her nose up, "so you took pity on me?" She sits back up, crossing her legs and playing with a loose thread on the covers.

"No," I shook my head, "I was worried..." I stall for a moment, licking my lips. "After running into you at the coffee shop and then seeing the marks I couldn't get you off my mind. Then you popped up in one of the newspapers and I saw your connection with Chord... well, I put two and two together and found you. Right place right time and all that..." I let out a low, gentle sigh of relief at the lie I just spun. It felt *too* easy.

"Oh," she breathes, her voice barely audible.

"I just needed to know you were safe."

She nods.

Silence crackles between us and I take that as my cue to leave.

"Stay for as long as you want or need... honestly." I smile but she doesn't see it, her eyes are fixed to the thread. "I work in the city, so it really is no bother to me," I roll my lips and turn to walk from the room. "You hungry?" I call from the door and her red rimmed eyes meet mine, she shakes her head.

"Okay," a small smile slips past my lips before I close the door on her.

Pulling out my phone I see a message from her dad. I should text him, but I'm not ready yet.

I don't want him knowing I have her.

Just a few more days.

CHAPTER FOURTEEN
CONNIE

THE NEXT COUPLE OF DAYS PASS IN A BLUR, I HARDLY VENTURE OUT of my room. I've set up camp in here and that's where I have been happy. Kaleb has kept his distance which I have been grateful for. I haven't switched my phone on since my first morning here and I am okay with that. I have no reason to look at my phone. No one of any importance to me is on there, well, apart from Robert but I have had no messages from him since I left my number at the front desk of the hotel he works at. I was going to give it until next week and then call again, but that thought soon diminishes. He was just being nice; he didn't want to be my friend.

Sighing as I flick through the channels, nothing is catching my attention. The one thing I could lose myself in is *The Vampire Diaries*. But I don't even think that would help me now. I feel myself getting agitated, feeling like the person I once was is slowly slipping away from me, and I am losing my grasp on her. Like she is drowning inside of me and no matter how much I pulled her to the surface, she just slipped straight back into the dark depths again.

Clicking the television off, I slam my hands down by my

side into the comforter and sigh. I need to pull myself together. But I just can't. Tears prick behind my eyes and instead of fighting them like I normally do, I let them fall. I let all the pent-up emotion I have been burying resurface, all the grief and heartbreak I feel I let out. I need to. I have to. Because if I don't all of this emotion is going to destroy me.

I've lost everything.

My dad

Reese.

My moms.

Tryst...

Everything I knew and loved is gone and why? Because of me.

Because I am too damn stubborn to swallow my pride and walk back. It's too late, I couldn't go back now. I have *nothing* to go back for.

I have no one.

Letting myself slip under the covers, I sob until I have no more tears left inside of me. My eyes are dry, my lips are cracked and chapped from the constant licking of them to catch the salty tears that cross them. My throat burns, my chest tight from the heaving gasps I've taken. I'm a mess.

LAYING IN THE BATH, MY INTAKES OF BREATH STILL SHUDDER FROM the amount I have cried. The hot bath is helping, my body relaxing in the lavender bath salts I poured in. Closing my eyes, I focus on my slow inhales as I try to calm myself down. A knock on the door makes me jump and I see the doorknob twist. I freeze, trying to cover myself as Kaleb pops his head round the door.

"CLOSE YOUR EYES!" I shout out, sinking a little lower under the water.

"I'm not looking!" he defends himself and I smile at him squeezing his eyes tightly. shut. "Dinner is here, I would really like if you could join me for dinner." His tone is soft.

"Okay," I whisper, my heart drumming in my chest. "I just need a minute..."

"Sure! Yes, of course," he rushes out. "I'll see you in a bit."

He closes the door quickly and I hear him muttering to himself. I let out a small giggle and submerge myself under the water.

Sitting at the table, I am wearing the hotel provided dressing gown. No words have been exchanged as I push my broccoli around my plate. Kaleb had ordered chicken, mashed potato and broccoli. It smelt delicious but my appetite just wasn't there.

"Everything okay?" Kaleb asks and I lift my eyes from my plate to meet his. I nod, dropping my fork.

"I need to try and get some of my stuff back," I say quietly as Kaleb takes a mouthful of chicken.

"Where is it?" he asks, cutting another piece of chicken and swiping it through the creamy mash. My stomach grumbles. Maybe I should just eat a little bit. Picking my fork back up, I spoon a small amount of mash onto the prongs of my fork and taste a bit.

"I have two suitcases at the hotel, I only took what I needed for the tour and the rest is at my moms'."

He nods, chewing slowly

"I'll get your clothes."

Smiling I take another small bite.

"I am really grateful for the bits you sorted for me, but it would be nice to have some of my own stuff, yano?"

"I get it, Connie." His eyes meet mine and I see the kindness that flashes through them, my heart expanding in my chest.

I feel a shift in the air, a loud crackling consuming me when a high-pitched ring pulls me from my moment. Kaleb's eyes pull from mine as he looks at his phone. His lips press into a thin line as he quickly picks the phone up and slides his chair back.

"Please, excuse me for a moment."

My eyes fall to my plate as he walks from the room.

"Yes," he barks into the speaker of his phone before slipping into his room and closing the door behind him.

Laying on the sofa, I let the noise from the television fill the large space, the sound of the *Salvatore* brothers surrounding the room. This show quickly became my comfort show. I watched it repeatedly on tour with Tryst, it helped fill the long and lonely nights. Kaleb has been working on his laptop since he got off the phone, I have no idea what he does, and I don't feel like it's my place to ask him. My wandering eyes can't help but watch him, but every time he moves, I tear my eyes away because I don't want him to catch me. His phone rings again and he is quick to answer and disappears.

Sighing, I roll on my side on the sofa. I feel out of place. Kaleb extended the room for another week but said we will have to move on soon. I like it here; it feels like home because I spent the majority of my time here before I ran from home. I met Reese here; my friends were here. This was *home*.

Maybe I could rent a room here for a while, find my feet then decide where to go after that. Something clicked and it felt like the right move to make. I just needed to tell Kaleb.

Turning the tele off and padding to my room, I decided to call it a night. Kaleb hadn't come back from his phone call, so I assumed he wasn't going to. Closing the door behind me, I crawl up the bed and fall flat. I feel like I'm lying on a cloud. Reaching across to the bedside table for my phone I debate for a moment or two whether to turn it on. I should really. What if something had happened within the family. Not giving myself another second to change my mind, I turned it on. It took a moment to come to life, but once it did I was hit with notifications. Mostly from Tryst but I ignored them. As I went to set the phone back down, I got the dreaded ping noise. This wasn't a good notification. Tryst set me up with a custom alert for when anything that mentioned the band or my name in the tabloids. I slowly lift myself up from the bed, my heart thumping in my chest. I tried to push the anxiety down that was creeping up my throat, but I couldn't.

My blood ran cold when I saw the headline

CHORD'S LEAD SINGER CAUGHT IN COMPROMISING POSITION! LONG TERM GIRLFRIEND CONNIE FLEES WITH MYSTERY MAN.

My heart is beating so hard I can hear it pumping through my ears.

"No, no, no..." I say to myself as I click the link and there in all his glory is Tryst behind the peroxide blonde haired girl's body and of course they've pixelated her face out.

Tryst looks wild, you can see how high he is. I felt sick, my stomach rolling. I continued scrolling to see me being kissed by Cal, another image being dragged away by Kaleb and an image of us pulling up outside The Plaza.

"What the fuck?" I whisper. I want to cry but I am too damn angry. This has been twisted around and the worse part, whoever papped us followed us to the Plaza which means...

"Fuck!" I shout, my eyes widened with panic as I throw the phone down and rush for my bedroom door. As I swing it open, my steps falter as I bump into Kaleb.

"Kaleb," I whisper, I am too panicked and worried to even get my voice out.

"I know," he nods, stepping back and clicking his phone. "Get the car," he bellows into the handset, clicking the call off and frantically rushing into his room, tossing his clothes into his bag.

"Where are we going?"

"Away from here," he grits whilst he continues stuffing his bag, "go pack."

I nod, turning and rushing for my room to pack the little clothes I did have and put them in the small duffel bag at the bottom of the wardrobe.

I am anxious and nervous; nausea swims at the bottom of my stomach and I'm worried if I move too quickly, I'll vomit over myself.

Kaleb is at my door, his eyes frantic. "You ready?"

I nod, zipping up the duffel bag. It's only when I walk towards the main door, I realise I am still in my pyjamas. I stop in my tracks and look down at myself.

"Don't worry about that now, we're going straight into the car."

Rolling my lips I follow him towards the lift, he grabs my bag from my grasp and continuously pushes the elevator button.

"You do know, that if you keep pushing it like that it doesn't make it come any faster," I twist my lips as I try to fight my smile.

His head snaps to face me and his glare is cold.

I go in on myself, dropping my head as I wait. The elevator pings and the door slides open. He pushes me in, then steps in close behind me. My breath wavers at the thought of him being so close to me.

His foot is tapping as his patience is wearing thin, his eyes move from the floor tracker to his watch. The silence is deafening. The tension and awkwardness is growing, my stomach is in twists of knots.

"They weren't out there this morning, hopefully they haven't got here yet." He mutters.

"But they followed us on that night, do you think the person who followed has been sitting here and because he didn't see anything, he tipped the newspapers off?"

"I have no idea."

"Like smoking us out?" My eyes widen, "He knew if he tipped the papers off we would be forced out," I gasp, reaching forward and pulling the emergency button.

"Connie!" Kaleb snaps reaching for the button, but I stop him.

"Please, I need a minute," I grab the root of my hair, tugging it as I pace the small square of the lift floor. My mind ticks over with memories from that night. The hallways are so narrow, it was only me, Cal and Kaleb. I still, my face whitening as the blood drains. My head snaps up and I glare at Kaleb.

"You took the photo," my voice shakes.

"Sorry?"

"You," I point at him, "you took the photo..." I stammer, "did you sell me out!?" I shove him, rage consuming me.

"What the fuck?!" he roars, his back hitting the wall of the elevator and I shove him again. "Why would I do that?" his jaw clenches, his back teeth grinding down.

"I don't know, Kaleb. Why would you?" My brows furrow, "I mean, you did just show up at the coffee shop, then at the show *conveniently* when Cal touches me." My eyes stay pinned to his, "You must understand where I am coming from right?!" my voice is growing louder as panic begins to grow inside of me. "Shit," I whisper, my chest heaving up and down. I hadn't noticed, but Kaleb was standing in front of me, his hands cupping my face as he holds me in place.

"Love," his voice is low and raspy as his face edges closer to mine, "I wouldn't do this to you, I promise you."

His eyes bounce back and forth between mine, my heart thumping in my chest.

I rub my lips together and make a small noise of agreement, but I can't believe him wholeheartedly, even though I want to... I inhale deeply, nibbling the inside of my lip to stop myself from saying anything.

"Now, can we go? *Please*?"

I could hear the desperation in his voice, every minute counts for the vermin to be hanging around on the sidewalks waiting.

I nod. He drops my hand and smashes the emergency stop button and the lift began its descent again.

"Do you trust me?" he asks as the lift lands on the ground floor. I suck in a breath and nod. He gives me a small smile, lifting one of the duffle bags onto his shoulder, he reaches for my hand and grasps it tightly.

Tugging me forward, I walk alongside him. I hated not having my cap on, but I was grateful that my eye had gone down slightly.

We approach the entrance to the hotel, and I can see the flashing lights, my eyes widening before I drop my head.

"Good girl, keep your head down," his voice is soft as we step out and into the pap's onslaught.

"Connie! Connie!" they call, and Kaleb tightens his grip around my hand.

They push forward, trying to get between me and Kaleb but he won't let them.

"Get the fuck off her!" he shouts, shoving one of the pap's cameras out of his face and pulls me closer to him. Another comes up from the side and pushes the camera in my face while shouting questions.

"How long had Tryst been cheating on you?"

"Is this the new mystery man?"

"Was Tryst with that girl for revenge?"

"Did he find out you were hooking up with his bandmate and that's why he retaliated?"

Said photographer grabbed my forearm trying to stop me and Kaleb snaps.

"Fucking touch her again and you'll die!" he shoves him away and I am grateful that there is a blacked-out car sitting close to the sidewalk waiting for us.

Kaleb shoves me into the car with force before climbing in and slamming the door behind us.

"Drive!" Kaleb orders his driver, and he pulls into a lane and heads away from the city. "Are you okay?" He asks, edging closer to me.

I nod slowly, my hands trembling.

I knew paps could be ruthless, but I never expected to be on the receiving end of it.

"We will be home in a while, don't worry darling, I've got you," he mumbles, wrapping his arm around me and pulling me into his side. "I promise."

CHAPTER FIFTEEN
CONNIE

WE WERE PULLED UP ON MADISON AVENUE, KALEB STANDING beside me on the sidewalk with the two bags.

"Welcome home," he smiles before stepping forward and climbing the stairs to greet the doorman.

"Evening Clive," he says curtly as I follow behind him. I give Clive a curt nod as I walk past. Kaleb keeps moving forward towards a private elevator. "Keep up," Kaleb orders as he slides a key card through the slot, the doors pinging open. Kaleb's eyes are on me as I stalk beside him. Once the doors close Kaleb instantly relaxes, exhaling a deep breath.

"Are you okay?" I ask, my stomach coiling in a tight knot.

He turns to look at me, his eyes soften then he drops his head forward, shaking it from side to side.

"No?"

"No, I'm fine," he smiles as he looks at me, "I just can't believe you're asking me if *I* am okay, when it should be me asking you."

I shrug my shoulders, "Not everyone can be like me."

He just smiles, his eyes pinning back to the lights that

are counting up. We come to an abrupt stop. Kaleb inhales deeply, the doors opening, and I follow him out. Walking down a short, narrow hallway, he turns, and I stall.

In front of me is a beautiful open planned layout. There is a large lobby area with a table that has fresh lilac and blue hydrangeas in. The floor is covered in square, high gloss white marble-streaked tiles, the table that sits in the middle is made from deep, red mahogany wood. It's not something I would put together, but it somehow works. The soft smell of clean cotton fills the room, and it instantly makes me feel at home. Kaleb walks forward after tossing his keys on a matching mahogany sideboard and kicks his shoes off next to the bags he dropped to the floor. He heads towards a lounge and dining area. The carpets are oatmeal, soft and plush. As he steps towards the small bar area in the corner, his foot imprints leave a trail behind. I follow, kicking my own shoes off and walking behind him. The room is dull until Kaleb clicks a light switch on. My eyes widen at the beauty of this room, the soft cream and gold chesterfield style sofas sit around a large, square coffee table. The hanging drapes match the sofa colour and scream lavish. There are little side tables dotted around with more hydrangeas and personal photos that I want to look at, but I let my eyes keep scanning.

Hanging above me is a large, ornate, gold chandelier. The reflections from the crystals scattered over the carpet and surfaces, and suddenly, panic arises inside of me. Does he have a wife? Did she design all of this? I don't know why, but it makes me anxious that I am in his home that he shares with a wife.

"Would you like a drink?" he asks, pulling the crystal stopper out of the decanter. He reaches for a glass and pours himself a drink.

I shake my head from side to side.

"Are you hungry?"

"No," I whisper, "I'm just tired," I yawn, rubbing my face with my hand.

"Okay, let me show you where the kitchen is, then I'll take you to your room." He swallows his bourbon down in one, then places the glass back on the tray he originally got it from.

I follow him out back into the lobby where I notice a sweeping staircase with an ornate cast iron handrail and railings. The stairs are mahogany hardwood but have a strip of oatmeal carpet running up them and gold carpet runners to hold it in place. We bypass the stairs and walk down a little hallway. He shows me the large laundry room, the downstairs restroom then the hallway runs into a large open planned kitchen with a large island with stools tucked underneath. The kitchen is all creams and neutrals, the work top is white which has gold specks scattered through. It looks unused. Everything is in pristine condition.

"Help yourself to anything you like, the fridge is always stocked. If there is anything you want or need, pop it on the list on the side of the fridge and Doris will collect it with the shopping," he smiles.

Doris?

Kaleb must see the confused expression on my face.

"My housekeeper," he smiles, giving me a gentle nod.

Ah, makes sense.

"Oh, okay," I smile at him as he switches the lights off in the kitchen.

We turn and walk back down the hallway, and I can't help but feel a sense of calm here. I'm not sure if it's because I've been on tour for months on end, or if it's because I'm with Kaleb but something about here feels right. *Home*.

I follow him up the stairs and come to a large square landing. He opens the first door on the left and steps inside, turning the light on. There is a four-poster bed on the back wall, French shabby-chic small dressers either side of the bed. The large windows open the room up and make it feel a lot bigger than it actually is. He moves forward, leaning into a closet and turning another light on.

"This'll be your closet whilst you're here." His lips roll into a thin line, his eyes moving from me to the room.

"Thank you," I nod curtly. He spins and behind the door is another large dresser with a television fixed to it, on the other side of the room is a dressing table and large mirror. My eyes move to the other closed door and Kaleb strolls over and opens it.

"This is a connected bathroom to the other spare room, it's only yours, but I wanted to explain what the other door was," he smiles kindly and switches the light on.

There is a large corner bath, a toilet, two basins sat inside a washer unit and a large mirror that takes up the whole back wall. Moving back, Kaleb shuts the door and rubs his hands together.

"I'll bring your bags up, and tomorrow I'll go about getting your things."

"Okay," I lick my lips, pressing onto my toes before rocking down onto my heels.

"I hope everything is okay here."

"Everything is perfect, thank you. I am so grateful," I blush as I knot my fingers.

"Hopefully you'll be here a couple of nights and I will help you on your way," he nods before walking out the bedroom.

I don't get a chance to respond because he is already gone.

I walk cautiously over to the bed and sit on the edge. The mattress is soft, the comforter is satin and feels amazing against my fingertips as I run them back and forth over the delicate material. I'm not alone long when Kaleb appears in the doorway again with my bag. He steps in over the threshold and places the bag down by the dresser.

"You sure you don't need anything?" he asks, and I shake my head. "Okay, well, get some sleep. I'll see you in the morning." He steps back, holding onto the door handle.

"Goodnight Kaleb," my voice is soft, my wide eyes on his.

"Goodnight Connie," and he is gone, the door closes softly behind him and I'm alone again.

I edge up the bed, pulling back the sheets and slip between them. The smell of fresh lavender fills me and suddenly, I am ready to fall into a deep slumber. Yawning, I roll on my side and tuck my comforter up and under my cheek. My eyes fall heavy, and even if I tried to fight it, I couldn't.

CHAPTER SIXTEEN
KALEB

I SIT DOWNSTAIRS IN THE DIMLY LIT LIVING ROOM AND SIP ON MY bourbon. It had gone one am, but I was too wired to sleep. My body wanted to sleep, but my brain did not. I hated the fact that she thought I leaked the picture. I took the photo for her benefit, for her own sake. I would never have released it. I wanted to threaten Tryst and that's exactly what I did, but now it has backfired, and she is dealing with the scandal of it all. I've had to talk myself out of going to see Tryst and beating him until all of my frustration has seeped out of me, but that wouldn't help and the last thing I would want is to push Connie away. She wouldn't go back to her dad's place or her moms' so all I would be doing is pushing her onto the streets. I have no idea if she has any money or whether Tryst paid for her lifestyle.

I know nothing about her so to speak.

Her dad has been ringing and messaging me, but every time he calls, I give him the fuck off by cutting him off.

I have nothing more to tell him. I messaged as soon as the article went live, letting him know that his daughter was safe and that I was helping her keep her head down until the scandal wears of. That's all I had.

Letting my head fall back, I inhaled deeply.

"I have no idea what I am going to do," I mumble to myself, lifting my head and taking a mouthful of my drink. "But sitting here drinking by myself isn't going to help anything."

I nod, pushing from the small, tanned leather chair that sits beside the bar, along with a matching armchair and a tall, bell lamp. I place my glass down on the surface. Bending and twisting the small light switch down, dimming the light out completely I pace up to my room. I still as I reach hers, the want that fills me to push her door open and make sure she is okay overwhelms me. I debate it but shake my head at myself.

Rule one of what we do.

You never sleep with or fall for a client.

Not that I would with Connie; she is over twenty years younger than me.

It would be wrong.

Picking up my feet, I march across to my room and close the door behind me. I need to sleep. Tiredness is making me delusional.

Sitting on the edge of my bed, I undress myself and fold my clothes away neatly. Wearing only my boxer shorts, I pull back the cotton sheets and comforter and snuggle down.

I will for sleep to come, but I spend most of the time with my eyes pinned to the ceiling.

It'll come eventually.

It always does.

Eventually.

Drifting in and out of sleep, I hear the distant sound of an alarm. Rolling over, I lift the spare pillow and smother it over my head. I groan when it doesn't stop, throwing the pillow and sitting up. It's coming from my phone.

"Fuck," I reach across and see the alarm for six a.m. flashing.

Shutting it off, I fall back down and lay for a moment. I need five minutes to come round. Once I finally got asleep, I fell into a deep slumber and now I feel groggy as hell.

Throwing the covers back, I sit up and stay on the edge of the bed as I let my feet sink into the plush, thick carpet. I reach my arms up and stretch my back out, hearing a satisfying click before letting them fall to my side. Clicking my neck left and right I stand, ignoring my morning wood and walk into my bathroom. I turn the shower on and stand at the basin. Splashing my face with cold water, I rub my hand over my dark stubble.

"You need a shave," I groan, dropping my boxer shorts and walking into the hot shower.

Once dressed in my suit, I style my hair and finish off with a spray of cologne and slap some aftershave on my face, wincing as the sting burns at the small nick I gave myself whilst shaving. My thoughts roam to Connie, I wonder if she is still asleep. I slip my watch on and look at the time, it's seven-thirty. Of course, she is asleep.

Opening the door quietly, I look out into the landing area and see her door is still closed. Edging quietly across the floor and to the stairs I try to avoid the creaking step.

Once downstairs, I relax and pace into the kitchen to see Doris and Connie.

"Oh, you're awake," I smile, looking at a bed head

Connie. She has pillow creases in her soft, rosy cheeks. Her brown hair is all over the place and her wide, green eyes are glistening. I have no idea why, but morning Connie is starting to become a favourite of mine.

"I am," she tilts her head to the side and takes a mouthful of coffee. "Morning," she chirps.

"Good morning," I give a warm smile and walk towards the coffee machine, "Morning Doris," I call as she potters about making breakfast.

"Morning Kaleb," she turns and looks at me before focusing on whatever is in her frying pan. Whatever it is, it smells delicious.

Taking my cup from the coffee machine, I grab the paper that Doris has left in my usual spot and perch myself on the stool. I place my coffee on the breakfast bar and open the first page.

Doris places two plates down in front of me and I watch as Connie looks up at Doris.

"Oh, you didn't have to," Connie's cheeks warm with a blush.

"I know I didn't, but I did," Doris winks at Connie before loading the dishwasher and walking out the room.

Folding my paper, I bring my plate closer to me. Bacon, eggs, avocado and toast. My stomach grumbles. I look over at Connie who just stares at the plate.

"Please eat," I say softly, and she nods, picking up her knife and fork.

"Do you have any ketchup?" she asks softly, and I nod.

"It's in the cupboard above the fridge," I would offer to get it for her but knowing Connie, she will want to do it herself. I don't think she likes being waited on.

She reaches up, her long tanned legs on show. She has changed since last night. She is wearing shorts and an oversized tee. I bat my eyes down, feeling wrong for looking at her that way.

She sits back down next to me and smothers every part of her food in sauce. I scrunch my nose up before lifting a brow.

"So, you like ketchup?"

"I do," she shrugs, putting the cap back on and digging in.

"I'll make sure to ask Doris to get some more." I smirk and pop a forkful of bacon and eggs into my mouth.

"How long has Doris worked for you?" she asks, not lifting her eyes from her food.

"About ten years I think," I smile.

"Wow."

"Mmhmm."

"Does she live here?"

"No, she goes home every night to her husband. I did offer to move them in, but she wouldn't," I shrug my shoulders up, "but it works this way too."

"She seems really nice."

"She is, she's the best," I whisper, "but don't let her know I said that," I wink.

"I heard you," Doris' voice is loud as she re-enters the kitchen and Connie giggles.

Doris is in her late fifties, her real name is Penelope, but I used to joke and call her Doris. She used to moan at me and give me crap at first, but now, I think she likes it too.

Finishing my breakfast, I push the plate away and I feel Connie's eyes burn into the side of my head as Doris takes my plate and cleans it.

I ignore her and continue my coffee and my paper before I have to leave.

My phone buzzes and it's Keaton, letting me know he is on his way up. I widen my eyes. *Shit.*

Downing my coffee, I push up and leave my cup as I look at my watch. I need to get out before Keaton sees Connie. He is a walking boner and there is no way he is getting near her.

I turn and see Connie just gawking at me, but I ignore her, rushing from the kitchen into the lobby.

"Good morning brother," Keaton comes strolling through the lobby, umbrella in hand.

"Morning," I grit, pushing past him and reaching for my own umbrella from the rack.

Keaton's eyes soon pass mine when he looks behind me and smirks.

"Well, good morning to you too," he strides past me and straight towards Connie.

"Keaton, come on. We've got to go," I grumble, turning and seeing him take Connie's hand, placing a kiss on the back of it. I roll my eyes.

"What's the rush brother? We only have a meeting with the two knob rots, let's make them wait a little," he turns to look at me and winks. Connie's eyes meet mine and I shake my head from side to side.

"So, do I get a name?" Keaton asks as Doris disappears in the lounge, "I would love a coffee Doris." She flips him off which causes a scoff of a laugh from me and wide eyes from Connie.

"You just can't get the staff these days," he laughs, "well, your name?"

"Connie," she says quietly, and he turns to face me, putting two and two together.

"Connie, what a lovely name," he turns up the charm, "it's a pleasure to meet you."

"I wish I could say the same," she pulls her hand from his, she was giving a carefree vibe at first, but now she's being cold and I'm not sure why, "have a good day." She gives him a curt nod before turning her attention back to me. "Kaleb, I'll see you tonight," she smiles and begins walking up the stairs.

"Hold on!" I call, rushing up the stairs behind her, "Are you okay?" I ask quietly, wanting to check in.

She turns to face me, hand on hip, the other wrapped and holding onto the handrail. She gives me a tight nod, her eyes not meeting mine.

"I've left my number on the lobby table, if you need anything then call me. Stay here today please, don't leave. Doris will be here all day, there are films, food, whatever you want. Just stay." I plead.

She nods again before I see her lips part.

"I was thinking of going to the book shop, would that be okay?" she bats her lashes and I groan.

"How about you text me what sort of books you like, and I'll grab them on my lunch and get them sent here, how about that?"

She rolls her eyes into the back of her head.

"I may aswell just tell you, I like romance books," she retorts and smirks.

"Good girl, perfect. I'll be home at five." I rush out as I step backwards towards Keaton. I watch as she turns and continues walking up the stairs and my eyes land on her peachy ass. I squeeze my eyes shut and turn to go down and rush to the bottom.

"Ready?" I ask, picking my umbrella back up.

"Oh, I am," Keaton smirks and walks beside me to the elevator.

Idiot.

CHAPTER SEVENTEEN
KALEB

Shaking off my soaked umbrella as I step into our office building, a shiver runs down my spine.

"Kept that one quiet didn't you," Keaton pipes up as he shakes his own off.

"There was a reason, now be quiet," I grit, dropping the umbrella into the basket by the door.

Keaton nudges into me but I don't retaliate. Pressing the button for the lift Keaton stands close to me.

"Have you slept with her?" my nostrils flare and I turn to face him and clip him round the back of his head

"She's the same age as Titus' daughter, for fuck's sake," I groan, stepping into the lift, the douche bag following me.

"And?"

"Keaton, please mate, give it a fucking rest." I grind my teeth, "You're exhausting!"

"I know, it's a full-time job," he shrugs his shoulders up, "but someone has to do it."

The doors ping open and Keaton walks out into the large open planned offices and I follow behind already agitated with my twin brother. We look nothing alike, and neither are our personalities. We just share similar DNA.

Keaton disappears into his office and I am grateful. I did not need that on a Wednesday morning. Wednesdays are bad enough without his constant noise.

"Morning guys," I say exasperated as I sit on the edge of Nate's desk. His head lifts out of his computer screen, and he smiles.

"You okay?" he asks, pushing his black glasses up his nose. He has mousy brown hair that sits in a tousled mess on top of his head.

"Yeah, not too bad," I mutter as Titus leans back on his chair.

"Keaton being a dick?" Titus has short, shaved black hair and a trimmed, neat black beard. He is broad, tall and a handsome little fucker.

"Yup."

"But when am I not a dick?" Keaton laughs from behind me, "Coffee?" he asks the three of us and we all nod.

"So, what's new?" Nate asks as he taps away on his keyboard. Nate is our IT guy, we would be lost without him. Titus is a bodyguard and Keaton is our accountant. And me? I'm a private investigator. I am CEO of Mills, Spencer, King. We've all been friends since kindergarten, and we stayed buddies ever since. I know you always get groups who seem to drift once they're grown and shit, but not us. We've been through so much as a group and I know if I needed to hide a body, it would be these guys I would call. Or Xavier. But he was a last resort.

I sigh, opening my mouth when Keaton swoops in.

"Well, he has his client living with him…" Keaton smirks, "isn't that right Kaleb?"

Titus and Nate lift their eyes to meet mine and I swallow.

"Shut. The. Fuck. Up," Titus smirks and Nate's eyes bug.

Keaton whistles, sipping his coffee and walks away.

Asshole. He is always the one to stir the shit pot.

"What happened?" Nate asks, sitting back in his office chair reaching for his cup.

"Just an absolute cluster-fuck," I rub my head, pinching my eyes closed for a moment.

"Bro, you shouldn't have brought her home," Titus chuckles, shaking his head, "rookie mistake."

I grind my back teeth and stand, deciding I have had enough of the third degree shit.

"I had to, it's just temporary." Pushing my hand into my suit pants, I grab my coffee in the other.

"Mate," Titus sips his coffee, "it's never temporary."

I turn, rolling my eyes and stalk to my office, slamming the door a little harder than intended when I hear Titus erupt.

The day was long, I checked in with Doris a few times to make sure Connie was okay. I don't know why she invaded my thoughts so much; it was time consuming. Sighing, I opened my emails. I had jobs coming up but until I was finished with Connie, I would pass them onto Titus. The door opens and I see Keaton.

"Go away," I roll my eyes and pin them to my screen.

"Oh, come on, I was only having a laugh earlier."

"Yeah," I nod, "but that's the problem, everything is a laugh to you." I don't allow myself to look at him.

"I'm going to grab some lunch; do you want some?" his tone was curt but I expected it.

"Just grab me a meatball sub please."

"Okay," Keaton mutters and closes the door behind him.

I sit back in my chair and let out an exasperated sigh. She was in my head and it didn't matter what I done, I couldn't shake her. Opening my drawer, I slip out my phone and see if I've had any missed calls from Doris, but I haven't. Dropping it back inside, I slam it shut.

It wasn't long before Keaton was back, he tossed the wrapped sub onto my desk and turned on his heel.

"Keaton," I call, and he turns to face me. "Look, I'm sorry for being a dick..." He nods. "No, honestly, I am. I was being a shitty brother." I see Keaton's brows pull and a hint of concern flash through his eyes.

"What's going on?" he asked as he slowly walked towards me and sits on the large, black leather armchairs that sat in front of my desk.

"I have no idea," I shake my head, letting my eyes fall to my lap. "I shouldn't have taken her home, no but I can't help but keep her protected. I know that whilst she is with me, she is safe. I don't want her ex getting to her again..."

Keaton says nothing, just presses his fingers into his chin and stares me down.

"I am scared of what he would do to her..." I swallow thickly, "but when she is with me, I can keep her safe."

He nods.

"But you can't keep her forever Kaleb, she isn't yours to keep."

And that sentence sucker punched me straight through my gut.

CHAPTER EIGHTEEN
CONNIE

LAYING ON THE SOFA, I AM LOST BETWEEN THE PAGES OF ONE OF the books that Kaleb got sent to me. I love living in these perfect romance stories with the beautiful happily ever after. That's what I want.

I want to be in my own romance book where I know I am guaranteed the happy ending. My heart thumps and my stomach twists. Closing my book softly I lay for a moment, my eyes closing whilst I just let my thoughts drift. I always see myself walking down the aisle, but I never seem to get to the stranger who is standing at the end waiting for me. Every time I get close, I wake up.

My eyes open and Doris is standing at my side, making me jump out of my skin.

"I am so sorry to startle you dear," her eyes are soft as she talks.

"It's okay," I smile, swinging my legs round and sitting on the edge of the sofa.

"I'll be doing dinner soon, Kaleb has asked for you to join him," she smiles, stepping away from me.

"Of course," I nod.

"He will be home in an hour," she states before she turns and walks away. Grabbing my book, I push from the sofa and make my way upstairs. I needed to get changed. I have been in my pyjamas all day.

Placing my book on my bed, I turn and stride towards the bathroom and close the door behind me. I needed a shower and to wash my hair. I can't sit at the table looking like this. I wasn't making an effort for him; I was making the effort for *me*. Lazing around all day had made me feel cooty. I liked how I felt living here, I felt safe here, I felt comfortable here. But it's just temporary.

Kaleb was just being kind.

Turning the shower on, I strip down and let the hot water wash over me, taking all of my tension and thoughts down the drain with it.

Dressed in skinny blue jeans and an oversized white tee, I gave myself a blow-out then run my fingers through the ends of my silky, brown hair. Sitting down at the dresser, I smiled back at my reflection. Reaching across for the small make-up bag that I travelled with. I couldn't wait to have all my actual stuff. I have no idea if Kaleb was still going to grab them today, but I didn't want to be pushy and ask.

Tipping everything out in front of me, excitement weaved through me at spending the time doing my make-up. I couldn't even remember the last time I actually done it.

Once finished, I felt amazing, my skin was glowing thanks to my foundation and highlighter. Plus, the purple bruising from my eye was nicely hidden. Standing from the dressing table, I moved for the door, my fingers wrapping around the handle when I felt the give on the other side. The door pushed open quickly at the same time I stepped forward and it hit me, right in the middle of my forehead.

"Damn it!" I shout, my hand falling from the handle as I press it against my head, the throbbing pain pulsing through me.

"Oh my god, Connie are you okay?" Kaleb rushes to my side, gripping my chin and lifting me up to look at him.

"I'm fine," I wince, dropping my hand from my head.

"I've marked you," his eyes widen, his fingers brushing my hair from my face. The tips skimming against my skin making me tingle all over.

"It's fine," I reassure him as I step back, trying to break the contact. The air was crackling between us, the tension growing, and it was making me nervous.

Kaleb clears his throat, also stepping back and fisting his hands deep inside his pockets. His eyes roam up and down my body, but mine stay on his. I watch as they sweep over me, the blood rushing into my cheeks. His lips twitch slightly before his eyes land on mine.

"You look lovely," he smiles proudly.

"Thank you," I let my head fall so I can hide my giddy smile.

"Ready for food? Doris loves putting on a feast," I can hear the smile in his voice before I see it.

"I am," I finally lift my head, my smile still plastered on my face.

"Then let's go," he steps aside and lets me walk out and we walk side by side to the dinner table.

He wasn't lying, Doris has laid out a wonderful meal. My stomach grumbles.

Kaleb rushes past me, pulling out my seat and letting me sit down first.

"Thank you," my voice is low and soft, but he hears me. He walks round the other side of the table and sits opposite me. He has a glass of red sitting at his place setting, but my glass is empty.

"Would you like some?" he asks, apprehension lacing his tone. I nod.

"Only a little please, I try not to drink much anymore..." I trail off and roll my lips. I don't want to open up to him about my previous struggles. I have an addictive personality and habits can change thick and fast.

"Of course," he lifts the bottle and I meet the opening with my glass. The glug fills the empty room, the lights are dimmed, and the candles burn softly on the table. I nod as he stops pouring and I lift the glass to my lips and take a sip. Its oaky, smoky and rich bodied. Very delicious.

Kaleb picks his knife and fork up and cuts into his chicken, and I mirror him.

"How was your day?" he asks once he has finished chewing. I cut into my potatoes, hovering the bit that's on my fork in the air. "I'm sorry I didn't get a chance to grab your clothes, work run away with me."

"It's fine," I wave him off, I didn't want to come across as bratty or ungrateful, "It was good, a little lonely, but good." I pop the potato into my mouth. "How about you?" I ask before chewing. He places his knife and fork down and takes a long, slow mouthful of wine.

"It could have been better," his tone is flat, his eyes fall to his lap for a moment.

"I'm sorry to hear that."

"Don't be, that's what happens when you work with family," I smirk back at him.

"Family and work don't mix," I snort a laugh.

"Have you done it before?" he asks, placing his wine glass back on the table before he goes back to his dinner.

"I haven't, but my dad used to offer me a job with him

all the time, but I always declined," I shake my head from side to side, "family and work..."

"I know, it can be a cluster-fuck." He scoffs and smiles.

"It can, I much preferred working by myself and finding a job I wanted to do, not *had* to do because it was expected of me."

His lips turn down, but I can see the smile he is fighting. "That's a good way to look at it."

"I loved working in the hotel, it was easy, the money was okay, but I was happy. I enjoyed going into work, and that's where I met my best friend Reese," the smile that was on my face begins to slip but I don't let it slip for long, and I force it back onto my face. This is not a topic I want to stay on.

"So, Keaton... is he older or younger?"

"I'm older by a minute," Kaleb smiles.

"You're twins?!" He nods.

"Luckily not identical, I mean, I am by *far* the better looking one," he puffs his broad chest out and sits tall and I nibble on the inside of my lip to stop my laugh.

"*Really?*" I wince, "'cause, I've got to say, I was leaning more towards team Keaton." I struggle to finish my sentence before I burst into laughter, and Kaleb joins me.

And that's when I realised, that right now was the first time in a while that I have felt a little like my old self.

The old Connie.

STRETCHING, I SLOWLY SIT UP. A SMILE SLIPPED ONTO MY LIPS, and I felt refreshed. I fell into a deep slumber last night and it seems like a lifetime ago that I slept that heavy. I needed it, clearly. I felt calm here and relaxed.

Reaching for the top drawer I looked at my phone, it had been off since Kaleb switched it off and honestly, I didn't miss it or the pressure of social media. My accounts haven't been updated in a while, I sort of lost interest a few weeks back, before all of this. I didn't want to panic followers but none of that mattered anymore. It felt nice to be able to relax and not worry about what was going on outside of these four walls and that's the way I wanted to keep it.

I was happy.

Really happy.

Letting my legs hang off the bed, I slipped off and pushed my feet into my pink, furry *Ugg* slippers.

Kaleb and Keaton went and got my things from Tryst's apartment late last night whilst the band were playing one of their concerts. It was nice to have everything here with me. Walking over to my bedroom door, I grabbed my silk kimono and slipped it on. Wrapping it round my body and tying it together. I didn't want to walk down in my silk pyjamas. I don't know why but I felt a little more self-conscious this morning.

Opening my door, I padded downstairs quietly. Kaleb's door was still closed. My brows pinched, maybe he wasn't at work today. I shrugged and made my way downstairs to see Doris putting a fresh pot of coffee on.

"Morning dear," she smiles at me, reaching for a white China mug and popping it under the machine. "Coffee?"

"Please," I smile at her, reaching for Kaleb's newspaper and looking at the jumble jargon that was printed on the front. Scrunching my nose, I pop it back in the place I got it from.

Doris passes me the coffee and I nod.

"Anything you fancy for breakfast?" Doris asks, pressing her hands flat on the worktop.

"I'm easy, whatever Kaleb likes," I shrug my shoulders up and lift my cup to my lips.

"Kaleb has already left for the day," she rolls her lips as my eyes pass her and look at the clock on the wall, it's already gone eight.

"Oh," I whisper, slowly placing the cup back on the worktop, then shaking the new feeling that seems to be creeping over me. "I'll just make some cereal, I'm not overly hungry yet," I push a big smile across my face.

"Okay dear, just call out if you need me." Doris says, turning and heading for the kitchen.

"Doris," I call quickly, her name rushing off my tongue. "Do you think we could go for a walk... or something?"

Her smile faded quickly, and she shook her head softly from side to side, "I'm afraid Kaleb wants you to stay here... you know..."

"I know," I whisper, nodding.

I see the grimace on her face before she rushed from the room. Sighing, I sit alone with the silence and enjoy my coffee.

CHAPTER NINETEEN
KALEB

I DON'T KNOW WHY, BUT MY GUT TWISTS AT THE THOUGHT OF leaving the house and not saying bye to Connie. I didn't want to wake her up, but maybe I should have hung around. I rub my hands up and down my face. She has me twisted and I don't know why. Darkness hangs over me, but I would never let that put out her light. She is a pure light in my life, in anyone's life and I would hate myself if I ever was the reason for dimming her light.

A knock on the office door pulls me from my thoughts and I see Keaton step over the threshold.

"You okay?" he asks as he sits on the arm of the leather chair in front of my desk and I nod.

"Just busy," I mutter, scrolling aimlessly through my emails. How do I have so many?

"Yeah? Need any help with anything?" Keaton presses, edging forward slightly.

I shake my head, "No thanks, I've got it."

"We need to go over this quarter's accounts at some point this month, any days better than others?" Keaton asks, standing now from the chair.

"Any day next week should work; things are starting to settle on my side. Titus always gets booked up in the autumn months and I have no idea why..." I pause, my eyes lifting from the screen to Keaton.

"You know why," he rolls his eyes, his lips slipping into a smirk.

"Do I?" I sit back in my seat, pressing my fingers together and pushing them out so they all click.

"Have you seen him? I'm sure nine times out of ten people pay him to be their date, not their bodyguard," Keaton scoffs. But he is right. Out of us all, Titus is the god of the group. Women and younger girls *love* him, and I am sure he *loves* them. Just not enough to break the contract and get *too* close. He has a daughter to think about and the money is too good to throw it away for a quick fuck because he couldn't keep his hands to himself.

"Have you heard about the woman who wants him to be her sugar daddy?" Keaton says non blasé, looking at his freshly manicured hands.

"No!" my eyes bug out my head and I laugh.

"Yup, she won't leave him alone, he said no of course."

"Stop it," I snigger, shaking my head from side to side. I push my shirt slightly up so I can see the time. "Fuck it, shall we go for lunch?"

"Yeah, just before we go, can I ask you something?" Keaton asks, lowering his voice.

"Yeah, course," I nod, locking my computer down.

"Why was it so urgent we needed to go to Connie's ex's last night?" his brows lift before he lets them relax and settle.

"I don't want him getting a sniff of where she is, I don't want to give her any reason to go back to him..."

Keaton's eyes pin to mine, I know that look. He is calling bullshit.

"Then why not just send her home to her *daddy*?"

"Because it's not safe, I promised him I would keep her safe. Don't you think Tryst will go straight there and look for her? I'm not putting her in danger, I know Tryst's kind. Once he gets his fingers dug back into her shoulders, he won't let her go. She will never get out and I can't do that. My job was to investigate and find her. To protect her. And that's what I am doing." I huff, pulling on my suit jacket as I stand, fastening the button. "I'm protecting her," I scowl at him, walking for my office door and out into the main office.

"Let's go to lunch, Keaton's treat," I chime, clapping my hands together and look over my shoulder at a thunderous Keaton. I wink and smile at him. Titus and Nate push up and walk over to us before we all head for the elevator.

I couldn't do this thing called life without these three men.

They were all my family.

My brothers.

FINISHING UP AT THE OFFICE, I LOGGED OFF AND WAS LAST TO leave. Turning the lights off and locking up, I headed to the basement parking lot. Unlocking my red *Mercedes-Maybach GLS*, the beep echoed around the emptiness. Settling in, I turn the engine on and pull out the lot. I didn't want to be here this late, that wasn't my intention but when I get into my job, I switch off and I can't just pull myself from it. It had just gone nine by the time I pulled into the parking lot under my penthouse, pulling into my space. I was glad it was Friday tomorrow, and I decided to stay home. I felt awful for leaving Connie festering at home, she must be bored out of her skull so at least I could keep her company. Once Tryst and his band fuck off out of New York she is free to go where she wishes, but not until I know he is away for good. Panic swarms my insides, my heart clenching. What scares me is that he will never be gone, not really. He may go away for a while but then he will be back for her. That's the thing with narcissists. They never really leave; they always have their hands on you. Controlling you. You're never really free.

I cut the engine and reach for my phone.

There is one person I could call. One person that could make this all go away for her.

Give her the do over she so desperately needed...

For her.

Scrolling my phonebook contacts, I stopped suddenly, my thumb hovering over his name.

Xavier Archibald.

Before I can change my mind, I let my thumb tap on his name and he answers on the second ring.

"What?" his gruff British accent fills the phone and suddenly it dawns on me that he is ahead of me... no doubt I have just woken him up.

"Hi, did I wake you?"

"Yes, but it doesn't fucking matter now does it," he snaps, and I can hear ruffling of bedsheets. "Go back to sleep baby, just got some imbecile on the phone, I won't be a moment Red."

Silence falls heavy over the line for a moment when I hear the sound of a door closing.

"What do you want?"

"I need someone gone... can you help?"

He sighs.

"I just want to retire; I am over this bullshit." He grumbles and the small hope I had slowly dwindles. "I'll email you details to reply to, then delete everything. I am nobody to you." He grits out then cuts the line off.

I let my phone fall from my ear and stare ahead.

For her.

That's what I must keep reminding myself. It's all *for her.*

CHAPTER TWENTY

CONNIE

I LAY ON MY BED, EYES PINNED TO THE CEILING. ROLLING ON MY side I looked at the time on the small, gold alarm clock. It had just gone nine thirty p.m. Anxiety rips through me, I hope Kaleb is okay. My memories flash back to when Reese told me that Elijah was killed in a car accident, the pain in her voice as she explained to me the loss of her love. I would never be able to comprehend the pain that she felt, I don't even know Kaleb, but my heart is already racing a thousand miles an hour at the thought of something happening. Falling onto my back once more, I try and steady my fast breathing. Is it wrong that I feel this anxiety with Kaleb but never with Tryst? I loved Tryst... I think? But he was convenient, a comforter if you will. But I don't miss him. At all.

An ache fills my heart making it heavy, but I have no idea why. I rub my chest trying to ease the ache, but it doesn't work. I'm tempted to turn my phone on, just to text Kaleb. I internally argue with myself then finally giving in. Rolling on my side I reach for the drawer, tugging it when suddenly I feel eyes on me. I turn my head slightly, looking towards the door to see Kaleb leaned up against the door frame, his broad, muscular arms crossed against his chest. My heart pirouetting, my chest slowly rising and falling as my breathing steadies.

"You're home," I whisper, pushing up and sitting at the end of the bed, my legs crossed underneath me.

"Yeah," he breathes out, a small smile creeping on his face, "I am."

Relief washes over me and I stop myself from running towards him and letting him envelope me in his large arms. Sighing, I fiddle with my fingers as my eyes are pulled towards him. I have to fight myself to let my eyes fall. Tension builds between us, crackling.

"Are you okay?" his deep voice breezes through the air, my skin erupting in goosebumps.

"Yeah, I am." I nibble on my full bottom lip, his bright grey eyes dancing with mine. "Are you?"

He nods, pushing off the door frame so he is standing tall, his hands stuffed into the pockets of his suit pants.

"I'm going to stay home tomorrow, thought we could spend the day together..." he trails off, his eyes widening as if a thought has flashed through his mind as the words tumbled from his lips. He rubs his chin. "Only if you want to of course."

My heart drums in my chest, a smile growing on my face. Being home alone every day with only Doris as company, a day with Kaleb sounds amazing.

"That would be wonderful."

"Good," he licks his bottom lip as his tongue darts out. Silence falls between us, the sound of the rain hitting the windowpane. I turn to look, it's almost stormy suddenly. "I'm going to get a drink; do you want to join me?"

I nod, "Let me just get a jumper on," I whisper, a chill

suddenly dancing over my skin. I was only wearing a tee and cotton shorts; I felt warm earlier but now I feel cold and all I want is to be cosy and warm.

Kaleb says nothing, just steps back and into his room and closes the door. I stand for a moment, rocking onto the balls of my feet. Turning I go into my closet, grabbing a pair of yoga pants, an oversized *Blink 182* jumper and slipping my feet back into my fluffy lined *Ugg* slippers.

Pinching my cheeks to let a bit of colour flush them, I didn't want to put make-up on. I run my fingertips through the ends of my hair, pulling a few knots out. I pull it up into a messy ponytail, then drop it back down, puffing my cheeks out.

I have no idea why I am fiddling and fumbling so much. Jesus, I need to pull it together.

Scraping my hair back up, I tie it with a hair tie and head for the door before I change my mind. Moving down the stairs quickly, my fingers wrapped around the handrail to steady myself.

Nerves bubble deep inside me; I press my hand to my stomach and inhale deeply. I have no idea why I am feeling so nervous and apprehensive about being close to him. Or is it excitement?

I roll my neck, then let my hands shake out in front of me. Moving to the lounge, I hover round the bar as I wait for Kaleb to join me. I stop at the floor to ceiling window that overlooks the city, the lights twinkling below me. I feel so high and away from the rest of the world up here. I like it. I don't want to go back down; I don't want to go back to the grind of day-to-day life. I lean forward, my fingertips press against the glass. The coolness making my skin tingle. Sometimes I wish I could fly. To just get away for a while, to just feel *free*.

"Hey," his voice rasps, making me jump.

I spin quickly, my eyes move up and down his body. He is wearing a tee and sweatpants. They're tight, in *all* the right places. Feelings stir deep in my stomach, the burning ache making itself known. I shouldn't be feeling anything like this towards this man.

I hold my hand up, waving gently.

"What was you thinking about, hope you wasn't thinking of escaping," he smirks as he takes long, slow, strides towards me.

I shake my head from side to side, stepping aside to put some distance between us.

"Good," he smiles, moving away from me and towards the cabinets behind the bar.

"Anything in particular tickling your fancy?"

"I'll have whatever you're having, I'm not fussy." I answer softly, picking a bit of skin that surrounds my nail.

"I was going to have an old fashioned, still want one?" He smiles, grabbing two short, crystal tumblers.

"Sounds delicious," I lick my lips.

"Take a seat on the sofa, I'll bring it over." He holds his hand out, gesturing for me to sit down. I do as I am told and wait for him.

I keep my eyes pinned to my hands, I wanted to look at him but I resisted it. I don't know what was wrong with me, I had only been here a few days and I felt myself all shy around Kaleb with no idea why. He wasn't my type; it wasn't even the age thing. I have slept with men my dad's age, even some of his friends, but I couldn't quite put my finger on what it was about Kaleb. He was handsome; beautiful even. A strong jaw line, bright, grey eyes that dazzled when he was happy. His nose was slightly hooked and a little wonky, and it made me wonder if he had ever broken it or if that was just how it was. He had a full, rosy, red bottom lip that I thought about how it would feel to sink my teeth into, his top lip bowed but thin. His cheek bones were high, I had never seen them that high on a man before, but they made his facial features much more striking, everything about his features was striking and defined, he really was the definition of perfect.

If you looked up perfection, handsome, striking and *dishy* in the dictionary, there in bold letters would be **Kaleb Mills**.

I hadn't realised, but he was beside me, looking down at me. His grey eyes glistened, his lips parted, and his gorgeous brown hair was messy and unkept. He wouldn't have had time for a shower, so I am assuming he run his large hands through it to mess it up. Holding his hand out, he passed me the crystal tumbler. I took it, thanking him as I did. I lifted the glass to my nose and sniffed it which caused me to cough as the strong aromas hit the back of my throat.

"It's got a punch," he winked, opting for the chair next to the sofa so he was looking out at the city.

"It certainly has," I cleared my throat and took a sip, my eyes bugging out my head. But not because I didn't like it, no, I loved the flavours, and I was surprised. I'm not a fan of whiskey, but this, this I *really* liked.

"It's good isn't it," Kaleb says as he rests his arms on the arm rests of his chair, his long finger tapping on the side of the crystal glass, his stormy grey eyes burning into me.

"It is, it's delicious," I admit, my tongue darting out and licking my lips as I savour the flavour for a moment more.

Silence fell between us, but it wasn't awkward. It was comfortable. We sat and sipped on our drinks, listening to soft jazz music that Kaleb had put on to fill the large room.

The ambience was relaxing and cosy, candles were lit, and the lights were dimmed giving the room a warm, orange glow.

I felt relaxed, I had forgotten what it was like living on the edge constantly.

"You look very lost in thought," Kaleb's soft voice pulls me away from my mind.

I scoff a small laugh, "I was," I murmur, my smile fading.

"Is everything okay?" he leans forward in his chair, shuffling forward so he is sitting on the edge of the armchair.

"Yeah, just thinking back to when my life wasn't as peaceful as this." I nod softly, even though I'm not agreeing to anything.

"I feel you; this is why I like just sitting here sometimes in nothing but silence, a drink in hand and soft Motown or Jazz crooning through the speakers. It relaxes me, makes me feel at peace somehow." He admits.

"I can understand that, I have never just sat and relaxed. I am always on the go, always doing something to keep my mind busy. Before now, I would be laying on the sofa, scrolling my phone and updating social media constantly worrying if my accounts were growing fast enough. It's an addiction, and until now it was something I craved, but now? I don't miss it at all. I feel like I have had a reset."

He says nothing, just listens as he brings his glass to his lips, taking a mouthful.

"I didn't want to do social media, I used to do it for fun, you know, uploading the odd photo of my weekends out but then as Chord grew, so did my following. I was the in girl, the girl that was *with* the band and people loved to see what happened when it wasn't all 'rock 'n' roll'..." I trailed off a moment, taking my own sip of my drink, wetting my tongue. My throat suddenly felt dry.

"It was fun at first, a new adventure and adrenaline spiked through my veins. I was constantly chasing the high, but with that high came almighty lows. And the pace that Chord grew, the lows came a lot more than the highs in the end..." I stopped talking when I felt the needles of a thousand tears prick behind my eyes. I blinked a few times trying to wash them away. My throat grew thick with a large lump which I tried to wash down with the remainder of my old fashioned. I frowned at the empty glass, looking at the orange peel and remanence of a brown sugar cube sitting at the bottom.

I feel Kaleb's fingers brush against the back of my hand and my eyes meet his. No words are exchanged. They don't have to be. He gets exactly what I am saying.

I smile, before pulling away from the situation. I push up off the sofa and pace over to the window once more, the condensation from the warmth of the penthouse showing. The weather was beginning to turn as the autumn months were creeping round the corner, but I was happy, autumn was my favourite time of year.

My skin tingled when I felt his breath on the back of my neck. My breath caught at the back of my throat, I pinched my eyes closed but pressed my fingertips against the panes of the cool glass, goosebumps erupting over my skin.

"Are you okay?" his voice was a whisper as it danced over my skin. I nod because words don't come when I open my mouth. "I'm going to get another drink, would you like one?"

I nod again.

He pinches the glass from my loose grasp, his fingertips

brush against my heated skin and I feel a shiver blanket me and it takes everything in me not to shudder against it.

He is gone as quick as he came and I gasp an intake of breath, trying desperately to fill my lungs.

"I'm just going to use the restroom," I rush out, turning and keeping my head down as I walk through the lobby and down the hallway. Pushing the door open, I quickly slam it shut and slip the lock across. I turn, pressing my palms into the panelled wooden door before sliding down it. I sit on the cold floor and just take a moment. I have no idea what is wrong with me, feelings stir deep inside of me, feelings I am unfamiliar with and a constant ache in my chest that just doesn't seem to ease.

I feel like I am being suffocated; trying to breathe around Kaleb is proving difficult but I don't want to be away from him.

Letting my head fall, my hands cradle my face, my fingertips pushing into the side of my hair line, up to my scalp.

"Get it together," I scowl out loud to myself. Inhaling deeply, I push off the floor and push the flush. I give it a minute before turning and opening the door. Pushing my chest out and my shoulders back I keep my head held high as I stroll back into the room and take my seat once more, reaching for my drink and falling back into that easy, relaxing, silence.

CHAPTER TWENTY-ONE
KALEB

I CRUSH THE BROWN SUGAR CUBE IN THE BOTTOM OF OUR tumblers then add a ball of ice. Topping with the mixture I finish off with a squirt of orange juice and lay the peel on top of the drink.

I take a sip of mine and hum in appreciation. I turn to look at the empty room and furrow my brows as I see Connie still isn't back. Have I upset her? No, no. I shake my head at my silly thoughts and walk over to where we were sitting, placing her drink down on the coffee table and I take my seat.

I turn my hand over, looking at my soft fingertips and frown expecting to see some kind of mark or sore but there is nothing. The shock and feeling that pulsed through me when I touched Connie was unexpected. I had never felt anything like it, except from the time you get a static shock, but this didn't feel like that. This felt a lot deeper, a lot stronger. My eyes fall to the carpet, then my cotton fibred socks and my brows lift, my lips turning down.

Maybe it was just a static shock, it makes more sense.

I nod to myself when I hear the sound of her slippers hitting the tiles. I don't turn round to face her, just keep looking forward because I know that once my eyes land on her pretty face I won't be able to look at anything else but her.

She clears her throat as she comes back into the room, reaching for her glass as we fall back into easy silence. I want to ask her more about how her life was before and what had happened to make her run, but I can't. Her dad gave me a very light run down of events, but I want to hear it from Connie's mouth.

But for now, I must appreciate what she has shared and hopefully within the next couple of days, just before I let her dad come for her, she'll tell me.

And hopefully, forgive me.

I HAVE NO IDEA HOW MUCH WE HAD DRUNK, BUT THE LINES BEGAN to blur and everything I felt so strongly about began to fade. I didn't care about *client protocol* anymore. There was something about Connie that drew me in, like a moth to a flame. I knew I was going to get burnt yet I still continued.

I watched as she stood, stretching up. Her head slowly swung round to me, and I watched the slow smirk creep onto her lips, her eyes heavy and full of lust and want. She felt it too. She grabbed the hem of her tee, lifting it over her head and dropping it to the floor. My eyes widened as I let them glide over her perfect fucking body. Her hips had a curve to them, her full breasts more than a handful and her pink hardened nipples inviting me to lock my hot and wet mouth around them. She curled her finger, calling me towards her. I licked my bottom lip, dragging it between my teeth. My cock was full and aching, it was hard and in desperate need for release. Standing, I place my empty glass down next to hers on the table and stalk towards her. Reaching up, I tug her hairband away and let her long, brown hair fall. It cascades down her back and I brush the loose, wispy bits from her face.

"You're so beautiful, do you know that?" I whisper, my lips edging closer to hers. Her deep green eyes steady on mine, but I break the contact and let my eyes fall to her lips as I kiss her, my tongue sweeping across hers as our kiss deepens and that's when I lose the little self-control that I did have. My hands skate down her sides, and under her ass. I squeeze her pert little cheeks before lifting her effortlessly, her long legs wrapping around my waist. I carry her towards the floor to ceiling windows, pinning her there with my hips.

"Do you know how long I have wanted this?" I nip at her jaw, my lips lazily trailing up to her ear and whispering, "Do you?"

She nods, her hands gripping the side of my face and bringing her lips back down on mine. I unravel her legs from me, tugging my sweatpants down as she undresses herself. I lift her back up, my lips trailing down her neck, past her chest before I lock my lips around her pert, hard nipple. She breathes a moan as I suck on her tits, licking and kissing before I drag my lips back to her mouth, taking her.

One of my hands hold under her, my other hand moving to her core, my fingers swiping through her wet folds, then tease at her opening.

"So ready," I groan, my hard cock bobbing and aching between my legs.

"Fuck me, Kaleb, please," she chokes, as I line my cock

at her opening, pushing into her. I have no idea how we got here, but fuck I am glad we did. Because she is everything I imagined and more. I pull to my tip, letting her adjust before I push deep inside of her again as she moans out.

"Fuck," I grit, burying my face into the crook of her neck, inhaling her scent of vanilla and cherries as I rock into her.

"So good," she whispers, her fingers digging into my shoulders as she holds on, her hips rotating over me, the sound of our skin hitting, I lift my head and let my lips find hers. Our kiss is messy, our teeth clashing as we lose ourselves in our heated moment.

I grip onto her ass, driving into her hard and fast.

"Keep fucking me hard, I'm so close," she breaks our kiss, her eyes fluttering shut before her lips are on mine again.

"You feel so good, you were made for me," I pant, my jaw laxed as I watch her come undone because of me. Her whole body stiffens, shuddering as her pussy tightens around my cock. Her eyes roll in the back of her head, her moans filling the room over the soulful Motown music, and it sounds like fucking heaven. My head tips back, I grit my jaw, the veins in my neck bulging as I tense, filling her with my cum.

Perspiration covers our skin; I slowly lower her onto her shaky legs. I fist myself into my sweatpants and reach behind me on the floor for her crumpled tee. I pass it to her, and she shyly covers her body, turning away from me as she quickly dresses.

She turns, a slow smirk on her face, her cheeks flush with a red glow from her orgasm.

"You okay?" she asks as realisation slowly creeps in on what I have done, a plaguing darkness coating my vision.

I panic, my throat tightening as I turn and run for my room, slamming the door behind me.

CHAPTER TWENTY-TWO

KALEB

I woke with a jump as a loud bang disturbed me, soaked in perspiration. Sitting up, my eyes widened as I looked down at myself. I was fully dressed. My heart was beating as if I had a drummer boy in there, skipping beats. It was a dream... right? I flung back the covers, darting from the bed and stopping outside her room, her door was shut. I sucked in a breath, moving down the stairs I see Doris and Connie sitting at the breakfast bar.

"Morning sir," Doris scoots up and bows her head.

"Doris, you didn't have to move," I grumble, rubbing my head and pulling out one of the bar stools next to Connie and slumping down beside her.

"Hungover?" she asks sweetly, sipping on her black coffee.

"Are you not having cream with that?" I turn my nose up, the smell of the coffee swarming my nose, it was overpowering.

"Nope," she shrugs and takes another sip of her coffee.

"Can I have some Advil?" I ask Doris as she slips closer to the exit of the kitchen.

"Sure thing," she turns and smiles before disappearing. My heart drums in my chest at the thought of being alone with Connie. I feel a thick tension between us, and I swallow down the lump in my throat.

"Are you okay?" she whispers, her head turning to me, her eyes searching mine for something, but I had no idea what.

"I think so... are you?" I stammer, panic still clawing at my throat, and I knew my tone dripped in it.

"I am," she smiles, "I slept so well last night, think the whiskey knocked me out," she scoffs.

"Yeah, yeah," I cough, clearing my throat, "me too."

I have no idea what to think, I dip my head, leaning towards her. "Did we, erm..." I rub my hand around the back of my neck. I stall, Connie's eyes bugging out of her head, her lips parting when she realises what I am asking.

"No, no, no," she rushes out, her cheeks pinching in the same crimson red as my dream last night.

"Oh, thank fuck," I place my hand on my chest over my racing, erratic heart, relief sweeping over me. Her brows furrow, her nose scrunching up at my words and I can see how I reacted has sparked some anger inside of her. "No, Connie, I..." I was interrupted by her voice.

"Well, I wouldn't want to sleep with you either, *Gramps,*" she bites, viciousness laces her voice and my skin prickles.

"I didn't mean it like that," but it falls on deaf ears because she is already gone, stomping up to her room like a teenage brat and I hear her bedroom door slam shut. I groan, letting my head tip forward as I let it rest in my clammy hands. That's the problem though, she is a kid.

Doris appears in the doorway, her lips twisted, her

brows high in her forehead and I can tell she heard everything.

"Don't," I snap at her, looking up before letting my head rest back in my hands. I hear the small pot of Advil being placed on the worksurface.

"Not saying a word," she says softly, pretending to lock her lips and walking into the laundry room.

I run my hands up and down my face.

"Fuck," I slam my hand on the worksurface and storm upstairs, slamming my own door.

CHAPTER TWENTY-THREE
CONNIE

I AM ANGRY. REALLY FUCKING ANGRY. HOW DARE HE.

"Oh, thank fuck," I mimic childishly out loud. "Silly old man," I groan, "he would be lucky to have sex with me," I continue.

Peeling my clothes off, I let them fall to the floor and head for the shower. I need to cool down.

I lather my hair up and rinse it off then shave and wash whilst the conditioner works its magic. I can't wait to get the hell out of here, I don't even know why I am still here. I don't need to be. Rinsing myself off, I step out and wrap myself in a bath sheet and pad to my room. Sitting on the bed, I reach for my phone out the drawer and turn it on. Anxiety creeps up inside of me, stirring my stomach into knots as I wait. My screensaver comes on, it's me and Reese at the champagne bar on our first night out. I smile fondly at the photo before my phone begins to ping into action. Missed calls, messages and social media notifications list on my phone and then comes the media pings and I know that chime, it means me, Tryst or Chord have been mentioned.

My eyes widen as I see the top story that mentions Tryst and I go numb. Article after article all with similar headlines.

LEAD SINGER OF CHORD, 24, FOUND DEAD IN APARTMENT.

REVENGE ACT FROM SCORNED SOCIAL MEDIA QUEEN EX?

WHERE IS EX GIRLFRIEND NOW LEAD SINGER OF CHORD IS FOUND DEAD?

TRYST, TALENTED LEAD SINGER OF CHORD FOUND DEAD.

LEAD SINGER'S GIRLFRIEND AND HIGH-END SOCIALITE FOUND HIM CHEATING, REVENGE?

UP AND COMING ROCKSTAR, DEAD AGED 24.

My heart thumps in my chest, nausea rocks through me and I scream. Kaleb bursts through the door, his eyes moving from me to my phone as he steps closer, closing the gap and his eyes widen as he takes the phone from my hand, his eyes scanning the screen.

"Fuck!" he bellows, grabbing my phone and turning it off. "This story was released about twenty minutes ago." He steps away from me, and my eyes just follow him. "We need to get out, now. We're going to be surrounded. I have no fucking idea where they got my address from" Kaleb's voice is rushed and I can hear the rage in his tone. He runs to the window, pulling back the curtain slightly until we see a couple of paparazzi are already forming and taking camp outside. "Shit," he grits.

I sit there, numb. I don't feel anything.

"Tryst is dead..." I whisper, fear spiking deep inside of me.

"Connie, it's going to be okay," Kaleb is kneeling in front of me, his grey eyes looking up at me.

"He's dead..." I stammer as a tear rolls down my cheek. I hadn't even realised I had started crying. I angrily swipe it away.

"They think I killed him!?" I choke, turning to look at my turned off phone again then back at Kaleb, "But I didn't, you know that right?"

"Connie," Kaleb's tone is exasperated, "of course I know, you haven't left the apartment. Tryst played last night, there are photos." He sighs, "We have an alibi and Doris is our witness, I promise you, nothing will come back to you," he reaches his left hand up and wipes one of my tears away with his thumb pad and I can't help but lean into his hand.

"Everything will be okay, but now, it's really important we get out of here before any more media get here," he whispers softly, and I nod numbly. "Pack essentials, just enough to fit in one duffel bag. I will meet you in the lobby in ten." And then he is gone.

His words swim round my head, but I can't seem to move, my legs feel like lead. I just stare into my closet and let what has happened replay over in my mind.

"Connie!" Kaleb shouts, pulling me from my hypnotic state but I don't move. "For fuck's sake," he grits, rushing into my closet and grabbing some clothes, stuffing them into the duffel bag. Then he moves to my drawers and grabs underwear and pyjamas. He rushes back to my closet and grabs my boots and trainers.

Zipping the bag up, he grabs my phone from the comforter and stuffs it in his back pocket before pulling me forward.

"Hey!" I call out, snapping out of it. "Get off me," I tug my arm out of his grip.

"Then move." His jaw is tight and I see him keeping it clenched. I cross my arms across my chest and stand in my spot. "I'm getting real sick of your bratty attitude," Kaleb steps towards me, grabbing the top of my arm again and dragging me out of my room.

"Get off me!" I scream as we get to the bottom of the stairs. Doris comes running out, her eyes shifting between me and Kaleb.

"What an earth is going on!?"

"We're leaving, Doris, stay here. Do not answer the door, get Derek here now and do not leave until I tell you it's safe." Kaleb rushes out, grabbing mine and his coat. "Do you understand?"

Doris nods quickly.

"Are you safe? Is everything okay Kaleb?" I can hear the worry in Doris' voice, and it breaks my heart.

"I am safe, I will be safe. I just need to get Connie out of the city for a bit." Kaleb calls out as he runs up the stairs, taking two at a time.

Doris' eyes land on me and I'm trying my hardest to swallow down the tears, my throat burns and my eyes sting.

"Oh sweetie," she soothes, pulling me in for a cuddle, "you'll be safe with Kaleb, I promise. He will not let anyone hurt you."

I choke a sob as the tears seep into her top.

"Connie, we've got to go." Kaleb's hands rest on my waist as he pulls me away from Doris. He ushers me forward before turning back to Doris and throwing an old burner phone on the table.

"Do not use landlines, I've put my burner phone number in there. I'll be at..." Kaleb pauses, pulling his phone out and looking at his emails, his brows raising then he gives a strong roll of his eyes. "The love lodge," and Doris scoffs.

I roll my lips, my eyes moving to Doris before they land back on Kaleb.

"We really need to get going," his tone is curt as he collects the duffel bags and I grab the coats off the lobby table. I hold my hand up to Doris and although I have only been here a few days, I have become fond of her.

Doris gives me a small wave then turns and walks away. Kaleb is waiting by the elevator in his penthouse, and I stand beside him. Damn he smells good.

The elevator doors ping open, and I step inside, Kaleb following before he presses the basement floor button and they close.

The elevator journey is short and within a minute, we're on the bottom floor. I follow Kaleb into the busy parking lot, walking quickly to keep up with his long strides. He unlocks a red Mercedes SUV. The boot opens and he throws the duffel bags inside before pressing the button and closing. He rushes to the passenger side, but I have already tugged on the door handle. I slide in and slam the door, hard. I felt infuriated, rage consumed me. I heard Kaleb tut, slipping in beside me and closing his door delicately.

"Please can you not slam my door?" He doesn't look at me, just pushes the start button on his engine.

I roll my eyes.

"Jeez, sorry…"

"Cut the tone," Kaleb snaps, turning to face me as he pushes down on the accelerator and pulls out the lot. I ignore him, turning my body to face out the window so I don't have to look at him.

My eyes widen as I see the flock of paparazzi beginning to camp outside the apartments.

"How did they find me?" I whisper, my eyes pinned to them until they were out of sight.

"I have no idea," Kaleb grits.

Silence falls between us and my chest feels heavy. I can't believe what's happened. I can't believe they're pinning this on me. Tears sting behind my eyes, but I won't let them fall. Grief hadn't even made an appearance yet, all that flooded me was anxiety and anger.

Tryst was gone.

And they're assuming I had something to do with it.

Kaleb senses the sombre mood, reaching and turning the radio on, *Labyrinth – Taylor Swift* filling the car. I close my eyes and that's when the tears fall.

CHAPTER TWENTY-FOUR

KALEB

PULLING INTO THE DRIVEWAY OF THE PICTURESQUE COTTAGE, I LET out a sigh of relief. I look over and see Connie curled up in the passenger seat, sleeping. Cutting the engine, I let my head fall back on the headrest of my car seat and I close my eyes for a moment.

I need to let my brain register everything that has happened over the last few hours. Turning my head once more, I look at her. And for the first time, I actually *look* at her.

Her chocolate brown hair has streaks of caramel blonde running through it. Her skin is a golden tone; she is a natural beauty. Her bare arms are dotted with the odd mole and suddenly I want to trace them like a dot to dot, just so I can trail a line over her skin and remember it. I will for her to open her eyes, just so her beautiful green ones can find mine. I could lose myself in them, her deep pools of green, and all I want to do is dive into them, losing myself in her soul.

"Darling," my voice is low and raspy as I try and wake her softly. The nickname that slips off my tongue with ease doesn't make me feel uneasy or weird. It feels right. She doesn't move, her soft snores fill the car and I debate sitting here a little longer to let her sleep. I look at the time, it's just gone one in the afternoon. The late night, the alcohol plus the rush of drama this morning has knocked it out of us both. I yawn, rolling my head back and letting it rest back on my headrest.

Moments pass and I turn to look at her once more as I hear her stir. Her head snaps up quickly before she rolls her head round to stretch the crook out of her neck. Her eyes slowly meet mine and she yawns.

"We're here," I smirk, stating the obvious. She nods, turning to look out the window at the pretty cottage that sits on a large front lawn. The outside panelled in white wooden slats, the front door a light sage green with matching shuttered windows. It really was a beautiful setting. The beach cove a stone's throw from the quiet road that lays in front of the lawn. The narrow driveway leads off the main road and bends and winds towards the house and stops outside a double garage.

"It's very pretty here," her voice is a whisper, her fingertips pressing against the window of the car causing the glass to mist from the warmth of her breath.

She turns her body, so she is facing forward, her eyes gazing in front of her.

"This is a complete shit show," she exhales deeply.

"It is, but today's news is tomorrow's trash," I say with a lightness of humor in my voice but it's wasted on her. She was too lost in thought.

I open my door and round the car, grabbing the bags out the boot. I hear the passenger door go and I see Connie by my side as she takes one of the bags from me. Her wide green eyes lift to mine, and I see a hint of a smile creep onto her lips.

"Let's get inside," I mutter, swinging my leg under the tailgate of the boot, the lid of the car slowly going down and closing.

I follow Connie up to the front door, moving in front of her as I pat around in my jeans to find the keys. Fiddling with the key ring I slip the key into the lock and twist, the door creaking as I push it open to see a cosy rustic home.

There is a small square lobby with a side table with dark oak accents. An ivory runner lays on the dark oak wooden floor leading down a narrow hall between the lounge and kitchen. The large double-door sized archways into both rooms allowing light to stream into the hall from both sides, making the space feel more open. To the left is a cosy lounge, two white material sofas sitting opposite each other with a large dark oak, square coffee table with a thin sheet of glass sitting over the top. A round gold, mirrored tray sits in the middle with faux flowers and thick designer books piled up.

It's warm and inviting.

I drop the bags at my side and begin walking through the house. The kitchen is to the right of the hall, a small square with white oak units and a solid, dark oak worksurface. The room is bright and light with a large, rectangular window that looks out at rolling green. Everything we need is here. I turn and see Connie hovering at the bottom of the stairs, her eyes finding mine over her shoulder. I give her a soft nod and she continues up the stairs, her fingers wrapping around the handrail as she disappears from view.

She isn't up there long before she appears at the bottom of the stairs.

"Everything okay?" I ask, my brows furrowing as I click the coffee machine on after checking for clean filters.

"Um, yeah," she nods, "there is only one bed though..." her cheeks turn crimson under her sun kissed skin.

"Fucking Titus," I growl low.

"Who's Titus?" her nose crinkles, her brows pinching before she smooths them out.

"Just a friend," I grit, my jaw tight and clenched, "well, he might not be a friend for much longer."

She scoffs a little laugh, then rubs her hands together.

"I'll take the sofa, you sleep upstairs," I smile as I reach for two cups.

"Honestly, I'll take the sofa. You have done so much for me... it's the least I could do..." she trails off and I feel like there is something more she wants to say. "Plus, you're old. Wouldn't want you to throw your back out now would we, Gramps?"

My eyes widen and I choke on my own breath as I cough.

She throws me a wink, strolling leisurely to grab her bag before turning and climbing the stairs.

"Fucking gramps," I scoff, lifting my takeout coffee to my lips and taking a mouthful, "I'll show her gramps."

WE SIT ON THE SOFA, HOT CHOCOLATE IN HAND AS CONNIE snuggles under the fur throw that she found in the blanket box. Her eyes are pinned to the television as she watches *The Vampire Diaries*. She is low key obsessed with this show, I feel like it's all I watch when she's around, but not tonight, my eyes don't move from her. I would much prefer to watch her than any television show. I love watching the range of emotions and facial expressions that consume her as she watches this show. Uneasiness twists deep in my stomach. She hasn't cried since the car, and I couldn't help but worry that she wouldn't grieve for Tryst. There has been no more emotion and it unsettles me because I don't understand why.

But that is just it. I don't understand her. I don't know her to understand her. I've asked her if she is okay and all I get back is a blunt yes.

I was out of my depth; I had no clue what I was doing and now I was second guessing everything. I have no idea what to do with her. Maybe I should have just dropped her straight back to her dad and be done with it. But I didn't want to.

I didn't want to give her back.

Sipping on the creamy, thick hot chocolate I reluctantly move my eyes from the beauty in front of me and turn to face the screen as I watch the television show. I didn't think I would, but I enjoyed the episode and when I look over, I see Connie curled up in a ball asleep.

Reaching for the remote, I click the television off and take our cups out to the sink. I debate washing them up, but I don't, I settle on leaving them in the sink till the morning. Padding back through to the living room, I notice she hasn't moved. I could leave her on the sofa, but I want her to have the bed. Before I can change my mind, I scoop her into my arms, her scent of cherries and vanilla filling my nose and it's quickly becoming one of my favourite smells. Once upstairs, I turned down the narrow hallway and nudged the bedroom door open with my shoulder. The room was bright, the walls painted in white. There was very little colour to bring some character into the room, but somehow, the whole white look was working. Laying her on top of the comforter, I readjusted the fur throw and lay it over her still body. Her breaths were shallow as she slept with ease. My heart ached as I watched her, I have no idea why I feel so protective over her, but I do. I can't explain it. It's like I've imprinted on her, or she's imprinted on me. She makes everything cloudy but so clear at the same time. It's chemical. A reaction. A disaster waiting to happen.

I lean down, pushing a strand of her caramel brown hair from her face and just watch her for a moment. Her lashes are long, light freckles are dusted against her cheeks, her perfectly red, full lips are parted as she breathes. Inhaling deeply, I step back and walk away. I still outside her room, looking over my shoulder at her one last time before I pull the door. Turning my head to look down the narrow hall, I see a bathroom at the end and a study to the left. Nibbling my lip, I fist my hands into my pockets and walk downstairs.

Raiding the cupboards, I can't find anything to drink. I need a night cap to sleep.

Strolling into the living area, I see my phone sitting on the coffee table. Reaching for it, I pick it up and press Titus' number.

Ring. Ring. Ring.

"Hello, how is the love lodge?" Titus' smug voice grinds me down instantly.

"Didn't feel like telling me there was only *one* bed?" I snap, looking back through the cupboards before slamming them shut again.

"That *little* detail must have slipped my mind," I hear his roar of a laugh.

"You're such a dick," I groan, rubbing my hand round the back of my head then clicking it side to side.

"You're welcome," he grumbles through a low laugh, "anyway, what do I owe the pleasure?"

"Drink. There is no drink."

"I have to hide it from Arizona and her friends when they go up there," his voice is low now.

"Isn't she twenty-one?" my brows pinch.

"Just, but still, no." I hear a sigh leave him, "I don't want her drinking when she is out there alone."

"But I can drink out here alone, right?" I tease, licking my lips as I pace back and forth from the kitchen to the living area.

"Obviously you big jerk."

"Well, there was no need for that was there," I smirk.

"Out the back, in the shed. There is a lock on it. 1234."

"Wow, because she wouldn't guess that," I scoff. He laughs.

"Now, fuck off," he snipes, cutting the phone off and I laugh to myself.

Heading towards the back door that's in the kitchen, I unlock it and rush to the shed out back. Pushing the code, the door unlocks, and I search for something to numb out my thoughts for a bit.

"Bingo." Smiling, I reach for the scotch and rush back into the house.

I shudder, the air cool. Locking the back door, I grab a glass before falling onto the sofa, kicking my feet onto the coffee table, I pour myself a large glass. Taking a mouthful, I wince slightly as the burn courses through me, and I instantly feel myself relax. I hate that some nights I have to rely on alcohol, but I need it. Sometimes my thoughts get too loud, and I need to shut them off and alcohol helps me.

Do I have a problem? Yes.

Will I do anything about it? Probably not.

Looking through my phone, it's filled with an outpouring of tributes towards Tryst. Most people don't agree with the headlines, but you get the odd keyboard warrior who is slandering Connie's name. I don't give a shit; I'll fight till I am blue in the face so she can win. I will always fight her corner.

The more I read, the more agitated I'm getting. Coming out of the web tab, I see I have fifteen missed calls from Killian and double the messages.

"Fuck," I groan, hovering over his name and pressing it quickly before I changed my mind. I swear, it didn't even fucking ring before his voice boomed down the ear piece.

"Kaleb," his tone was curt and blunt, and he had every right to be pissed at me.

"Killian," I sat up, shuffling in my seat as I place my glass on the table and clear my throat.

"What the fuck are you playing at?" his voice was a little louder now as I heard the sound of a door closing behind him.

"I'm not playing at anything," I scoff, standing from the sofa and pacing back and forth and I hear the low grumble from him. "Connie is my priority. She will *always* be my priority. It wasn't safe for her; you knew Tryst was going to be an issue hence why I've had to look out for her. It had nothing to do with her seeing the world and running out, it had everything to do with Tryst, didn't it? You didn't trust her around Tryst."

The line falls silent.

"I don't have kids; I don't think I'll ever have kids, but I can understand why you're anxious. She's your baby. I get it. I really do. But you hired me, you trusted me to get your daughter home and I will. But I can't risk it yet. She hasn't cried about Tryst. She may not, but I am worried about the media and what they're saying. They'll hound her if I bring her home and neither of us want that do we? Let me keep her safe for a while longer, no one knows she is here..." I trail off and I hear him heavily sigh.

"I paid you to bring her home," his voice is quiet for a moment. "I understand why you're doing it; I do. But I didn't ask you to hide her away, I asked you to bring her home."

His tone soon changes, and it instantly gets my back up.

"Well, old man, she isn't coming home yet and if my memory serves me right, she wants nothing to do with you as of yet, so I think she'll be happy to stay with me."

"Don't push me Kaleb."

"I'm not pushing anything, Killian. Your daughter is with me, let me do my job and stop fucking questioning me." I cut the phone off then turn it off. "Stew on that you fucker."

I fall back onto the sofa, cradling my glass. My thoughts echo in my mind, replaying the conversation I had with Killian. I shouldn't have reacted. I shouldn't have let him get a rise from me. But I did.

Tipping my head back, I let my eyes focus on the ceiling for a moment as I pondered over my next move. I needed to keep her safe. Just for a few weeks. Was Tryst's death at the hands of Xavier? If so, why is Connie being tarnished? I need to speak to him.

I am waiting for the other shoe to drop for her, waiting for the colossal wave of emotions to hit her like a tsunami. I needed to be ready.

But how can I be ready when I don't know her? I would sit down with her tomorrow, start light conversation and see what she is willing to tell me. I need her to trust me. She has no idea who I am and who hired me and that's the way

I want it to stay. She doesn't need to know. She never needs to know.

It's just a few weeks and she will be up and out of my life. Back home where she belongs.

But until then. She is with me.

CHAPTER TWENTY-FIVE
KILLIAN

I PACE BACK AND FORTH DOWN THE HALLWAY, BREATHING HARSH breaths through my nostrils like some raged bull who has had a red flag waved in front of him. My blood boils as it pumps through my veins.

I hear her footsteps before I see her.

"Baby," she whispers, grabbing my hand and stalling me in my place. I turn to look at her and I swear she can see the turmoil in my eyes.

"He put the fucking phone down on me," I grit, my jaw clenched, my back teeth grinding. I'm surprised I have any molars left since hiring that jumped up prick.

"I know, and that was a dick move but you're missing the bigger picture here..." she trails off, wrapping her arms around my waist, her head tipping back so her opal eyes are all I can focus on. A small smile graces my lips as I look down at her, momentarily forgetting the anger that is coursing through me. Her dirty blonde hair is pulled into a messy bun, a few golden strands have fallen and frame her pretty face. She is truly beautiful and all mine.

"She is safe. What would have happened if the press got

to her? They've tarnished her name; they could ruin her life and reputation with this rumour. So, Kaleb done what he thought was the right thing, which *is* the right thing and I know you're angry about it..." she trails off, squeezing me tight, "but you know it was the right thing to do. You paid him to find her, well he did... and now he is keeping her safe until this all blows over. He has good intentions Killian..." she pauses, and I bow my head, my eyes closing.

"You would be angrier with him if he *didn't* do anything. Imagine how you would feel if he left her there? Left Connie to deal with all of this? It would break you and it would break her, only pushing her further away from the both of us, further away from her coming home. You need to think of the end goal. Connie coming home." Her voice is soft, I let my eyes open and immediately see her eyes darting back and forth between mine.

"I know," I whisper, admitting defeat. She is right. My anger is still bubbling deep inside of me, but it'll simmer. She presses on her toes and kisses me softly on the lips.

"She'll be home before we know it," Reese whispers against my lips.

"I hope so," I whisper back.

CHAPTER TWENTY-SIX

CONNIE

I WAKE AND IT TAKES ME A MOMENT TO REALISE WHERE I AM. Sitting up slowly I let out a shaky breath. My stomach is in knots, my heart racing in my chest like a racehorse that has bolted from its stall. It takes everything in me not to reach for my phone. I don't want to read what they are saying today. I don't need to hear it.

The anxiety ripples through me, my breathing fastening. Part of me feels like walking to the local police station and giving a statement, but would it help? I know I didn't do it; Tryst was troubled. He had been for the last year and his addiction had gotten out of hand, but I never thought he would kill himself. He had so much going for him, but not enough apparently. Tears prick my eyes at his selfishness and guilt consumes me.

What if I had never left?

Did he do this because I broke up with him?

Why?

The questions ricocheted round and round; my thoughts noisy. I palm away a stray tear that rolls down my cheek, whatever his reason and whatever happened, it was still devastatingly heart-breaking. I wanted to reach out to his mother, she had a rollercoaster of a relationship with Tryst, but I wanted to know that she was okay. I scoffed; she isn't going to want to hear from me. In her mind she believes the papers, of course she does. It won't be long until I am found and questioned. I have an alibi; I have witness statements. I know I'll be fine, but it's daunting. My influencer career is over, I don't need to check my phone to see that my followers are dropping by the second, or growing, because the world is sick and fucked. People love to watch the lives of others unfold behind a screen. They don't know what really goes on in our lives, yet they love to watch someone's downfall, it won't be long before speculation starts, and rumors grow. They become detectives, looking for signs that somehow point them to an outcome that isn't true.

I don't want that.

I started my social media for *me*, for fun and to document my travels but now, the fun has been sucked out of it.

Throwing back the covers, I swing my legs round and let my toes spread into the carpet. Stretching up, I slip my feet into my slippers and grab my robe. Hesitation sweeps through me as I walk down the stairs. Stopping on the bottom step, I turn my head in the direction where Kaleb is sleeping. His leg is hung over the back of the sofa, one of his arms is tucked behind his head and the other is hanging off the edge, whilst his other leg is laid straight. I just stare for a moment, tiptoeing closer to him just so I can look at him for a while. The fur throw that must have been covering him is now on the floor in a heap and I wonder if I should cover him back up but decide against it. My head tilts to the right and I stop in my tracks. My eyes roam over his face, his dark hair soft and messy, the product non-existent now. His dark stubble dusted over his chin and jaw which neatly stops at his sideburns. My eyes trail down and I see a light dusting of dark chest hair and suddenly I feel the urge to place my hands there, just so I can feel his skin under my fingertips, the soft drumming of his heart beating under my fingers. I shake my head from side to side before stepping back when I see a bulge growing in his boxers. My eyes widen and a rush of scarlet pinches at my cheeks. I turn quickly, letting my head fall as I focus on my feet and move to the kitchen to turn the coffee machine on.

I feel the heat swarm in my tummy, a pulse deep down that is begging to be relieved but it mustn't. Not by him.

I open the cupboard doors and close them quietly as I look for cups to make me and Kaleb a coffee. Reaching for two large mugs, I spun to see Kaleb leaning up against the door frame. His eyes pinned to me. I inhaled sharply, the colour of his eyes changing from green to grey.

"Morning," his voice was gruff as he rubbed the sleep from his eyes whilst yawning.

"Morning," I kept my voice low and soft as I finally moved my anchored feet from the ground and poured us a cup of coffee. "There isn't any cream... so I hope black is okay," I hold the mug out for him to take, which he does.

"We will head to the shops today," his voice is full of sleep still as he brings the mug to his lips and takes a mouthful, wincing.

"Yeah, there isn't much here," I shrug my shoulders up softly and take my own mouthful.

"I don't think Titus uses it much anymore, it's more for his daughter and her friends during their summer breaks."

"Oh yes, Titus. And how do you know him?" I ask as I pass him and sit on the sofa, Kaleb following.

"Well, he is my friend first, but we work together. He is a..." Kaleb pauses for a moment, "insurance broker." He mumbles taking another mouthful of coffee.

"Is that what you do?" I ask, leaning back into the pillows on the sofa.

"Something like that," he smirks, sitting back too. I let my eyes sweep down and I am grateful he has clothes on. I don't think I could focus if he was still semi naked. Something about him lures me in, maybe it's because he is double my age; it's forbidden. Or maybe it's because he is hot as fuck and I know he would know how to work my body.

My eyes widen at my thoughts. I can see Kaleb's lips moving but I can't hear anything he was saying.

"You okay?" he edges forward so he is sitting on the edge of the sofa.

"Yeah, sorry, just lost in thought..." I blush and drop my head, hoping that he doesn't notice.

"It'll be okay you know, all of this..." he trails off for a moment, "I won't let anyone near you, okay?"

I nod, nibbling the inside of my bottom lip.

"I promise, Connie. I will keep you safe, and once all of this has blown over, you're free to go." He sits back in the sofa and crosses his right leg over this left thigh.

Silence fills the room as I lose the ability to string a sentence together. I don't know what I am meant to feel, or how I am supposed to act.

"Grief works in funny ways, some people don't cry... some people cry for weeks, even months. But don't beat yourself up over your version of your own grief." Kaleb's words slice through me.

"I think it's the shock..." I whisper, keeping my eyes pinned to my mug.

"I know, and the shock will pass and then I'll be here when you're ready to let it all out." Kaleb stands and strides over to the sofa I am sitting on and falls down beside me, his large hand landing on my thigh, and he gives me a gentle squeeze.

"Guilt is eating me alive," I admit, still not looking up.

He says nothing, he just listens. "I just feel like this is all my fault, that I pushed him into this, and I also feel guilty that I haven't cried."

"You have nothing to feel guilty about." Kaleb's voice is soft and comforting.

I sniff as a tear escapes, rolling off my cheek and dissolving into my lap.

"He had demons, I knew that, but maybe I shouldn't have been selfish and left... if I would have stayed..."

"He would have still died. You couldn't save him Connie; you couldn't be his hero. He was his own downfall, it all got too big too quick for him to be able to keep up with the crazy schedule he had without the help of drugs. No doubt the drugs were at the hand of his manager, a little bit of cocaine, just to help the tiredness... In the end, cocaine is least of the problems. He had an addiction that he couldn't curb." Kaleb stalls for a moment, his arm reaching round my shoulders as he pulls me into him. I look up, my eyes stinging as I hold back the tears. "You were never going to be his saviour Connie," he whispers, and the tears fall from my eyes.

CHAPTER TWENTY-SEVEN

CONNIE

WE HAD BEEN HERE A FEW DAYS, BOTH ADAPTING TO LIVING together. Kaleb kept his distance unless he was checking in on me. Most of the time he was on his laptop losing himself in work. I was bored, I pottered about and kept the little cottage tidy but it didn't take long.

Sighing exasperated, I lay on the sofa and watch the cheesy love films. They wouldn't have been my first choice, but I didn't have much else to choose from. The evenings were getting cooler, the days getting darker earlier, and it felt like autumn had really kicked in. Thanksgiving and Christmas were always my favourite times of the year, but now, now it all seems tarnished. I had no family or friends to spend it with, I was going to be alone.

I see Kaleb sit on the sofa opposite me, beer in hand, a loud sigh leaving him too.

"Bad day?"

"Not bad, just not good either." He shrugs and brings the beer bottle to his lips.

I nod along as if I know what he is talking about, I don't.

He doesn't talk much about work, just occasionally talks about his friends, Nate, Titus and his brother Keaton.

"You hungry?" I ask when the movie pauses for an ad break.

"Yeah, but I was going to cook, you cooked last night so let me cook tonight," he turns to look at me and smiles, "I can't promise it'll be any good but, I would like to cook," he takes another sip of his beer and I smile.

"I'm looking forward to it."

I liked Kaleb. Yes, he was easy on the eye, but I liked what was inside so much more. He was kind, caring and very giving. He could be a bit of a grump, but I think that was more because he felt out of control. Well, apart from the first time I met him at the coffee shop, but I was in my own head space there. I wasn't happy and everything used to push me over the edge. It didn't help with how Tryst used to be.

Tryst.

There had been no movement, people were speaking about it, but it had quietened down slightly. I still wasn't brave enough to turn my phone on. I didn't think I would cope with anything if I read something out of context.

Kaleb had been checking in with Doris, just to make sure she was okay. I had no idea how the press knew I was at his place, but all it would take is one shot of him to piece it all together. The good news was the police hadn't asked to see me yet. I knew I would have to give a statement but once I had, I was hoping that would be the end of it.

Kaleb pushes from the sofa and heads into the kitchen just as the film starts again. I reach down and grab the fur throw out of the rug basket and cover myself up. I pull it up to my chin and inhale, Kaleb's scent is all over it. I don't know why, but his scent reminds me of tobacco and suede with hints of vanilla laced through it. I smile as I inhale deeper, filling my lungs with his scent.

I'm not normal.

It's like I am addicted but I don't know what I am addicted to. I try my hardest to focus on the film, but I can't. My mind is too busy with everything else that is going on around me. My heart hurts when I think of Tryst, not because I once loved him and he is now gone, but because of the way he died. I would never have thought he would have taken his own life. He never came across as feeling low, but then, he never told me anything before I left. He was living on a constant high. That was the problem. He was always on a high. Doubt kicked in, my stomach twisting and turning. I felt like I didn't know him near the end of our relationship. The Tryst I knew and loved would have never have treated me the way he did, he would have never done the things he did.

It's times like this I wish I could pick up the phone and call Reese. Just to vent, to get another female's perspective on the situation. Just to have someone who could maybe *understand* what I was going through. But I have burned those bridges. Nothing would build them back to the way they were. They were well and truly broken, nothing but cinders and ashes.

I am snapped from my thoughts when I hear the sound of dishes smashing together. I rush from the sofa and walk to the kitchen to see Kaleb standing flustered with dinner plates surrounding him.

I nibble the inside of my lip, the corners of my mouth pulling into a smile.

"Do you need any help?" I step into the kitchen, asking softly when I see the mess he is in.

"No, no," he shakes his head as he grabs the handle of

the saucepan and spoons lumpy mashed potatoes onto the plate, followed by some vegetables and chicken. I watch as he tugs hard on the kitchen drawer, pushing his hand into the cutlery and he fists out two sets of forks and knives.

He drops them onto the plate and turns to hand me one. I thank him and take it as we walk to the dining table. Placing the plate down and pulling a chair out at the dining table, I sit and wait for Kaleb to sit with me so we could eat.

I'm not waiting long when Kaleb joins me, sitting opposite and I let my eyes settle on him for a moment. Picking his knife and fork up, I place my elbows on the table and clasp my hands together. Kaleb stabs an underdone carrot with his fork and hovers it in front of his lips, his eyes batting back and forth between mine.

"Do you mind if we say grace?" my voice comes out small.

He lowers his hand slowly, placing his knife and fork back on his plate and not moving his light grey eyes from mine.

"I just think..." I stammer, "with everything that has gone on, well..." I shrug my shoulders up and swallow the growing lump in my throat.

"Of course," he mumbles, clasping his hands together, he bows his head.

Once finished, I cut into my chicken and my eyes widen the same time Kaleb crunches down on his vegetables. I stifle my laugh then push my fork down into the chicken breast and lift it up to show him.

"It's pink," I roll my lips and I see the realisation on his face, dropping his knife and fork down onto the plate.

"Don't eat it," he shakes his head, leaning across the table and snatching my plate away from me then taking my fork with the raw chicken still impaled. He pushes from the table, his chin lifted high as he drops the plates into the sink, dry heaving.

I try to stifle my laugh, but I can't, I snort it out and cover my lips with my hand to try and mask my laugh but it doesn't work.

"Do you think it's funny that you nearly died!?" he spins from the sink and stalks towards me, hands on his hips, his mouth laxed as he waits for my response but his manic eyes dart back and forth between mine.

I roll my eyes in an over exaggerated manner. He was being *very* dramatic.

"I didn't nearly die, Kaleb. No need to be over the top," I smirk, not letting my eyes break from his stormy gaze.

"You nearly ate raw chicken Connie; you would have died."

"I didn't nearly eat it; I cut into it and saw it was raw." My eyes focus on him for a moment, and I can see the sheer panic on his face, my smile quickly slipping. I push away from the table and walk over to him until our bodies are practically touching for how close I am to him.

"I'm okay," I whisper, and he closes his eyes for a moment, inhaling deeply.

When his beautiful grey eyes open, I can see the glisten to them. He seems petrified.

"Let's get pizza and watch crappy cheesy love stories," I bump into him softly and smile.

"That sounds like a plan," he nods, stepping away and pulling his finger and thumb across his upper lip stubble then dragging the rest of his hand down his chin. "Sorry for fucking up dinner, I wanted to do something nice," he kicks the floor with his toe, his hands fisted into his pockets.

"Kaleb, you have done nothing but nice things since I met you," I rush towards him and wrap my arms around his torso and hug him. He doesn't hug me back; his whole body stiffens but I don't let go. I want him to know how grateful I am to him.

KALEB

Her touch feels strange. I clench my jaw together, my back molars grinding down hard on my bottom ones. I am scared I am going to grind them down to nothing more than stumps. My jaw is tight and wound as if it's tightened with wire and the only way to release it is by having it cut. Her arms wrapped around my torso make me feel like I am suffocating but I don't let her know that. I want to feel the comfort from her, I want to feel something other than terrifying fear.

Her fingers draw circles on my lower back before they link behind me. My skin prickles in goosebumps, her touch burning me. I want to pull away, but I don't. I stay put and ignore all the warning signs to push her off me.

She needs this, and honestly, so do I.

CHAPTER TWENTY-EIGHT

KALEB

I PACE UP AND DOWN THE SMALL LIVING AREA LISTENING TO Keaton harp on but stop and look out the window. Connie is sitting out front reading a book in the fresh autumn air. She is wrapped up in a blanket and has a hot chocolate resting on her lap whilst she loses herself in her story and I smile before stepping back away from the window.

"I know, but I can't be there. You're big enough and ugly enough to deal with them yourself." I sigh but I understand his frustration. We both grew this business together and have always dealt with the bigger meetings together, but today, I can't.

"Can't you just leave her?" he asks when I hear his office door shut and I flare my nostrils.

"No, I can't just *leave* her, there is too much going on. It'll only be for a few weeks, and it'll be business as usual."

"I don't get it." He sighs but his voice is low.

"You wouldn't," I grit out, tugging the hem of my black and white checked flannel shirt.

"I never want to either," he bites back.

"Set up a video meeting and I can join you."

"No fucking point," and he hangs the phone up before I can respond. I clutch my phone tight in my hand and squeeze my eyes shut for a moment.

"Is everything okay?" Connie asks as she stands in the doorway, clutching her book in her hands with the large, woven blanket wrapped around her shoulders.

"Yeah, fine," I clench my jaw and throw my phone onto the sofa. I feel my rage bubbling, but I don't allow it to boil and spill out of me.

"Shall I go and grab us a couple of beers?" She asks as she walks and places her book on the coffee table in the living room.

"I'll go, sit on the sofa and continue your book," I smile, and she nods.

"It's so beautiful out here and so quiet. You can hear yourself think, I forgot what it was like to not be in the hustle and bustle of the city. I can actually see the stars above me dancing in the sky. I would move here in a heartbeat," she sighs blissfully as she falls into the sofa and reaches for her book.

"Yeah, I could too. Just move away and start over."

"Let's just stay here forever," she snuggles down.

"Sounds like the best plan," I chime as I push out the back door and into the crisp, autumn air.

Sitting opposite Connie I sip my third bottle of beer; we're not talking, she is too lost in her book. My eyes pinch as I scan the cover, it's discreet and tells me nothing of what it could be about. I'm intrigued.

"What is your book about?" I ask, sitting up on the sofa. She doesn't lift her eyes from the pages.

"Romantic stuff," she sings, her lips curling into a smile.

"Like..." I pry.

"Like... romantic stuff," she smirks at me and this time she lifts her eyes from her book to me.

"Well, are they riding a tandem bike through the daffodil meadows on their way to a picnic? Holding hands whilst skipping through Paris? Dancing and kissing in the rain?" I fire the questions at her and she just blinks at me before laughing and shaking her head from side to side.

"No," she blushes, dropping her head as she focuses on her book.

"Then what?"

She sits up and spins to face me, closing her book. My eyes roam up and down her slender but curvaceous body as she stood. She's wearing chequered baggy pyjama shorts and a white ribbed vest that has a scalloped trim neckline. Her eyes are glued to me as she slowly stalks towards me. I swallow down the dry lump that felt lodged in my throat.

"Well, the guy has just grabbed her round the base of her throat, pushing her against the wall. She keeps pretending she doesn't want him and vice versa..." she stalls as she sits her pert little ass on the edge of the coffee table, her legs crossing over one another. My cock stirs in my pants, and I pray that she doesn't notice. I shouldn't be getting aroused over her. She is twenty-two. I am forty-seven. She sinks her top teeth into her bottom lip and slowly pulls at it.

"Then he pushes his knee between her legs, knocking them open so he can get just that little bit closer to her..."

I shuffle forward so I am sitting on the edge of the sofa, my eyes pinned to her completely hooked on her story, "And then what?" my voice is barely audible, my throat thickens and I can feel my cock throbbing as the blood rushes there.

"Then she smirks at him, her eyes dark and hooded as she waits for him to make his move..." she stalls, her small hands running round the back of her neck before she scoops her brown hair into a high ponytail then rubs the palms of her hands across the bare skin on her thighs.

I sit waiting with bated breath.

"Then," she licks her top lip, pressing her hands behind her so they're pressed against the glass of the coffee table, her chest pushed out so her pert little tits are all I can focus on.

"Then...?" I whisper.

She smiles, leaning forward so our lips are inches from each other's, her eyes dropping to mine before her sapphire green eyes penetrate through to my soul.

"I'm about to find out."

My eyes widen as I'm pulled from the trance she has put me under as she stands from the table, sashaying her hips towards the sofa she was lying on and grabs her book before disappearing up the stairs.

"Fuck," I groan, sitting back into the sofa, my erection evident, "fuck," I scoff again, shaking my head as I take a sip of my beer.

LAYING ON THE SOFA, I CAN'T SLEEP. ALL I CAN THINK OF IS HOW fucking beautiful she looked when she was sitting on the edge of the coffee table, all innocence I once saw seeping out of her pores as she described a mild scenario from her dirty little book. Does that turn her on? Is it like porn but on pages? I groan as my cock throbs. Palming myself through my pants to try and relieve some of the tension but it does nothing.

Throwing the fur throw off me, I storm upstairs towards the bathroom, but I'm mindful not to slam the door. Sexual frustration is pumping through my veins making me short tempered. I can't ever go there with Connie. I don't care how much I want it, how much she may want it – I will not give in.

She has trauma, I have my own trauma.

We wouldn't work.

We're both too broken to work.

Catastrophic.

Disaster.

Broken.

Twisting the shower faucet, I pull my pants off and let them fall. Stepping under, I hiss as the cold water coats my hot skin and goosebumps erupt. My erection feels heavy between my legs and I wrap my fingers around my thickness as soon as I can. I tighten my grip, the whole time imagining it's her petite hands wrapped around me. I suck in a breath and tip my head back as the pleasure erupts deep inside me. The warm water trickles over me, but I don't care. I am too submerged in my pleasure to care about anything else. I imagine her wide, green eyes watching me the whole time. I slow my strokes up and down my cock as my toes curl over the shower tray.

I don't want it to be over this quick, but I can't hold off. My mind is filled with her and only her. Squeezing a little tighter and moving my hand faster to get the friction I so desperately crave; my head falls forward as I watch. My breaths are ragged and harsh, my spare hand splaying against the cool tile as I feel my orgasm begin to build deep inside of me, the sweet tingle of ecstasy that is about to take over my body as pure euphoria consumes me.

"Fuck, Connie," I groan, clenching my jaw tightly then let out a roar as I come, hard. I don't stop, I keep pleasuring myself until I have nothing else to give.

I drop my hand, my cock bobbing and throbbing as I pant. It takes me a moment to come down from this almighty high, but when I do, I turn to see Connie standing wide eyed staring straight at me.

CHAPTER TWENTY-NINE
CONNIE

I couldn't move. I was anchored. I willed for my legs to walk but they wouldn't.

"Connie," Kaleb was breathless, grabbing the white towel off the towel rail and wrapping it round his waist. His eyes were wide and bulging, his mouth open as he clutched onto the top of the towel. "It's not, erm, it's not," he stammers and my eyes are pinned to the bulge under the towel.

His body is glorious, toned and sculpted with the perfect Apollo's belt. I wanted to kiss him everywhere then run my tongue all over every inch of him. And I mean *every* inch.

What was wrong with me?

"It's not what it looked like," he finally managed, crimson pinched at his cheeks, or was that just from the scalding water? Possibly his post orgasmic glow?

"Okay," I managed, shrugging my shoulders up, trying to not let him see how much this has affected me. I turn to walk out the bathroom. I needed a minute or three.

I had just caught my minder—a man twice my age—

pleasuring himself with *my* name falling from his lips as he came. It was hot. So, so hot. I continue downstairs to get some milk, I was wide awake and not tired in the slightest. I was only waking up to use the toilet.

Opening the fridge, I grab the carton of milk and pour some into a mug. I should warm it but I don't. I take a mouthful of the cold milk, instantly cooling my burning insides. I hear footsteps approaching behind me, but I don't look round. Embarrassment suddenly swarms deep inside of me, anxiety crippling me.

"Connie," his voice is low, but I stay forward and stare out the window. I need my blush to leave my cheeks. All I can think about was how he stroked himself, his dipped head watching as he continued. I don't think I have ever felt so turned on before. "I just want to say I'm sorry," he stammers, his voice getting louder as he is approaching behind me.

I spin quickly to face him, both of my hands wrapped around my mug as I give him a soft smile.

"You have nothing to be sorry for, I should have knocked..." I shrug my shoulders up softly, tilting my head to the side, "risks of us sharing one bathroom," I scoff a laugh, my lips curling at the corners as I sip my milk.

Kaleb nods.

"I'm going to go to bed," I whisper, stepping forward as I brush past him, our shoulders barely touching. Kaleb grabs the top of my arm and pulls me back, my skin erupting in goosebumps, and I instantly miss his touch when he drops his hand from my skin.

"Are we okay?" his eyes search mine.

"Of course," I nod, placing my small hand on his chest, the warmth of his skin scalding my fingertips. I remove them quickly; afraid he had burned me. "Goodnight," I whisper, suddenly my chest hurts and I feel like I am unable to breathe being so close to him. I needed to get away from him.

I rush up the stairs and close my bedroom door. Clutching my mug, I press my back against the door and let my head tip back, it softly banging against the wood.

I'm doomed.

I WOKE FEELING HEAVY HEADED AND MISERABLE. I COULDN'T SLEEP and I have no idea why. Oh no, wait. I do, it was because of Kaleb and his cock. It's all I could think about. How good he would be, how bad he would be, how fucking reckless it would be. Anxiety swarms me, my stomach twisting as pain radiates through my body. My emotions peak and I swipe a tear away. I don't even know if I could be intimate with someone else since Tryst. He broke me. Mentally, physically and emotionally. Would someone be able to pick up the pieces and make me whole again? Would someone be able to deal with the trauma that haunts me? The way Tryst changed so quickly, manipulating me, *forcing* himself onto me. Nausea rolls in my stomach at the flashbacks. He loved me. Or so he said. But those three words are so easily said. So, just because he loved me, must that mean that he can't do the things he did? No, of course he could. It was so much easier for him to get to me and manipulate me in the way he did. He was a narcissist. He gaslit me. How could I not notice it? I knew him when we were younger teens, he was never like this but then...

I jumped when I heard a knock on the door, and I swear I felt my soul leave my body before it came back. I swipe an angry tear away that rolled down my cheek.

Knock.

My heart raced in my chest.

"Come in," I call out softly, my voice trembling and it doesn't matter how much I try and calm it, I can't.

The door opens slowly and Kaleb pops his head round the door frame.

"May I come in?" his black hair is pushed from his face, but it's tousled and messy.

Unkept. His grey eyes seek out mine and I swear I could fall into them. He is just so devastatingly handsome.

"Yeah," I mumble, letting my eyes fall before the tension gets too much. He has a magnetising force around him, and it doesn't matter how hard I try, I am pulled to him whether I like it or not.

He pushes the door open a little more and strolls in. I don't look up.

"Doris has just called," his voice is gruff, I don't even have to look at him to know he is grinding down on his back teeth. I automatically begin nodding, I didn't even need him to finish his sentence.

"Okay," I whisper, lifting my face up to look at him, "I'll just get dressed."

I slip off the bed and into the bathroom, slamming the door shut. Curling my hands around the edge of the sink, my head falls forward and I cry. I knew this day was going to come, I knew I had to give a statement but now it's finally here, I was terrified. Squeezing my eyes shut, I try to stop the tears but it's no use. The days of bottling up my emotions has got too much; I couldn't put a lid on them even if I wanted to. I used to be so good at shutting off anytime emotions threatened, but since everything has happened I have no control over them.

I choke out, turning my face to the ceiling of the

bathroom and inhale deeply. My chest heaves up and down, my heart racing to the point it's skipping beats which only causes me to catch my breath. It's a vicious cycle. This continues before a tight band wraps itself round my chest. My fingers turn white from the tightness of my grip, and I gasp for air to fill my lungs, willing for a breath not to knock another one straight out of me. My lungs burn as I try and force as much air through them but it's no use. I can't breathe. Clutching the thin material of my pyjama top I stumble back and fall to the floor, my head in my hands as I close my eyes trying to still my racing heart.

A soft knock on the door has me turning my head and I see Kaleb's wide eyes. He rushes in, pulling me into his embrace and holding me tight as my trembling begins to ease, Kaleb's large hand rubs my back in soft circles causing the tightness in my chest to settle.

"I've got you; it'll be okay," he whispers, pressing his lips to the top of my head, "I promise you."

Sitting in the questioning room, Kaleb at my side, I drum my fingers on the wooden table. I'm nervous. Anxious. Nauseated. My right leg bobs up and down quickly as I try to focus on my anxious mind on anything but this moment right here. But how can I when this is plaguing me? The door opens and a young lady enters, Kaleb's hand moves under the table and rests on my moving leg, curling his fingers round my thigh and squeezing it in a soothing manner.

"Connie," The young female officer sits down opposite me, holding a piece of paper and a pen.

"Hi," I swallow down the thickness and ignore the sickly feeling that swarms in my stomach.

"You're only here to give a statement, we don't see you as a suspect, but we need to get statements from people who were close to Tryst, and we know you were a couple until you recently broke up." Her warm honey eyes pin to mine, I can see the kindness in them, but I don't drop my guard.

"We just need you to write your version of events as you know them and where you have been since the night of Tryst's death."

"She's been with me," Kaleb's voice is low as my leg begins to shake again, he doesn't remove his hand.

"We just need her to statement it," she turns her face towards Kaleb, her eyes glowering at him. He stares her down until she gives in and breaks her glare. "Like I said, we just need you to write down your version and sign it," she smiles, "I'll pop out for a moment, take your time."

She stands from the chair and pushes the piece of lined paper over to me and a pen before turning and walking out the room, closing the door behind her with a little more force.

"I don't think she likes me," Kaleb nudges me and smirks.

"I don't think she likes you either..." I mumble, not lifting my eyes from the paper in front of me.

"Take your time," his grip tightens on my leg, his fingers digging in slightly and I turn my face to look at him, "you've got this, just write the truth..." he trails off for a moment and licks his bottom lip, "every, single, truth, Connie."

And I swallow the large lump down, my stomach knotting and coiling.

"No need to hide anymore, love, he can't hurt you."

CHAPTER THIRTY

KALEB

CONNIE HASN'T SAID TWO WORDS SINCE WE'VE BEEN IN THE CAR. Cruising down the highway back towards our rental home, the silence is deafening. I go to open my mouth but then stop myself. The officer told us she would be in touch if she needed any more information, but given Connie's statement and witnesses, they feel like they have enough to keep her away from the case. I am just praying it stays that way. Once I know Connie is settled, I need to call Xavier. I am beyond pissed at how he handled this situation, I've had no calls and the way he done it was shoddy. He has caused carnage because he didn't deal with it like I was assured.

I tighten my grip round the steering well as frustration brews deep inside of me.

"Can we stop for food? I'm hungry," Connie's soft voice pulls me back from my rage, I turn to face her, my furrowed brows smoothing out.

"Of course, what do you want?"

"Fast food, I want French fries and a burger," she sighs before turning to look out the window.

"You got it darling, as soon as I see a drive-through, I'll stop."

I needed noise, I hated being alone with my thoughts. My mind was a dark place, until Connie. Now she is a little bit of lightness at the end of a dark tunnel. Reaching forward, I push the button on the dash and my phone playlist connects to the car as *This – Megan McKenna* begins to play. My chest tightens, my heart drumming to the beat of the song. Emotions swarm me and I cough slightly to clear my throat. I have no idea what is happening to me, but I am beginning to feel something other than numbness. It's been that way for as long as I can remember. I have never felt anything for anyone.

Until now.

Turning my blinker on, I pull into the fast-food parking lot as I join the queue for the drive-through.

"Any specific burger?" I ask, turning the music down slightly.

"Cheese, no onion but extra pickles," she smiles, tilting her head so it's resting more into the car seat.

"You can have my pickles," I grunt, pushing the window down as we approach the speaker. Her eyes widen, her mouth open in pure shock.

"You don't like *pickles?!*" she gasps, "they're the best part!"

I shake my head, turning my nose up.

I place our order and ask for extra pickles for *my* darling and pull into a car parking spot. She holds onto our large cokes until I put the brake on. Placing the cup holder on the dash, she unplugs herself, crosses her legs underneath her and turns to face me holding her hands out.

"Patience," I smirk, fisting my hand into the brown paper bag and grabbing her carton of fries, handing them along with her barbecue and ranch dips. She grabs a handful and eats them before grabbing a couple more and dipping them into her dips.

Smiling, my heart thrums at the sight of her. She really is beautiful. To be honest, beautiful isn't a strong enough word to describe just how *beautiful* she is. Beautiful still seems an injustice.

I reach for her burger and hand it to her. She places the cardboard carton of chips in the small gap between her legs as she unwraps her burger and lifts the bun to see the extra pickles.

She hums in appreciation then takes a bite.

"Good?" I ask as I lift the bun of my burger for her to pick the pickles out. Her eyes light with glee, making them glisten as she leans across and picks the pickles up and pops them straight past her lips.

"No one has ever shared their pickles with me," she nibbles her bottom lip, her stunning green eyes finally connect with mine and I feel every fibre of my body vibrate, causing a ripple to course through me.

"Well, let it be known…" I chew the inside of my lip as I reach for a couple of French fries, I lean across the centre of the car, and she edges closer to me, "I don't share my pickles with *just* anyone."

"Well, I'm glad." She shuffles back in her seat, continuing her food and a comfortable silence blankets us. And for the first time in a while, I feel content.

CONNIE TOOK HERSELF TO BED WHEN WE GOT HOME, HER MOOD diving drastically when she caught a glimpse of my phone on the news section, Tryst was still filling the columns and so was she. I wanted to follow her, comfort her in the best way I knew how, but I decided it would be best to let her have some time out. It has been a long day for her, and I don't want to make it worse by poking into something she may not feel comfortable talking about.

Slipping my shoes off, I fall onto the sofa with my whiskey and reach for my phone. Finding Xavier's number, I let it ring.

"What?" he snaps.

"Hello Xavier, it's Kaleb."

"Who?" his disinterested tone bites at me.

"Kaleb..." I trail off and look behind me to make sure the coast is clear, "I spoke to you about *Tryst*?" I whisper his name and cover my mouth as I speak into the speaker of my cell.

"Oh, yes, *you*." He snipes, his attitude fucking stinks.

"Was there a little miscommunication between us? I thought I made it clear..." I stall my words as he begins talking over me.

"I didn't do it. Someone beat me to it by the looks of it."

I stood from the sofa quickly, my eyes bugging out my head as I run my hand over my mouth and down over my stubble.

"What?" I hiss, pacing back and forth between the sofas.

"You heard me, I sent my guy, but your guy was already brown bread."

"Brown bread?" I ask confused, "Wh..."

"Dead." His tone harsh, "Your guy was dead."

"And you didn't do it."

"Are you thick?" he laughs.

No, not thick. Just confused as hell!

"Anyway, I would say it's been a pleasure, but it hasn't.

And I don't lie. I didn't kill your bloke, and I am pretty sure I told you to lose my number."

"Well..." but it's too late. He has cut me off. "Rude, arrogant fucker," I seethe, wrapping my fingers tightly around my burner phone and throwing it on the sofa.

"Was someone here?" her soft voice breaks through my harsh mood, making my skin erupt in goosebumps.

"No, love." I shake my head softly from side to side, "I was just talking to Keaton," I roll my lips.

"Oh."

"Are you okay?" my brows pinch, and I walk towards her but then stall. I run my hand round the back of my head, just so I am doing something with my hands other than reaching for her and pulling her close to me like I so desperately want to do.

"I just wanted some milk," she stayed on the bottom step as her nervous fingers played with the hem of her oversized tee that sat on the top of her thighs. It was a cream *Nirvana* tee, her brown hair was down and messy from where she had been asleep. Her skin dewy but her eyes heavy and still full of dreams. I just hope they were happy ones and not ones of sadness or hurt.

I had come to realise in the few days that we had been here, that if Connie couldn't sleep, she would come down for milk. My mind flashes back to the early hours of the morning when I followed her down here after she caught me in the bathroom. I clench my jaw at the memory of her innocent eyes seeing me like that.

"Go sit down on the sofa, I'll make you a warm cup of milk," already strolling across to get the saucepan from the drawer, Connie grabs the milk from the fridge. "Shoo," I flick my fingers outwards, indicating for her to go and sit down but she rubs her lips together and leans over the work surface on the other side of the kitchen. My wandering eyes leave the saucepan for a moment as they trail up her long, toned legs before I turn my head away and focus my attention on adding the milk.

"I'll make it how my mom used to make mine," I cough softly, clearing my throat, "I hope that's okay," I take a moment before I give in and turn to look at her, her eyes are batted down, but she gives a small nod.

Guilt crashes through me, I shouldn't have said about my mom. She is probably missing her moms more than anything right now and I've just mentioned mine. I inhale deeply as I whisk the milk softly. Turning the stove down low, I raid the cupboards until I find some cinnamon powder. I look for a sell-by date but there isn't one. Can cinnamon powder go off?

Popping the lid, I tap a small amount on my finger and taste it. Giving it a moment, and after internally battling with myself I decide it's fine. Sprinkling cinnamon on the top of her steaming milk, I turn on the spot and glide it across the work surface to her. I have to keep my distance, because the way she is looking at me with them hooded, dark eyes is tempting me. They're pulling me towards her, and I cannot go there with her. She has already caught me in a compromising position and that's already gone one step too far. I step back, turning the stove off and placing the used saucepan in the sink.

"I hope that makes you sleepy," I give a soft smile as I pad towards the living room and grab my phone. Walking back towards her, I stop at the front door and make sure it's locked. I need to sleep, and I need to freshen up. I feel stuffy and dirty. Stepping down the narrow hallway and back towards the kitchen I turn to see Connie standing, her tee slightly risen as the crease of her pert ass cheek is on show.

My eyes widen, my cock instantly going hard as it strains against the material of my pants.

What is she doing to me?

I drop my head and rush for the stairs, I need a cold shower and a wank. The rate I am going, I'll have no dick left.

CHAPTER THIRTY-ONE
CONNIE

I LAY IN THE TUB, MY BIG TOE PUSHING INTO THE OPENING OF THE faucet as a few warm drips of water run down my ankle. The wind howls outside as bitter rain hits the glass pane. There is something comforting about sitting in complete silence whilst warm and cosy when the weather is cold and miserable outside. I thought I would miss the city when we first came here, but this feels more like home than the city ever did. I am content here. Reaching for my glass of wine, I take a sip and place it back on the bath board and pick my book up. Kaleb is out grabbing groceries and I hope he returns home soon; I am anxious him being out there in this horrendous weather. Once more, my thoughts fly to Reese and how she must have felt when she was told that Elijah had died in a car accident. My heart aches and my chest falls heavy. I rub the ache out as much as I can, steadying my breathing that is suddenly harsh and ragged. I hear a soft knock on the door, but it doesn't open.

"I'm home, no rush, just wanted to let you know." My heart slows as well as my breathing. My stomach swarms with butterflies and I internally scold myself for allowing myself to even feel remotely anything towards that man. The whole situation is wrong. So wrong. But I can't help but wonder what it would be like to be with him, if only for one night.

"Okay!" I call out, I feel the heat swarm my cheeks. Shaking my head from side to side at my schoolgirl behavior, I open my book and pick up where I left off. I feel heat burning through me, the apex between my legs begging to be touched. My eyes skim over the pages where the main male character is eating the female out. She is sitting on the edge of the bed, her legs wide as the tall, dark and handsome man runs his tongue up and down her folds, lapping up her arousal whilst pumping two of his fingers deep inside of her.

I feel the heat rush to my cheeks as I swallow another mouthful of the chilled wine. I turn my head slightly to side eye the door, making sure it is definitely shut. I lean forward, placing my wine back on the bath board as I let my fingertips gently skim over my sensitive skin, letting them dip under the warm water before I swirl them over my swollen clit.

My eyes roll in the back of my head at my touch, pleasure rolling through me thick and fast as my mind is filled with Kaleb. I take the scenario from the book and imagine it as me and him. Me looking down at him as he fucks me with his fingers, his tongue rubbing and swirling over my clit as I feel my stomach tighten and coil, my wet pussy clamping down over his fingers as I feel my orgasm threatening to crash through me. Normally I would try and stop it, slow down as I work myself up, but I needed this release. I need to rid myself of some of this tension. Letting my head fall forward, I open my eyes as I watch my fingers rub over my clit, working me the way I like. Fluttering my eyes shut, I see Kaleb's grey eyes on mine as his head is between my legs, and I come. My orgasm rolling through me with such force, I jolt forward, my whole body trembling as I come down from my high.

THE EVENING DRAWS IN AND THE WEATHER ONLY GETS WORSE. Kaleb paces back and forth across the small floor space of the house, running his fingers through his hair.

"What's going on in that head of yours?" I ask, wrapped under my fluffy blanket as my eyes continue gliding across the words on my pages, blushing at the memories of me getting myself off.

"Just whether I need to board the windows or something, the wind is getting worse..." he spins to face me then shrugs, "maybe I'll just keep an eye on it."

"You just going to sit at the window all night?" I click my tongue at the top of my mouth and twist my lips.

"Well, I sleep down here so it won't be hard will it," the sarcasm drips from his tone, the gruffness of his voice present and that's when I know he is grumpy. But I love grumpy Kaleb.

"Would you like the bed tonight? I don't mind..." I say coyly, my eyes lifting as I watch him turn to face me, the corners of his lips pulling.

"No, the sofa is fine." He grunts, turning round and heading to the kitchen, opening the fridge and grabbing two bottles of beer.

"You're very grumpy tonight," I say as he strolls towards me, standing over me and handing me a bottle and I can't stop the small smile that graces my lips.

"I'm tired," he yawns, rubbing a palm over his face.

"Not sleeping?" I ask, placing my book page down on my chest and let my face fall to the side to look at him.

"Not really, but then it's nothing new."

"How so?"

"My mind is always so…" He stalls for a moment, his words trailing off as he looks out the window again.

"Hectic?"

"Yeah, something like that," he shrugs his shoulders up and that's when I see his facial expression change, a coldness glazes his eyes, his jaw tightening. I take that as my cue to stop poking the bear and pick my book back up but I'm not reading long when he speaks.

"What's your backstory?" he surprises me with his question. I roll on my side, propping up on my elbow and resting my head on my hand as my eyes fall to him.

"There isn't much to know," my tone is flat as I sigh, "grew up in a fairytale only to find out last year none of it was real," Kaleb shuffles in his seat, his interest piqued.

"In what way?" Now it's his time to poke me.

"I don't want to talk about it," I snap, rolling onto my back and lifting my book over my face.

"Why don't you put the book down and talk to me like an adult."

"Because I don't want to talk about my life, I would much rather read about a story that is a lot happier than the life I am currently living," I wince at my harsh answer and realise how bad that must sound to him.

"Is it really that bad?" Before I can turn to look at him, he is crouched down next to me, his large hand moving to my face and I feel like everything moves in slow motion as he pushes a strand of my brown hair from my face, his eyes volleying between mine.

"Yes," I whisper as I struggle to breathe from the

closeness of Kaleb. I have never had the air knocked from my lungs by someone before. "I don't feel like grief has hit me yet," I whisper because that's all I can manage.

Kaleb falls back slightly, a puzzled look on his face as his brows knit.

"I should feel that all-consuming grief... right?" a small laugh leaves me before a lump forms tight in my throat.

"Everything that you feel or may not feel is okay, Connie. Not everyone cries, not everyone feels painstaking grief..." Kaleb trails off for a moment, rubbing his fingers across his stubble, "you just have to take each day as it comes, darling."

I nod, rubbing my eyes that suddenly sting.

"Tea?" Kaleb pushes to his feet, clearing his throat.

"Only if you're making," a small smile plays across my lips as I pick my book up and try to lose myself between the pages once more.

"I wouldn't be asking if I wasn't going to make one..." his voice trails off as he disappears into the kitchen. I sit up and look over my shoulder at him, my eyes trail up and down his back and I must admit, he is *so damn fine*. He is wearing a black fitted tee that allows me to see the muscles ripple under his skin every time he moves, which makes my skin come alight, a fire burning deep inside of me that I hadn't felt in a long time. It makes my stomach knot and twist. My eyes continue to roam, and I fixate on his toned ass and legs that are being hugged by a khaki pair of sweatpants. I know I shouldn't be looking, and I know for definite that I shouldn't be feeling the way I do about this man... but that's what makes it dangerous... because he is forbidden to me, as I am to him.

We will never work.

Guilt consumes me. I am angry and disgusted with

myself in an instant. My ex-boyfriend died a little over a week ago and here I am fighting with temptation over someone I can't have.

Am I broken? I choke on a sob, a tear rolling down my cheek as I angrily swipe it away before Kaleb can see. I sniff and lay my back against the arm of the sofa as I pick up where I left off in my book, acting as if everything is normal.

"Here we go," he stands before me and holds out the white mug filled with hot tea, and I smile as I take it from him.

"I hope lemon and honey is okay," he half smiles as he takes his own seat and sips a fresh bottle of beer.

"I thought you were making a tea," I pinch my brows together.

"Nah, just making one for you, thought it might make you feel better... and if I said I wasn't making one then you wouldn't have had one."

I chew the inside of my cheek and smile.

"Well, thank you."

"You're welcome."

It had been a week since I had given my statement and we still hadn't heard anything from the police. I was getting anxious, and Kaleb was on his phone a hell of a lot more to try and find out information. He was getting more frustrated as the days were going on. He couldn't even get a response from the officer that I gave my statement to and that unnerved me even more.

I stare out the kitchen window at the calm sea, the rolling grey clouds getting heavier. It was the real life visual of the calm before the storm. I lose myself in my thoughts as I replay the last couple of weeks in my head and how much has happened, things that I never thought I would witness but here I am.

My ex-boyfriend is dead.

I am still avoiding my family and best friend.

And I am living in the Hamptons with a stranger who showed up at the right time when I needed someone.

I am pulled from my thoughts as the smell of burning wafts through my nostrils. My eyes widen as I grab the pan from the stove and turn it off.

"Fuck it," I groan, getting my spatula and flipping the grilled cheese and looking at the burnt side.

"What's burning?" Kaleb rubs his hand over the top of his head as he appears in the doorway. All six foot four of him looking incredibly handsome and I sigh.

"Your lunch," I throw the pan onto the worksurface and spin round to face him. My back resting against the edge of the worksurface as I cross my arms in front of my chest and pout.

Kaleb smirks, his grey eyes on me as he stalks towards me. A small gasp leaves me as my breath catches in the back of my throat. He stands in front of me, his warm, minty breath that is laced with a hint of coffee swarms me and my heart flips. I drop my arms and let my hands wrap around the edge of the work surface as I try to balance myself. He cocks his head to the side, one corner of his lips lifting into a smirk as he reaches for the grilled cheese sandwich from the pan and drops it on a plate. I wince in humiliation at how loud it sounds when it hits the China plate, my cheeks pinching a rosy red.

He brings the burnt slab of charcoal to his mouth,

parting his lips then takes a bite, the crunch echoing round the room.

"Please don't eat it…" I cover my eyes, but I can still hear him crunching.

"It's the best grilled cheese I have ever had," he winks when I peek at him, a playful glint flashing in his eyes before he turns and walks away to the living room.

I breathe out a heavy breath and turn the kitchen faucet on, as I let the water run for a bit until it is hot. Filling the sink with dish soap I sink the pan into the bubbles and let it soak.

Opening the fridge, I grab a bottle of water and pad towards the living room. The days are growing shorter, darkness creeping in earlier and earlier as winter approaches. Kaleb is sitting on his phone, his brows furrowed as he continues chewing on his inedible food. I am sure he is just being kind; I think he is worried that one wrong move and I'll dissolve into a puddle on the floor.

"Everything okay?" I ask, picking up on the tension that is vibrating round the room. I sit on the sofa, crossing my legs underneath me as I pick the skin round my nail bed.

"Ugh," he exhales, locking his phone and tossing it on the seat beside him, "yeah, just work, the guys are struggling…" he sighs, rubbing his hands over his face.

"Why don't you go back for a while…" I stammer, knotting my fingers together.

"I will *not* leave you here. I can sort something, they'll survive." He nods, popping the last part of his lunch into his mouth and suddenly I am jealous of a burnt grilled cheese.

"Will they though? You look like you have the weight of the world on your shoulders, and I can't help but thinking that's because of me." I chew my bottom lip, nerves ripping through me.

"Connie," he says exasperated, his mouth laxed, his eyes soften as he stands and walks slowly over to me, his large hand cupping my cheek, "none of my weight is because of you."

His touch is soft and cold against my burning scarlet cheeks, and I automatically lean into his hand, my green eyes lifting to his.

"My weight will never be because of you," he whispers, his thumb brushing across my cheek bone and I swear I feel something shift between us, but before I can get accustomed to this new feeling that is stirring deep inside of me, Kaleb's phone rings. He drops his hand from my face quickly as if my skin burned him.

"Yeah," his tone is flat as he picks his plate up and walks it to the kitchen, "speaking."

I stand, curiosity getting the better of me as I walk slowly behind him. "This is good news, so everything to do with Connie is closed?" He nods, his eyes fixed out the window as the rain begins belting down onto the glass, nothing but that sound fills the house for a moment. "Okay..." he stalls, his smile that was once on his lips slipping for a moment, "Perfect, I'll let her know. Thank you, Detective."

He cuts the phone off and he gives me a small smile, stepping towards me.

"They're not taking you any further with the Tryst case, following your statement and witnesses, you're not a suspect..." he trails off and before the slither of relief swarms me, I am waiting for the *but*.

"But?" I ask, my dark green eyes widening, my heart drumming in my chest fast.

"But, they have had Tryst's autopsy results..." he licks

his lips, rubbing his hand round the back of his head. I have noticed when Kaleb does this, he is nervous.

"And..."

"He did take his own life Connie, he overdosed. They've found a note..."

I swallow down the bile that burns my throat, my eyes stinging as tears prick the back of them.

"A note," I whisper, stepping back as the air is knocked from my lungs. Suddenly I feel winded as I gasp for air, and I realise what is happening. I'm having another panic attack. My legs buckle beneath me, and Kaleb catches me, moving me to the sofa as he holds me tightly like he did before. No words are exchanged, and this time, I let it all out.

I SIT IN THE TRAY OF THE SHOWER, COMPLETELY NUMB. I DON'T even realise that the water has run completely cold, but I don't care. It has hit me. Well and truly hit me that Tryst is dead. He is gone. Sure, in the end, he didn't treat me great, *but* he did love me at some point in his downfall. I just never thought Tryst would take his own life. He had so much going for him, and even when the low of his addiction hit him, he was still upbeat. It just didn't make sense.

"Connie," I hear Kaleb's voice, but I don't lift my head. I keep myself in the same position I have been in. My knees pulled to my chest, my arms wrapped around my legs and my chin resting on my knees. My wet, dark brown hair frames my face as it's stuck to my skin. My eyes hollow and dull.

"Connie," he calls again but I don't have the energy to

even respond. Any ounce of energy has been drained from me. My thoughts have been consumed by nothing but Tryst for the last hour. I shouldn't have left.

I should have never come with Kaleb.

If I hadn't, Tryst wouldn't have killed himself.

The papers are right to blame me.

Because it was my fault.

I killed Tryst.

CHAPTER THIRTY-TWO

KALEB

I HAD NO IDEA WHAT TO DO. I FELT HELPLESS. I COULDN'T PULL her out of this hole. She was slipping from my grasp, and I didn't know what I could do to help her. I pace back and forth outside the bathroom; the hallway is only narrow and short so it doesn't take many strides for me to reach the other side but I can't stop. What was I thinking telling her about the note? I should have kept it to myself until I knew she was strong enough to handle it. Running my hand through my hair, I pull at the root in frustration. My mind whizzes at a hundred miles an hour. I could smash the bathroom door down; I don't even know what she is doing in there. I know the shower is running, that's about it. What if she tries to harm herself? Is there a razor in there? Fuck, what about the shower hose? My eyes widen, I stand outside the door and bang hard.

"Connie!" I shout as panic begins to stir deep inside of me. She doesn't answer. "Fuck!" I growl, banging on the door again.

I take a couple of steps back before I lift my leg and kick

the door in, it swings off its hinges and bangs against the wall behind it.

"Connie," I gasp, rushing to her where she is sitting in the shower tray, the water cascading down over her and falling to my knees in front of her.

"Kaleb!" she cries, her eyes widened as she realises I'm in the room. I grasp her pretty little face in my hands as my frantic eyes search hers.

"Are you okay! Fuck Connie, you scared me half to death."

She doesn't answer, her eyes just focus on mine as she trembles in my grasp.

"It's okay," I pull her into me, her wet body against mine as the shower water cascades down over both of us. I am grateful she isn't naked; it would be awkward to stand here trying to comfort her with an erection. It's bad enough that she is wearing a white tee which I am sure is mine and little shorts which have both gone sheer from the water.

"I killed him," she mumbles, snapping out of her trance and pushing away from me.

"Killed who?" I question, my face screwed up as I listen to her.

"Tryst," she chokes, her back against the tiled shower.

"You didn't..." I shake my head from side to side, droplets of water running off my head and down my nose before eventually falling and hitting the shower tray.

"I did! And it's your fault!" she shouts at me, her eyes burning through me, the venomous tone to her voice throws me off. "You should never have taken me away from him." She begins to tremble again before sliding down the wall. Her knees are back up to her chest, her head dipped as she cries.

I want to stay but I need to go. She is angry and she is

lashing out at me. It's fine. She is grieving. I *get* it. But I would be lying if I said it didn't hurt me.

I turn and walk away from her, leaving her heart-breaking sobs behind. I don't grab a towel; I just keep walking until I can't walk anymore. I still at the front door, looking out the window at the dreary weather in full swing. I can hear the wind howling across the choppy sea. I debate going out there, just to take a minute or two but the thought of leaving her in here terrifies me.

Shaking my head from side to side I see my phone screen flashing on the coffee table. It's Doris. Sighing, I answer.

"Is everything okay, Doris?" I ask quietly, trying to hide the betrayal in my voice.

"It was," I hear her pause, "we haven't had any reporters here for the last few days, anyway, Derek went down to check the mail and they have set up camp again..." she trails off and I literally face palm myself, but I don't remove my hand. I rub my index finger and thumb into my eye lids and push a little harder than intended.

"It's okay, it's because they've got wind that Connie has been dropped from the case..." I stall for a moment, dropping my hand and lifting my head to look up the stairs and I sigh. "Tryst killed himself, Connie is..." I pause.

"Not taking it well?" Doris finishes my sentence for me.

"No, not taking it well at all," I puff out my cheeks and let out a slow, exasperated breath. "I think I have bitten off more than I can chew with this one."

"Nonsense." Doris scoffs, "She's just not making your job easy. Give her some time. Stay in the Hamptons for a couple more weeks... there is no rush to get back is there..." I don't know whether she is telling me or asking me.

"Apart from my company is falling apart beneath my

feet because the incompetent idiots who also own the business cannot seem to run it without me." I snap at Doris and that's when I realise how wound up I am.

"Are you okay, Kaleb?" her voice is soft and suddenly I miss home. I fall onto the sofa and pinch my eyes closed whilst inhaling deeply through my nose and then out of my mouth.

"I will be," I grit, "just stay on the phone for a minute, I am trying to calm my heart rate. My lips pull at the corners, and I know she will be panicking.

"Don't say that!" she scolds, and I let out a small laugh.

"I'm joking Doris, I am just exhausted," I yawn and stretch.

"Are you not sleeping?"

"Not any less than usual." She hums.

"I'm on the shit sofa which doesn't help."

"Well, that is certainly going to play a part in your foul mood," I can hear the smile in her voice, "I'm sure Connie will swap out with you for a couple of nights, or you know..."

"Don't. Finish. That. Sentence." I warn, my tone clipped, and she belly laughs down the end of the phone which in turn, makes me laugh.

"Get some rest, Kaleb... that's an order."

"Okay," I whisper, "stay in the penthouse... that's an order." And I cut the phone off.

I stay sitting on the sofa for the minute. I am completely out of depth here. I have no idea what to do to help her. I don't know her. I can't suggest her favorite movie, because I don't know what it is. I don't know what her favorite colour is, her favorite food, her favorite animal. I know *nothing* about her other than the little bits of information that her dad gave me to find her. But her as a person, I know nothing.

Lifting my head, I press the screen on my phone to wake it up. I needed help. And there was only one person I could call.

CHAPTER THIRTY-THREE
KALEB

IT RINGS, AND RINGS, AND RINGS. UNTIL FINALLY, IT STOPS.

"Hello?" I can hear the hesitance in her voice.

"Hi, Reese?" I stammer, but keep my voice down so Connie doesn't hear me.

"Yeah, it's me. Who is this?" she asks, her own voice lowering as I hear the sound of a door close behind her.

"Kaleb."

The line falls silent.

"I need your help, but Killian *cannot* know about this. Connie is already going to hate me even more than she does right now, but I *need* you." I plead, my mind is busy, and I am frantic with worry. I didn't know who else to call.

"What's happened, is she okay?" The panic is evident in her voice; that was not my intention.

"Yes, yes, well, no... no she isn't. But she is safe, if that's what you mean." I'm rambling. I have never been so worked up before. "How quick can you get here?"

"I can't just up and leave, what would I say to..." I hear her footsteps, "Killian," she whispers.

"I don't know, all I know is that Connie needs you. I

need you. I've tried but she won't listen. I'm suddenly the bad guy." My voice is low as I pad into the kitchen.

Silence crackles down the line, I am ready to get on my hands and knees and beg.

"I'll be there as soon as I can, text me the address," she whispers and cuts the phone off.

Relief swarms me. Slipping my phone into my pocket, I pour her a drink and make my way back upstairs. She already despises me, now she will even more.

CHAPTER THIRTY-FOUR

CONNIE

MY EYES ARE PINNED TO THE WIDE OPEN BATHROOM DOOR. KALEB booted it so hard, the hinge has bent. He hasn't come back in, but then again, why would he? I shouted at him and blamed him for something that wasn't his fault. I am embarrassed and hurt. I have these mixed feelings that I know I shouldn't be feeling, plus these feelings combined with guilt, anger, grief... it's just a cluster-fuck. I drum my fingertips over my temples as I hold my head in my hands. I am in shock, complete and utter shock at the news I heard today. There was always that inkling in the back of my mind that Tryst could overdose which made my stomach roll.

I have no idea how long I have been sitting here for when I hear the sound of footsteps approaching. I still, my eyes not moving from the open door when I see a pair of high-top converse. My eyes widen and my heart races in my chest. I know those shoes.

"Reese?!" I shriek, and then my heart sinks.

He called them.

Her eyes are rimmed with tears as she walks cautiously

towards me. My eyes stay on her as she crouches down in front of me, her hand reaching out and clasping over mine.

"Hi," she whispers but I turn my face from her because I don't want her to see the tears that are rolling down my cheeks. "Your dad isn't here... he doesn't know Kaleb called me..." her voice is soft as I feel her fingers brushing my hair out of my face. I turn to look at her and I choke.

"How did Kaleb call you?" I ask, ignoring the constant roll of tears.

"He must have gone through your phone," she says, her head tilting to the side. I suck in a breath, and lunge myself at her, her arms wrapping around me tightly as I grip onto her as if my life depended on it. "I promise to keep it that way too," she whispers as I feel her hug tighten. "I've missed you so much."

I lift my eyes and see Kaleb standing in the door and as soon as our eyes meet, he turns and walks away and my heart breaks a little. I've hurt him.

SITTING IN MY BEDROOM IN FRESH CLOTHES AND ONE OF REESE'S English breakfast teas I feel slightly better. I cried, *a lot*. I didn't realise I had that many tears to cry until I was a full-on sobbing mess.

"Talk to me, Connie," Reese sips her tea but her eyes don't leave mine.

"About..." I act dumb and I annoy myself instantly at this stupid charade I am putting on.

Her brows knit as she shuffles on my bed, stretching one leg out and stretches her back. "The weather," she rolls her eyes and laughs.

"How did you sneak out past my dad?" I ask, my bottom lip trembling.

"Just told him I needed a few hours out from your baby sister..." she sighs, "he didn't question me, I do take some down time every now and again when being a mum is a little overwhelming."

I nod, but I'm not sure what I am nodding at.

"He would understand you know..." she trails off, reaching her hand out to touch mine but she retracts it quickly, "he misses you..."

Still nodding, the burn in my throat evident and only growing thicker and more painful as the seconds pass.

"I really miss him too..." I manage, barely, "but I'm not ready yet..." I shake my head from side to side.

"I get it... I do," she smiles weakly, and I can see that she doesn't get it, I mean, why would she? "It's just, you've never met your baby sister," Reese's eyes cloud and I watch as she tries to blink the tears away and guilt consumes me, the pain searing through my stomach.

It feels like a knife has been twisted deep and keeps winding until I can't take much more. Reese fiddles around in her bag and pulls out her phone, turning it to face me. The screen lights up with a beautiful brown haired little girl, her big opal eyes just like Reese's, her glowing skin like my dad's and I can see so much of me in her.

"She is beautiful," I whisper, swiping a stray tear that rolls down my cheek, "I'm sorry."

"Don't apologise," she swipes her own tear away, "we just want you home."

I nod, "One day I will be, just not today."

She turns the phone back around and locks it, slipping it back into her bag again.

"Another tea?"

"Please, you make the best tea," I beam at her, even though on the inside I feel like I am dying. Reese winks, grabbing my cup from my hand and making her way downstairs.

Once she has gone, the smile slips and I fall back into the pillows and my eyes fixate on the blank, white ceiling above me. I am beyond annoyed at Kaleb, but also, extremely grateful that he called Reese, I'll have to remember to ask him how he got her number and if what she said was true. I was a bitch to him, downright rude... I should never have blamed him for Tryst. He saved me.

And even though I haven't told him yet. I am so thankful to him. So fucking thankful that he was there that evening.

When Reese re-appears, she hands me a fresh cup of tea. Silence fills the room for a moment as she sits back on the bed in front of me.

"So, talk to me, what is going on?"

I inhale deeply and drum my nails on the mug to try and think on where to begin.

"I don't really know... I have been fine, and then when I was told I was no longer needed in the case, Kaleb told me that there was a note found with Tryst... it just hit me like a freight train."

Reese says nothing, just listens and keeps her eyes focused on me.

"Grief can hit at any time..." Reese's voice is a whisper and I realise that I am talking to the girl who lived through, no, *lives* through her grief.

"Reese... I..."

"Stop it," she leans forward and swats me, but I can see her eyes glassing over.

"I just feel..."

"Empty." Reese finishes my sentence for me. I nod.

"But we weren't together, he hurt me. Broke me in ways that a girl should *never* be broken..." I swallow, the familiar lump lodging itself deep in my throat once more.

"Connie..." Reese trails off, shuffling closer to me and cupping my hand with hers, "What did he do to you?"

Silence blankets us, my eyes fall to my lap, I feel humiliated, and I focus on my cup of tea before my eyes lift and penetrate through hers.

"He used me when I didn't give him permission to."

I wasn't ready to say what it was just yet. Couldn't say *that* word. I couldn't.

CHAPTER THIRTY-FIVE
KALEB

I sat on the sofa, my eyes pinned to the staircase. They had been up there for what felt like hours. I had to stop myself from going up there so many times, but it wasn't my place. She had her friend. She didn't *need* me.

My phone buzzes and I see Keaton's name.

"Yeah," I exhale heavily, my mood heavy and my sombre tone drips out of me.

"Woah... you okay?" Keaton asks.

"Yeah, just tired." I give him what feels like my go to response lately, nodding as if he can see me.

"You not getting any rest?"

"Yeah, I am. It's just been a rough few hours," I rub my hand over the top of my hair, my eyes not moving from the bottom of the stairs.

"With Connie?" I nod, he has no idea of course, but I don't respond and that seems to be enough. "I've seen the headlines," his voice is dull and flat.

"Yeah, it's spooked her and now she is blaming me for it all."

"What?!" Keaton barks down the speaker and I roll my eyes, frustrated with myself for opening my mouth.

"Never mind, it's sorted," I grit, even though it's not sorted at all. "Anyway, onto more important matters," I cough softly, clearing my throat as I stand from the sofa, "can you and the boys get down here tomorrow at all? I can't work these fucking zoom meetings."

Keaton chuckles down the phone and I hear the pop of his decanter lid and my throat burns at the craving of drinking his amber poison with him.

"You sure are showing your *old* age," his sarcastic tone drips through the phone.

"We're the same age," irritation laces my voice as I reach for my bottle of bourbon from the top cupboard and pour myself a glass.

"Ten a.m. work?"

"Ten a.m. is perfect, make sure Nate brings everything that's outstanding, I need the client list from Titus too. May as well spend the day here, be more productive."

"Agreed," Keaton hums.

I move back to the sofa, sitting in my seat that now is imprinted with my ass.

"See you tomorrow," my tone is curt as my eyes burn into the bottom step.

"Bye," Keaton just gets out before I cut my cell off and turn it face down on the sofa, and this is where I stay.

CONNIE

Tears are streaming down my face, but they're not tears of sadness, no, they're tears of joy and happiness.

"My first one-night stand after Elijah, and I get the champ that is a shit lay and only cares about himself," Reese swipes a tear from her cheek, her hand pressed against her stomach.

"Stop it," I howl, my head tipping back.

"Never have I ever faked an orgasm like I did with Colt," she shrieks.

"Then you kicked him out and said if you were meant to see each other again, fate would allow it," I choke, "poor Colt."

"Poor Colt!? What about poor Reese?! First time back in the saddle and I get a one pump chump who couldn't find my clit or g-spot for that matter even if he had step by step instructions!" she swipes her ring finger under her eyes to stop the stream of tears that were threatening to fall. My eyes focus on her beautiful engagement ring and my stomach twists, my heart dropping.

"Oh," I breathe out, trying to calm myself of my laughter, when suddenly, the wide, beaming smile slips from my lips. Realisation hitting me hard.

"Con?" Reese's smile slowly fades as well as mine; she leans over, scooping her hand in mine, "What's wrong?"

"I've missed you so much," I whisper, tears pricking my eyes for a completely different reason now, "and I've missed out on so much." Sighing, I pull Reese towards me and I throw myself at her, wrapping my arms around her slender frame. I don't let go. I'm not ready to let go of her yet, I needed this more than she could know.

"So, the hot hunk of a man you're staying with..." she wiggles her brows up and down.

"Nothing to tell," and I immediately blush giving myself away.

"Oh, there so is!" Reese laughs and shuffles in her spot,

"Tell me, because he is so fine, honestly, he is a walking, talking god."

I feel the heat pinch at my cheeks even more, causing a burn to radiate through me.

"Okay," I let out a shaky breath, "we've had a few little moments..." I admit and I watch as Reese's eyes go wide.

"Nothing like that..." I roll my lips and let my eyes fall for a moment. "He asked me what the books were that I read... so I sort of explained it and teased him a bit," the flames hit my cheeks again and I hide behind my hands.

"Hey!" she exclaims, her hands pulling mine from my eyes, "None of that, did you say they were super smutty?" she is grinning like a Cheshire cat, her eyes wide and full of glee.

"Sort of," I smirk, "and I also walked in on him... well..."

"You didn't!" she snorts a laugh, covering her mouth as she lets out a deep belly laugh.

"Mmhmm," I just about manage before I laugh along with her.

"What did you do?" she edges closer to me.

"I stood there just staring at *it* for a moment... then turned and walked out the bathroom."

"So, you got a good look then," Reese's smile doesn't slip at all.

"I did," I whisper.

"And?"

"Huge," I mouth before I fall back into the pillows and laugh until my stomach and cheeks ache.

THE HOURS HAVE SLIPPED AWAY FROM US AND AS MUCH AS I DON'T want Reese to leave, I know she has to. I can't be selfish.

"You sure you don't want to come with me?" She asks as

we reach the bottom of the stairs, my heart is jack hammering in my chest as my steps bring me closer to facing Kaleb.

I nod, my breath catching as I try to speak.

"Okay," she smiles, pulling me in for an embrace. Tears fill my eyes and I let them fall. The burn in my throat scalding but the tears help to extinguish it.

"Tell Dad I miss him," I sniff and smile as I pull away from her, wiping my nose on the sleeve of my jumper. Disgusting, I know.

"I..." Reese's eyes widened as she stammered.

"We both know Dad wouldn't have let you out without telling him where you were going..." I smirk, my green eyes glassy and Reese smiles softly. "Drive safely, I love you."

"Love you more," Reese hugs me one last time before she walks out the door, giving Kaleb a small nod and smile as she leaves.

My eyes fall to my feet. I can feel Kaleb's stare burning into me, but I refuse to look up at him because I am embarrassed at my behavior and especially after everything he has done for me over the last week. I knot my fingers in front of me, the tears brewing once more. I couldn't stop these ones even if I wanted to.

His scent surrounds me, his footsteps closing in on me. "Connie," his deep voice is soft as he stops in front of me.

"Kaleb," I whisper, lifting my head and baring my soul to him, my green eyes red and rimmed, my cheeks tear stained but they continue to fall. His hand is cupping my cheek, the soft pad of his thumb catching and wiping my tears away. "I'm sorry," I choke, sucking in a breath as it catches.

"Connie, you have nothing to be sorry for..." he trails off, his neck craned as he looks down at me, my lips part as

I feel the air between us crackle. He edges his lips closer to mine but doesn't take his eyes off me.

"I have everything to be sorry for," I whisper, his grip on my cheek tightening slightly. I lean into his warm hand, my lips lifting and silently begging for him to kiss me.

His phone beeps, making me jump and pull back. His hand falls from my face and his eyes squeeze shut, a deep sigh leaving him. He turns and walks towards the sofa where his phone is lit up. I take that as my cue to leave. I spin and disappear up the stairs before shutting my bedroom door.

That was too close. A single moment of weakness, my guard slipped. My chest heaves fast, my breaths harsh as I try and control my breathing. I couldn't even be with him if I wanted to, after what Tryst done to me, I am adamant I am broken. *Dirty*. Tryst *raped* me, someone who was meant to *love* me hurt me in a way that I never imagined.

My fingertips brush across my cheek and I feel the wetness caused by finally admitting to myself what he did to me, finally thinking the word. *Rape*.

Anger courses through me. I am sick of crying. Sick of wasting tears over my narcissistic and abusive boyfriend.

Falling back into my pillow, I tug my comforter over my head and cry myself to sleep.

STEPPING OUT OF THE SHOWER, I WRAP MYSELF IN A WARM TOWEL and wipe the condensation off the mirror and sigh at my reflection. I look and feel like crap; ignoring it, I brush my teeth before padding into the bedroom and rooting through my panty drawer. I pick a black thong and matching bra. Slipping them on, I pull black yoga pants on and an oversized tee. Brushing my hair into a high ponytail, I finish my look off with my pink slippers.

I look at myself in the mirror again, turning to the side and sighing. I'm bloated and feel sluggish. I need to work out. I am pent up; that's not helping with my emotions. I feel like a ticking time bomb, ready to implode at any second. Shaking it off, I catch the reflection of my phone sitting on the bedside unit. I turned it on to make sure Reese got home last night, but now it's back off again. Maybe that's the problem. Maybe I am being held back because of it. How can I truly feel free when I am imprisoned by a piece of technology. My life and job are in that phone, but that's a life and job that I no longer want to be part of, that part of me died with Tryst. I turn, marching over and snatching the phone off the table and I storm downstairs.

"Morning," Kaleb calls from his makeshift office in the cosy lounge, his laptop open on the coffee table, his fingers tapping quickly. "Hey, hey!" He calls out, his tone panicked as I ignore him and pull the front door open with force, the cold, harsh air burning my lungs as I inhale deeply. I tip my head back and let the rain fall down over me.

Kaleb follows, but he just stands and watches me. I let my head fall and my eyes focus on him.

"What are you doing?" he asks quietly.

"Something I should have done last week," I rasp, turning and marching towards the water's edge.

"Connie!" he shouts as he runs behind me. He grabs the top of my arm, tugging me towards him.

"Let me go, I *need* to do this," I hiss, pulling my arm from his tight grip and he drops his hand.

I stop in my tracks when I get to the wet sand, looking down at my feet. I frown. Taking my slippers off and leaving them on the sand, I continue towards the sea. The icy rain is pelting down on top of me, the bitter wind picking up and howling across the crashing waves.

I close my eyes for a moment, inhaling the fresh sea air, letting it fill and burn my lungs. Once my eyes are open, I pull my arm behind me with my phone gripped in my hand, and I throw it forward with everything I have. I scream out, my voice hoarse as I watch my phone leave my hand and flip through the air, eventually falling into the deep, dark sea, the waves crashing over it as it sinks.

I pant, tears streaming from my eyes as I scream out again. I fall back, sitting on the wet ground and fall back so I am laying on my back. I close my eyes and let the rain wash over me. I focus on my breathing and listen to the wind dancing with the ocean, its waves crashing in a rhythm.

It's peaceful.

It's calm.

It's perfect.

CHAPTER THIRTY-SIX

KALEB

I JUST STAND AND WATCH. I WANT TO GO AND STOP HER, BUT SHE said she needs to do this and if it's going to help with her trauma, then who am I to stop her? I watch as she throws her phone into the sea, screaming out as she does. I step forward a few steps as she falls down, laying on the wet ground as she lets the rain wash her pain and past away. *I hope.*

Connie deserves so much happiness and I hope this is the first step she is taking towards healing herself.

My phone buzzes, it's Keaton telling me they're thirty minutes away. I sigh. I need to go get her. Pushing my phone back in my pocket, I slowly make my way over to her. She hasn't moved, her eyes are closed, she is soaking wet but I can't stop staring. She is beautiful, even when she thinks she looks a mess, she is *my* beautiful mess.

I don't speak, just bend down and scoop her up in my arms and hold her tight. Her arms wrap around my neck, her face turned into my chest as I carry her home.

Both warm and dry, Connie's hands are wrapped round a hot cup of coffee. She has the fur blanket wrapped around her shoulders. She looks so small sitting there. We haven't spoken since, but I am content, and she seems to be too.

I look at the time, they'll be here any minute.

"My brother and friends will be here shortly; we have a meeting... I hope that's okay," I look at her over the top of my laptop. Her head slowly lifts as our eyes connect.

"Of course, I'll take myself upstairs and out the way," she pushes from the sofa, letting the blanket fall to the floor and before I can tell her she doesn't need to, it's too late, she is gone and they're at the door. I inhale, rubbing my hand over my face before standing and walking to the door to let them in.

Keaton barges through, his eyes darting round the room, and I roll my eyes, already feeling myself getting pissed at him. Titus smirks and pats me on the back as he passes me, and Nate just gives me a small shrug of his shoulders before he pushes his glasses up his nose and walks into the living room.

Puffing my cheeks out and exhaling a long, heavy breath I close the door. Nate is already setting up on the coffee table, Keaton is sitting with a cocky smirk on his face, one of his legs bent as his foot rests on his other knee and Titus is sorting the coffee machine.

"So, where is she?" Keaton eventually asks.

"Upstairs," my answer is blunt, but I don't want him sniffing round her.

He nods, his lips turning down as he cranes his neck, his head dipping so he can look up the stairs, "And where is the bathroom?"

"Keaton," I grit.

"What?" he laughs, holding his hands out, "I need to pee."

"Stop winding him up," Titus snaps as he walks in with

four cups of coffee, handing me mine first, "I didn't make one for Connie, wasn't sure she would be down whilst we're here."

I nod, silently thanking him and he nods back.

Nate sits up, taking his own coffee and smiles, "I'm all set up, ready when you lot are," his voice is smooth as he takes a sip of his coffee.

"I'm just going to use the toilet," Keaton rushes up and I stand quickly, Titus shakes his head from side to side, his broad shoulders lift as he rests his hand on my shoulders, holding me in place.

"He is doing this to get a rise out of you, when will you realise that?" he rolls his eyes and chuckles softly.

My jaw is tight, my stomach in knots. I don't relax until I see his shoes appear on the stairs. His eyes move straight to mine, and he wiggles his brows up and down then wipes his bottom lip with his fingers.

Ignore him. Ignore him. Ignore him. I constantly remind myself.

"Now we're all here, let's begin shall we?" I chime, before we all sit and lose ourselves in business.

WE STOP FOR LUNCH; TITUS RUNS AND GETS TAKEOUT. I HAVEN'T been shopping and we're running low on supplies. Connie made herself a sandwich before the guys got here, then disappeared upstairs. I am grateful that Connie has stayed in her room, but my insides twist at the thought of her being bored up there. We're all standing in the kitchen, tucking into our subs and I hadn't realised how hungry I had been. I have been so focused on making sure Connie is okay, that I have been forgetting to look after myself.

"When are you coming back to the city?" Nate asks as

he bites into his meatball sub, wiping his mouth with a napkin.

I shrug, "Soon, I think..." I chew my mouthful before continuing, "we just need to wait for the morons that are still printing about it to fuck off, I honestly don't think Connie can take much more of it, it's been a lot for her..." I swallow, my eyes moving to my three best friends, "once the funeral is done, I think she will feel a little better. She has been through a lot with this dude, it's not like a normal kind of death..." I trail off and Titus is smirking.

"What you smirking at?" I snap.

"Nothing dude," he scoffs before taking a big bite and I choose to ignore him. I don't want to open myself up for a conversation that I don't want.

I hear the sound of footsteps coming down the stairs and my heart thumps hard in my chest. My eyes are wide as she turns the corner of the kitchen and stares at me. I swallow hard. She looks so fucking beautiful. Her eyes tear from mine as she scopes out the three faces standing with me.

"Here she is," Keaton pushes his tongue into his cheek, and I swear I want to fight him.

"Sorry," she blushes, tucking a loose strand of her brown hair behind her ear before her eyes land on me again, "I thought you were finished, I just wanted to do some yoga," her voice was like velvet as it danced over my skin, smothering it in goosebumps. She thumbs behind her, her cheeks a beautiful shade of pink. "I'll just go..." she nods to herself and turns.

"It's fine, we can work in here," Keaton jumps in, and she stills, her wide, doe eyes on mine awaiting confirmation from me.

"Yeah, fine," I nod, my fingers wrapping around the edge of the work surface as rage seeps out of my pores.

"Only if you're sure," she smiles at me.

"I'm sure," I just about manage, my voice constricted and tight as I force the words out. I let my eyes roam up and down her body, her clothes different from this morning but still as fucking hot as hell. Her toned legs and peachy ass are being hugged by light grey yoga pants that sit high over her curvaceous hips and sit just under her pierced navel. My cock twitches and I press myself forward and into the kitchen units. She is wearing a black, long sleeved, crew necked crop tee and I have never been so glad that her chest is covered. I snap out of it, shaking my head from side to side quickly before taking a bite from my sub that is now cold.

Side eyeing the rest of the guys, it seems she has them under her trance as well.

I nudge into Titus a little harder than I wanted which causes a domino effect to the other two idiots.

"Okay, I'll set up," she beams at me, spinning quickly and moving into the lounge.

Once she is out of sight, I feel three pairs of eyes burning into the side of my head. I slowly turn to look at them, brows raised in my head as I wait for them to tell me what the problem is.

"Are you trying to torture us?" Keaton groans, his eyes moving to the lounge and back to me.

"How the hell are we meant to focus on anything but *her*?" Nate rushes out and Titus just lets out a deep, slow chuckle.

"Easy, don't fucking look," I snap, suddenly losing my appetite. I turn, throwing my plate with the contents of my lunch into the sink.

"Go and get the shit from the lounge," I order looking out the kitchen window at the sea, Keaton and Titus talk amongst themselves quietly.

"I'll clear this side of the work surface and we can all work here, that way none of us are tempted to watch her stretch and... shit," I clench my jaw, my molars grinding.

Keaton laughs, "I am not fucking standing facing the wall because you don't want us looking at your little pet."

I turn, my nostrils flaring as my eyes widen.

"My little *pet*?"

Titus just steps back and inhales deeply.

"Yeah, you're acting as if she belongs to you," Keaton steps forward, closing the gap between us.

"She doesn't belong to *anyone*, nor will she belong to *anyone* in this room." I step forward, our heads pressing against each other, "She is off fucking limits."

"We will see about that," Keaton taunts and I have to step away before I knock my brother out cold.

I turn, storming out the front door and slamming it behind me. I should know better by now not to let him get to me but he knows what buttons to press to get under my skin and cause a reaction. Twin power and all that shit. I tip my head back and listen to the waves crashing against the shoreline. I only need a minute or two for my rage to leave and my breathing to slow.

Letting my head fall forward, I gaze out at the gloomy, grey horizon and inhale deeply before I make my way back inside. Closing the door softly behind me, I rub my hands together and still as I watch Connie. She stretches up, her head tilted before she reaches down to touch her toes, then walks out with her hands and I am assuming she moves into downward dog. *Fuck.*

I rush through to the kitchen, the boys all facing the wall.

"This is going to be torture." My voice is low.

"Did tell you that," Keaton whispers.

"Fuck off."

"Will you two just pipe down?" Titus groans, opening his spreadsheet. "Heads back in the game," and Nate nods along, his head bobbing up and down.

I look over my shoulder at her, she looks at ease and relaxed and that makes me happy. When I turn my face back round, I catch the three of them looking at her.

"Head back in the game," I snap, repeating Titus' words and they all laugh.

I have no idea how long we have been facing the wall for but I feel her before I see her, looking over my shoulder, my lips spread into a wide, toothy grin. She has a sheen of sweat covering her skin, her brown hair is slightly wet at the front and her cheeks are reddened.

"Never knew yoga could make you so..."

"Hot," Nate drawls out, stumbling over his words and she laughs.

"It's a really good work out, especially for your mental wellbeing and I feel like I need it." None of us say anything and she nods. "Let me just get a drink and I'll be out your way, I'm going to jump in the shower," she tells the room as she opens the fridge and grabs a bottle of water. I just give her a small nod and then she turns and walks out the room and I finally feel like I can breathe.

"Shall we move to the living room? My back is killing me," Titus groans, rubbing his lower back as he grabs his paperwork and laptop.

"Maybe you need to do some yoga stretches old man," I jibe, following him with my own laptop. Nate and Keaton join us shortly after with fresh coffees before losing ourselves in work for the rest of the afternoon.

When we're done, we sip cold beers while we lose ourselves in easy conversation and it feels like a long time since we have sat and spoke.

"I never want to leave here," I admit, letting my head rest on the back of the sofa, "I feel so relaxed, and under different circumstances I could see it being the perfect place to live, the city is going to seem so noisy when we eventually go back."

"Would you move out here? Or somewhere like this? Away from the city?" Nate asks, sipping his own beer.

"Yeah, one hundred percent, especially once I am settled down. I love the city, but I don't want to grow old there."

They all hum in agreement, the four of us taking a sip of our beers at the same time.

I hear her giggle, turning to look behind me at her standing at the bottom of the stairs.

"May I join you?" she asks as she slowly strides towards us. She's wearing her flannel pyjama bottoms and a long sleeved, cotton tee.

"Of course," I smile at her, turning my head back around as I eye the guys. She falls between me and Titus, shuffling then crossing her legs under herself. Silence blankets us as she rubs her ring finger.

"What you guys been talking about?" she asks, trying to break the silence as her eyes move to all of us around the room.

"Just about moving out to somewhere like here instead of the city..." Nate pipes up.

"I like it here, I feel relaxed..." she nibbles her bottom lip and a laugh bubbles out of her, "most of the time," she leans into me, giving me a gentle nudge in the ribs.

"You've had a lot going on," my voice is quiet, and suddenly I wish it was only me and her in the room.

She turns her face to look at me, blinking a few times and I watch as she tries to blink the tears away.

"So, what have you been doing whilst here with Kaleb?" Keaton swipes in, trying to take her mind away from wherever it is.

With her beautiful smile back on her face, she turns to face Keaton.

"Not a lot, Mr Grumpy here doesn't let me out of these four walls, so a little exercise and reading my book," she shrugs her shoulders up.

"Well, that isn't good is it," Keaton tsks, shaking his head from side to side as he eyes me, "I can see it now, Connie falls for you because of Stockholm syndrome; you are keeping her a prisoner here..."

"Dickhead." I roll my lips, "She reads *romance* books," I quote romance with bunny ears and I smirk, trying to change the subject that feels heavy on my shoulders, and I swear if looks could kill, I would be six feet under. Her cheeks burn a deep scarlet, and her eyes widen. She swats me in the arm with the back of her hand, hard. "Ow," I laugh but more out of shock I think. "What was that for?"

"Telling them I read *'porn'* books," she swats me again, this time a little harder.

"Hey! I didn't say porn... you did," I wince and hold my hands up before she hits me again, "Stop it," my laugh grows.

"Porn books?" Titus scratches his head before turning to

look at Nate and Keaton who give him just as much of a puzzled look as the one he has on his face.

"Dirty books," I wiggle my brows and she grabs the scatter cushion from behind Titus and hides behind it.

"Like, *dirty* books," Keaton shuffles forward so he is on the edge of the sofa, legs apart, elbows resting on his knees, and I nod.

"Have you read any of it?" Nate asks me, his own interest growing.

"Nope, but I'm going to."

"You are not!" she shouts, pulling the cushion from her face and swatting me once more.

"Stop hitting me," I laugh, tugging the pillow from her grip and throwing it, "just own that shit, you read porn."

She rolls her eyes, "So what?" suddenly brazen as she stands and strides towards the small cabinet in the corner of the living room. All eyes are on her. She opens the door and pulls out her book, holding it out.

"Want me to give you a little snippet?" she continues to open the book, flicking through the pages.

"Yes," Keaton smirks, rubbing his hands together.

Connie's brows lift, the corner of her lip lifting.

"No," I growl, standing and placing my beer on the coffee table.

"Shut up," Keaton groans and I throw him a dagger stare.

"*He pushes her against the wall, his fingers wrapped round her delicate throat...*" Connie starts, lifting her eyes from the pages and settling them on mine. I clench my jaw.

I say nothing, ignoring the deep burn that's beginning to stir.

"*A raspy moan leaves her as his lips brush against hers, she knew this was wrong but yet...*" her eyes lift to mine once more, "*she doesn't want him to stop.*"

Her breath catches as she lowers the book from in front of her, rolling her lips before pushing her spare hand through her hair at the root.

"Sorry boys... I don't think you could handle it," she shrugs, bending down and putting her book back in the cabinet. She stands quickly and spins. "I'm going to grab a beer, anyone want one?" she exhales linking her fingers, pushing them out and cracking them.

"Please," I nod, falling back into the sofa, pulling at the crotch of my jeans. I don't know if it's just my mind playing tricks on me, but it seemed like the line she read was aimed at me.

"I'll have another please," Titus calls out.

"Here, I'll help," Keaton chimes, standing from the sofa and following Connie into the kitchen. The aggravation is swarming deep inside of me, but I ignore it, I can't rise to him. "Nate," Keaton calls, "are you having another?"

Nate turns to look towards the kitchen, "I better not, I've got to drive."

"You can all stay if you want," Connie's head pops round the door frame and my eyes widen.

"There isn't really much room," I cough, rubbing my chin.

"Thanks for the offer," Titus calls out, "you know, as much as this is *my* house, I think it's best we go after this drink," he smiles.

"Of course," Connie blushes before she disappears again. My eyes are pinned to the doorway, waiting for them to come back. I don't trust Keaton with her. Not that I think he would do anything with her; no, more that he doesn't hold his tongue and I don't want him to ask or say something that will make her fall back down again.

"You okay?" Titus asks quietly, patting me on the knee.

"Yeah," I nod, but not pulling my eyes from the doorway.

"Okay," Titus gives me another pat. He never oversteps with me, he knows if I want to talk I will.

Connie bounds back into the room and sits back between me and Titus, but she leans a little closer to me and I am glad. We fall into easy conversation until the guys leave.

Once they've left, Connie potters around, tidying up. I follow her out the kitchen, stepping behind her I place my hand on her hip and I hear a soft gasp that she inhales.

"I'll do this, go to bed," my voice is low, my breath dancing across the back of her neck. She turns quickly to face me, her eyes volleying back and forth between mine, her lips parted.

I crane my neck, my eyes falling to her lips. If I was to edge slowly forward, my lips would be on hers. The burning desire swarms through me like wildfire. My fingers move slightly, my hand reaching out for hers slowly which are down by her side, the tips of my fingers brushing over her warm skin on the back of her hand, but I instantly pull away as if my touch would burn her.

She ducks away, rushing past me and towards the stairs.

"Goodnight Kaleb," she calls but I don't respond.

She is already gone.

CHAPTER THIRTY-SEVEN

CONNIE

I LAY WIDE AWAKE. MY SKIN STILL TINGLES FROM HIS TOUCH, MY insides burn to just let myself feel what it's like to be loved by him. But I can't. We can't. You never play with fire. My thoughts are hectic, and it doesn't matter what I do to try and settle myself, I can't.

Sighing, I roll on my side. When did my life get so complicated? I miss the old Connie, the carefree Connie who didn't give a shit about what she done as long as it made her happy. I felt so whole when Reese was here, it felt like old times as we laughed and joked about our antics, but I chose to walk away, or more like run away. Everything happened so quickly. I was just coming to terms with Reese and my dad having a baby, but to then find out the wicked witch of New York was my mother... my thoughts silence for a moment as bile thickens in my throat. I swallow, willing to ignore the taste that is threatening. The hate I felt for Adele didn't seem natural but at the same time it did. She was always a constant in my dad's life. I should have connected the dots, every birthday, every Christmas she would show up with him. My moms were polite enough to let her join us, but I always wondered why. Honestly, I thought her and my dad were hooking up though it never seemed that way.

She had her claws dug so deep into my father's back that you could see the marks and the blood from where she never let go. And when my dad used to date, she got worse. He used to moan to my moms about her all the time, but I was so young and naive I never really understood. She was always awful. She spoke down to me, never smiled at me and I could see the hollowness behind her eyes. She didn't have a soul or a heart and my dad telling me what the tie was between us altered me. Her and my dad slept together, I never asked if it was once or more because as soon as he told me she was my mom, I was out of there like a bat out of hell. She wanted to terminate the pregnancy, but my dad didn't want her to. He knew that my moms wanted a baby and agreed with Adele that as soon as the baby was born, Katie and Lara—my moms—would adopt me. But they failed to tell me any of that.

I always wondered why there were never any photos of one of them with a bump or any scan photos. The only picture they had was when my mom was holding me as a new born and she wasn't in a hospital gown like you would expect, she was in a tee or a jumper and her and Katie were overjoyed as my mom Lara smiled for the camera, Katie staring down at me in awe. Adele signed a closed adoption until she wanted it to be known I was the tie. I grew up in a happy and loving home, but all of that just felt empty deep inside of me now because it was all a lie, a lie that I had to run from. I didn't want to swallow the bitter pill that was the truth, because my life before the truth was so much better than the life after, the life I am living now.

I still remember how I felt when my dad was telling me

that she was it, that I was the tie between him and the whore. The reason why he couldn't just walk away. My heart was ripped from my chest as soon as the words left his lips, nothing else mattered from that moment on. Everything I once knew was a lie, a lie that he and my moms spun. They don't know what it is like to feel like you don't quite belong somewhere and that's how I always felt. Like I didn't belong, until Tryst.

My stomach knots, my heart rate spiking.

As soon as I rushed from my dad's office he was the only person I wanted to go to. By the time I got to his front door, I was a crying mess. My eyes bloodshot, stained cheeks from my mascara that had run as the tears constantly fell. His mom opened the door, her eyes wide with worry, her mouth slightly open at her shock. She didn't question me, just let me in and held me whilst I cried into her sweater, letting my tears soak into the material as if it would help with the pain I was feeling. They may as well have stuck a knife into my back, twisting and pushing it up until they hit my lungs. The burning becoming a normal feeling as I gasped for breath.

His mom was panicked; she cried out for Tryst. She slowly moved me from her arms to his and he held me tight until I was ready to move, until I was able to take the steps up to his room.

I moved in with him and over time, I pushed my emotions to the back of my mind where they stayed until the night Tryst died. It was as if he was the vault of my emotions and trauma, the only one who had the key. But now he was dead, it all came flooding back. I choke out a sob at the thoughts that haunt me, my heart breaking as I think of how different we are now, how different he was to the man I met two years ago.

He was so excited to tell me that they had been signed and were going on a world tour. Of course, I was elated for him. I wanted to be by his side for it all, and that's where I stood until he began slipping out of my grasp. The boy who was once my comfort blanket left me in the side stage, and as each show went on, he pushed me further and further away. I was his addiction until he found something new to give him a better high. He had no use for me anymore. I wasn't his number one, I was a burden.

I didn't want to admit that I had lost him, so I still clung onto the hopes that he would come back. But he didn't.

The Tryst I grew up with as a teen and fell so deeply in love with was no more. He was replaced with a narcissistic prick who abused me. Maybe it was my fault... maybe I could have done more to feed his habit, but all I done was let him get me addicted to him. The first six months of tour were a blur in the end, but it helped numb everything out. Until it didn't.

Until he raped me, he didn't care that I was crying and screaming for him to stop. He didn't care that I dug my fingernails so deeply into his skin that I made him bleed.

He didn't care.

But I do have some things to thank him for.

His love.

His kindness.

His abuse. Because if he never hurt me the way he did, I would have stayed and even if the outcome was the same and he died, I would have still clung onto him for dear life.

Because he was my comfort blanket.

"Connie," he whispers, and I know that voice, his large hands gliding over my hip and rests on my stomach through the silk of my Cami vest which makes my skin tingle all over.

I don't respond, I let his fingers trail over my stomach as they glide back and forth from my stomach to my hip. The weight shifts next to me, his lips brushing against the shell of my ear, my skin breaking into goosebumps.

Bang.

I still, forcing my eyes shut, the rain coming with the rolling thunder as it hits the glass pane.

"Let me make you forget all the bad memories, darling," the rasp in his voice twisting my stomach with a delicious burn, "just for tonight, let me do this for you." My racing heart slows slightly as his fingers glide over my hip and follow the curve of my ass. I still as his fingertips trace me through the thin, silk material of my shorts. My breath catches, his fingers moving and circling over my clit.

I don't move, I stay laying on my side, Kaleb pressed up behind me, his lips still sitting at the shell of my ear. My eyes flutter shut as the ripples of pleasure course through me, the thunder rumbling in the distance, the bolt of lightning lighting up the room as Kaleb's soft strokes continue to undo me in the best possible way. His lips move from my ear as he places butterfly kisses along my temple and cheek. I fight the urge to look behind me, I'm too scared to meet his eyes.

"Do you know how hard it has been to stay away from you, to fight with my mind every hour of every day that we have been together?" His voice is soft as he speaks between kisses, his fingertips rubbing a little harder now. My legs fall open slightly, making it easier for him to get to where he needs, where *I* need. I want to scream that I have felt the same, but I don't. Because this can't happen again.

My breaths turn to pants, my hips rotating softly to match his strokes.

"Lose yourself, Connie, let it all go," he whispers in my ear as my head falls back against him, the delicious build up teetering. My hand moves behind me as I dig my nails into his bare skin, looking for anything to grip as my orgasm crashes through me like a lightning bolt, a soft moan passing my lips as the room lights up, and this time, I give in and look at him. His hand cups my face as he lowers his lips over mine. I roll my body towards him, our kiss deepening as I let his tongue explore my mouth before my tongue dances with his.

A loud crash wakes me; I sit up startled, my heart racing in my chest as I look over at the time. *2am.*

I have no idea how long I have been asleep for, I cried myself to sleep again. *How sad and pathetic am I?*

Another crash echoes around the room, and this time a strike of lightning lights up the sky and the room at the same time. My body trembles, pulling the cover up around my chin. I reach out for Kaleb, and I'm confused he isn't here. *Was he ever here? Or did I just have a sex dream?*

My cheeks flame, and suddenly I jump when the door swings open, Kaleb's eyes searching for me in the dark, but he isn't searching long when another crack of lightning illuminates my room. My eyes are wide with fear; I hate thunderstorms.

"Connie," he breathes, rushing towards me but stopping when he reaches the bed. "Are you okay?"

I half nod and half shake my head as the thunder crashes, my head shaking side to side quickly.

"Scoot over darling," his raspy voice pebbles my skin.

He is only in his boxers, and I have never wanted for lightning to strike so much as I do at this moment, just so I could see a little more of him. I lay on my back as he lays next to me, pulling the sheets over us. My racing heart slows slightly, just having him next to me is enough to calm me.

"Not a fan of thunderstorms?" His voice is full of sleep, muffled and raspy.

"No," I whisper just as the light illuminates, the thunder cracking making me shudder. He turns towards me, pulling me towards him as his arms envelope me.

"I've got you," he whispers, his lips pressing into my forehead.

We're facing each other, his head a little higher than mine as I nuzzle into him. My heart is skipping beats at being this close to him. I inhale him as subtly as I can, his scent comforting.

"What don't you like about thunderstorms?" he asks after a moment of silence.

"It stems from when I was a little girl, I got woken one night by a storm and it instilled a fear in me that I have never felt before." Silence falls again as another rumble fills the room. I squeeze my eyes shut and wait until all I can hear is Kaleb's steady breath.

"On that night, we got broken into. They took everything. I was so scared but my moms were so brave..." I trail off, the word *moms* feeling foreign on my tongue. "My mom, Katie, ran downstairs to confront the robber, whilst my other mom, Lara, called 911..." I tremble, "I sat in the corner of my room, there was a lot of commotion and I waited for both of my moms to come back up the stairs. I still remember my little heart beating ten to the dozen, worried that whoever was downstairs was going to take them from me. My wide eyes stayed pinned to the top of the stairs, my room was opposite the staircase and I remember feeling so relieved when I saw my mom, Lara, walk up the stairs, holding her arms out for me. Katie scared them off before she even got downstairs, but it just brings that small bit of trauma to the surface whenever there is a storm..." I lick my lips; I hadn't noticed but a single tear was rolling down my cheek. I shuffle and cough softly, trying to clear my throat.

"So maybe that has something to do with it..." I whisper, not even sure if he is still awake.

"You don't need to be afraid anymore, love." His breath is warm on my lips as his eyes level with mine. I roll over, suddenly *this* feels too intimate. I catch my breath, my gaze averted to the window as the thunderstorm reflects in my emerald eyes. He doesn't let me go and I have never felt as safe as I do right now, in his arms. The thunder soon dissolves around us, and I fall into a heavy sleep.

———

MY EYES SLOWLY OPEN, BUT THEY FEEL HEAVY. BLINKING A FEW times, the low winter sun is shining through the window. A smile graces my lips when I feel the weight of Kaleb's arm over me. He felt like home, here felt like home but we both knew this wasn't where we were supposed to end up. This was just a safe house until Kaleb thought it was safe for me to go back.

My thoughts stopped suddenly, an aching pain radiated through my chest at the thought of having to leave here and go where? I had no home. I wouldn't be one of those girls that would go running home to mommy and daddy as soon as I was in trouble. No, I would deal with it.

You can't always walk on water, sometimes you have to slip and fall. It's up to you whether you keep fighting to reach the surface or let yourself sink into the depths of the ocean.

"Morning," the rasp to his voice smothers my skin and suddenly I want to be twisted in these bedsheets with him.

"Hey," my voice is quiet and timid as I roll on my side. I let my eyes roam over his face, his beautiful eyes closed and disappointment at not seeing them surges through me.

I could study him all day, taking my time to let every single feature of him burn into my brain.

"Stop staring at me," his grumpy tone makes me smile, my cheeks pinching a crimson shade.

"Sorry," I nibble the inside of my lip and roll on my back.

His arm wraps over my body, pulling me towards him as he buries his nose into my neck. This is too close. I can't breathe.

It didn't matter that I needed him like water. That I needed him like the air that I breathe, like the heart that keeps beating, keeping me alive. That's how *much* I needed him.

"Coffee?" I ask, rolling away from him and out of the bed.

"Yeah...?" I can hear the confusion in his tone, but I ignore it. Slipping my feet into my slippers and wrapping my dressing gown around my frame I leave the room in a rush. I'm terrified, my breathing is hard when I am close to Kaleb, and I have no idea why. It's as if I hyperventilate around him before falling into a panic attack, but I am happy when I am with him. It doesn't make sense and even trying to get my mind around it is confusing enough.

Filling the coffee machine up, I stare out the window.

The clouds are breaking, the rays of sunshine beating down into the horizon and a glisten of a rainbow is appearing. Mad to think that a few hours ago it was storming, but they always say a rainbow comes after a storm.

Maybe, *just maybe,* Kaleb was my rainbow after my storm.

We didn't speak about him comforting me during the night, I felt embarrassed for some reason, though I have no reason to feel embarrassed.

Kaleb has been working most of the morning and all I want to do is cosy up next to him, but I feel like he has made it very clear that he isn't into me like that. I just have a silly little crush. Once I am away from him and not living in his pocket like a needy child, these butterflies will crash and burn.

His phone rings, and I lift my head to look in his direction. His brows are furrowed, his hand rubbing under his chin as he listens, hardly saying a word back but then his eyes lift to meet mine; the harshness that is normally so prominent slowly starts to fade, softening.

"Okay, thanks for that Doris," he nods softly then cuts the phone off.

"What is it?" I just about manage; I know that look.

"Tryst's funeral arrangements have been made…" he grasps his phone between both his hands, his legs parted as he lets his arms fall between them.

"And…"

"It's tomorrow," his tone is flat, I can see the grimace on his face. He doesn't even try to hide it.

"Oh," I whisper, closing my book softly and sitting on the edge of the sofa.

"Are you okay?" he closes his laptop and stands from the sofa, cell still in his hands.

I nod, "I think so."

"Okay," he licks his lips, his hand pushing through his brown hair before he sits next to me, "Did you want to go?" His tone wasn't harsh or malicious, it was soft, kind and caring.

I turn my face to look at him, my eyes welling, and I couldn't stop them even if I tried. I nodded, not saying a word.

"Okay, I'll get all the details from Doris." He wraps his arm around the top of my shoulders, pulling me into him as his arms cocoon me in a safety grip. His lips press into the top of my head, a small, simple gesture that I am coming to love more and more each time he does it. "Then, if things have calmed down, we can leave here and you can get back to your life, a life with no more pain and hurt..."

I sniff, wiping my tears away with the sleeve of my jumper.

"I have no idea what I am going to do," I half laugh, half cry.

"Kid..." he pauses for a moment, "I'm not kicking you out, come and live with me." I pull away, looking up at him. "Just until you're on your feet again."

I laugh, swiping my tears away before wiping my sniffling nose on the cuff of my jumper. I really do need to stop doing that.

"Honestly, darling, I would love to have you there."

Love.

"Okay, only if you're sure... and just until I have my shit together," scoffing, I smile at him.

"Of course, I am sure." He smiles back down at me then stood and made a call to Doris.

Anxiety ripples through me at the thought of tomorrow. I know I said I wanted to go, but did I? Did I really want to put myself out there for the vultures to circle me and feast on me when they get their opportunity?

If I don't go, I'll be insensitive, but if I do go, I'll probably be seen as the guilty ex-girlfriend trying to prove herself.

I didn't want any of that. I want to go because I want to go. Not because I have to, not because I have anything to prove. I want to go to mourn for the boy I had loved. The boy I was friends with, the boy that stood by my side when we were younger, the boy who I used to watch jamming in his garage with Callaghan and Rox. The boy that I used to blame for my rocky teen era because it was easier for my dad and moms to be angry with him than me.

I want to mourn my friend.

Laying in the bath, I have felt numb all afternoon. Tomorrow was the day this chapter of the book ends.

That part of my life will be buried with Tryst.

Wrapping my fingers round the edge of the tub and pulling myself up, the water splashes over the edges but I don't care. I stand, closing my eyes as I tip my head all the way back. My skin erupts in goosebumps as a cold chill smothers me. Stepping out cautiously, I reach for the bath sheet and wrap it around me. Tugging the door open with force I bump into a body and freeze. I lift my face to look up to see Kaleb. His grey eyes burning into mine.

"I was just coming to see if you were okay... you have been in there a while," his eyes move behind me before they fall to me once more.

"Yeah," I whisper, his hands moving to the top of my arms, holding me in place as I try to move past him. My heart races, my chest rising and dipping fast.

"Tryst's funeral is at eleven, do you need something to

wear?" he asks, his voice soft like a blanket. I shake my head from side to side.

"Okay, go get warm and I'll sort dinner."

He lets me go and I instantly miss the burn from his fingers on my skin. I watch as he turns and walks away, and I don't move until he is out of sight.

Dressing in a cream lounge suit, I slip my feet into my slippers. My hair is now dry and twisted into a messy bun. I took my time doing my skin care and re-painting my nails black. I could smell dinner from my room and my stomach groaned. I have no idea what Kaleb is cooking but I am hoping we don't end up with raw chicken again.

Opening my door, I head downstairs to see the dining room table laid, two small candles burning, and I smile. Approaching the kitchen door, I freeze. Kaleb is standing with a hand towel over his shoulder, stirring the contents of a large saucepan on the stove, but his eyes are not focused on what's cooking; no. His eyes are skimming across the pages of my book.

The porn book.

Shit.

I cough, clearing my throat, "Ahem." Hands on my hips, foot tapping, I eye him with wide, bug eyes.

"Oh sorry, just doing a bit of *light* reading," he beams at me.

"Put it down," I snap, surging forward and trying to grab it from him but he lifts his arm up high so I can't reach.

"Uh, uh, uh..." he shakes his head, smirking, "I need to see what happens between these two," he lifts his chin, tipping his head back slightly as he continued reading. "*My fingers swipe through her wet folds, slowly rubbing her clit. Her delectable moans fill the room as my lips press against the soft skin on her neck, my fingers gliding into her soaked pussy,*" his eyes widen, his voice slowly trailing off, his mouth agape as he looks down at me.

"Kaleb!" I shout, jumping and trying to grab the book from his grasp.

"Connie..." his tone is low; with his spare hand he turns the gas from the stove off.

His eyes move from me back to the book and he continues reading out loud. "*Her back arches from the bed as I continue fucking her with my fingers, curling and rubbing her g-spot as her arousal runs down my hand. 'Shit, baby, you're fucking soaked'. Her pussy clamps around my fingers, I know she is getting close. Pulling out of her, I push my two fingers between my lips and lick them clean,*" his brows raise high in his head, but he doesn't stop.

My cheeks are a flaming red, but the burning ache is between my legs, my pussy throbbing at his deep, delicious voice reading a sex scene. It's a lot to take.

"*Fisting myself, I line my tip at her entrance, pushing my hips slowly, her mewls hypnotizing me as I drive into her completely, filling her to the hilt.*" He coughs, closing the book and turning to face me. His eyes are ablaze, his jaw clenched as he stares deep into my soul. "Connie," this time he has a certain rasp to his voice, as if he is struggling to even speak my name.

"Kaleb," my tone matches his, and I am breathless suddenly. Throwing the towel from his shoulder and landing it on the work surface he stalks towards me, his eyes growing darker as he gets closer. He takes one last step towards me, all the time my heart is thumping in my chest, and with each step he takes it thumps that little bit harder. I step forward, our eyes volleying back and forth, his hands are on my face, holding me a little tighter as his lips hover

over mine. It's not rushed like I thought it would be, he takes his time... he is *hesitant*.

But before our lips even touch, his phone screams from the living room.

"Let it ring," I whisper against his lips, I can't believe the words are even leaving my lips but, in this moment, I don't care. I could nudge forward, and my lips would be on his but he stills, his eyes closing before dropping his hands from my face. He steps away, keeping his head bowed as he disappears into the living room.

I feel *rejected, humiliated, frustrated...*

Suddenly I have lost my appetite. Snatching my book from the work surface, I turn and storm up the stairs, slamming my bedroom door in temper.

CHAPTER THIRTY-EIGHT
KALEB

Fuck.

My hands push through my hair, tugging at my root in frustration. I'm a fuck up, my insides are dark and twisty and the first ray of light that tries to break through, I put it out instantly.

Pacing back and forth, my thoughts are whirling when I stop at the bottom of the stairs and lift my face to follow them.

Part of me wants to go up there and make it right... but it was a *heat of the moment* kind of thing. She is probably regretting her choices right about now. I shouldn't have teased her, I knew what I was doing, I was playing with fire, but it wasn't me that got burned. It was her.

I ignore the pull to go upstairs and head for the kitchen to clear away dinner that never got eaten.

"You're a fucking idiot," I mutter to myself whilst I scrap the food into the trash then continue to wash up. Once done, I fall onto the sofa and eventually, I fall asleep.

. . .

I WAKE WHEN MY HEAD HITS THE SOFA AND THE SCATTER CUSHION I was sleeping on was thrown in my face.

"Hey!" I call out, lifting the pillow and throwing it on the floor. In front of me is a pissed off Connie, her hands on her hips of her high waisted black jeans. I let my sleepy eyes trail up and down her body, she has her skinny jeans tucked into her chunky doc martens and a black v necked jumper. Her long brown hair is loose, cascading down her sides. She has a black NY cap on, her skin dewy and glowing.

"Get up," she pressed the sole of her shoe into my thigh, rolling me.

"What's biting you?" I snarl, sitting up and tossing the shitty cover off me.

"Not you, clearly." She flicks her hair over her shoulder and turns away.

I scoff, rubbing my face with my hands then standing up and stretching. I reach for my phone and watch from the coffee table and look at the time, it's just gone eight. I yawn, padding towards the stairs and up to the bathroom. I needed a shower, I needed to wake up. I felt exhausted. After sleeping in the bed the night before, the sofa was shocking. I've been on it just over a week and I've had enough. Is it selfish of me to hope that we can go home tonight and leave this all behind?

Yes, it is, you selfish bastard.

I ignore my subconscious and step under the scalding water, letting it wash all my tension away. Once dried, I see my phone screen light up, Killian.

KILLIAN

Look after her today, it's taken everything in me not to be there for her but I need to respect her wishes. Just bring her back to me soon, each day without her is getting harder and harder. Keep her safe, Kaleb.

I tap a quick response letting him know that my only job today is to keep her safe. Tossing the phone back on the bed, I grab my suit that Doris had sent to me.

I dress in a black suit jacket and trousers and wear a simple white shirt underneath and finish it off with my black oxfords.

Rubbing product through my hair, I mess it a little. It feels weird being smartly dressed, we haven't been anywhere apart from when I leave to get essentials.

Puffing out my cheeks I head downstairs to see her picking at the skin around her nails.

"Have you got much to pack?" I ask, walking straight through to the kitchen.

"No," her voice is quiet as she appears in the doorway.

"Okay, let's make a decision once we've been to the funeral, plus I need to get my Cinderella on and sort this place out," I smile at her as I take a sip of water,

"Won't take us long," she quips, her stone-cold expression grating on me, but I let her bratty behaviour go because of what today is. Today is the goodbye she needs to say so she can move on.

"Let's go," I mumble, grabbing my keys off the side table and open the front door. She barges past me and down the driveway. Locking up behind me, I unlock the car and she slips in the front.

"You okay?"

"Mmhmm," she hums, plugging her seatbelt in and looking out the window.

"Great," I roll my lips, irritation growing inside of me. Starting the car, I pull out of the garage and down the drive, the music from my phone automatically starts playing

She Hates Me – Puddle Of Mudd.

I roll my eyes, clutching one hand on the steering wheel whilst my other arm is resting on the window edge of the car, my fingers covering my lips. You couldn't make this shit up, even if you wanted to.

The two-hour car journey was agonizingly awkward. Connie didn't say two words the whole way. Pulling into the church parking lot in Brooklyn, I watch as Connie stiffens in her chair. Reaching across, I place my hand on the inside of her thigh half expecting her to move it, but she doesn't. I give her a small, reassuring squeeze.

Pulling into a space, she pushed her large black glasses up her nose. The skies are blue, the winter sun low as it shines over the graveyard. Nothing can make this day better, but at least the sun is shining down on Tryst.

I didn't like the way he mistreated her, he deserved to pay for it, but honestly, not the way he did. Not the way that his demons dragged him to a place where he never thought he would be free from. She sniffs then coughs to clear her throat.

"You ready, darling?" I ask, my voice soft as I cut the engine. She turns to face me, and I don't need to see her eyes to know that the tears are filling her beautiful, green ones.

"I'm right here, I'll be by your side and if you need me to, I'll hold your hand."

She gives a curt nod before turning away from me, opening the door and I watch as she gasps the cold winter air into her lungs. My lips press into a flat line as I exit the car. I have my own feelings brewing deep inside of me at being here, it unsettles me.

Closing my door, I grab both coats from the boot and lock the car. Shrugging my long, wool black coat on, I walk over to Connie and place hers over her shoulders. She slips her arms in before looking at me, I see her bottom lip tremble and I give her a small nod.

"It's going to be okay," I whisper to her as we begin walking.

She stops suddenly, her steps faltering as she looks up at the church in front of her, the outside is panelled in white slats, four pillar columns sit flush on the front of the church. Two large, sash windows sit either side of the tall, black doors. The steeple reaches high, a compass sits proudly on top. I notice the paparazzi perched and ready to get the worthiest image for the front page. Averting my gaze across, I notice the black funeral car sitting alongside the church and we both watch as an older woman steps out dressed in a black knee length dress. Her black hair twisted up and her face covered by a black veil. My heart thumps and I feel Connie's fingers brush against mine. I turn my face to look down at her and as I go to grip her hand, she pulls it away and begins walking slowly. The older woman turns as Connie approaches. Neither of them moves, neither of them says a word until the older lady rushes towards Connie and wraps her in her arms.

Tryst's mom.

I stand still, not wanting to approach or encroach on this moment.

Tryst's mom pulls back, holding Connie's face in her hands, her red rimmed eyes filling with tears. She kisses Connie on the forehead then turns and walks into the church. Connie doesn't step forward, just stands staring. Walking slowly behind her, I see what her eyes are focused on. It's Tryst's casket.

He has a wicker casket, laced with white calla lilies spilling over the sides. Subtle but beautiful. *Purity, holiness, and faithfulness.* I chew the inside of my cheek, if only they *knew*. Tryst was none of those things. I know I shouldn't speak ill of the dead, but that man was the *fucking devil.*

"Baby," I whisper, and I am unsure why that name has slipped off my tongue, I had never called her that before but it somehow felt right. Wrapping my arm around her back, I usher her forward.

She walks slowly beside me but her eyes stay pinned to his casket and my heart is obliterating in my chest for her. I've been here. I've felt this kind of hurt. I know what it is like to bury someone you love but despise at the same time. As we approach the church the paps start clicking on their cameras. Narrowing my gaze on them, I feel my rage bubbling.

My eyes move from the vermin that they are and focus on her. *I only care about her.*

"Connie, over here!" One of the paps shouts out and I feel my anger beginning to grow.

"Were you invited, or have you crashed Tryst's funeral?" another bellows and I snap my head round to face him. Dropping my arm from Connie's body, I walk in slow strides over to the cameraman. Crouching down to my knees I cock my head to the side, a small smirk lifting at the corner of my mouth.

"Have a little fucking respect, either shut up willingly, or I'll shut you up." I grit, and the pap just stares at me, wide eyed and blinking.

I pat him on the shoulder a little harder than intended.

"There's a good boy," I wink, gently slapping his cheek before I stand tall. She drops her head, turning away as I take her hand in mine and lead her into the church.

She slips into one of the pews at the back so she can go unnoticed. Turning, she looks over her shoulders before letting her eyes scan the rest of the room. The room is full, but I expected it to be, and I am eternally grateful that no paps have been let inside.

Shuffling in my seat, I look down and see her picking her skin around her nails again. I scoop her small, cold hands into mine and hold them there so she doesn't pick anymore. The piano begins to play the tune *dancing in the sky,* and I feel Connie's hands begin to tremble. I hold them tightly, when all I want to do is pull her into me and let her sob into my shirt and take all of the pain she is feeling away from her. If I could do anything for *her* it would be that.

Everyone stands and I hold onto Connie because I am terrified that if I don't, her legs will give out beneath her. She turns slowly, looking over her shoulder and I see her crumble. Her beautiful face screws up as Tryst is carried in by the pallbearers. The tears that I feel like she has been holding in for what seems like a lifetime finally break the dam. She pulls her hand from mine and angrily swipes her tears away as if she is ashamed or even guilty for feeling emotion.

Tryst's casket is placed on the catafalque, the pallbearers stepping back and sitting in the front row. A tall blonde guy looks over in Connie's direction and she clutches onto my hand, pushing herself into me and I realise who it is. It's that dickhead that tried to make a move on her the night I found her. I lift my arm, letting her in as I wrap it around her small frame and hold her close.

"Breathe," I whisper as I feel her shoulders lift a little faster than normal.

The pastor stands, his eyes moving to the large photo of Tryst. He looked nothing like he did when I saw him. He was full of life, his eyes glistened, and he had a full, round face. When I saw him, he was gaunt, his eyes blackened and full of horrors.

A prayer was said and then the second song began to play. I didn't know it, but it seemed Connie knew what it was. It must have been one of his songs. She sat, a shell of herself, her head down, her hands clasped as she rocked back and forth.

It's okay darlin', better days are coming,
I won't always be plagued with demons,
I know this all feels numbing
but for now, they're here for a reason.
You're my light, my life, my becoming,
it's okay darlin' I know we're always in disagreement
but better days are coming.

I turn to look at her and the tears have stopped, her eyes are wide, her perfect bow lips parted. Lifting my head, I listen to the bridge of the song again. *It's about her.*

My arms are by my side, and I miss her being in my embrace. My fingers flinch and wiggle slightly as I feel her pinkie finger brush mine.

Her eyes are still focused forward, a small smile gracing her lips as Tryst's mom walks to the stand. She looks so fragile, as if she is ready to break at any given minute.

"My son, Tryst..." she swallows as her voice cracks, she tips her head back and looks at the ceiling and I am assuming she is trying to stop the sting behind her eyes as the tears threaten to fall.

"He was kind, caring, considerate..." she trails off as her eyes connect with Connie's, "but as time went on and he *finally* got to live his dream, he was constantly chasing the next high... but nothing was ever enough for Tryst, he always wanted more, the life he was living in that moment was never enough." She sniffs, wiping a tear away from her face. "But that didn't mean I didn't adore him. He was my son, my baby boy..." her voice breaks again, "no parent should ever have to bury their child, no matter the circumstance or lifestyle," her eyes move to the front row, "but he was loved, he was happy and he lived his life to the fullest. I was *proud* of him. I know people have said this was *revenge*, but I don't believe that. Tryst had demons, very dark and bad demons but he unfortunately couldn't win the battle against them," she chokes, letting her head fall forward she shakes it from side to side and the blonde-haired jerk from the concert stood next to her, putting on a show. I didn't know the guy, but from what I saw of him, I didn't like or *trust* him.

"Connie," I hear Tryst's mom say into the microphone, all eyes focus on Connie. She shrinks, her eyes wide and full of shock. "Could you come and say a few words about Tryst? It would mean the world to me, and to Tryst... if he could have chosen his funeral, he would want you up here telling everyone your love story."

She grips my hand tightly.

I avert my gaze from the broken woman on the stage and look down at Connie who hasn't moved. It is as if she is anchored to the ground.

"You don't have to do this if you don't want to," I whisper, rubbing my thumb over the back of her hand, "you can say no, just say the words and I'll whisk you out of here."

She nods softly, then I feel her hand slip from mine. She moves past me cautiously and stands in the aisle. Every single pair of eyes are on her and suddenly I feel protective of her, I don't want her to be in this vulnerable position and I can't help but think there is an ulterior motive here. She wants to do this.

She *needs* to do this, and I need to *let* her.

———

CONNIE

My palms are sweaty. My heart is drumming along to its own, hectic beat in my chest. Anxiety swarms in my stomach, stirring up a wave ready to crash over me at any minute. What am I doing?

I falter, looking back over my shoulder at Kaleb. His eyes are pinned to mine; he looks worried. I give him a small, reassuring smile, even though it's fake I don't want him worrying about me. He nods his head slightly, before I turn and walk towards the front of the service.

Tryst's mum, Colette, pulls me in and holds me tight. Cal giving me a sad smile as he opens his arms for me to fall into but I don't. I ignore him. Once on the stand, my eyes seek out Rox's. He looks broken, completely and utterly *broken.*

"I... um..." I stammer, rivers of tears are all I see in these people's eyes, Tryst's mum is standing beside me crying into Cal's arms. "I'm..." I cough, clearing my throat. I close my eyes for a moment, inhaling deeply as I try to calm my erratic heart. When I open them, all I see is *him.*

Kaleb.

Suddenly, my heart rate slows, my anxiety settling deep within me.

"Tryst..." I start, turning to face the casket and my heart sinks. Sniffing, I turn to focus on Kaleb.

"I met Tryst in school... we were friends, always up to no good," I half laugh, my brows pinching as I remember the past, "well, it was more me up to no good..." I smile at Colette. "Sorry," I mouth and she wipes her eyes whilst smiling.

"Tryst was there for me..." I swallow as my throat thickens, a lump slowly growing by the second, "when I had nobody else to turn to." I sigh. "I just..." I feel my insides burning, I try to stop the feeling that is taking over me. Nausea swarms me, my eyes widen as I begin to panic. "I just..." but I can't finish, my bottom lip trembles, my nose scrunches up as my eyes begin to fill with tears.

"I can't do this," I just about manage as my legs buckle beneath me, but I don't get a chance to hit the ground because Kaleb is there holding me up.

"I've got you," he whispers, "I've got you."

"Ashes to ashes, dust to dust," the pastor says as he throws dirt onto the coffin, then everyone else follows. Slowly people one by one begin to leave, Colette gives me a sombre nod before turning and walking away with Cal and Rox. It stung that they didn't talk to me, but then did I really want to still have them in my life? This was my fresh start, my do-over, this was my goodbye.

I have no idea how long I have been standing here for. The air is crisp, the sun setting in the distance and yet, I can't seem to move my legs. They're heavy and anchored as if I am being held here by gravity.

I turn to face Kaleb, he just stands, his hands clasped in front of him. He had the patience of a saint to put up with me. Turning, I look into the hole that my ex is in, and grief hits me like a freight train. Recalling the love we had, it was sweet, naive and reckless. I can't deny that I didn't love him because I would be lying to myself. It's weird, I sometimes feel like I can hear his voice in the wind as it blows past me, but I know it's just my mind playing tricks on me. He was my life lesson, the one to show me that I had so much more growing to do. He taught me things about myself that I hated.

I sniff, a tear rolling down my cheek. I always thought he was going to be the hero in my story, my prince who rides in on his white horse, whisking me away but it's as clear as day... he was the *villain*. I feel like I am drowning in a sea of tears, I don't want to cry anymore. I don't want to feel broken.

"You broke me," I whisper angrily, "you took everything good that was inside of me and sucked every slither of it away," my voice grows louder. I hear Kaleb's footsteps approaching behind me.

"You were meant to be the hero, I can't forgive you for what you have done to me, for how *you* made me feel. You've ruined every piece of me," I sniff, I don't wipe the tears that are relentlessly running down my cheeks. "I will miss you, but the *old* you. I won't cry over you anymore; you can't break me anymore Tryst... I will *never* forgive you," I step back from where he was laid to rest. But I retract, and surge forward once more.

"No, Tryst, I *will* forgive you, and I just hope that's enough for you to not spend eternity in hell where you should be, I really do pray that God washes all your sins away and lets you live in peace in heaven. That's what I wish for you, Tryst." I choke out, full on sobs leaving me. My lungs burn, my throat thick as I cry out loud, falling to my knees, "You done this to me, everything I once loved about myself I now despise." I cry out, "You would have taken me down with you, letting me fall into that darkness that you couldn't escape, you were happy to do that..." I whisper, my nose streaming, my breath catching on every other word. "I want to believe you're at peace Tryst, after watching me drown in an addiction I didn't want, but because of your actions you pushed me to get clean. And do you know what, you assaulting me in that way was the best thing you could have done for me, so *thank you* Tryst," I grab a handful of dirt and throw it down onto his coffin, screaming loudly but I have no idea if it's anger, grief or relief.

I feel large arms covering me, pulling me to my feet and Kaleb holds me until I honestly have no more tears left to cry.

I SLEPT THE WHOLE WAY HOME, I FELT MENTALLY DRAINED FROM today and all I wanted to do was climb into my bed and spend the rest of the evening there, soaking my pillow with tears. Kaleb was amazing, just like he has been from the moment he stepped into my life, saving me from something I didn't even know if I was sure that I needed saving from. But little did I know, Kaleb was saving me from my own death. Because after today, I am sure that I would have died along with Tryst. Two fucked up souls, destined to die together like a darker version of Romeo and Juliet.

But he saved me.

And that's what I was going to spend my life remembering. I didn't want to remember the hurt, the shame, the guilt and grief that Tryst made me feel, I left those feelings when I watched them bury Tryst into the ground. My feelings were dead and buried along with him.

Now it was my time, I needed to take this as my sign for my fresh start. I was one of the lucky ones that got a chance for my do-over, so I was going to make sure I lived it.

I'm going after what I want for my own happiness.

The first thing I am starting with is Kaleb. And just like that, the tears that were haunting me had disappeared.

CHAPTER THIRTY-NINE
CONNIE

"You want this you little whore, why are you fighting me?" Tryst's venomous tone slashes through me.

"Please Tryst, please don't do this," I gasp, my eyes wide as tears fall. But he doesn't listen, his hands are grabbing at my nightdress that I am wearing.

"Please," I beg, but he doesn't stop. He pushes my dress around my waist, Callaghan and Rox stood behind Tryst, but they were faceless. Like mannequins. Tryst grips my cheeks, squeezing them tight, his stale alcoholic breath glossing over my face. I close my eyes, holding my breath and ignoring the burn that spreads through my lungs. A dark, hooded shadow glided towards us. I tried to turn my face so I could see who it was, but I was met with the resistance of Tryst.

The hooded figure floated through Rox and Cal, his hands removing his hood and Kaleb's eyes met mine.

Relief swarmed me, but every time he tried to stop Tryst, he couldn't. My heart was frantic, eyes darting round the room when I saw Callaghan pull a gun, turning towards Kaleb and shooting him in the side of the head.

Screams left me, my throat hoarse as I watched Kaleb's

lifeless body drop to the floor. Callaghan gave me a sickening smile before shooting Rox and Tryst before turning the gun on me.

But I couldn't speak. My ability had gone.

Tears streamed down my face, my head shaking from side to side in a silent plea. But nothing stopped him. He pulled the trigger; the sound of the bullet being fired echoed causing my body to fall...

WAKING WITH A JOLT, MY HEART RACES IN MY CHEST, SKIPPING beats and making my breath catch. I clutch my tee over my chest, pulling at it. I'm dripping in sweat. I pat around me, relief swarming me that it was just a dream. A bad fucking nightmare. I jumped, my bedroom door flying open with a panicked Kaleb.

"Are you okay?" he rushes over, his hand pushing the hair that is stuck to my face away, his eyes scanning over my face. "You were screaming."

"Yeah," I whisper, "it was just a dream..." I roll my lips, my eyes penetrating through his. He reaches for me, pulling me into him as he holds me tight.

"Your pyjamas are soaked," he whispers, pulling away as his brows furrow, his eyes back and scanning over my face. Standing from the bed, he grabs the hem of his tee and lifts it over his head in one, swift movement.

I try to stop my jaw from dropping as my eyes roam up and down his toned body. He throws his tee at me, smirking as it hits me in the face.

"Pick your jaw up darling," his voice is low and raspy making my insides spark. He crawls back onto the bed, rolling onto his back and resting his head on my pillow. "Go put that on."

I say nothing, just scramble off the bed and into the bathroom, slamming the door a little harder than intended.

Lifting his white tee to my nose, I inhale his scent, my body warming before pooling on the floor. He smells delicious. The musky tobacco and suede filling my nose and finished off with a dusting of vanilla. It's such a strange combination, but I am obsessed. I undress quickly, the cold air in the bathroom nipping at my skin as I let his tee blanket me. It comes down to my mid-thigh, it's oversized and baggy. Scraping my hair into a ponytail, I tie it with a hair tie.

Stepping nervously out of the bathroom, I walk down the small narrow hallway towards my bedroom.

Why am I so nervous about him seeing me?

Tiptoeing round the bedroom door, a small smile graces my lips when I see him laying on my bed with just his cotton pyjama bottoms on.

"That's better," his eyes roam over me and I feel myself blush under his heated gaze.

He curls his finger, enticing me over. I fiddle with the hem of his tee as I walk slowly over to him, sitting on the edge of the bed when he leans up and reaches for me, pulling me into him so he is spooning me. I still, his arms wrapping me up in him, his scent suffocating me in the best way.

"Now sleep, baby," his voice rasps out before soft snores surround me. It doesn't take me long to doze in the safety of his arms.

"No!" I scream, "Tryst please," choking on sobs, I wake.

"It's okay darling, I've got you, I've got you."

He envelopes me into his embrace and I welcome it. His fingers stroke through my hair and I feel the tingles erupt over my skin.

I roll over, my glassy eyes seeking out Kaleb. His grey eyes fall to my lips, staring. I feel the internal battle with myself at wanting to kiss him, at wanting him to kiss me and I can't help but feel he is doing exactly the same. My eyes fall to his lips, his breath low and slow as he strokes his bottom lip with his tongue, wetting it. His fingers that were in my hair now skim down my cheek, his thumb and finger grabbing my chin as he tilts my head back.

"Can I kiss you?" he breathes, and it takes me a moment to register what he has asked. I nod, I feel my whole body trembling at the thought of him being intimate with me, the fear that this may be too fast but then again, I need this. I need to feel something other than crippling fear.

"Yes," I whisper, letting my eyes flutter shut slowly as his lips brush against mine gently. I flinch slightly, my eyes shooting open to see the pained look in his eyes, his lips lifting from mine instantly. "I'm sorry," I admit but he says nothing, just lowers his mouth over mine once more and this time I welcome them. Our kiss is slow and gentle, no tongues; it's just a kiss but it feels like the best kiss I have ever had.

He breaks away, his thumb gliding over my cheek as he wipes a tear away from his thumb pad, his grey eyes burning into mine. I swallow, my heart is beating hard in my chest as he pulls me closer to him, my face burying in his neck as I inhale his heavenly scent. I splay my hands against his bare chest, ignoring the spark that courses through my fingertips I lift my face to his, my eyes volleying back and forth as I swallow the thickness away.

"Make me forget," I whisper, "fix me..." I can barely get the words out, "please."

He inhales deeply, his hand cupping my face as his thumb swipes away another tear, "Baby, I will spend the rest of my life putting every broken piece of you back together if that's what I need to do."

I nod, sinking my teeth into my bottom lip. I roll onto my side, propping myself up with my elbow, his hands framing my face. His eyes gaze into mine before he lets them drop to my lips, his tongue darts out as he runs it across his bottom lip. My chest rises fast but falls slow as I try and eradicate my racing heart.

Edging forward, his lips meet mine again. His grip on my cheek tightens slightly as our kiss goes from soft to hard. Teeth clashing, tongues dancing in a hot, heavy and messy kiss. This is all I have wanted from the moment I laid eyes on him. I've wanted his lips on mine; I was desperate, as if he was the oxygen I needed. A delectable, gruff groan vibrates in his throat as he moves his hand from my face, down the side of my body, his hand cupping and squeezing my hip before his fingers trail softly between my pussy lips through my panties. His tee that was once covering me is now bunched around my waist. I gasp a moan into his open mouth as his fingers press against my clit, rubbing softly as my body comes alive with feelings I haven't felt deep inside of me for what feels like months.

"Kaleb," I whisper, pulling away slightly, I rub my lips together, my hand pressing against his chest.

"I know, love, I've got you," he smiles before our lips meet again, his fingers brushing across the front of my cotton panties, rubbing a little harder over my clit in a rhythm. He stills when he hooks his fingers round the side of my panties, as if waiting for my permission to go there. I nod, looking down at him and fluttering my eyes shut as his cool fingers glide through my folds causing a gasp to leave me.

"Tell me to stop if it gets too much," his voice is soft,

and I can just about nod as he pushes me into my own pleasure pool.

"I need more," my fingers splay against his bare chest before I dig my nails into his skin. His tongue slips between my cushioned lips, the tip of his finger swirling and teasing at my opening. My head falls forward as he pushes deeper into me, my body shuddering as a course of electric zaps through me, my stomach knotting as the delicious sensation smothers me, a current that only he has ever made me feel pumping through my veins. Gently he pulls his finger out, pushing another into me in a slow, torturous way. "Kaleb," I whisper, his thumb brushing across my sensitive clit, moaning out into the empty room.

"Your moans are…" he rasps as he trails kisses along my neck, down my collar bone then stills at the neck of my tee. He pulls his fingers from me, leaving me whimpering at the loss of him. Pushing my tee up around my neck, he smiles as his eyes fall to my full breasts.

"Hold your tee up," he mutters against my skin, his fingers slipping between my legs once more, filling me.

I do as he asks, holding my tee up so his hot as sin mouth has access to my breasts.

He smirks before he licks and sucks my pink, pert nipples. My stomach tightens, twisting at the pleasure that's taking over my body.

Covering my nipple with his mouth, he sucks and licks tentatively, his fingers pumping in and out of me, his thumb stroking my clit as he works me up.

"Stop," I breathe out, my skin erupting in goosebumps. He does, instantly. His eyes meet mine, our gazes steady. He doesn't question me, just waits for my next command.

"I'm clean…" I rush out, my cheeks heating, "I got tested after I found out Tryst…"

"Baby," he rasps, cutting me off.

"I just needed you to know…" I whisper and he gives me a slow, lazy smile. Pushing him back gently so he is laying on his back, I sit up and throw my leg over his torso so I am straddling him. My breath is shaky, my tee falling back down and covering me up.

He smirks up at me, his hands moving to my hips as he pushes my tee up slightly so his fingers can dig into the skin on my hips. I rock myself over his hard cock, I can feel him through the thin cotton of his pants, working myself up until I'm ready for the next move.

My hands are pressed into his chest, the need to have our skin touching is too much, I need to feel the connection between us constantly.

"Baby, I need you," he whispers, his grip on my hips tightening as I continue to ride him through our clothes.

Lifting my hands from his skin reluctantly, I push off him and stand, my feet either side of him as I hook my fingers into my panties and slip them down my legs.

"Your turn," my voice is sultry and seductive. He winks, lifting his hips and discarding his pants. My mouth goes dry as my eyes take in *every single inch* of him.

His large hand wraps around the base of his thick cock, his fingers gliding up and down himself, but he doesn't tear his eyes from mine. It's intimate and hot. He stops, his fingers still wrapped around the base. I lower myself down slowly, hovering over the tip of his cock which he rubs through my soaked pussy folds.

"Oh…" is the only word that leaves my lips breathlessly.

Pressing his thick head at my opening, I lower myself down a little more, taking some of him. My head tips back at how full he is making me feel. I ignore the sting that is caused by his size and focus on the pleasure. His spare hand pushes my tee over my hips, his fingers wrapping around my hip bone, his eyes watching between our bodies. I let my fingers skim down my body as I rub over my clit slowly.

"Baby, you can take more than that... I need you to sit, not *hover.*"

I moan, his jaw clenching as I roll my hips over him then lower myself a little more.

"There's a good girl, you can take it all... show me," he praises me, lifting his hips, pushing into me as I grind down onto him filling myself to the hilt. "Fuck," he rasps, his grip on my hip tightening as I rock myself over him slowly, my fingers pressing and rubbing over my clit.

My eyes flutter shut as I take a moment to appreciate this feeling that is bubbling deep inside of me. This feels *so right.*

He lifts his legs, bending them behind me. I lean back using him as support, lifting my hips then lowering myself back down on him.

"Connie," he groans, his hips meeting my lifts.

"I'm close," I choke, my eyes filling with tears.

"I've got you," he whispers, I lower myself over his body and kiss him, but his cock doesn't stop slipping in and out of me. His tongue swipes over mine, his thrusts getting harder now as his own rhythm begins to get sloppy; his kisses messy.

"Fuck, baby, I am so close to coming," he grits, his jaw clenched. "Do you trust me?" he asks. Anxiety ripples through me at his question but I nod. "I need you to say the words baby."

"Yes, I trust you," I breathe, his cock still filling me, slipping in and out with ease.

His large hand pushes me up and off him, lifting me and turning me over. He shuffles up the bed, resting his back against the headboard. I watch as his eyes darken, but my eyes fall to his beautiful dick, covered in my arousal and I am desperate to have him back inside of me. His long arms reach forward, tugging me back onto him, my back to his front. Widening my legs as I hover over him, I wait for him to line himself up as he pushes the tip of himself into me. I lower down, this time taking him in one move.

"Oh," he moans, one hand curling back around my hip, the other moving up my torso, across my sternum before he is groping my breast and rolling my hardened nipple between his fingers. Letting my head fall to the side, his lips are on my neck in a flash, kissing and nipping at my sensitive skin. Rocking over him a little faster now, his thrusts meet mine harder and faster. I feel his hand move between my legs, and I am needy to have him touching me. Tilting my pelvis up, I mewl.

His fingers rub over my clit, my hands squeeze my breasts, my head tipping back as pleasure consumes me.

"Bend your legs and bring your knees up," he pants. Steadying myself, I bend my legs so my feet are flat to the bed, one of my hands reaching behind and pressing against his chest as I lift my hips up and down over his cock.

"Yes," he pants, his fingers still rubbing over my clit, his cock hitting me deeper and the tip of him rubbing against my g-spot. I clamp down around him as he slips in and out of me.

"I..." I pant, my eyes closing before I watch his fingers work me whilst his thick cock fills me deep.

"Let it go baby," he groans, removing his fingers from my clit, both his hands are on my hips as he helps me, lifting me up and down faster for his own pleasure and mine. I move my fingers down to my swollen clit and rub as I feel my orgasm building fast.

"Shit, oh, Kaleb," I cry, my head falling back against him as my orgasm shatters deep inside of me, I moan, my hips lifting up his dick and rocking them over his tip.

"I need more," he groans, slamming me back down over him as he pumps his cock deep and hard inside of me, pinning me still as he uses my body to reach his orgasm.

He growls, lifting me and slamming me down one last time before I feel his cock throb and pulse inside of me as he comes, his fingers digging into my skin marking me, but I don't care at this moment, I am still coming down from my own high.

He made me feel things I hadn't felt before. He brought me back to life when I hadn't even realised I was dying.

CHAPTER FORTY

KALEB

Watching her sleep is something I never knew I needed until today. Laying on her front, her face turned towards me and her long, chocolate brown hair fanned out and cascading down her back. I study her every feature, not wanting to miss a single detail on her face. The light dusting of freckles that branched over her nose. They were barely visible, but to me, I saw every single one. Her plump bow lips parted, soft snores passing them which made me smile.

Sighing blissfully, I rolled onto my back as my mind flashed back to last night. A very small part of me was disappointed in myself that I gave in to her temptation, gave in to the forbidden fruit that I have wanted to taste since the moment I laid eyes on her. The thing about Connie is that I feel so protective over her. The thought of her leaving to go back to her normal life terrifies me, but she isn't mine to keep. She isn't mine for me to have that possessiveness over. She is a job. A client. Once she is ready to leave, that will be it. No more rays of the sunshine that she is in my life. I'll go back to being the grumpy, miserable fucker I always was. I scoff, shaking my head from side to side softly.

I wasn't always grumpy. If anything, I was a lot like my brother, Keaton, until he married the spawn of Satan herself. I was so carefree; I didn't give a shit. Until it all went wrong.

I had a client five years ago, she was a little older than Connie, but in the same situation, just not with the vermin paps following her around and snooping. I kept her safe, moved her in with me whilst I made sure she was away from the devil that abused her day in, day out. She wasn't a paid client, her case was right time, right place. I saw her boyfriend getting handsy with her, saw the fear in her eyes and the way she held herself. I stood in the shadows until he left to go and get another drink for his already poisoned and intoxicated bloodstream. As soon as he was out of sight, I made my move. Laying here next to Connie, my thoughts can't help but slip into the past, recounting the memory of that day.

"Are you okay?" my voice was low, but loud enough for her to hear over the music that was softly playing in the background.

She nods but I can see her trembling in the low light of the room.

"I can help you," I hushed, my voice a little more rushed now as I worried that he would be back any second. Looking over my shoulder, I caught sight of the dickhead paying for his drink, urgency spiking within me.

"We need to move, now," the panic was evident in my voice, "please, come with me, I can keep you safe," my hand squeezes the top of her arm reassuringly, and she nods. "Come," I whisper, pushing her away from me and turning her to face away. "Head to the back of the room, we will go out the back exit."

She was a quivering mess, but she began to walk, and with each stride her steps grew faster.

But I let her go too soon... I was her downfall.

MY HEART RACES AT THE MEMORY OF HER, THE DARKNESS THAT was slowly being lit from the sunshine that was in the form of Connie, was starting to creep back inside of me. I pant, my eyes pinned to the ceiling. I stare into the abyss before I let my eyes shut as I try to calm my breathing. I feel her twist and turn in the bedsheets, my heart suddenly stilling.

"Hey," she whispers, her eyes still shut, her breathing slow, her voice drawling.

"Morning sunshine," a smile pulls at the corners of my lips, "how did you sleep?" my voice is husky.

"On my back," I wiggle my brows and she rolls her eyes, "nah, like a log, best night I've had in ages," she blushes. "How about you?"

"Like a fucking baby," I beam, letting out a soft chuckle. I reach forward, wrapping my arms around her I pull her into me. She rolls so her pert little ass is resting on my cock. Fuck, I can't believe we crossed that line last night, but it was worth it. She was worth it. She was all I imagined she would be. No, I'm lying; she was *so much more*.

A soft moan leaves her lips as I cocoon her in my arms, nuzzling into her hair and inhaling her addictive scent. She wiggles her ass over my hardening cock.

"Baby, don't be doing that to me..." I groan, leaning up and placing a kiss at her temple, trailing them down to her jaw. Slipping my hand between her legs, I rub her clit through the thin material of her panties, a little surprised at how wet she is. "Baby, you're so wet," I whisper, smiling against her skin as she moans. Lifting my fingers from her, I grab the duvet and throw it back, my eyes widening when I see my fingertips are bloodied. "Erm, baby…" I stammer, not moving.

Connie hums, slowly turning her head to face me and her eyes widening.

"Did I cause that?" I ask, my brows pinch at my idiotic question.

"Of course, you didn't, it's a period *Kaleb*." Calling out, she rushes from the bed, her cheeks scarlet.

"It's okay, what can I do?"

"Go and clean yourself up," she huffs, tugging at the covers as she begins to strip them. I shake my head from side to side, rushing towards her and reach out for her, stopping her in her tracks.

"Let me get the shower on, I'll sort this." I press a kiss to her forehead. She nodded, nibbling her bottom lip to try and stop the tremble. "It's okay," I pull her in for a hug then take her hand and lead her to the bathroom. Dropping her hand, she sits on top of the toilet lid as I twist the shower on.

"Do you need anything?"

"Tampons," she sighs, "in the rush of us leaving… I didn't even think," she shakes her head from side to side as if she is annoyed with herself.

"That's fine, I'll nip to the shops. Anything else?"

"No," she whispers. I step towards her, pulling her up. I grab the hem of her top and lift it over her head slowly and cautiously. I was half expecting her to stop me, but she didn't. Putting my thumbs into the side of her panties, I push them down, moving to my knees. Her hands rest on my shoulders as I slip her shorts from her ankles. I place soft kisses on each of her thighs. Standing slowly, I cup her cheek and cover her lips with mine.

"I'll be back before you're out the shower," I whisper against her lips, "is it wrong that I am hard for you? Wrong that all I can think about is fucking you raw?" Her eyes widen. "But I won't. Get in the shower," I kiss her again before leaving her in the steam filled room.

Pacing up and down the sanitary aisle, I have no idea what I am getting.

"Tampons," I mutter to myself, "why are there so many?" I stop and look at the different types. "Fuck it," I groan after five minutes, swiping the shelves with all the options. Smiling smugly, I walk around to grab some chocolate, sweets, a hot water bottle, Advil, and some new pyjamas.

Walking back to the car, I floor it back to the house, panicking a little more until I am on the drive. Rushing through the door and straight up the stairs I see Connie standing in the bathroom with just a towel wrapped around her slender frame.

"Hey," I call, nodding my head towards the bedroom for her to follow me. Tipping the bag out, the contents falls onto the coverless comforter.

Connie's eyes widened, before laughing. "How many did you get!?" she swats me in the arm.

"I didn't know what you needed," I smiled, "I'll leave you be," reaching for the hot water bottle before stepping back, I close the bedroom door behind me.

Filling her hot water bottle up, I hover at the bottom of the stairs and wonder if I should go back up again. I have no idea what this is between us now, we crossed the thin line and now I feel like I am in unknown land. I would be lying if I said I didn't feel something for her, because I do. But then again, I was there for her last night when she needed me. That's all. I was just being a friend, well, if you can call us friends.

I go against my thoughts and climb the stairs; her door is still ajar. Pushing it gently I see her curled up on the bed.

"Connie," my voice is hushed as I step into the room. She doesn't answer. Padding towards her I smile, she's asleep and cuddling into a pillow. I gently lean over, pulling it away softly and replacing it with the hot water bottle. My frown crinkles when I see the sheets still wrapped up in a ball on the floor. Picking them up I turn and leave her to rest.

I scratch my head as I stare at the washing machine. I have no idea how to work this. Connie has done all the laundry, and I know how that sounds... like I am some chauvinistic pig. Which I'm not. Slipping my phone from my back pocket I dialled Doris' number.

"All okay?" she asks in way of greeting.

"Yeah fine," I rub my hand over my head, "how do I work the washing machine?"

I hear Doris' laugh.

"Read the settings out to me, what are you washing?"

"Bedsheets and duvet cover," I mutter, spinning the dial of the machine round and round.

"Okay, so it only needs to be a light wash."

"Connie got her..." I cough.

"Oh, say no more. You want to put it on a hot wash, choose that setting then push start."

"Okay, thanks."

"Not a problem, when are you home? Just so I can get things sorted here for your return."

"Are there anymore vermin outside?"

"A couple, but they don't stay here long. I think they've given up."

"Good," I rub my chin, smiling as the machine clicks and begins to fill. "We'll be home tomorrow."

"We?" I can hear the change in Doris' voice; excitement.

"Yes, myself and Connie."

"Oh lovely, that's perfect. I'll get everything sorted for your return; I'll get lunch ready as well."

"Thank you Doris, see you tomorrow."

"See you tomorrow, Kaleb."

I cut her off and head to the kitchen. I'm starving. Opening the fridge, we don't have a lot left. A few eggs, milk, onions, tomatoes, and some cheese. Everything I need for an omelette.

Dishing two servings up, I place them on the coffee table in the lounge with a beer. Not ideal but might as well use them up. Heading back upstairs, I step into her room and sit on the edge of the bed. Brushing her hair away from her face, I say her name softly. Smiling when her beautiful green eyes land on mine.

"Hey," my heart flutters in my chest. There is no point denying this, I'm smitten with her.

"Hey," she rolls over and stretches, her hand moving to the hot water bottle before her eyes move to mine once more.

"Thought it might help with cramps?" *Hello, who are you and what have you done with Kaleb?*

"Thank you," she beams, sitting up and kissing me on the cheek.

"Brunch is downstairs when you're ready. It probably tastes like garbage, but I gave it a go."

"I'm sure it'll taste delicious." She smiles, her eyes bright and it's nice to see a little of a spark back in them.

257

We ate every last mouthful; it was actually good. I surprised myself.

"I was thinking," I say, turning to face her on the other sofa, "we will head home tomorrow, if you're okay with that?"

She nods, "Yeah I am."

"Still coming to stay with me?" *Please say yes, please say yes.*

"Only if that's okay?"

Bingo.

"Of course, it is, I wouldn't have offered if it wasn't."

"Only until I am settled of course."

"Of course," I nod and my gut twists.

"I'll start packing tonight," she reaches for the remote and flicks through the channels when *How to lose a guy in ten days* catches her attention.

"Could you do this?" she asks, not moving her eyes from the screen.

"Could I do what?"

"Make someone fall in love with you in ten days then break their heart?"

I scrunch my nose up, scoffing.

"Could you?" I ask, knowing full well she could.

"One hundred percent," her smile is wide as she shows her full set of pearly white teeth.

I know, because you have caught me, hook, line, sinker.

CHAPTER FORTY-ONE
CONNIE

I woke alone and disappointment surged through me, after our night together I assumed Kaleb would have slept with me, but he never came to bed. That evening was everything and more but now I felt like a stranger to him. We sat in silence on the way back to Kaleb's and the whole time I was battling with the questions that were firing round in my head. But the loudest one was, *have I done something wrong?*

Pulling into the underground parking lot of the apartments, I was relieved to be getting out. I needed space between us. Once the car was parked, I opened the door and gasped as I sucked in the air into my lungs. I felt suffocated suddenly.

"Connie?" He calls out, my skin erupting in goosebumps at his voice blanketing my skin.

"I'll meet you up there," I shout back, my voice echoing around the large space, but I don't look back at him. I just keep walking. Pressing the button continuously for the elevator praying it comes before he gets to me, but it doesn't.

"Everything okay?" his lips twitch, his eyes roam over my face.

"Yeah, just girl..." he holds his hand up and gives a slow nod. The doors ping and I slip in, letting my head drop forward and knotting my fingers in front of me.

The question was on the tip of my tongue to ask if he was okay, but I couldn't. Every time I wanted to; the words failed me.

I will for him to kiss me, to feel the electricity course through me that only he has made me feel. But he didn't budge. Just stood scrolling on his phone which grated on me.

I was grateful when the door opened, I knocked my shoulder into him with a little more force than necessary and slipped down into the lobby, smiling when I saw Doris. Suddenly the foul mood that had surrounded me began to lift.

"Connie," she beams at me, holding her arms out ready to embrace me and I have never thrown myself at someone so fast. "How are you?"

"I'm okay," I nod, tears springing to my eyes.

"Are you sure?" she asks and I can hear the concern in her voice.

I nod, my throat thickening. Stepping away when I hear Kaleb's feet hitting the tiles. I bow my head and walk up the stairs, not looking back.

Once in my room, I let out a heavy sigh. I feel like I have put a wedge between me and Kaleb, but I don't know how or why. Have I read into this a little too much? Maybe he was just tired? Or could it be as simple as some miscommunication?

I rub my hand over my face, annoyance burning deep in my tummy. Was I being a brat?

Walking gently over to my bed, I sat on the edge as my eyes fixed on the closed bedroom door. I wasn't sure how long I sat staring into the empty space but my heart skipped a beat when I saw the door handle shake slightly.

Sitting up, my shoulders no longer rolled forward and slouched, I see Kaleb's head pop round the door.

"Can I come in?"

I nod, nerves rip through me, and it unsettles me.

"I just wanted to make sure you're okay..." he walks cautiously over to me, his fingertips brushing across his bottom lip and suddenly I am jealous. Of a lip. *What the fuck is wrong with me.*

"I feel like you've had the hump with me since I woke... or have I read that wrong?" He sits next to me, his hands resting on his thighs.

"I just felt like..." I still, lifting my eyes to look at him for a moment but his eyes don't avert to mine, and I feel my heart splinter slightly. I exhale heavily, my breath shaky.

"You just felt..." he repeats my words.

"Forget it," I nibble my bottom lip.

"No, Connie... tell me," he turns his body towards me, and now he looks at me. His eyes scalding my skin as they rake over my body.

"You didn't come to bed last night..." I just about manage, the humiliation of my confession burning my cheeks.

"I didn't think you wanted me to, I just assumed it would go back to normal..." he admits, rolling his lips then locking his fingers together.

"Oh, *normal,*" my tone as a little sting to it.

"Is that not what you wanted then?"

"For an old man, you're not very wise," I lick my upper lip ignoring the burn in my throat.

"Old man?" he snaps his head round, "I'm not *old.*"

I snigger. "I think you are," I stand, placing my hands on my hips as I turn to look at him once more, "you're definitely an old man to me," I shrug my shoulders up.

"I'm forty-seven, hardly an old man."

"You see, Grandpa, you are old. You're two decades older than me."

He says nothing, just twists his delicious lips.

The slight bit of humour that was slowly starting to creep into the room was shut down by silence.

"I didn't want you sleeping on the sofa," I finally say when the truth is, the silence hadn't been that long.

"I was just trying to do the right thing..." he stands, inhaling deeply as his gorgeous grey eyes lock on mine.

"But it wasn't the right thing..." I just about manage a whisper, my breath catching at the back of my throat.

"No?" he steps closer to me, the gap that was between us is now non-existent. His hand lifts slowly, gripping my chin to stop me from letting my eyes fall to my feet. "What should I have done, Connie?" he rasps, his voice has quickly become one of my favourite sounds.

"You shouldn't have left me in the big, *old* bed alone."

His lips edge closer to mine, my cheeks blush a crimson red. I don't know what it is about him making me blush like a schoolgirl. I want to admit that it annoys me, but it doesn't. I like the effect he has on me.

Love the effect he has on me.

I feel his full lips brush against mine ever so softly, my eyes flutter shut as his butterfly kisses make my tummy flip.

"We shouldn't be doing this..." he whispers through our kiss.

"I know, but no one has to know..." I breathe.

"You'll be my secret."

"Your secret, Kaleb. *Yours.*"

My heart races, as he finally gives into temptation and kisses me. His tongue slowly stroking against mine, his hand cupping my cheek as he holds me still whilst he kisses me long and hard. I have never felt the way Kaleb is making me feel from this one kiss. It's as if I can finally see this mediocre world in vibrant colour. The life that I haven't cared about in the last two years finally feels like a life worth living. I want the dream. The fairytale and the happily ever after.

I want it all.

And I'll get it.

LYING IN BED LATER THAT NIGHT, MY EYES ARE GROWING HEAVIER, but he promised he would come, but how long do I wait? Flicking through the channels, anything to keep me awake but I lose the fight, giving in to sleep.

I'm awoken when I feel the bed dip, his arm wrapping over me and pulling me back, so his front is against the back of my body.

"Hey darling," his voice rasps, awakening me and I smile.

"You're late."

"I know sweetheart, but I had some things to tie up."

"Okay," I just about manage as I feel my body grow heavier, sinking into the mattress. His lips brush against my shoulder, trailing up my neck slowly until his lips brush across my cheek.

"Goodnight, baby."

Rolling over, I smile when I see Kaleb still asleep. I take this little quiet moment to look at him, his long lashes fanned against his cheeks, his golden skin aglow, his bow lips parted as soft snores fill the room. I instantly miss his touch on me, the way he brings me to life by a stroke of his fingertips on my skin.

I have no idea what this is between us, but whatever it is, I want it.

He stirs, his pupils dilating before they fix on mine. His eyes are dark and deep, a beautiful open window to his soul.

"Morning."

He rolls on his back and a heavy sigh leaves him when his phone begins ringing.

"Back to reality," he rolls to sit on the edge of the bed and grabs his cell, but before he climbs out of bed, he falls back and leans across, kissing me on the forehead. Then jumps up, smiling as he answers the phone.

"Hey Titus," his voice is cool as he walks towards the door, checking the hallway before he sneaks out. I sit up, letting my eyes rake up and down his bare back, the muscles rippling under his skin making my stomach knot.

Falling back into the pillows, I smile. I feel happy, inside and out. My eyes pin to the ceiling and for the first time in what feels like forever, I want to call Reese.

Throwing the duvet back, I climb out the same side that Kaleb did and frown when I don't see my slippers. Pulling my messy brown hair into a high ponytail, I catch my reflection in the mirror as I move towards the door and smile. I feel like my glow is back and it's all due to Kaleb. My eyes fall and my heart thumps. I'm wearing one of Kaleb's tees that has become a favourite of mine. Lifting it to my nose, I inhale sharply, disappointed that his scent is not as prominent as it once was. Pushing forward, I make my way downstairs and hear Kaleb's deep, beautiful voice echo around his apartment. Butterflies swarm, my heart races and I smile. The feelings this man makes me feel are overwhelming but wanted. So, so wanted.

I round the corner and see him pacing back and forth in nothing but his pyjama bottoms and my pink glittery slippers that are way too small for him. I smirk, a scoff of a laugh leaving me as I cross my arms across my chest and watch him.

His head snaps up, his head turning as his eyes dance with mine. The corner of his lips lift before winking at me.

"Yeah, I'll be in the office in an hour."

I pout and his smile widens.

"Make it two," he cuts his phone off and walks towards me, his eyes darken as his phone falls out of his hand and onto the sofa.

His body is flush with mine, his hands skimming down the side of my body reaching the hem of my tee and slipping his hands inside.

"You look so good in *my* tee," his forehead presses against mine and my breath catches, he is the definition of *take my breath away.*

"I feel good in your tee," my breath dances over his skin.

"You feeling okay?" his large hand rests on my lower belly, making me jump slightly at the intimate piece of contact.

"A bit of a stomach-ache, but I'm okay," I nod.

"Go and get back into bed, choose a film and we will chill before I *have* to leave for work."

I nibble my bottom lip, my wide eyes focused on him, the fire burning through my veins.

Doris turns the corner and Kaleb jumps, pushing me

away before running his hand through his thick, brown hair, his fingers parting through the strands that fall softly.

"Morning Kaleb, Connie," she smirks, keeping her chin high as she walks past us. She isn't silly.

"She knows," I whisper as she disappears through into the dining room.

He scoffs, "No she doesn't," he shakes his head from side to side. I rock onto the balls of my feet, giving my eyes a soft roll before I turn on my heels.

"Whatever Grandpa," I chime, smirking to myself knowing he won't chase me because he doesn't want Doris to catch on, but she has already caught on. She knows exactly what is going on.

Silly, naive man.

Taking the stairs, I head straight to the shared bathroom and brush my teeth. Bending over the sink, I rinse my mouth out when I hear a low whistle. I stand abruptly, turning to see Kaleb resting against the door frame. His eyes are pinned to me, and I feel the tension growing.

"You startled me," I admit, my voice small as he steps towards me and stops behind me, his hands rubbing the curve of my ass cheeks which causes a soft gasp to leave my lips.

"I didn't mean to startle you baby," his lips press against my neck, and I lean my head to the side to give him better access. I love feeling his lips on mine. His soft hands continue round the front of my thighs, kneading his fingers into the skin gently.

"I know," I whisper, my head falling back onto his bare chest.

"Look at us in the mirror darling," he rasps, his eyes pinned to my reflection. I slowly turn to watch, my cheeks flushed, and he hasn't even touched me sexually. I never used to be this timid and tame, but since Tryst... I block out that thought before it consumes me whole. I watch as his hands move higher, lifting the hem of my tee around my waist so I can watch as he strokes me through my cotton panties.

"I've heard orgasms help with the cramps," his voice is slow and low.

I shiver against his warm body as his fingers rub a little harder over my clit, his teeth nipping at the sensitive skin on my exposed neck.

"Kaleb," I whisper, shuffling my feet further apart.

"Yes baby?"

I exhale, my breath shaky as I lose my trail of thought. I am too focused on the pleasure that is rippling under my skin.

Turning my head towards my shoulder, I meet his lips. His spare hand holds my hip as I allow his tongue to stroke mine before they entwine.

I spin, making him lose his rhythm on my clit, my hands grasping his face as I deepen my kiss, our teeth clash, our lips slide as it becomes messy.

"Take me, Kaleb," I moan into his mouth between our kisses. Groaning, his hand skims under my ass lifting me up with one arm and I lock my legs around his waist as he walks back towards the bath.

"I need to..." I pant, realisation kicking in suddenly.

"I know baby, I know."

He reaches behind and turns the shower on, the steam filling the room quickly. Placing me on my feet, he grabs the hem of my tee and tugs it over my head in one, swift movement.

His hands move to my chest, his thumb brushing over

my hardened nipple then kneads my full breast. Leaning down, his hot, wet mouth covers my nipple as he sucks and licks causing a pang of pleasure to rip through me deep in my stomach. His other hand skims down my sides, slipping into the side of my panties as he pushes them down my legs. I kick them off as they hit my ankle. His tongue continues to stroke my hardened nipple, his fingers pinching and rubbing the skin as he caresses my breast.

Trailing his fingers up the inside of my thighs, he presses his finger into my skin a little harder and I step aside, giving him access to where he wants to be. His wet mouth pulls away from my skin and I whimper at the loss of him over my sensitive nipple. His grey eyes find mine as he falls to his knees in front of me, batting his lashes at me as he smirks. Two fingers press against my clit making me choke on my intake of breath, my fingers resting on his shoulders as I steady myself.

"Does that feel good?" he asks as his lips press against my sternum; words fail me, my head falling forward.

His spare hand runs down my back, skimming over my hip before he lets his hand glide across my ass cheek. Kaleb's fingers continue stroking me, slowly. Moving underneath me, his fingers find my tampon string and he pulls, discarding it in the bin beside us. As much as I want to call him out on the action, I don't because as soon as it's out, his fingers are deep inside of me, my insides tightening as I clamp down around him.

"Kaleb," I breathe out, digging my nails deeper into his skin.

"You thought I was going to stop a little blood getting between us, love?" he mutters against my skin as he stands, towering over me, but his fingers continue to fuck me.

"Let's get you washed, shall we?" he smirks, my doe eyes wide as I look at him through my lashes.

I nod, his fingers slipping out of me and the sting of the loss slices through me. He doesn't break his eye contact as he pushes his fingers between his lips and sucks them. My cheeks heat under his gaze and he notices, smirking, and his thumb brushes against my cheek.

"I am obsessed with you," he breathes, his eyes falling to my parted lips, "so, fucking obsessed." My heart jack hammers in my chest, electricity sparking through my veins, his voice like velvet against my skin.

Lifting me, he carries me into the shower, placing me under the large shower head as the hot water cascades over me. He stands in front of me, pushing his pyjamas down, his swollen, thick cock bobbing between his legs and my mouth dries, my eyes widening.

Water droplets hit the bridge of my nose, running down and dropping off the tip. He steps towards me, lifting me up and backing me against the wall.

"As much as I want to spend all day in here, I have a very *important* meeting I need to get to..." he rasps, gliding two fingers through my parted pussy lips, swirling the tips at my opening.

My eyes roll in the back of my head as he pushes them a little further into me, his thumb brushing against my clit.

"You're mine, Connie..." he rasps, and I nod through a moan. Slipping his fingers out, I feel the roundness of his tip edging into me.

"Yes," I whisper.

He edges into me slowly, filling me and causing the most delicious burn to radiate through me.

"Tell me, pretty girl, tell me that you're mine."

"Yours, Kaleb," I pant, as he fills me to the hilt, stilling for a moment.

"Good girl," he pulls out to the tip and slams back into me. "This is going to be hard and fast baby," he grits out, edging me, stilling then thrusting deep inside of me. I moan, my hands locked around his neck as he fucks me hard and fast.

I feel myself tighten, my pussy clenching round his thick cock.

"I'm going to come," I moan, the pleasure erupting deep inside of me, my orgasm teetering on the border, ready to free fall into my own sea of pleasure.

"Come baby, I want to fill you with everything I have," his lips crash into me, as he slips in and out of me, his hand reaching between our bodies as he brushes his finger over my clit causing me to come undone, my second orgasm coming on quick and exploding from deep inside of me, overwhelming me so completely that my whole body trembles in his arms.

He follows, his cock twitching as he pumps his cum inside of me, his lips lifting to my forehead as we both pant, coming down from this almighty high.

That was the moment I knew.

I've fallen for Kaleb Mills.

CHAPTER FORTY-TWO

KALEB

A LITTLE LATER THAN I PROMISED I'M WALKING INTO THE OFFICE from the elevator with a huge smile spread across my lips.

"Good morning, lads," I call out and all three of the guys heads pop up.

"What the fuck is that on your face?" Keaton scowls, his eyes burning into mine. My smile slips, I stop and rub my hand over my face, confusion filling me as I stare at Keaton when I find nothing.

"What are you going on about?" I let my arm fall in frustration, my brows knitted.

"That thing on your lips? I think some call it a... smile," he sits back, kicking his feet onto the desk looking proud as fucking punch.

"You're a dickhead." I roll my eyes, storming into my office and slamming the door so hard the frame rattles.

"Welcome back brother!" Keaton calls out and I flip him off behind my door. *Can I go home?*

The morning slipped by, and I was uninterrupted which I was surprised about. Keaton normally bounds around me like an excited puppy dog.

I hear a gentle knock on my office door, my eyes lifting from the screen. Sitting back in my chair, I rub my finger along my bottom lip.

"Come in," I call out, I watch as the door handle moves, and I see Titus.

"You busy?" he asks as he steps into my office.

"Not overly." I smirk, giving him a wink.

"Glad to be back?" Titus pulls the chair out opposite my desk and sits down, crossing his leg over the other and linking his fingers round his knee. Titus has light green eyes that pop against his darker skin. He gives me a slow smile, his brows raising slightly.

"Yes..." I breathe out, "and no..."

"Is that because of Connie?" All I can do is nod.

"I've seen that things have settled down, are you finished with her now?" his question feels like a knife twisting in my gut and it doesn't matter how much I try, I can't remove it. My brows pinch when I feel my hand move across my stomach, I pull it away quickly.

"Not quite yet," I shuffle in my chair, the urge to snap out against him and protect Connie at all costs is overwhelmingly strong, but I bite my tongue.

"Why's that?" Titus scoffs his question, hiding his pearly whites behind a closed, tight lip smile.

"Because she has nowhere to go, she isn't ready to reconcile with her father or her moms for that matter..." I exhale heavily, "I'm not a heartless bastard, I can't throw her out on the streets."

Titus says nothing but his facial expression tells all. I know he is wondering why she can't spend her money on a little apartment, why she can't stay at the hotel she used to work in and more importantly, why she can't stop acting like a brat and make peace with her family. I know he is thinking it because I thought it too. But not anymore.

"But..." he counterparts and I stop him, holding my hand up.

"But nothing Titus, she's safe with me, I know where she is at all times. And until I am ready and until she is ready, she can live with me." I finally drop my eyes, breaking our stare that had grown more intense. Titus holds his hands up in surrender, a soft chuckle leaving him as I gaze at my computer.

"You like her then, huh?"

I snap my head round to face him once more, narrowing my dark eyes on his light greens.

"What makes you think that?" I have no idea why my back is up so much in regard to Connie, that's annoying me even more.

"I'm not an idiot. You may as well have a '*I heart Connie Marsden*' tee on," he sniggers, covering his mouth with his hand as he continues to laugh.

"Don't be a dick man, you're the one who always has my back with things like this," I sigh, angrily shaking the mouse of my computer to wake it up.

"Mate, I'm only reacting to you..." he gives me a playful wink and I feel my shoulders sag with ease as I relax a little.

"Sorry."

"No need to apologise, just own it, we can all see it... we saw it when we came to visit you."

"Yeah?" I ask, his comment piquing my interest.

"Yeah, she seems good for you man... a little young for my liking, especially as she is my daughter's age..." he frowns and I shrug.

"I don't see her as a twenty-two-year-old..." saying it

out loud makes realisation smack me round the face, dazing me.

"But her dad might..." Titus leans forward, drumming his fingers on the desk.

"Her dad doesn't need to know," I shake my head from side to side, my defensive wall slowly building back up.

"He will know, what's going to happen when she decides to take you home?" Titus leans back into the chair, and I see the smug look on his face. "Hi Dad," he mimics Connie's voice, "this is my boyfriend, Kaleb, Kaleb, this is my daddy, Killian," Titus belly laughs and I feel rage consume me. "Oh, hi Kaleb, thanks for keeping an eye on my daughter, how's the money in the bank? Bought anything nice?" he continues as he stands. He leans over the desk and swats me round the back of the head with his hand.

"Wake up and smell the roses, this isn't going to work out. You either need to come clean and tell all... or you need to just say goodbye to her." Titus fists his hands deep into his light grey suit pants, his head dipped slightly. "Either way you're going to hurt her."

"I can't say goodbye," I choke out, fear creeping up my throat, clawing at it.

"Then you better put your big boy pants on and tell her," he gives me a small shrug, his head cocking to the side, "she'll find out soon enough," he sighs before he turns and walks out my office, closing the door behind him.

"Fucking Titus," I groan, ignoring his shitty warning.

I pull my phone out to message Connie but realisation swarms me, she doesn't have a phone. Sighing, I push away from my desk. Locking my computer, I grab my wallet and cell and head into the main office.

Nate looks over his computer screen and gives me a smile.

"I'm popping out to grab some lunch and a phone, fancy joining me?" I ask as I approach his desk. He looks down at his watch and nods.

"Yeah, let me grab my coat."

I step towards the coat rack and grab my own coat before passing Nate his. Nate is the shortest of the group and always refers to himself as the *little* guy, but from what I have heard from his past lover, Nate is not a *little* guy. I snort a laugh at the memory, causing a blinking Nate to stare at me.

"What?" he asks.

"Nothing bud, come on, let's go before the other two of the groovy gang want to join us," smirking, we walk towards the elevator and wait.

Nate side eyes me, his brows furrowed.

"You're being weird."

"Am I?"

"You sure are."

I shrug my shoulders up and step into the elevator, Nate following.

WALKING INTO APPLE, I APPROACH ONE OF THE WORKERS. A younger woman with a huge grin on her face.

"Hi, welcome to Apple, how can I help ya'll today?"

"Hi," I smile, pulling my leather gloves off and stuffing them in my black coat pocket, "I need an iPhone 14 please, in rose gold if you have it?"

The young girl taps on her iPad and her smile grows before she lifts her eyes to meet mine. "Yup, I've got that, what size storage?"

"The biggest you do."

"Perfect, I'll get that put behind the cashier desk for you."

"Can you also add an iPad and MacBook Air please? All in the same colour if you have it."

"Same with the storage?" her eyes alight with dollar signs, Nate just turns to look at me, gawking.

"Please," I give her a smile.

"Lovely, sir. That's all done, your items will be behind the desk, and I'll take payment from you now if that's okay?"

I nod, reaching inside my coat and pulling out my wallet from my inside pocket. Sliding out my black Amex, her eyes widen.

"American Express, okay?" I smirk.

"Amex is more than okay."

"Perfect," I reach out and insert my card and wait. The receipt prints and she tears it off then hands my black card back to me.

"That's all done sir."

"Thank you..." my eyes drift to her name badge, "James."

"The pleasure is all mine," she spins round, her long red hair swishing as she bounds away.

"Well, I bet her commission will be nice," I say with humor lacing my voice, shoving the receipt into my wallet, turning to face Nate but he isn't there. "Nate?" I look round the shop, but I can't see him. I tsk, walking over to collect my bag of goods and head out of the shop. I look down the sidewalk and see him leaning against a wall, scrolling on his phone.

"Everything alright?" I ask, sucking in an intake of

breath, the cold air filling my lungs, I dip my head to try and get into Nate's eye line.

"Yeah, fine," his tone is blunt.

"Why did you come outside?" we begin walking back towards the office, Nate quieter than usual.

"Just needed some air."

"Okay," I nod to myself, not wanting to push him anymore. One thing I've learnt with Nate, you don't push him out of his comfort zone. Because once he snaps, he blows like a gasket.

We walk in comfortable silence back to the office. Nate shrugs his jacket off, hanging it up then sitting at his desk, he pushes his earphones in and that's how he stays until five p.m. Uneasiness swarms me that I've upset him somehow, but I know deep down it isn't me. Maybe he did just need some air.

I don't let it consume me anymore, I had work to catch up on and I was desperate to get home and see *my* girl.

WALKING INTO THE LOBBY OF THE APARTMENT, I LOOK ROUND FOR her, but I don't see her.

"Connie?" I call out and I'm not waiting long when I see her walk down the stairs, her hand gliding down the handrail, her beautiful face lighting up with her pretty smile. "Hey baby," my voice is low as she stands on the bottom step, I close the gap between her and pick her up, inhaling her heavenly scent. "I got you a present."

"You did?" she asks surprised as I put her down gently and I nod, passing her the shopping bag.

She looks down, before her beautiful green eyes find mine, glassy.

"Kaleb," she whispers, opening the bag and gasping.

"I thought you might be missing a phone... it's a new number."

"Thank you," she throws her arms around my neck, still clinging to the bag and my arms wrap around her delicate waist.

"You're so welcome."

She pulls away from me and my body aches at the loss of her.

"How was your day?" she asks, placing her bag of goodies down on the bottom step and hopping off, walking close to me as we head into the kitchen.

"Long," I groan, rubbing the back of my neck to try and ease the tension.

"I missed you," she whispered, just as Doris walks round the corner.

"Not as much as me, kid." I mumble loud enough that only she hears and a small smile creeps onto her perfectly plump lips.

"Hungry?" Doris asks as she pulls the large, heavy double doors to the fridge open.

"Famished," my eyes darken as they rake up and down my pretty girl. She is wearing yoga pants and one of my tees. Fuck, I would pay to have her in my tees every single day.

I watch as the blush that I have grown to adore pinches her cheeks.

"Salmon okay, Kaleb?" Doris asks, spinning to face me, cocking her brow.

"Yup," I nod, locking my fingers together as I rest over the breakfast bar, fighting the urge to pull my gaze so I can look at Connie. She's a dangerous habit, a torturous addiction, an unstoppable craving. It didn't matter how

278

much I told myself we were bad for each other, I was like a moth to an open, naked flame when it came to her.

Swallowing down the thickening lump in my throat, fear creeping deep inside of me at the thought of having to come clean, but I didn't want to. Because as soon as those words leave my lips, I knew I was going to lose her forever and I was too selfish to do that yet. I didn't want her out of my life, now I had her I didn't want to let her go. I know that was wrong of me, yet I didn't want to do anything about it.

"Kaleb," Connie's angelic, sweet voice pulled me from my sombre thoughts.

"Yeah," I stand tall, stretching my back up and giving the lower part of it a rub.

"Doris asked if you had a good day back at work." I lazily move my eyes between Connie and Doris.

"It was good, took me a while to get back into the swing of it but once I got my head down it was like I never left," I take the glass of water from the middle of the breakfast bar and take a small sip just to wet my lips, I have no idea why but suddenly my throat feels dry.

"That's good, you will be back to it in no time, I have no doubt. How are the boys?" Doris asks as she potters about the kitchen, prepping dinner.

"Yeah okay, Keaton kept his distance which was a little unnerving but needed. Went for lunch with Nate and Titus dropped in, we had a little..." I stilled for a moment, clearing my throat softly to not make it seem intentional... and failing.

"Excuse me for a moment," Connie dips her head and walks out the room, but by the time I go to call after her she is already gone.

"Shit," I curse under my breath and I see Doris'

furrowed brow. "She is going to think I didn't want her listening to my conversation."

"Did you?" she goes about her task.

"I didn't mind, but it's not something I wished to discuss in front of her if I am being honest."

"Why, was something said?"

"No," my tone is clipped and curt but I don't mean it to be.

"Then why are you worrying?" she stops in her tracks and stares me down.

"I'm not," I shuffle on the spot from foot to foot. I exhale heavily and drop my head.

"Kaleb," Doris' voice is soothing. My eyes meet hers and I can see the concern that is filling them.

"I'm okay," I nod, "just been a day."

She nods, going back to coating the salmon in a dressing.

"How is Arizona?"

"Titus didn't say, I didn't ask."

The tray clatters loudly as she places it in the hot oven and begins prepping the vegetables.

"Go and see Connie," she urges me, and I don't have to be told twice before I turn on my heel and climb the stairs two at a time.

I hesitate, hanging back outside her bedroom door. Lifting my hand to knock, I shake my head from side to side and push the door open to see her sitting in the middle of her bed, her legs crossed underneath her as she sits typing on her laptop.

"All set up then?" I ask her, edging closer to her but cautiously. Connie has a temper, and I did not want to get on the bad side of her.

"Yup," she chirps, not even looking at me, she just keeps her gaze forward.

"Connie."

"Don't need an explanation, I can tell when I am not wanted Kaleb. I'm not a child, you do not have to tiptoe around me acting all delicate and shit."

Rage burns through my veins.

"It's not like that."

"No?" This time she turns to look at me, a small crease in her forehead from her frown lines.

"It was just work shit, nothing for you to worry about and it has no concern around you."

"But yet it did Doris?"

"Doris knows the ins and outs of my work life Connie; I don't want to drag you into the shit I have to deal with on a daily basis."

"I know, but to stop mid conversation and let out a stupid, little cough..."

"Yes, I agree, I shouldn't have done that..." I drop my head, ashamed of myself.

"I get there are times you aren't going to want me to listen in... just give me a heads up." She slips off the bed, stalking towards me, her tongue swiping across her bottom lip. "I get you have *important* things you have to talk about... Captain."

"Captain?" my brow cocks high as my neck cranes, looking down at her,

"Sorry, would you rather sir?" she bats her fucking eyes at me, pressing her tight little body up against mine. My hands move to the curve of her ass, squeezing through her yoga pants.

"No, baby, I think I prefer Captain."

"So do I, *Captain,*" she purrs and my cock is straining against my tight suit pants.

"Fuck," I rasp, gliding my hands up the side of her body and cupping her face, lowering my lips to hers but she shakes her head from side to side, pressing her hands against my chest and pushing me away.

"Wh..." but she presses her finger to my lips.

"Shh," one corner of her lip lifts as she breaks into a smirk before falling to her knees.

My pulse quickens, dancing under my skin. Her greedy hands pull at the button of my pants, tugging them down. Sucking in a breath as I watch her eyes widen as her fingers stroke up and down the underside of my length. A blanket of coldness covers me, causing a slight shiver to dance up and down my spine. Edging forward, her tongue flicks across my tip, my cock bobbing as she licks the pre cum from me.

My fingers twitch, unsure where to put them. She hollows her cheeks, her eyes on mine as she slowly presses her plump lips against my swollen head and slips down my thick length.

I groan, my head tipping back as pleasure rips through me, my whole body vibrating causing my nerve endings to spark and fuse.

"Shit," my hand moves to her hair, bunching a fistful of her soft brown hair in my grasp as I pull her head back and push her further down my cock, expecting her to gag as I fill her but she doesn't. "Such a good girl," I smirk down at her, rocking my hips forward into her hot, wet mouth.

My eyes roll in the back of my head, her fingers grip the base of my cock as she glides her hand up and down my length, her lips meeting her hand as she continues to suck me.

"Shit, Connie," I pant, my grip tightening in her hair, pulling her off me but holding her head back so she has no choice but to look at me. Wrapping my fingers around my throbbing cock, I stroke myself slowly, not lifting my eyes from hers for a single second. "Do you see what you do to me, baby?" I rasp, my voice tight as I try to hold off my impending orgasm.

"I do Captain," she mewls, her lips parting as she reaches out for me, her hand replacing mine as she swallows me deep.

"Fuck," my jaw tightens, my back teeth grinding as I squeeze my eyes shut. "I'm going to cum."

She widens her mouth, flattening her tongue on the underneath of me as I explode, spurting my cum down the back of her throat, my cock pumping and twitching as I empty inside her sweet mouth.

She sits back on her knees, a proud smile on her face as she wipes the corners of her mouth with her fingers.

"How much longer do I have to wait before I can taste you?" I groan, palming my aching cock.

"Only a couple more days, Captain," she winks, pushing to her feet before scrambling towards the bed but I lunge forward, wrapping my arms around her waist and tugging her back towards me so her back is flush with my front.

"Not so fast," I smirk into her hair, "I haven't even kissed you yet."

She stops wriggling in my arms, slowly turning to face me. Her head cocks to the side as her eyes fall to my lips.

"What you waiting for?" her breath on my face intoxicates me.

Cupping her cheek with one hand, whilst the other wraps round her and rests on the small of her back, I lower my lips over hers softly. This doesn't need to be hot and heavy; I just want to feel every moment of this kiss through to my soul.

AFTER DINNER, WE LAY ON THE BED WATCHING *TANGLED*. I LAY behind her, her body close to mine as my hand rests softly on her stomach. Connie's cramps were back so I grabbed chocolate and told her she could choose the film, so now we're watching Rapunzel and Flynn Ryder. I can't even pretend that I am mad, I'm a sucker for a fairytale.

She sighs when Rapunzel is in the boat, watching the lanterns.

"What is it?" I prop myself up and look down at her, her eyes glued to the television.

"One thing I loved about the Hamptons were the clear night skies..."

"They were something weren't they?"

"I miss looking at the stars," she turns her head back to look over her shoulder at me, "don't you?"

My eyes soften and I nod, but the truth was I didn't. Because who needed a clear night sky when I could see the constellation of stars in her eyes whenever I looked at her.

"Can we go back?" she whispers.

"Of course, baby," I lean down and kiss her on the tip of her nose, "soon."

She smiles, lingering for a moment before turning over and watching the film again. I snuggle into her, my face buried in her hair and that's how we stay for the rest of the evening.

CHAPTER FORTY-THREE
CONNIE

THE LAST COUPLE OF WEEKS HAD FLOWN BY, I WAS STILL LIVING with Kaleb and truthfully, I never wanted to leave. We were still sneaking around like teenagers, stolen glances across the room whenever we were in company, our fingertips brushing as we walked past each other; the air crackling between us, a magnetic force field that surrounded us. I knew Doris knew, but still playing along with Kaleb was fun. I loved feeling the fire burn through my veins and the heat blossoming between my thighs from just a grazing of our fingertips. No one else knew what was going on. He was my secret, I was his.

I still hadn't set up the phone that Kaleb bought me, it felt like a piece of the old me and I didn't know if I was ready to go back there just yet. I was enjoying finding myself again and having the fresh start that I so desperately needed, I just didn't know how much I needed it.

Closing my bedroom door, I let out my bated breath. Kaleb was in a meeting until late, so I was going to get myself ready for bed and get an early night. Kaleb still sneaks into my room once Doris leaves, and as sad as it is, that is my favourite part of my day.

Flopping down onto my bed after my shower and teeth brushing, I let my mind wander. I couldn't wait to get some sort of exclusivity with Kaleb, but I was also enjoying keeping him to myself. My laptop pinged, the unfamiliar sound making my brows crease as I slowly sat up and turned to look at it sitting on my bedside table. Pushing off the bed, I grab it and slump down on the large pillows at the head of the bed, resting against the soft headboard. Lifting the laptop lid slowly, I see one notification sitting in my emails at the bottom of the toolbar.

Hesitation creeps over me, my finger hovering over the track pad.

It's most likely a welcome email. My subconscious screams.

Tapping the track pad, the email opens and my heart swells in my chest, a huge smile spreading across my lips as I see his name.

Kaleb Mills.

I swear I have never opened an email as quick as I did with this one.

From: *Kaleb Mills*
To: *Connie Marsden*
Thursday, 20:47
Subject: *I miss you xo.*

Baby, I hate that I am at work still and not with you.
I am counting down the minutes until I see you.
I have no idea if this email still exists, but if it does
then just give me a quick reply if you can.

Love, Kaleb xx

My smile only grows as I hit reply. I hover over his email to see if it's his company one, but it's not. It's a personal one. I know he works in insurance, but he has never delved into what kind. I shake the intrusive thoughts from my head.

From: *Connie Marsden*
To: *Kaleb Mills*
Thursday, 20:55
Subject: *RE: I miss you xo.*

Damn it, you found me. I didn't even know this email address was still live, but that's the joys of the World Wide Web, nothing is ever gone once posted. Slightly off subject there, sorry.
I miss you too, can't you just sneak out? Do you really need to be there? I mean, how can you speak about insurance for this long?
My door will be ajar, your side of the bed empty and ready for you. But can I ask for one thing?
Wake me up with a kiss when you're home.

Love,
Connie xx

I hit send, the whoosh indicating that the email has sent. I drum my fingers in a rhythm on my laptop as I wait, and within what feels like seconds he replies.

From: *Kaleb Mills*
To: *Connie Marsden*

Thursday, 20:56
Subject: *RE: I miss you xo.*

I promise to wake you with a kiss, love xo.

I sigh, slowly closing the lid on my laptop when I decide against it and push it back open instead. I hold my breath as I stare at the internet search engine. I type my name in, my heart thumping as I see all the suggested search topics, my eyes moving from side to side quickly as I read the lies. It was too much. Slamming the lid down, I reach over the bed and slip the laptop underneath it.

That was enough internet for tonight. Jumping from my bed, I head for the walk-in wardrobe and dress in cotton pyjamas. Okay, they weren't the sexiest, but they were comfortable.

Anxiety bubbles away deep inside of me, like it does whilst I am waiting for Kaleb. We took our first few times slow, and Kaleb, I feel, still hasn't shown me just *how* he can fuck, but I am grateful. I get myself worked up sometimes and worry that I am *broken*. That there is something *wrong* with me because of what Tryst did to me. Part of me will always be scarred, even though they're not visible, they run deep so I can feel them. Like a knife being pushed into my windpipe, choking me.

But Kaleb always understood.

He *never* pushed me. I wanted him to make me forget everything, but sometimes, he couldn't. I get too in my head, too consumed by the demons that plagued me from my past, and on the days it all got too much and he couldn't get me out of my head and forget everything, he held me tight until the wave of anxiety left me. He never let me go.

If it wasn't for Kaleb, I would have never made it

through these last few months. I would have wound up down the same path as Tryst, because without Tryst, I had nothing. I gave my heart and soul to that man, but he destroyed me, piece by piece and now Kaleb is piecing me back together little by little. He saved me. He never questioned my emotions, never made me feel like a burden to him.

Sighing heavily, I pull back the covers and slip under them, my body feels heavy suddenly. Snuggling down into the soft mattress, my eyes flutter shut. I tried to fight it, but I couldn't. I gave into the sweet solitude of sleep.

I am gently woken when I feel the mattress dip, a warm body slipping behind me and I smile. "Hey, you," my voice is muffled and full of sleep. I will for my eyes to open but they're too heavy.

"Hey, my baby," his face nuzzles into my hair, I feel his shoulders rise as he inhales deeply and takes in my scent.

"What's the time?" I breathe, shuffling back into his body, his arms draping over me and pulling me closer to him in a tight embrace.

"Just gone midnight," the rasp of his voice is thick, I can tell he is tired.

"Oh," I just about manage, my voice slow as sleep threatens to take me once more. I feel his fingers clutch my chin as he turns my head backwards, he shifts onto his elbow and lowers his face slanting his lips over mine. A soft moan vibrates in my throat as his kiss intoxicates me. His lips move across my upper lip, to my nose and up the bridge until his full lips land on my forehead.

"Now sleep, my sweet girl," he whispers.

"Goodnight Kaleb," I whisper back, my soul and heart so full I'm scared they will explode at any second.

CHAPTER FORTY-FOUR

KALEB

I WAS READY FOR MY WEEKEND AWAY WITH CONNIE, WORK HAD been kicking my ass and we were still no closer to finding out what happened to Tryst. We know he didn't kill himself, but Connie doesn't know any different. She has grieved the loss of her ex through suicide. I wanted to keep this from her as long as I could, but the weight of carrying all these secrets round with me was bringing me down. I want to come clean, but the crippling fear that she will leave is too much. What she doesn't know can't hurt her, she's already had too much hurt in her life and I don't want to be another one to cause that.

"Did you hear me?" Keaton asks, flicking me on the forehead. I frown, rubbing where he touched and swatting his arm.

"Idiot."

"You've been in *LaLa land* for the last ten minutes, care to share with the rest of the class?" his snarky tone gets my back up instantly. His head cocks to the side, his eyes slanted slightly as his lips twist into a lopsided smirk.

"Yes, I heard you," my jaw tightens as it clenches, my

blood boiling. Fuck, I love my brother, but he infuriates me at the same time. We have some weird twin shit, like I know exactly what he is thinking and feeling. And I know he feels the same as me but it's like a love and hate thing. A very thin line between us that is so easily crossed. More on his part than mine. He likes to push my buttons in the worst way, gets under my skin and has me in a blind rage ninety percent of the day.

But I would die for that fucker. Every single time.

"So, what are your thoughts on it?"

"On what?" There is no point lying, I may as well admit defeat. I wasn't fucking listening to a single thing they said.

"So, you wasn't listening," Keaton's lips twist and I can't help but smirk back.

"Nah," I drop my head, laughing and shaking my head from side to side.

"Right, let's get back on track then shall we." Titus claps as he stands up, his deep voice booming round the room.

"Let's," I cough, shuffling in my seat and silencing my thoughts for a moment whilst I listen.

"I have been contacted by someone, his daughter is in a bit of a situation with the Knight brothers..." Titus trails off, his eyes scope around the room but then stop on mine. "I believe you have spoken to him before." His eyes widen a little, his fingers locking together as he lets his hands rest in front of his groin.

"Have I?" I ask a little confused, my brows knitting as I sit tall in my chair. I was clueless.

"You have indeed," Titus breaks eye contact, looking down at the piece of paper before his eyes penetrate through mine.

The room falls silence and confusion fills me, but so

does dread. Because the next name that left his lips was not somebody I thought would ever ask for help.

From what I heard, he never needed help. He was *the help*.

I swallow thickly, my palms slightly sweaty as I wait with bated breath.

"Xavier Archibald."

"Fuck," I mutter, rubbing my hand down my face. I don't scare easily, but something about the guy installs an ice-cold fear inside of me.

"Yeah..." Titus sighs, "fuck."

"And what does he want from us?" I lean forward in my chair, crossing my leg over the other.

"Protection for Amora."

"From the Knight brothers?" I reach for my coffee cup and take a mouthful of the now cold coffee, screwing my face up.

Titus nods, then points at Nate. I twist in my chair to face Nate. He fumbles with his laptop, then pushes his glasses up his nose as he hits some keys, connecting his screen to the large screen in the meeting room.

My eyes narrow on the image of the three young guys who are on my screen. I scoff.

Twisting back round to look at Titus, I raise a brow.

"And we're worried about these punks because..."

"Because believe it or not, these *punks* are ruthless and it seems that Xavier crossed the wrong people when he killed their dad."

"Well... fuck," I rub my chin.

"The Knight brothers are from a small underground gang in London," Nate chirps and our attention turns back to him. He runs his fingers through his hair, "They have the power of their dad's men underneath them; he was known as the King Pin and for whatever reason, Xavier took him down after an anonymous job came in."

Keaton stands, pushing his hands deep in his pocket as he paces the room and whistles through his teeth.

"Our job..." Titus begins, "if we decide to take it on..."

"How much?" Keaton asks, stopping in his tracks as his dark gaze averts to Titus.

"$800,000."

I cough. My eyes widening as I spin to look at Titus.

"Fuck," I whisper, turning to eye Nate and Keaton. Keaton's brows knit before his eyes fall to his feet.

Nate sits back in his chair, linking his fingers together and letting his hands sit in his lap.

"Ask for a million," Keaton pipes up and I scoff.

"You're delusional. Is eight hundred thousand not enough for you Keaton?" Titus gripes, rolling his shoulders forward and placing his hands palm down on the conference table.

"You don't have kids do you Keaton?"

My eyes volley back and forth from Keaton to Titus. I sit back and try to stop the smile from spreading across my lips.

"Is that a rhetorical question?" Keaton quips, tilting his head back and laughing softly.

"Imagine not having any money to hire someone to protect your daughter, what would you do?" Titus' voice is low and slow, but you can see the rage in his eyes as they burn into Keaton.

"I would go to the end of the world to get them, then I would burn it all to the ground."

Titus smirks. "Yeah, you would burn the world to the ground," Titus repeats, "and I would sell my soul, no *give* my soul to the devil for my daughter's safe return. Xavier is in the position to pay us a generous payment, and honestly, I don't even want to take the money. I just want Xavier's daughter safe." Titus stands tall.

Me and Nate nod and Keaton steps towards Titus, patting him on the back before standing next to him.

"What does he want us to do exactly?"

"He wants us to keep tabs on her phone, laptop, socials..." his eyes lift to Nate, "Nate, that's your expertise so I want you on it as soon as possible."

Nate gives a tight nod, his lips twisting as he starts tapping his laptop keyboard.

"Keaton," Titus looks to his side, Keaton looking up at him, "I want you keeping tabs on those fuckers, do what you need to do. We just need to make sure they don't get her, because I am scared to death that if they get her, we will never get her back." Keaton says nothing, he pulls his cell from his inside pocket and starts tapping the screen.

"I think we should book a flight, get her here. We can put her on a private jet, Titus, you can go over and get her? We're too far away to do anything if needed..." Keaton rambles.

"Look into it, let me know as soon as you can," Titus nods, Keaton nodding back and heading out of the meeting room to disappear into his office.

"And Kaleb," I spin in my chair, leaning back and giving him a smile.

"Yes, sweetie pie."

"Do nothing, you already have one girl you need to look after, this one is on me." And with that, Titus follows Keaton's footsteps and leaves the room.

"Oh right, like that is it," my brows raise, sitting high in my head as I turn to face Nate, but he doesn't look at me, he is too focused on his task. "Am I not relevant anymore?" I look around the room when Nate looks up at me.

"You're relevant, just not on this case," he scrunches his nose up then pushes his glasses back up his nose before his eyes re-focus on his screen.

"Excellent." My voice echoes round the room, sarcasm lacing my tone as I push out of my chair in a strop and grab my coat and bag to head for the elevator.

"Where you off to?" Titus calls out just as I push the button for the elevator. I spin and flip him off.

"Home," my tone is flat and dull as my eyes scan past the three of them, "where I am *relevant*."

As soon as I am home, my bag is dropped to the floor, my coat thrown over the table in the lobby and I climb the stairs two at a time to get to my girl. Pushing the door wide open to see her room empty, I hear singing, and I'm pleasantly surprised at how sweet and angelic her voice is. A soft belly chuckle tickles the back of my throat. The corners of my lips lift as I twist my lips, fighting the smirk that is threatening to play across my mouth. Pushing the ajar door, I pop my head round to see her in the bath.

"Baby," I call out, but she doesn't respond and the smile I have been fighting has come out in a full, teeth bearing grin. She has her wireless headphones on, singing along to *Another Love – Tom Odell.*

I lean against the doorframe, my arms crossed against my chest and just watch her, counting in my head to see how long it will take her to notice me.

One.

Her eyes are closed, her head is swaying from side to side to the beat.

Two.

Her arms come up, her small hands open and her fingers spread as her fingers tap the air.

Three.

Her beautiful face scrunches up, her lips parting and her brow furrowing as she gets ready to belt the notes round the tiled bathroom.

Four.

She sits up, bubbles covering her silky, wet skin in all the places I am desperate to see and feel beneath my fingertips as she curls her fingers in front of her lip to form a microphone.

Five.

She fucking screams out the chorus. And that's when I realise, she doesn't sound like a screeching cat, or an angel being choked, she sounds phenomenal.

My smile drops from my lips, my jaw slacking and my eyes widen.

I've lost count.

That's when she looks at me.

Wide eyed, crimson pinched cheeks and a goofy smile on her face.

Shit.

And that is when I realise that I am completely, irrevocably, in love with her.

CHAPTER FORTY-FIVE

CONNIE

KALEB'S FINGERS LACE THROUGH MINE, HIS THUMB RUBBING across the back of my hand in a soothing manner. Every time this man touches me, my soul alights with a burning ember. I have never felt as free as I do with him now. I always felt like a caterpillar awaiting to grow and break free from its cocoon and become a beautiful blue butterfly, then finally spread my wings and fly away.

My life before was the cocoon.

Kaleb was my life after.

"You okay darling?" he asks, the rasp in his voice causes heat to swarm between my legs.

"Yeah, just looking forward to getting away for the weekend and spending some time with just you," I nod, turning my face to look at him as he drives us to the Hamptons. I was looking forward to going back to *our* place. The place where he protected me and comforted me even when I didn't know I needed him to. Taking me back to the place where I began to fall in love with him. It was our place, my *favourite* place. The place that feels more home to me than New York.

"Me too, baby." He smiles, lifting the back of my hand to his lips as he brushes his lips across my sensitive skin. My heart flutters.

"I think I need to call my dad soon," I nibble my bottom lip, breaking my eyes from him as I focus out the windscreen.

"Yeah?" Kaleb clears his throat before answering.

"Yeah," I sigh happily, "I need to clear the air between us, I've frozen him out for long enough..." I trail off for a moment, my mind ticking with the flashbacks of my dad telling me that Adele was my birth mom. My stomach churns with nausea, bile clawing at my throat, but I swallow it down, the acid burning.

"That's good," Kaleb's tone is flat, and I sense I've missed something.

"What's wrong?" I pull my hand from his, turning in my seat as I question him.

He stays quiet for a moment as he drums his long fingers on the steering wheel then a heavy, deep sigh leaves him. I watch as his chest falls and his shoulders sag.

"You're scaring me," I whisper, tears pricking my eyes.

"No, no, baby," he ushers, his hand reaching for mine and scooping it in his. "Nothing to be scared of," he shakes his head from side to side.

"Then what is it Kaleb?" my voice is shaky as I try and hold off the tears that are threatening to fall.

"Everything is going back to normal, and I'm just not *ready* for it to go back to the way it was before. I'm being selfish..." he stalls as the car rolls to a halt at the lights. He turns to look at me, "I know I'm being an ass, but I have been so used to just having you to myself that I don't want things to go back."

A smile pulls at my lips as I shake my head from side to side.

"Mr Mills, you're stuck with me. Fact." I squeeze his hand tight, "But I need to do this for me, for my journey. I've had a do over and I need my family back in my life..." my eyes well, "all of them."

"I know baby, and do you know what, I don't think I have even said it before now and that guts me to my core but " he leans across the centre of the car, cupping my face as he pulls me towards him so our lips are close. "I am so fucking proud of you," he breathes, his minty breath filling my senses as he kisses me softly only for us to be interrupted by the sound of a horn. Kaleb sits tall, holding his hand up in the rearview mirror to apologize for stalling and not driving when the lights changed to green.

I giggle and relax a little in my chair only to be filled with confusion when we miss the turning we should be taking.

"Kaleb?" I whisper as I watch our turning disappear.

"Yes darling?"

"Where are we going?"

"It's a surprise."

My insides bubble with excitement, but also slight apprehension.

Kaleb taps his phone as we sit at another set of traffic lights and a familiar song begins to fill the car and my heart drums in my chest. *Hunger – Ross Copperman.*

"I love this song," I choke, my eyes staring at the screen in Kaleb's *Mercedes* SUV.

"I know," his hand finds mine once more, his fingers lacing through mine as he brings my wrist to his lips and places a soft and delicate kiss at the point where my pulse races under my skin, which only makes it quicken more.

ASHLEE ROSE

The rest of the car journey is in comfortable silence and my eyes bug when Kaleb pulls through a barrier that looks private.

"What are you doing?" I ask as I take in the surroundings. Widening my eyes when I see the private jet sitting on the tarmac. "Is this yours?" I snap my head to look at Kaleb as he rolls the car to a halt in front of the tarmac and an impeccably dressed man opens his car door.

"Mr Mills," the stranger smiles a knowing smile at Kaleb as he hands the keys over.

Kaleb is round my side within a flash, opening my door, holding his hand out for me to take which I do, gladly.

"What are we doing here?" I ask another question seeing as he hasn't answered a single one yet.

"We're going for a weekend away," he wiggles his brows, pulling me into him as his hand wraps around my back and holds me close. His lips hover over mine before kissing me. I don't want to move from this moment, I want to stay here with the cool air wrapping around us, the sound of the jet engines whirling in the background as everything else blurs into nothing. It's just me and him in this little pocket of perfectness.

Sitting on the private jet, a young air hostess comes over and offers us both a glass of champagne. I take one gladly and smile as Kaleb takes his.

"Thank you," his eyes don't leave mine, but as I take a sip of my bubbles I eye the air hostess who curtly nods her head and turns on her heel, disappearing down the aisle. In all my romance novels you always see the other women drooling over the lead female's man, but not this girl, she didn't even bat an eye lid at him.

"So, where are we going?" I shuffle in my seat, pulling on my seatbelt to tighten it. This jet is a lot bigger than

Tryst's; the seats are wider apart, and these are more like sofas than individual chairs. My heart constricts against my chest.

"You'll find out in just under three hours," he winks, taking his own mouthful of champagne.

"You tease."

"Oh baby, you've not even met the tease in me yet." He edges forward, perching on the edge of the lavish chair.

I smirk, uncrossing my legs as I let my eyes roam up and down his body. I will never get over how deliciously handsome he is.

"Miss Marsden, are you undressing me with your eyes?" he smirks, his eyes hooding in darkness and my insides twist.

"Maybe, what you going to do about it, Mr Mills?"

I hear the guttural moan that vibrates deep in his throat and my cheeks flush as heat swarms between my thighs. Pressing my thighs together to try and relieve a little of the tension that is growing.

"Oh, I can do a lot about it... we're on my plane. *My* plane." He edges closer to me, his large hand reaching for my knee, his fingers digging into my skin. The burn radiates through his fingertips, spreading slowly and teasingly across my skin.

Our moment is interrupted when we hear the pilot speak.

"Mr Mills, Miss Marsden, welcome aboard. Our flight time is two hours and thirty minutes, give or take. Conditions are clear, the sun is shining on this cool autumn morning here in New York. So, sit back, relax and enjoy the flight."

"Oh we will," Kaleb's smooth voice makes my skin pebble, his fingers still digging into me.

He reaches with his spare hand for his glass of champagne, bringing the glass to his lips as he takes a small mouthful, but all the time not lifting his eyes from me. The plane accelerates down the runway before we're climbing through the clouds. I mirror him, swirling my champagne in my glass before taking a mouthful to dampen my suddenly dry throat.

The ding indicates it's safe to move around, the air hostess smiles at us as she approaches, Kaleb finally pulls his eyes from mine, and I feel like I can breathe easy again.

"Would you or your girlfriend like anything Mr Mills?"

"No thank you, we're going to take a little rest in the state room," Kaleb slices his dark eyes back to mine and I swallow hard, sparks of excitement shooting through me.

"Of course," she dips her head, nodding before turning and walking away.

"Kaleb," I breathe, my cheeks flaming.

"Have you ever been fucked whilst flying, baby?"

I shake my head from side to side, draining my champagne flute.

"Good," his voice is low as he stands, placing his glass on the small table then taking mine from my fingers. He helps me up, laces his fingers through mine and gently pulls me towards the bedroom all whilst my heart drums beneath my skin.

He pushes a small door open, revealing a quaint bedroom. It's neutral and bright. A small smile slips onto my lips. But that soon goes as Kaleb wraps his arms around my waist, lifting me and dropping me on the bed, his hand slipping between my legs as he pushes me up towards the headboard.

"Welcome to the mile high club, darling."

CHAPTER FORTY-SIX
KALEB

HER NAKED BODY IS COATED IN A SHEEN OF SWEAT, GLISTENING AS the sun shines through the oval windows of the plane. My fingers are wrapped round the base of her throat, my other hand wrapped around the curve of her hip as my eyes fall between us. Her hips lift and roll as she rides me at her own pace, slow and torturous.

"Fuck, darling," I rasp, my head tipping back as pleasure rains over me, my hips rocking up to meet her every movement.

"I know," she pants, her hand splayed against the warmth of my chest.

What was meant to be me fucking her turned into her riding me and making me fall even deeper and harder in love with her. *Fuck*. Did I just say I'm in love with her?

I swallow down the burn that creeps at my throat, the words coating my tongue, but I can't say them yet. Not yet.

"I will never get over how fucking good you feel," I sigh, lifting my head to watch her take all of me.

"It's all you, baby," she coos, leaning her body over

mine as her lips brush over mine. I slowly unwrap my fingers from her throat and skim them down the side of her body, cupping her full, rounded ass and press my fingers into her skin and slowly lift her up and down my hard, throbbing cock.

"Fuck," I groan, edging my lips closer to hers again as our tongues messily dance together.

She breaks away, her arms either side of my head as she lifts her upper body up and I smile up at her, lifting my head as I lock my lips around her full, pert nipple. Sucking and licking as I fuck her.

"Kaleb," she breathes, her hips slowing as I feel her pussy tighten and clench around me.

"I know sweetness, I know."

She is so close, I can feel her body tremble under my fingers as I slow my hips, lifting her to the tip of my thick cock and slowly sliding her back down me.

"Oh," she shudders, her eyes rolling in the back of her head as I do it again.

"Let me fuck you," I rasp, "how I want to, how I *need* to."

She moans, sitting up as she takes me deep and rocks her hips forward slowly.

"Please." Never did I think I would be begging someone to fuck them, to take the reins in the bedroom. But with Connie? I would kneel on hot coal, kneel on broken glass and fucking crawl to her if it meant she would say yes.

She nods, her hands cupping her breasts as she gropes and kneads them.

I sit up, wrapping my arms around her waist as I cradle her in my arms, placing hot kisses on her collarbone, trailing them up to her neck and continuing until I get to her lips and kiss her as if I am starved of oxygen and kissing her is the only way to breathe.

I gently lift her off me and lay her down. Kneeling back, I push her legs wide and my eyes fall to her pretty, plump, pussy.

A devilish smirk breaks across my lips as I lean down, my hot mouth hovering over her pussy before I swipe my tongue through her wet lips, then flick over her swollen clit.

Her hands are in my hair, her pelvis tilting and her hips gyrating over my face. Teasing a finger at her opening, I rest my head on her inner thigh as I softly glide my tongue back and forth over her clit.

"Kaleb, oh," she moans, her back arching as I continue. Her wetness coats my fingers, her pussy clenching around me and I know she is close. I lift my lips from her, her eyes falling to my glistening lips that are covered in her arousal. She pulls me up to her by my hair, my fingers still fucking her slowly as she covers her mouth with mine.

"I needed to taste you, your pussy looked so fucking good to just ignore," I mutter against her lips and her breath catches, her chest rising and falling fast. "Don't come yet, baby," I smirk as I kneel back, slipping my fingers out of her and pushing them past my lips, sucking them clean. "Fuck you taste so fucking good," I groan, letting my hand fall as I fist myself.

Her eyes widen as she watches me touch myself, her lips parting as a moan slips past.

"Oh, baby, do you like watching me pleasure myself?" I rasp, kneeling up so she can see me better as I stroke myself up and down my cock.

"Yeah," she whispers, her own fingers skimming down her body as she dips them into her hot, wet pussy and suddenly I am jealous.

"Want me to keep doing it?"

She nods eagerly, slipping her fingers from her tight

opening and swirling her arousal over her clit as she rubs softly.

"You look so fucking beautiful rubbing yourself, darling."

She pants, her hand grazing over her skin before she rolls her hard nipple in her fingers.

"Kaleb," she cries, dipping her finger back inside herself before dragging her coated fingers to her clit.

"I've got you," I groan as I reach for her hips, flipping her over on her front.

"Kaleb," panic creeps up her throat and my heart hurts.

"Do you trust me?" I ask, slipping two fingers inside her pussy, she trembles.

"Yes," she breathes, her lips pressing into her inner arm as she looks over her shoulder at me.

Removing my fingers, I wrap my fingers around her hips as I push myself into her slowly, giving her a minute to adjust. Pulling out to the tip then thrusting back into her again this time with a little more force, giving her everything she needs. I do it again, causing her to whimper, her pussy clamping around my cock, sucking me in.

"Shit," I grit through clenched teeth, removing my hands from her hips and digging my fingers into her peachy ass cheeks, pushing into them and spreading her wide. Sinking my cock into her deeper and faster, her hips move with me, fucking me as I fuck her.

"Kaleb, I'm going to come," she cries out, I lean forward wrapping my fingers round the base of her throat and pulling her up so her back is against my front and I can pound up into her.

"That's my good girl, come for me darling," I whisper in her ear as her body begins to tremble, her head falling back against my hard chest as her pussy tightens around me, her orgasm rippling through her slowly. "That's it baby, take what you need," I praise, not slowing until I feel my own orgasm brewing deep inside of me, my cock twitching. As much as I don't want this moment to stop, my orgasm splinters through me; my skin pebbling as pleasure rips into me and I throw my head back as I continue my hard pounding into her soaked cunt, roaring out.

After coming down from our bless we lay silently in each other's arms, my fingers running up and down her forearm as I draw circles on her sensitive skin.

"I could stay on here forever," she hums, smiling as she turns to face me, her eyes focused on my lips.

"Me too baby, me too," I smile back, lowering my lips to hers. "But we have a weekend to look forward to," I soothe, kissing her temple before slowly sitting up, "and we will be landing soon by the looks of it, so we better get dressed," I wink, throwing the covers back and reaching for my clothes.

"I can't wait," she beams, climbing out of bed herself.

"I promise, you're going to love it."

"I would love anything you plan," she turns to face me, her cheeks flushed as her beautiful green eyes seek out mine.

My smile grows, my lips parting to say what I have wanted to for so long, but I choke.

The moment is ruined by the captain calling for everyone to be seated for landing.

"Come," I stand at the end of the bed, holding my hand out for her to take which she does gladly, and I lead her back to our seats.

CONNIE

Climbing into the SUV that was waiting for us on the tarmac when we landed, I had no idea where we were. It was nowhere I recognised. Kaleb kept tight lipped, just smirking as he placed our luggage into the boot of the waiting car.

"You ready for our weekend?" he asks as he climbs into the back of the car and grabs my hand, cupping it with both of his.

"I am," I smile, leaning into him and resting my head on his shoulder, the driver shut the door, gave Kaleb a curt nod in the rear-view mirror before pulling off. "I don't like surprises though," I admitted, my stomach twisting, "I get anxious."

"Baby, you have nothing to get anxious about, I promise."

He turns, placing a kiss on the top of my head and my erratic heart settles slightly, but still skips a beat every once in a while, reminding me that it's found its own rhythm since Kaleb and eventually I drift off to sleep.

"Baby," I hear Kaleb's distant voice, and my eyes slowly lift, "baby, we're here."

I sit up, looking around me a little disorientated. It took me a moment or two to realise I was in the car.

"You okay?" he asks, his head dipping as he grips my chin to look at me.

"Yeah, I'm okay," I nod, nuzzling back into him for a moment. The door is pulled open, the driver standing with our luggage.

"Connie," he whispers as my eyes begin to fall heavy again.

"Mmmhm," I hum.

"Open your pretty green eyes baby," the softness in his voice swarms my insides with butterflies. He laces his fingers through mine as he slides across the seat and out of the car, taking me with him. I step out of the car, lifting my head as my feet hit the ground, my eyes bugging out of my head, my mouth agape and tears prick my eyes.

"No way," I choke, hiccupping through sobs. "Kaleb," I tear my eyes from the *Mystic Falls* sign to look at him, "Kaleb," I just about manage as a hot tear rolls down my cheek and before I can swipe it away, his thumb is there, brushing it away.

"It's all for you, baby," he faces me, his fingers still laced in mine.

"We're in Mystic Falls," I choke, my smile spreading.

"We're in Mystic Falls darling, I have no idea what sort of hold these characters, or should I say these two brothers," he rolls his eyes in an exaggerated way and I swat him which causes a laugh to roll past his lips, my chest blooms with love.

"You saved me," I turned to nudge him in the ribs, "but so did they," I wink. I break my gaze from him and look back at the road that takes us into that world.

"Let's go and have an adventure," he wraps his arm around my waist and pulls me into him, kissing my temple tentatively. I twist, pushing onto my tiptoes as I lock my arms around his neck, brushing my lips against his.

"Let's have an adventure, and Kaleb," I whisper, my breath catching at the back of my throat, "you'll never know how much this means to me, thank you." Pushing my lips softly into his, my tongue slips past his lips and suddenly, the ground feels like it falls away beneath me.

When we break, his eyes are glistening as we gaze deeply into each other's souls.

"I love you," his words ricochet off me, my heart racing as it skips a beat, and my eyes fill with unshed tears.

"I love you," my voice sounds pained, but that's because it is. I have never loved someone as fiercely as I love Kaleb.

CHAPTER FORTY-SEVEN
CONNIE

The last seventy-two hours have been a whirlwind, but the best kind. This weekend has been everything and more. I dragged Kaleb round to every part of the town. I didn't want to miss a single minute of it. My little *Vampire Diaries* heart is so full. I sigh as I zip my bag up.

"You okay, darling?" Kaleb asks as he reaches for my bag. I nod, looking round the beautiful room we're in. Kaleb couldn't understand why he couldn't find the *Salvatore Mansion*, so booked a hotel a little down the road that had the same feel.

"I am perfect," I smile at him as I step towards him, placing both my hands on his chest and kissing him. "Thank you, Kaleb."

"Anything for you, baby," he lets his arm fall as he leans into me, scooping me up, "I would give you the moon and stars, if that's what you wanted."

"All I want is you," I smile against his lips, as he walks me to the bed until it knocks me in the back of my knees, "what time is check out?" I tease.

"We've got thirty minutes."

"Let's see what you can give me in twenty minutes, Gramps."

"Gramps!?" he pulls back, his brow furrowing as he fights the smile, "I'll show you gramps, darling," he roars, throwing me to the bed as I scream. "I've changed my mind," he smirks, wrapping his fingers round my ankles and tugging me down the bed.

"Kaleb," I scream, my rumble of a laugh filling the room as he scoops me up and perches me on the edge of the cherry oak desk.

"I am so glad you've got this pretty little skirt on," he groans, falling to his knees as he pushes my legs wide, his lips pressing against my skin as he trails up to the apex of my thighs and licks through my thin, lace panties and against my clit. The feel of the material and his tongue indescribable as I curl my fingers round the edge of the desk.

"Fuck me," I whisper, trying to get him to remove his hot as sin mouth from me, but he ignores me, hooking his finger round the material that's covering me and pulling it to the side as his tongue swept through my lips, teasing at my opening before focusing on my clit.

Moans escape me, my fingers tightening as he eats me, his tongue buried deep inside of me then gliding to my clit, swirling over with the tip of his tongue and sucking.

"Kaleb," I cry, "I need more." Lifting my pelvis, my hips rotating. He groans, standing in a rush and unbuttoning his pants, pushing them down to his thighs as he fists his thick, hard cock.

"I could fucking eat your pussy all day Connie, I am fucking *addicted* to your taste." Shivers explode over my skin at his words, and I swear I feel my arousal drip through me, but Kaleb's fingers are there, swirling and filling me.

"You like my dirty mouth don't you, darling?"

I nod, mewling as I try and fight against my body as my orgasm teeters on the edge of the cliff.

"I am going to fuck you hard and fast," he promises, his lips pressing against my collar bone, nipping at the skin that covers it.

"Please," I beg.

"Beg me again, baby," he smirks as he teases me, rubbing the head of his cock through my folds, edging into me slightly before he slips out.

"Please fuck me Kaleb, I need you," I choke, my voice thick as I ignore the burn that radiates in my throat and my breath is snatched from me as he slams his cock deep inside of me. His hands press into my inner thighs, keeping my legs wide as he slips his cock in and out of me hard and fast, our skin clapping when he fills me.

"Shit," I sob, my eyes falling as I watch him fuck me, my body vibrating as pleasure bubbles.

"Your cunt is so tight, so fucking wet for me baby," he pants, digging his fingers in deeper to my skin. I watch with eager eyes as my pussy stretches around him, taking him with ease as I see my arousal beginning to show on the silky skin of his cock. I uncurl one of my white knuckled hands, and place my fingers over my clit, rubbing hard and fast, giving my body the little helping hand it needs for me to orgasm fast.

"There's a good girl, I can feel how close you are," Kaleb breathes, his eyes on mine for a moment before he watches himself fuck me, suddenly pulling out to the tip, and slowly pushing a little into me before pulling back out.

"Oh fuck," I cry out, the feelings too overwhelming, my pussy clenching as he teases me. "I'm going to..." and I can't even finish my sentence as I he pounds into me, his cock spearing in and out of me with speed, the desk rocking and creaking as he fucks me through my earth-shattering orgasm.

"Yes, fuck," he cries out, letting go of my skin; it instantly feels bruised as he wraps his hands around my hips, tugging me further off the edge of the desk as he ploughs into me, knocking the air from my lungs as I feel the sweet build-up of another orgasm that's about to crash over me like a tsunami.

"I'm going to come again," I cry as the tip of his cock rubs my g-spot.

"Let it go," he growls, his punishing pounds into me send me into oblivion as my orgasm explodes deep inside of me, covering my skin in goosebumps, Kaleb moaning with me as his own orgasm detonates, filling me full of him.

He collapses onto me, his forehead sweaty, his heartbeat racing underneath his skin.

"How long have we got left?" he pants, looking up at me, his dark brown hair flopped onto his forehead.

I smile, pushing it away from his beautiful face. "Ten minutes," I smile shyly, as he stands up, pushing himself back into his pants and fastening the button.

I go to move, and he shakes his head from side to side, dropping to his knees as he swirls his fingers in our mixed arousal and pushes it back inside of me.

"I want you full of this baby, we don't want to waste any of it now do we," he winks, as two fingers fill me causing my eyes to roll in the back of my head.

"Kaleb," I breathe.

"I know baby, just want to make sure none of it escapes," he smiles as he pulls his fingers out, leans forward and places a kiss on my bare pussy then covers it with my lace panties.

"You're so dirty," I giggle, crimson creeping on my cheeks.

"Only for you," he whispers, sucking his fingers clean, "always, only you." He smiles, helping me stand as he kisses me with everything he has. And it really was one of those ground moving, earth shaking, once in a lifetime kisses.

The ones that show you've found your soulmate. Like something in the universe finally slots into place.

BEING BACK HOME AND IN THE SWING OF LIFE MAKES OUR weekend away feel like a distant memory. A delicious, distant memory but nevertheless, a memory. Kaleb is back into the thick of work and I finally decided to turn my phone on, slowly adjusting to being connected to the world again. I need to find a job, or something because I would never be a kept woman, staying at home whilst the man works. No thank you, not for me.

Pulling a cotton, V-neck tee over my head, I tuck it into my mom jeans and scrape my brown hair into a messy ponytail. I head downstairs to find Doris when I see letters piled on the centre table in the lobby. My brows pinch, that's unusual.

"Doris?" I call out, walking past the table and into the lounge area but she isn't in there. I walk back out into the lobby and into the kitchen but, she isn't there. "Doris?" I call again but silence is the only answer I get.

Pacing back down towards the lobby I reach for the letters and gasp when I see one made out to me in handwriting. No one knows I am here apart from my father and Reese; I am assuming. I know my dad's writing, and this isn't it.

My heart races in my chest as I flip the plain white envelope over and run my finger under the fold. Pulling the sheet of paper out, I open it out and my heart fucking sinks in my chest. It's Tryst's suicide note, but the handwriting isn't Tryst's.

My hand covers my mouth as tears spring to my eyes, my throat burning as I try and swallow the growing lump that feels like it's about to suffocate me.

"Fuck!" I scream, just as the lift pings and I see Doris with concern and worry etched over her delicate face.

"Connie!?" She drops her bags to the floor and rushes to me, just as my legs buckle beneath me. As soon as her arms surround me, I choke out my sobs.

"Let me call Kaleb," she ushers, reaching around for her phone and I shake my head.

"No, no," I tremble, "I'll go to him. I can't breathe. I need air," I gasp, suddenly feeling claustrophobic and needing out.

"Okay sweetie."

"Who dropped these letters off?" I manage as I stand from the broken mess I just was, swiping my tears away angrily.

"The mail man," her brows pinch in confusion, her eyes moving from me to the letters.

"There was no stamp, I don't get it," panicked chokes leave me as I try and breathe through the tears that fall.

"Connie."

"I'm fine," I snap. "I need Kaleb," I turn to grab my coat and scarf, wrapping it round my neck and shrugging my coat on. I pace towards the elevator and slip my feet into my black, platform *Ugg* boots. Realisation coats me suddenly that I have no idea where Kaleb works.

I turn to face Doris, and she smiles softly.

"Thirty-sixth street, midtown," she gives a small nod.

"Thanks," I rush out, pressing the button continuously for the elevator whilst clutching the letter in a white knuckled grasp.

After waiting for what feels like a lifetime, the doors ping and I step inside and once the doors are closed, I crumble once more.

STANDING ON THE BUSY AND COLD STREETS OF NEW YORK WAS not what I had planned for today, but here I am trying to hail a cab to get to Kaleb. I see a taxi with its light on heading towards me and hold my hand into the road to try and gain its attention. Swooping into the sidewalk and slowing, I jump in before it has fully stopped.

"Thirty-sixth street, midtown Manhattan please." The taxi driver grunts, tapping the meter as he swings the taxi round and heads towards my destination.

I read the letter over and over, my heart shattering a little more each time. If Tryst didn't write the letter, who did? The thoughts bounce round in my head and new fears creep inside of me, if he didn't write the letter, was it actually suicide? I feel sick, my mouth feeling watery as I try my hardest to ignore the feeling of nausea that swirls deep in my stomach.

I look up, leaning to look out the windshield to see thirty-sixth street approaching, I fumble in my bag and grab some notes ready. The taxi slows and I throw him the money without checking it as I push the door open to get out onto the sidewalk. Slamming the door behind me, the taxi driver pulls away in a hurry, most likely because I overpaid him. I bend over, my hands on my thighs as I try and breathe. Nausea overwhelms me, forcing my eyes closed I slowly stand up and inhale deeply, trying desperately to fill my lungs with air.

Moments pass and so does the nausea. I open my eyes, my shaky hands clinging onto the paper as I see Kaleb's name on the door of one of the office blocks.

Stepping forward, I push through the door and walk into a small square lobby. I head for the elevator and see the company name, Mills, Spencer, King. It's the only one on the board.

Pressing the button, my heart is in my throat, my pulse thumping through my ears. The ride is short, the doors ping open, and I gain the eyes of the office. Titus and Nate see me first, Titus slowly standing from his chair as he walks towards me.

"Connie, shit," he rasps as he gets to me, his eyes scanning over my face. No doubt my mascara has bled down my cheeks, my nose red and my eyes swollen.

"Kaleb," I choke, wiping my tears away that won't stop falling.

"This way babe," Titus wraps an arm around my shoulders as he begins walking me towards Kaleb, but Keaton comes into view first.

"Connie?" he rushes over to me, making me stop in my tracks as he cups my face, lifting me to look at him. His eyes bat back and forth to mine then move to Titus, they exchange looks and I hear him before I see him.

"Baby," the panicked tone that seeps from him makes my erratic heartbeat spike. He is wrapped in a dark navy suit and a crisp white shirt, looking devastatingly handsome. I see his hand pull Keaton out the way as his hands replace his brothers. Titus gives a gentle nod and steps back, taking Keaton with him.

"Did someone do this to you? If so, who?" his voice is

low and steady, but I can see the pure rage in his eyes, his jaw clenched as he holds onto me.

I shake my head from side to side, closing my eyes as more tears begin to cascade down my cheeks. Lifting my left hand slowly, my knuckles white from the tight grasp I've had the letter in.

Kaleb's eyes drift from mine to the letter, his brows pinching before smoothing back out when the penny drops. It takes a moment before he drags his eyes back to mine.

"Where did this come from?" he asks, but his tone is clipped as he takes it from my hand.

"It was in the lobby," I hiccup through broken sobs.

I watch as the colour drains from his face, his eyes widening as he continues reading down the page.

"The fuck!" he roars, stepping back and running his hand through his hair, pacing a few steps in front of me before stalling. Realisation crashing through him like a freight train as he turns on the spot, his eyes softening as they find mine. "Baby," he chokes, rushing towards me and pulling me into his embrace, clinging onto me. "Are you okay?" he whispers, his lips brushing against my cheeks as I sob in his arms.

Kaleb's thumb swipes across my cheek, catching the tears as they roll across my skin. Holding his other hand up in the air, Titus swoops past and takes the letter before walking over to Nate.

"Who would do this?" I whisper, lifting my head.

"A sicko," Keaton shouts out, then takes a bite into an apple, the crisp sound echoing round the office. Kaleb slices his gaze over to Titus and Nate but something in his expression is throwing me off.

"Kaleb," I whisper, my eyes not leaving his and I see his jaw clench as he faces me. I volley my eyes back and forth, my gut twisting and rolling in nauseated spins. "Kal...," struggling to even get his name out past my lips, my breath shakes as I feel like the air has been snatched from my lungs, my windpipe burning as I will for the air to course through.

My teary eyes search the room when I see Titus, Keaton and Nate's eyes on me, but none of them can look me in the eye.

"What the fuck is going on?" my voice vibrates, shaking me to my core, but my question is aimed at Kaleb.

He inhales deeply, sucking in a breath.

"We've known about it for a while..." I hear Titus' voice slice through me like a sword.

"Have you?" Again, my question is directed towards Kaleb, and I can feel the betrayal ripping me apart piece by piece. I didn't care about anyone else, I only cared about him. He drops his head, and that's all the confirmation I need. "And you didn't think it was important to tell me this!?" I choke, hot tears rolling down my cheeks and the heat swarms my face.

I suddenly realise where I am, I can feel their eyes burning into me but I can't move to look at them.

"Connie... I..." Kaleb stammers over his words as he steps towards me, but I shake my head from side to side.

"Don't," I snap, the tears that prick in my eyes drying up and now all I feel is rage. Pure, venomous rage. I step towards him, lifting my hand and slap him hard against his cheek, the loud clap echoing round the room.

"Oh fuck," I hear Keaton chuckle, I snap my head round to face Kaleb and narrow my gaze on him.

"You're an asshole," I spit, stalking towards Titus before reaching for the letter and grabbing it from him.

"Connie," Kaleb calls out as I turn and march towards

the lift. I hear him behind me, reaching for me and grabbing my wrist to pull me around to face him.

"Get off me!" I shout, smacking my balled fist into his chest.

"Listen to me," he growls, not even attempting to stop me from assaulting my fists into him.

"No!" I spit, pushing off from him but I can't get out of his grip that he now has me cocooned in.

"Listen," his voice vibrates through me, "I didn't tell you because we don't know. It was my plan to tell you *everything* once I had the information," his voice lowers, softens as each word drips from his tongue.

"You hid it from me, you let me go all these weeks with me thinking Tryst took his own life? But you knew, you knew that it wasn't like that," I feel the unwanted needles beginning to prick behind my eyes again, the burn coursing through my throat as the large lump bobs up and down.

"I did it for you," he whispers, his grip slowly loosening on me.

"For me?!" my eyes widen, my voice lifting one or two octaves.

"Yes, Connie," his tone was flat as his eyes bored into mine, the tension building.

"I don't know *who* you did this for, but it wasn't me Kaleb. Don't fucking fool yourself." I see his face slip, his eyes narrowing as the crow's feet at the corners soften. His hands fall away from my body, and I don't know why, but that hurts more than the letter for a moment.

I give a gentle nod, stepping back.

"Well, that's that then." I swallow down the lump as my voice trembles, tears threatening to fall. Turning quickly, I press the button for the elevator, and I am grateful I'm not waiting long.

"Connie," Kaleb's voice brushes over me and it takes everything I have to ignore him. Stepping inside the elevator, I turn with blurry eyes to face him.

No words are spoken, the air crackles between us, but it slowly fizzles out into nothing. I feel like I am waiting for something, but I just don't know what. I inhale sharply as the doors begin to close, but Kaleb lurches forward, sticking his foot in the doors before clamping his hands round the edges.

"I don't want to lose you," his voice is thick, his eyes are bloodshot as I see the glassiness in them.

"I was never yours to lose, Kaleb," I whisper, and that admission has him stepping back, the doors closing instantly.

And once I know I am alone, I slide down the elevator wall and break, my face screwing up as the tears finally fall again.

CHAPTER FORTY-EIGHT
KALEB

I STAND NUMB AS MY EYES ARE FIXED ON THE CLOSED ELEVATOR. What the fuck had just happened? What the fuck had *I* just let happen?

One hand clasps over my mouth, the other runs through my dark, messy hair.

"Kaleb," I hear Keaton's voice and I spin to face him.

"Leave me alone," I groan, striding away but knocking my shoulder into him as I walk off and head for my office. Slamming the door behind me I sit and fester. I have no one to blame but myself. I can't even be angry with anyone but me.

I should have told her, she was right. It wasn't fair on her to have kept this to myself. I watched her mourn Tryst, I watched her rip herself to shreds over his death and blame herself in some way. Guilt consumed her for weeks, and all of this time, I knew he didn't do it. And what's even worse, I originally paid for someone to kill him. He was just beat to it.

Fuck. My heart races in my chest, skipping beats as I squeeze my eyes shut.

I hear my office door close gently, and I exhale deeply. I don't even have to open my eyes to know who it is.

Who it always is.

Titus.

As much as Keaton is my twin and I love him, Titus is my best friend and the first person I would call if I needed help.

"Kal," his voice is gruff as he drags the chair out across the floor, my eyes lifting to look at him.

I sigh, leaning back in my chair before rubbing my hands over my face, slowly dragging them down. "I've fucked up," exasperation laces my tone.

"You've fucked up," Titus repeats, his lips pulling into a thin line, lifting slightly in one corner as he nods his head.

I feel my anger bubble as I sit forward and slam my hand on the desk, hard.

"Calm down," Titus reaches forward, grabbing my hand. "Don't go down this road again," he warns, and I know exactly what he is referring to.

The one client that changed how I worked... until Connie.

"I won't, but I feel like I have just pushed her back into that world, just like I did with Ruby; I pushed her back into that monster's arms and I trusted that she was going to be okay, trusted that she wouldn't let that asshole manipulate her again but he did. Like always. Until he took her last breath, beating her to a pulp." I swallow, the images flashing in front of my eyes of her laying there.

"Kaleb," Titus' deep voice pulls me from my nightmares. My eyes slowly focus on him. "Connie's situation was different... fuck, it *is* different. Her abuser is gone, dead. He isn't coming back for her."

I nod, knowing he is right. But it doesn't ease the ache in my chest.

"What am I going to do?" I ask Titus, because since meeting Connie, she has twisted me inside out. I am nothing like I was before her.

"You're going to get on your fucking knees and beg her for forgiveness."

"I would crawl across burning embers, slice myself open with glass so she can watch me bleed out to show her how sorry I am, I would sacrifice myself for her. Sacrifice all of this." I swallow, my stomach dropping, my heart thumping. "What if she doesn't forgive me?" I whisper; that's all I can manage. The thought of losing her completely scares me, I couldn't live in this world without her.

"Then you let her go," the thick grimace masking his face makes the knife that is slowly being plunged into my chest go deeper, making it hard to breath as I gasp at the thought.

"I can't let her go."

"For her, Kaleb... you would *need* to let her go." I shake my head from side to side. "It's not about what you want buddy, it's about Connie. It's always been about Connie. It *will* always be about Connie." He sighs, pushing to his feet and standing. My eyes follow him, watching as he walks to the door, he pushes the handle down before turning to face me, "Now stop wallowing in self-pity and go find her." And with that last sentence echoing round the now empty room, he is gone.

CHAPTER FORTY-NINE
CONNIE

I HAVE NO IDEA WHERE I'M GOING, I JUST WALK. THE ICY NEW York air is harsh against my face, causing me to catch my breath several times. My whole body is numb making this walk a little easier than I would normally find it. Realisation sinks in as I stop at The Plaza, lifting my eyes to see the place that once was like home. I have nowhere to go. I toy with the idea of going inside but I'm not ready to face them yet. I'm not ready to answer questions I clearly don't know the answers to. Because what I was made to believe was that Tryst took his own life because he was so unhappy and down with it all. I always knew it didn't quite make sense; he had his moments, but he was high on life, living his dream that he always wanted and now I know that he didn't even write the suicide letter. Okay, sure, he *could* have taken his own life, then someone found him and wrote the letter to make it a little easier on his loved ones, or my deepest fears become a reality when in fact, someone took his life.

It didn't make sense. Who? Who would do this? Police ruled out foul play, didn't they? Or did Kaleb lie to me about that? I scrunch my nose up when I feel coldness on the tip. I stop in my tracks and look up to see snow beginning to fall. Sighing, I drop my head and continue walking, I needed out of my head. I need out of it all.

My heart races as I stall outside the beautiful town house, tipping my head back as I take it in. Scoffing, I step forward until I reach the steps. I have no idea why I walked here, no idea why my legs brought me here, but I know it wasn't because of my dad. No. Pushing through the black iron gate, I climb the steps and give myself a moment. My finger hovers over the doorbell, arguing with myself if this was the right thing to do or not, but before I could change my mind, my finger was on the button. The wait felt like hours, when the door finally swung open Reese's opal eyes widen, her fingers still wrapped round the edge of the door as her lips part.

"Hi," I whisper, my eyes moving from hers to the beautiful little girl sitting on her hip.

"Connie," she breathes, stepping forward and wrapping her arm around my shoulders and pulling me into her. I feel the unwanted tears prick at my eyes, but I blink them away, I wasn't going to cry again. Especially not in front of Reese, I didn't want her to see me upset.

"You're frozen!" she exclaims, pulling me into the house and closing the door behind me.

I nod, my eyes scanning round the large lobby space. Natural, warm beiges and grieges wrap round the walls and I instantly feel cosy. I shrug my coat off, then unwrap my scarf and stuff it in my coat pocket, looking for somewhere to hang it.

"Here, let me take it," she smiles at me, taking it from me and opening a door in the lobby.

My eyes are pinned to Celeste's and hers to mine. I cannot get over how much I can see myself in her, but also, how much she looks like her mom.

"Tea?" Reese's warm smile radiates as she stares at me.

"Please," I nod, following her down the long, narrow hallway that leads us to the large kitchen area. "Where's..." I struggle to finish my sentence, choking.

"Your dad? Work," she smiles, "he will be sorry to have missed you," her smile soon slips as she fills the kettle and places it on the stove, turning on the gas.

"I know, but I came to see you... not him..." I swallow the thickness down my throat as I pull a seat out at the table.

"Is everything okay?" she spins, her brows furrowed on her pretty face, Celeste grips onto her top as she shyly snuggles into her mom.

"Yeah, fine..." I trail off, tapping my fingers on the table as I pull my eyes from her and turn to look at the back yard.

"Connie," her tone is stern and I drag my eyes round to face her. Her blonde hair is pulled into a high ponytail, loose, golden blonde strands tumbling round her ears. Her petite frame is hidden behind a knitted V-neck sweater and black skinny jeans. She looks amazing.

"Reese?" I counter back at her. The corners of her lips twitch as she fights her smile.

"Let me get little miss down for her afternoon nap, I'll be five minutes, okay?" she speaks softly as the kettle begins to whistle.

I nod and watch as she walks out the room, her lips pressed against the toddler that is clinging to her, but Celeste's eyes are on me and my heart rushes through beats. *My sister.* I hear the soft, tired whines of Celeste as Reese takes her to her room.

The silence is soon replaced with the loud whistle, I push off the chair and walk towards the stove, lifting the kettle and turning the gas off then placing it back down.

Sighing, I face the room and take in the large, airy space. It has Reese's stamp all over it and I smile when I see the photos scattered across the back wall. Stepping over to them, I place my hands on my hips as I examine them.

The first one is a black and white one, Reese is smiling at the camera and my dad is kissing her on the cheek, the snow falling over them. They look so happy. The next one is of Celeste, wrapped in a swaddling blanket and a little flower headband on as she sleeps, her plump, pert lips slightly open. She looks adorable. The third picture is Reese, Celeste and my dad. Sitting under the trees in central park having a picnic. They really were the picture-perfect family. The fourth picture was me and Reese. It was the night we went to the concert to see Tryst for the first time. My heart races as I swallow the nausea down that is creeping up my throat, my stomach rolling. I tear my eyes away, spinning to see Reese enter the room.

"Hey, sorry about that," she smiles, baby monitor clutched in her hand.

"It's fine, I'm sorry about just turning up," I shrug my shoulders up, running my finger over the edge of the dining table.

"Connie," she sighs, twisting to look at me as she holds two cups on her fingers. "Never apologise, you are always welcome here, you have always been welcome here."

"I know," I whisper, suddenly feeling vulnerable. "Look..." I stammer over my words, anxiety swirling deep inside of me.

Reese steps closer, handing me my cup of tea. I smile, taking it from her, wrapping my fingers round the cup as it warms my ice-cold hands. Reese sits at the dining room table and I pull my own chair back out and sit down.

"I'm sorry for being gone for so long, sorry that I haven't made contact..." I can't even look at her as the embarrassment colours me. I feel her hand on mine and lift my head, her small hand placed on top of mine.

"Don't be sorry, we get it..." her slight hesitance has me thinking my dad *didn't* get it.

"Or you get it and Dad just had to put up with it," I smirk, sitting back in my chair and lifting my cup to my lips, taking a small sip.

"Your dad is your dad. He has been non-stop worrying about you, but knows you're in good hands."

I nod, not wanting to even think about Kaleb because I know once I do, the tears will fall and I'll have to tell all to Reese.

"Have you seen your moms at all?" she asks and I begin shaking my head before she has even finished her sentence.

"No," I breathe, "I don't even think I am ready to yet."

She nods.

"I get it," she rolls her lips, sitting back in her own chair and silence sweeps over us for a moment.

"I've just had enough, it's been one thing after another," I finally admit.

"Care to elaborate?" she pushes gently.

I puff my cheeks out, my eyes pinned to hers and I shake my head, slowly exhaling the breath that was filling my cheeks. "I will be ready... soon..." I blink away the tears that are starting to fill my eyes and I see the worry on Reese's face.

"Oh, Connie," she breathes, pushing from her chair and

rushing to my side. I stand and let her arms wrap around me as I sob into her sweater, my tears soaking through.

"Let it all out, *all* of it." She whispers as she holds me, and I have never been more grateful for her than I am now.

Once the tears stop flowing, Reese makes us a fresh cup of tea and I feel a lot better after letting the tears free fall until I had nothing left to give.

"How is Kaleb? Are you still living with him?" she asks, the rim of her cup sat on her pursed lips.

"Kaleb is..." I twist my lips, "Kaleb," I shrug my shoulders up.

"Men; pains in the asses," she smirks, and I laugh.

"How is Dad?" I finally ask, guilt wrapping its ugly hold on me.

"He is good, misses you," she winks, "but he is good, busy with the company."

"Are you still working there?" curiosity kills the cat, I also want to know about that bitch Adele.

"When I can," she glances lovingly over at the monitor, "but finding a decent child minder is hard, I struggle letting her go to *just* anyone and your dad is even worse."

I laugh, rolling my eyes, "I can imagine."

"I love working, it has been nice being home with Celeste, but my god." Reese sighs, "Being with her every single day and having no other adult interaction is *hard*."

"I bet," I mumble, "I get lonely being cooped up at Kaleb's whilst he is at work," My eyes bug out of my head at my little slip.

"Oh," she smirks, wiggling her brows up and down in a flirtatious way, "like that is it?"

"Oh my god," I whisper, my hand over my mouth as flames hit my cheeks.

"Connie! I want to know all about that beautiful man wrapped in his expensive suits."

I sigh. "It's..." I stall for a moment, looking away from her wide eyes. "Complicated," I whisper.

"It's only as complicated as you make it. Jesus, look at me and your dad and what we went through to get here," she holds her hand out, gesturing to the perfect life she is living.

"I know, and I would love all of this with him, but I think it's all over now anyway."

"So, there was a thing."

"Oh, there was definitely a thing," I nod, swallowing the lump down.

"Like, a thing *thing*," she whispers.

"Oh, yeah..." I smile.

"Well..." she whistles, sitting back and taking a mouthful of tea with a satisfied look on her face. "Maybe don't tell your dad that..."

I shake my head, "Wouldn't dream of it... plus, there is nothing to tell anymore. I need to find somewhere to live and get a job."

"We have..."

"No," I shake my head, "I *need* to do this for myself, I really appreciate the offer, but I need to move on. I have been held back since I left with Tryst, and I don't ever want that again."

"I get it," she smiles, and I see the tears shining in her eyes. *Elijah.*

"And now look at you," I sniff, feeling her grief.

"Look at me now," she chokes, swiping away a stray tear that rolls down her cheek.

"I am so proud of you," my voice wavers for a moment

but I mean it, everything she had been through and now look at her.

"Connie," she sobs, placing her head in her hands as I watch her shoulders shake. When she finally looks at me, her eyes are rimmed with tears, mascara staining her cheeks. "I have missed you, so much. Please don't leave again."

"I won't, and I was thinking if okay with you of course..."

"Yeah?" she sniffs, wiping another lot of tears away.

"Could I spend some more time with Celeste, so she gets to know her big sister and then, if you would like, maybe I could be her nanny kind of thing, I'll look after her whilst you go and work."

"Of course! I want you in Celeste's life so much, and Connie, that would be amazing."

I stand at the same time she does and we hug, both shedding tears that have built up over the last year.

"I want her to know me, I want to be in her life." I whisper and Reese nods.

Our moment is ruined when Connie's phone begins ringing with *Taylor Swift – Blank Space*. She breaks away, smiling as her phone dances across the table.

"Sorry, it's your dad," she pauses and she must see the look on my face, "and you're not here, I know," she adds before sliding her finger across the screen to take the call. "Hey baby," I watch as the smile slips from her lips, the colour draining from her face, and she turns to look at me. "Okay, I'm on my way," she rushes out, cutting the phone off.

"What is it?" my own panic coats my skin in perspiration.

"It's Killian, he's been in an accident," I watch as she

grabs the back of the chair to stop herself from buckling at the knees. "I can't, not again… I can't lose him Connie," she chokes out. I rush to her, pulling her up.

"You won't. Go and get Celeste, where are the keys?" I ask.

"Side table in the lobby," she hiccups through her sobs.

"Go get the baby, I'll get the car warmed," I say soothing her, and walking her down towards the stairs. "He is going to be okay, Reese," I nod trying to hide the worry that is currently destroying me inside. One, because it's my dad and two, I don't want Reese having to go through anything like this again.

Once I know she is out of sight, my trembling hands tug the drawers out and grab the keys. My heart is racing in my chest as I gasp for breath, needing to fill my lungs.

Reaching for my phone out of my coat pocket, I see messages and missed calls from Kaleb, but I ignore him.

I am not interested in anything he has to say at the minute. Shrugging my coat on, Reese appears at the top of the stairs with a sleepy Celeste. I watch as she yawns, her little chunky fists rubbing her tired eyes before she begins crying.

"It's okay baby," she coos. "My mum has finished work," she says as she grabs the baby bag by the front door, "I'm going to drop her over to her, I can't take her to the hospital," her bottom lip begins to tremble and I grab the top of her arm.

"It's going to be okay," I reassure her, even though I have no idea what state my dad is going to be in.

I open the cupboard and grab Reese's coat and Celeste's. I automatically swoop in, taking Celeste off Reese and hold her against my chest as she dozes in and out of sleep. I wait for the cry, but it doesn't come. A little shudder leaves her as she breathes out but that's soon replaced with dozing snores.

"Hey baby," I whisper, dropping my chin and placing a kiss in her thick, blonde hair on the top of her head as I inhale her scent.

Reese wraps her scarf round her neck, and I pull mine out from my coat pocket. Reese reaches for Celeste and wraps her in her coat before covering her with a blanket. I grab the baby bag off Reese and pull it up my shoulder.

"Ready?" I ask on a shaky breath.

Reese just nods and I can see if she speaks, the tears will consume her.

"Come on then," I say softly, ushering her out the door and locking it behind me.

He was going to be fine.

He has to be.

CHAPTER FIFTY

P<small>ULLING OUTSIDE</small> R<small>EESE'S OLD APARTMENT, SHE PUSHES THE</small> hazards on and rushes out the car. She opens Celeste's door, unstrapping her and grabbing the bag.

"I'll stay in the car," I rub my lips, my palms sweating, and she nods at me, slamming the car door. I watch as she disappears into the building, waving at Frank as she walks past him.

This apartment block holds such bittersweet memories for me, memories that have changed my brain chemistry. Some for the better, some for the worse. But it's all part of the journey of me becoming the person I want to be.

I feel my phone vibrate again and see Kaleb's name flashing up. I cut it off. I should know it's him, no one else has this number. It vibrates again and I see another message. Hovering my thumb over the screen, I debate opening it but Reese climbs back into the car, putting her blinker on and pulling out into the road.

Slipping my phone back in my pocket, she decided that for me. We ride in silence, I can see how frantic she is, her fingers tapping on the steering wheel, and if they're not tapping, she is biting the skin around her nails. I know that her anxiety will be doing overtime because of what happened with Elijah. She lost him to a car accident, stopping her world from turning in an instant. But in losing Elijah, she found my dad. My dad received Elijah's heart, talk about meant to be and a twist of fate huh? They were destined. That heart has only ever loved Reese, and Reese has only ever loved that heart.

I am snapped back to reality when Reese sharply pulls into the parking lot of the hospital and abandoning the SUV in the first spot she sees.

"I'll get the meter," I nod, not giving her a chance to argue, opening the door and walking to the meter, throwing my coins into it.

She meets me at the meter, and I link my arm through hers as we walk towards the hospital. My heartbeat is thumping against my chest, the pounding in my ears as the blood pumps through and with each step I take, the faster my heart races.

Her grip tightens on my hand as we walk through the doors, her eyes scanning the room for the desk. Pulling me with her, she drops me once she gets there.

"Killian Hayes, I had a call to let me know he was here," she manages, her voice shaking.

"Straight through to ER, he will be in there somewhere," the lady points to the left, down a long and narrow corridor.

She turns, rushing and I follow as we run towards the ER. Pushing through the door, a nurse comes over to us, a smile on her face. "May I help you?"

"I'm looking for my fiancé, her dad," Reese nods towards me and the way the nurse's facial expression slips, I elbow Reese.

"Oh, erm," the nurse's eyes bounce between me and Reese.

"Killian. Killian Hayes," Reese begins to panic, her fingers fumbling and twisting her engagement ring on her finger.

"Oh, yes, come with me," the nurse turns quickly and walks us to a small room by itself. The curtain is pulled round the bed as the nurse enters the room quietly. I reach for Reese's hand, grabbing it and lacing my fingers through hers.

"Everything is going to be okay," I whisper as we follow the nurse into the room.

"Mr Hayes, your fiancée is here," The nurse smiles as she pulls back the curtain and my eyes widen, Reese's jaw drops and my dad's eyes land on me.

"Connie!?" he rubs his eyes as if in disbelief. He is fucking sitting there, with sutures over a cut on his head, sutures on his top lip and his arm is sitting in a sling.

"Are you fucking winding me up?" Reese is enraged, her British accent thick and Killian moves his eyes from mine to his fiancée.

"I'll give you a moment or two..." The nurse says softly, giving me a glare before backing out the room slowly, closing the door.

"What?" Killian snaps.

"I thought you were hurt! Why did the doctor call me and not you?"

"Because I was in an accident, Reese! A car accident; it's not a little scratch is it?"

My fucking eyes bug, I step back and lift my hand, cutting it across my neck to get my dad to shut the fuck up. His eyes slowly move to mine, his brows furrowed as I mouth *Elijah* and realisation smacks him in the face like a shovel.

"Oh shit," he whispers, holding his hand out for Reese. "Baby," he coos, "come here, I'm so sorry... I didn't mean to scare you... I didn't think."

She takes his hand and chokes out heart-breaking sobs as he comforts her. His eyes move to mine as her tears soaks into his shirt, his lips pulling into a smile and my heart constricts in my chest.

"I'll go and get some drinks... give you two a minute," I nod, dropping my head quickly as I spin so he can't look at me in that way that pulls on my heart strings. Closing the door behind me, I feel my own bottom lip begin to tremble as the adrenaline from the shock begins to wear off. Tears threaten to fall as my eyes brim with unshed tears, my throat burning as the unwanted lump continues its climb, clawing at my throat until I give into it and let the tears fall. I push forward, keeping my head down as I walk out of the ER, heading towards the main lobby before pushing through the sliding doors. As soon as the icy air hits me, the sharpness in my breath filling my lungs causes me to gasp on my breath. Tipping my head back, I let the new snowflakes fall over me as the hot tears begin to roll down my cheeks. And this time I don't stop them. I let everything out, letting the tears wash all my anger, resentment, embarrassment, hurt and betrayal away.

After pulling myself together, I make my way back towards dad's room, holding three black coffees. I stand quietly on the other side of the door, inhaling deeply before using my elbow to push the handle down.

"I'm back," I plaster a smile on my face not to give them a chance to see the façade slip and show my real emotions that are threatening to give me away once more.

I hand a coffee to dad, then grimace when I pass one to Reese. "I know you don't like coffee, but they didn't have a tea option…"

She sighs, taking the coffee cup from me, bringing it to her lips and taking a mouthful before screwing her face up at the bitterness.

"Nah, that's vile," she shakes her head from side to side, turning and looking for a bin. She walks over to a large, green leafed plant and lifts the plastic lid from her cup, pouring the whole contents of it over the soil of the plant. "Have a drink little bud," she says softly, smiling as she gives the plant a complete caffeine rush.

"I don't think it's going to appreciate the drink, hun," I wince, "you've given it an overdose of caffeine."

"It'll be fine, it needed a little pick me up," she spins, beaming a smile at me.

Rolling my eyes, I step closer to dad. His eyes search my face, looking for something, I just don't know what.

Reese falters her steps as her eyes bat between me and dad. I don't know why, but it feels like awkwardness and tension begins to seep out of both of us, and I get it. I left with no warning and have been out of contact ever since. My heartbeat races in my chest as I swallow constantly, willing for my mouth to produce saliva.

"I know you wanted me to come back, but getting into a car accident *just* to get me here…" I smirk, my heartbeat spiking, now going ten to a dozen. "It's a little much isn't it?"

His eyes widen as he coughs on his mouthful of coffee, spluttering as Reese rushes over to him and hands him a tissue from the side cabinet.

"I did not…" he trails off before he realises, I'm being sarcastic. "Oh," he lets out a deep rumble of a laugh, his eyes slicing towards Reese for a moment. "Baby," his voice is low and soft, but Reese already has her phone in her hand.

"I'm going to call my mum, make sure Celeste is okay, and of course update her on you, *old man*," she rolls her eyes, "let her know that my brave soldier has a couple of scratches," she goads him, a condescending tone lacing her voice.

"I have sutures! Have you not noticed?" he counters back, pointing to his face, "And not to mention my dislocated shoulder!"

Reese sniggers, placing her hand on his chest, "Like I said, a few scratches," she lowers her lips over his and kisses him softly, "but I would much rather a scratch than anything life changing," she whispers, her eyes filling with tears as she kisses him again.

"I love you," dad rasps, thumbing one of her tears away.

"And I love you, so much more," she manages, her voice cracking.

She stands, walking past me and giving the top of my arm a supportive squeeze, I look at her over my shoulder as she continues for the door and give her a smile. I wait until the door closes, exhaling heavily as my feet finally move towards the chair next to dad's bed. My anxiety stirs deep inside of me, my palms twitchy and sweaty as I try and wipe them against my jeans.

"So, all jokes aside," I finally muster the words, "are you okay?" He nods, his eyes not lifting from mine. "What happened?" I pry, shuffling in my seat as I take a mouthful of the shit coffee, making my mouth instantly dry with its bitterness.

"Some jackass pulled out on me, I swerved to avoid them and ended up in the side of one car, then another went into the back of me. Smashed into the steering wheel, only then did the airbags deploy," he shakes his head from side to side. "No idea how I done my shoulder, maybe the force of the crash and the seatbelt," he sighs, "honestly, have no idea," he shrugs his shoulders up.

I rub my lips together, my eyes scanning his face.

"I'm glad you're okay," I reach my hand forward slowly, creeping it towards his but then stall and retract it back.

"I'm glad you're here." He smiles, his hand slowly uncurling and turning it palm up. My eyes prick with tears as I place my hand in his, his fingers wrapping round it and giving me a squeeze.

"I'm sorry..." I whisper, because suddenly the words feel like too much to speak, the weight of those two words heavy on my shoulders.

"Connie," he chokes, squeezing my hand tighter.

"I am, Dad, I was selfish and thinking about myself." I begin to tremble as the admissions seep from me.

"You were *not* selfish, Connie. I would have acted the same, I, we..." he pauses, "me and your Moms, we kept you in the dark thinking it would be best for you. But as Ad..."

"Don't," I close my eyes, grinding my back teeth as my jaw clenches and tightens.

"As *she* got more demanding, targeting Reese... I couldn't have it going on anymore. She was taking everything from me, she was draining my company and treating Reese like nothing more than dirt on the bottom of her shitty shoe."

I keep my eyes closed as he continues, his grip not loosening at all on my hand and I am grateful.

"And whilst she dangled the tie between us all like a carrot, she knew I would let her do whatever, to whomever. She fucked with the wrong person, and then she threatened to tell you. The day I missed our gender reveal and Reese's birthday, I was with her, pleading and begging for her not to go anywhere near you. It went from platonic to heated within minutes. She was crazed, and all she wanted was to see my downfall. Threatening Reese and making her life hell was not acceptable, but what she was threatening to do to you, it was the straw that broke the camel's back."

I swallow the thickness down in my throat, my eyes burning but I refuse to blink because I don't want another tear to fall.

"So, I done what I should have done years ago, I told you the truth." He sighs as I feel his eyes burning into mine. "Albeit I went completely the wrong way about it, but it was my plan to tell you. Your mom, Lara, wanted us all to sit down together but after you came into my office and launched your sneaker at my head," he smirks, "you were already pissed with me, so I took my shot..." his voice is tight, his hand gripping mine as tight as he could. "And I'm sorry for the way I did it, I have beat myself up every single day since. You're my world Connie, I know I have never been dad of the year, but it was always agreed that once you were with your moms, I would step back. As soon as you began to recognise me though, your big, beautiful green eyes always finding mine as soon as I stepped into the room, how the hell could I stay away from you?" he chokes, his voice cracking as tears brim in his own deep, brown eyes.

"And I am so sorry for everything that has happened to you since the day you walked out of my office. And Tryst," his eyes close for a moment, shaking his head from side to side, "I can't even begin to imagine what you are going through," he whispers.

You have no idea, Tryst's death is just the beginning.

I nod, slowly standing from my chair and throwing myself over my dad, wrapping my arms round his neck. I hear his breath catch, his arm slowly wrapping round me as he holds me.

"I love you Connie," he whispers.

"I love you, Dad."

———

I sit in the back of the car whilst Reese drives us all to her mom and dad's. They chat amongst themselves and suddenly I feel like a spare part. I slip my phone from my pocket and see all the notifications.

"Shit," I whisper under my breath as I click on the messages.

"Everything okay?" Dad's eyes find mine in the rear-view mirror and I nod, keeping tight lipped. Now was *not* the time to bring up Kaleb.

"Connie," his voice rasps as I ignore my phone for a moment.

"Yeah?"

"Can I ask a favour?"

I nod once more.

"Go and see your moms; if you can forgive me, they deserve your forgiveness too."

"I will dad, I've just got some bits I need to sort first."

"Okay darling," he smiles at me, his hand slipping across the centre of the car and resting on Reese's thigh.

Pulling into the underground parking lot this time of Reese's old apartment block, dad groans as he reaches for the permit in the glove compartment, tossing it onto the dash.

"You okay?" Reese asks.

"Yeah, think the whiplash is beginning to set in," he sighs, and her small hand rubs his shoulders as she puts the parking brake on in the car.

My phone begins to ring, and I cut it off, sighing. "I'm going to head off," I suddenly feel out of place.

"Oh," Reese's surprised tone pulls my eyes from my lap to her, "I was going to see if you wanted to come in and see my parents and Celeste."

I swallow, love swarming to my heart.

"I would love to," I manage, "only if that's okay of course," and Reese laughs, shaking her head.

"Of course, it is," she smiles, unplugging herself and hopping out the large SUV, then opening my door. "Give me a minute," she says as I step down from the car, "let me just help the old man from the car," I hear dad curse under his breath.

"Don't *old man* me, Buttercup. We both know what happens," and before he can finish his sentence, I push my fingers into my ears.

"LA LA LA LA," I shout out and see dad laugh, Reese elbowing him in his side and mouthing 'sorry'. I shake my head and feel my phone go again, seeing Kaleb's name.

"Who is that?" Reese asks as dad hobbles off in front and I scoff.

"I have never known a more over dramatic man than my dad," I laugh, and Reese laughs with me as we slow our steps.

"Don't change the subject," she keeps her voice low, and I shoot her a look. "Oh," she nods knowingly.

"But he is being an ass, so I'm ignoring him."

"Once your dad is feeling brighter, how about we get a wine night in... I am assuming you're in the city still?" I nod. "Then let's get a date in," she chimes, "have you got a new number? I have been texting your old one, but they never deliver," she sighs.

"I do have a new number; I've not long turned my phone on." I say, "I launched my old phone into the sea when I was in the Hamptons... then Kaleb," whispering his name round the echoing parking lot, "bought me a new one a few weeks back but I've not wanted to connect with the real world, until now..." I turn to look at her and smile.

"I'm glad," she links her arm through mine, laying her head on my shoulder.

"Me too," I nod, my heart swelling in my chest, "me too."

CHAPTER FIFTY-ONE
KALEB

I AM FUCKING FRANTIC.

I have no idea where she is and it's been hours.

I've been home and to The Plaza. I have no idea where else to look. Something inside me niggles at the possibility that she may have gone to her dad's but then again, I don't think she would have. She didn't seem ready.

What is even more annoying is that she is reading my messages and leaving me on read. I press her name again and bring the phone to my ear as it rings a couple of times before she gives me the fuck off button.

"Fuck!" I scream, running my hand through my hair. I've already started going grey but by the time I find her, I'll have a full head of grey.

"No luck?" Keaton calls out.

"Obviously not," I shout back, aggravation bubbling inside of me.

"Was only asking," he snaps back.

"Well don't ask such stupid questions!" I growl, pulling up a message.

KALEB

Answer your phone, I am losing my temper.

I send the message then instantly regret my tone.

Baby, I'm sorry. I am just frantic with worry.
Just let me know you're okay.

I watch as three dots pop up and relief swarms me.

CONNIE

Fuck off Kaleb.

And I fucking lose it. Roaring, I swipe my desk clear of anything that is on it, watching as my computer slips and smashes to the floor. My chest heaving, my nostrils flared as I breathe raging hot air through them.

My bloodshot eyes dart to the doorway when I see Titus leaning against the door frame, a stupid smirk on his punch-able face.

"Fuck off Titus, not today, go and focus on getting Archibald's daughter to safety," I grit.

He ignores me, of course he does because he is a walking, talking, dickhead. He has to be involved in everything and normally I am here it, but not today. The closer he steps towards me, the more I see him as a red flag, waving in front of an enraged bull.

"Titus," I warn.

"I know," he nods, still stepping closer to me, in slow, small steps.

"Please go away," my voice cracks as I practically beg him.

"I know," he whispers as he stops in front of me, my hand gliding down the side of my head, and cupping round the back of my neck.

"She's infuriating." Titus nods. "So fucking infuriating."

And before I know what's happened, the broad shouldered six-foot seven guy has me in a bear hug. "I know," his voice is soft, "and I get it, you're protective, you're allowed to be annoyed..." he stalls.

"But," I grit, still standing pinned by him,

"But you going all cave man on her is not going to bring her back any quicker, if anything, you're pushing her to keep defying you. Which is what she is doing right now. You have not stopped messaging and ringing her, she has replied, you know she is okay now just let her simmer down and she will reach out when she is ready."

I breathe out on a shaky breath as I try and contain my anger.

"But she has nowhere to go," I counter against his logical solution for Connie's behaviour.

"She will go home when she is ready."

I sigh, my shoulders finally dropping down as I relax.

"Give her space, you're suffocating her," his arms still wrapped round me while he speaks.

"You're suffocating me," I grit, and he lets out a deep roar of a laugh.

"Ah man, look at you two..." Titus clicks his tongue to the roof of his mouth, "Smile," I hear Keaton's voice as I look over, and he has his phone in his hand, snapping pictures.

"I swear to fucking god, Keat."

"Fuck off Keaton, I've just calmed him down," Titus grits, his head turning to Keaton and now Nate who has popped his head round the doorframe.

I don't know how Titus knows I need this. But he does. He has always done it, most of the time I would spend ten minutes fighting him off, but some days, I let him hold me.

"Let me get in," Keaton bounds over like an excited puppy dog, wrapping his arms round Titus and then looks behind him at Nate.

"Come on Nate, come and get involved in the group hug."

"No, thanks anyway." Nate snipes, giving us a smirk and a wink then turns on his heel and walks away.

"Ah, well, his loss." Keaton shrugs then gets involved again.

I roll my eyes, but internally I am smiling. I would truly be lost without these fuckers.

My phone buzzes in my pocket and I try to fish it out.

"Guys, I need my phone, it could be Connie," Keaton groans as he drops his arms from Titus, who then peels his arms from me, freeing me.

I give him a thankful nod and he flicks his two index fingers from the side of his head in a salute.

Pulling my phone out, my brows furrow and knit together as I see Killian's name, my heart drums in my chest as I open his message.

KILLIAN

No need for your services anymore, Connie is safe. Send me the invoice and I'll get you settled up.

"Like fuck," I shout at my phone, my hands trembling as I launch the phone at the wall and before I know it, Titus has thrown himself back into me, restraining me again as I scream.

CHAPTER FIFTY-TWO

CONNIE

Walking nervously down the corridors of Reese's old apartment block, I hook my index fingers together. Dad slips his phone back in his pocket, wrapping his arm round my shoulders as he places a kiss on the side of my head.

"Feels weird being back here," a nervous laugh bubbles from me as we get closer to her parents' apartment.

"I get it," Reese chirps as she stops outside the front door.

"How much did we go through in that apartment," I sigh, memories flooding me.

"I know, most of the time I was moaning about this pretentious, possessive asshole boss that wouldn't take no for an answer."

Dad rolls his eyes so far in the back of his head it makes me laugh.

"It's true! You wouldn't take no for an answer would you," Reese taps her sneaker on the carpet, hands on her hips.

"But I knew I wanted you, so I wasn't going to stop," he shrugs his shoulders up as if it wasn't a big deal.

"It was a little weird…" I whisper, edging away from him and giving him the side eye, "stalker," he pushes me a little harder than intended, knocking me off balance.

Reese knocks on the door as our laughter dies down, her mom opening the door and pushing Reese out of the way to throw herself into dad.

"Jesus Christ," Reese's thick British accent comes through as her eyes widen pinning them on her mom.

"I am so glad you're okay," her voice is panicked as she clings to him.

"I'm sorry I gave you a fright Liz," Dad pats her on the back and gives me a tight-lipped smile.

"Mateo and I were so worried," she pulls away, pressing her hand against her chest then taking dad's hand and leading him into the apartment. I walk up to Reese and a giggle slips past my lips as I lose the will to hold it off.

"You would think that they were married to him, wouldn't you?" she scoffs, rolling her eyes as she holds her hand out for me to walk in, "After you."

"You would," I agree and step into the apartment, my breath catching as I am throwing back to last year, old emotions surfacing. Nothing had changed. Everything was just how I remembered it. I found out so much inside these four walls that altered me, some for the best, some for the worst. But either way, they changed me.

"Oh my god, Connie!" Liz beams, her mouth agape as she looks between dad and Reese. "Is it really you?" she asks.

"It is," I smile, my eyes watery.

"Oh, it's a day full of miracles," she clasps her hands together, her own eyes brimming with tears as she makes her way over to me and hugs me. I wrap my arms around her and hold onto her tight.

"It's so good to see you," I mutter, and my eyes focus on Reese who is being held by my dad and I find that my smile only grows. It's good to see them together and happy.

"Mi amor, Celeste has been an angel," Mateo coos as he looks at my little sister sitting on the rug, playing with her toys. Her brown hair has small tuft curls that sit at the base of her head, she has a little pink clip slipped into the side. She is wearing a light grey velour lounge suit. The concentration on her face is adorable as she stacks the blocks up one by one before knocking them over and giggling away, clapping her hands.

"She is an angel, that's why," Reese beams as she looks over at her daughter, and Liz finally lets me go.

"Who wants tea?" she asks, already walking towards the small kitchen area.

All squeezed on the sofa, I can't take my eyes from Celeste, she is so beautiful, and I am gutted and wracked with guilt that I have stayed away for so long.

"How have you been, Connie?" Liz asks me, disturbing me from my loving gazes. I snap out of it, turning to face her.

"I've been okay, I'm slowly getting back to the girl I once was," my voice is small as I take a sip of my tea.

"I am so glad to hear that. Reese told me what happened with your boyfriend... we're so sorry for your loss, please accept our condolences," she moves to the edge of the armchair that she sits in and places her hand on my knee.

I cough, trying to clear the lump that feels as if it is blocking my throat.

"Thank you," I manage to squeak out, my stomach knotting. I slowly turn my head to look over my shoulder to see my coat hanging there, the letter burning a hole in the pocket.

"It'll get easier, just look at Reese," Liz averts her loving gaze towards her daughter and my dad, and I just nod.

"I know," I whisper, because if I speak, my cracked voice will give everything away. I'm not ready for that yet. I've only just begun to let the dust settle between me and my dad, I didn't need to bring up everything else that has gone on.

I look at my watch and see it's early evening already.

"I better get going," I say softly as I finish the mouthful of tea left in my cup.

"Why? Where are you going?" My dad asks, standing and wincing as he does.

"Sit down, baby," Reese reaches up touching his arm, but he ignores her.

"Where are you going?" Dad asks me again, his brow furrowed, his tone is a little sterner now.

"Home, Dad." I whisper, heat burning my cheeks.

"But we're your home," he looks at me puzzled.

"I know, but Dad, I've *just* got you back in my life, today has been..." I look round the room of eyes that are all pinned to mine.

"It's been a lot for her," Reese finishes my sentence for me, and I smile at her, thankful that she stuck up for me.

"I just need to go home and let everything sink in."

Dad sighs, placing his one hand on his hip, the other still sitting in its sling.

"The penthouse is yours if you want it, it's been empty since Reese had Celeste." He begins walking towards me, "It was my plan to give it to you as a surprise, but..."

"But," I nod quickly, swallowing as I drop my head to look at my feet.

"It's there for when you want it," he gives me a tight smile, then pulls me into a hug, holding me a little tighter, my arms wrapping round him as his lips press to the top of my head.

The noise of jangling keys has me looking up and pinning my eyes to Reese. I break away from my dad, shaking my head from side to side.

"I'm going to walk, I need some thinking time," I give her a small smile as I step away. "Liz, Mateo," I rasp, "it was lovely seeing you again and thank you for your warm and kind hospitality." They both give me a nod and a smile.

Reese re-appears with Celeste, and I lean in, giving her a kiss on the forehead.

"Bye baby," I whisper, grabbing my tan trench coat and wrapping myself in it.

I see a small notepad on the kitchen surface, and I grab the pen, jotting down my number.

"Text me when you want to get that drink," I smile at Reese before turning to face my dad. "Dad," I whisper, my eyes filling with tears, "I'll see you soon."

"I'll see you soon," he nods, wrapping his arm around Reese and pulling her close to him, Celeste reaching out for him and she starts to cry when he doesn't immediately take her.

With one final nod, I turn and exit the apartment, finally able to breathe again. Rushing down the corridor to the elevator, I pull out my phone and nibble the inside of my lip as I see no more notifications from Kaleb. I finally give in and click on his name, the phone barely rings.

"Darling?" the rasp in his voice makes my heart skip a beat.

"I'll see you at home," I just about manage before I cut the phone off and step into the elevator.

My strides are slow, the cold air pinching at my skin as the day begins to fade with the lowering sun. I feel frozen to my core, but I need the thinking space. So much had happened today that I don't feel I really had time to process it. I feel numb. Fisting my frozen hands into my pockets, my fingers brush against the folded letter and my heart hurts. The need to rub it out overwhelms me but I push it down, letting the ache slowly dull and die out.

I falter my steps as I approach Kaleb's building, my heart rushing in my chest. My dad's words ring out in my ears *'the penthouse is yours if you want it'.*

I love Kaleb, but maybe we need the separation to grow. My heart plummets into the depths of my stomach and I choke on my own breath at the thought of being without him. We were forced together at a time I needed protection, I'm not in need of that anymore.

My feet begin moving towards the main doors, and with each step I take, my heart drums a little harder and a little faster deep inside my chest. I inhale sharply, before exhaling a slow, long breath which is visible, dancing through the cold air. The warmth of the apartment block hits me, my cheeks instantly flaming with heat. Nerves crash through me as I close in on the elevator, keeping my head down as I wait.

I have no idea what I am walking into, I know he is going to be angry with me. I have ghosted him all day, but I needed space. He fucked up. He kept something from me that wasn't his to keep. This was a big deal. This letter could potentially mean Tryst's death is changed from suicide to murder. Just like that.

The case would be reopened and me, his friends and his poor mom would have to go through all of this heartache and grief again because of one little piece of kept communication.

"Miss," the concierge calls out as he walks over to me, my head snaps up and my eyes widen as he closes the gap between us. "Are you a guest of one of our residents here?" His brow lifts, his eyes slowly sweeping over me.

"Yes," my tone is curt and short, I am tired, cold and anxious. I really don't need this right now.

"May I ask whom?" he pries, his face edging closer to me as I pinch the bridge of my nose and inhale deeply.

"Kaleb Mills."

"Ah, Mr Mills... our penthouse owner."

"Yes."

"Let me just call through and make sure he is expecting you," his eyes dance over me once more before turning and walking towards the desk. I let out a loud groan of exasperation, my head tipping back as I drag my heavy legs towards him.

"Ah, yes, hello Mr Mills," his chin lifts a little higher as he looks down his pointy nose at me, his beady eyes pinned to mine. I let my eyes do a quick sweep over him as he wears a boxy suit jacket that is miles too big for his slender frame, a crisp white shirt, and a maroon tie. His hair is greased back to perfection with no chance of a stray hair escaping.

"I have a young girl here claiming to be coming to your penthouse, what with..." he stops abruptly, his eyes widening as his cheeks colour crimson. "Oh, yes... I understand, no, no sir, that will not be necessary. Yes, okay, I'll send her up now," he stammers, placing the phone back into its cradle. "Mr Mills said for you to go up."

"Yup," I wink, turning on my heel and heading back for the penthouse elevator, not once looking back behind me.

Once inside, I place my hands back inside my pocket, the letter reminding me of everything that had happened today. The bad, and the good. If it wasn't for this letter turning up this morning, I would never have found out about Kaleb's involvement, I would have never ended up at Reese's and I certainly wouldn't have reconciled with my dad. A small smile pulls at the corner of my lips at the thought, but it soon disappears when the lift comes to a halt, the doors pinging open and suddenly my heart is in my throat. I hang back, trying to muster up the courage to step out, and just for a moment I will for the *old* Connie to make an appearance. The carefree, strong willed, no fucks given Connie. But she doesn't come out and I fear she will never return. Tryst made sure she was dead and buried right alongside him.

"Babe?" I hear the deep rumble of Kaleb's voice before he comes into view, my eyes pinned to his. He steps over the elevator threshold, his hands in his pockets. His stormy grey eyes have lost their glisten, and my stomach knots. Removing his hand from his pocket, he rubs it over his chin, the sound of his stubble scratching across his skin. We haven't seen each other for a few hours but it feels like days, and the tension only continues to grow between us.

Holding his hand out for me to take, I step forward, a little hesitant but eventually place my hand in his, the tingle spreading and coursing through my body, sparking a little piece of hope deep inside of me. His lips purse into a smile, clasping my hand a little tighter as I step towards him. No words are exchanged as he leads me to the living room, his brows furrowing as he rubs his thumb across the back of my knuckles.

"You're frozen," his voice is low as he lets goes of my hand, pulling my coat off my shoulders and throwing it onto the sofa. He reaches for me, but I throw myself at him. His large, strong arms wrapping round me as I let the heat from him radiate through me, warming me through to my core. "Are you okay?" His lips brush across the top of my head and my body warms as he does.

"I've been better," I mumble into his chest, my arms still locked round the back of him not wanting to move.

"Connie," his voice cracks as he says my name, but he stops suddenly, his arms loosening, and I hear a light cough. I freeze, my eyes widening but I dare not move.

"Well," I hear Doris' voice breeze through the room. I go to move, but Kaleb doesn't let me.

"Don't move," he whispers, "if we don't move, she won't notice us," I can hear the playfulness in his voice and I giggle into his shirt, trying to muffle any sound.

"I can see both of you, anyway..." she pauses for a moment, "do you think I am blind? Or stupid?" she scoffs, "I have known something has been going on between you two, honestly, you're not discreet, and your *sneaking*?" She lets out a loud laugh, "Honestly," she shakes her head from side to side, "I'm really happy for you both," she smiles, turning to continue into the kitchen before calling out, "dinner will be ready in twenty."

We wait till she is out the room and both burst into laughter, but I can feel the almighty weight of the thick tension that is filling the room as the seconds pass.

DINNER IS QUIET, THE ROOM FALLING SOMBRE THE LONGER IT GOES without us clearing our minds to elevate some of the tension. I don't want to leave any words unsaid and let the tension grow even more than it already has.

I stand, reaching for my plate then leaning over to take Kaleb's but he shakes his head, stopping me from lifting it.

My brows furrow as he stands and lifts his own plate, walking towards the kitchen and I follow him like a lost, little puppy. Placing the plates in the sink, Kaleb's arms snake around my waist as he lets his lips brush against my neck.

"Kaleb," I whisper, my eyes closing as I let my head roll back into him, giving him full access to where he wants to be.

"Fuck, I missed you," his lips graze over my skin as he talks, the vibration of his voice making my heart race.

"And I missed you," I breathe, but I'm not going to let him try and seduce me into forgetting what has happened.

I place my hands over his, lifting them from my skin reluctantly then spin to face him, shaking my head from side to side.

"We need to talk," my voice is low as his eyes volley back and forth between mine before finally letting his head drop and inhaling deeply. "Come," I take his hand and lead him upstairs, pushing the door of my room open.

Dropping it as soon as we get to the bed, I sit in the middle, my back against the headboard as I tuck my leg under myself, and Kaleb sits opposite me. Silence crackles between us, his eyes not lifting from mine, and I can feel the tension brewing once more.

"I'm mad at you," I just about manage before I have to look away from him, his burning gaze too much for me to bear.

"I know," he breathes, "it was my intention to tell you," scooting closer to me, he grips my chin with his thumb and finger as he lifts my face to look at him. "I promise, I just wanted to make sure we had everything and left no stone unturned before I did."

"This could change everything, Kaleb," I shake my head from side to side, his fingers slipping from my chin, "and not just for me, but for Tryst's friends and family. This is not just about me," my heart begins to drum in my chest, skipping beats.

"I know, and if we found out it wasn't suicide, we would do everything to work with the police and everyone to find out what happened to Tryst."

"Do you think it was suicide?" and that's when he looks away from me, inhaling deeply as he links his fingers together.

"Honestly?" he asks me, his head slowly lifting, our eyes meeting.

"Honestly," I whisper, the air being knocked from my lungs as soon as I speak the words.

"No," his rolls his lips, shaking his head from side to side and I choke on the gasp of breath that hits the back of my throat. "Connie," he shuffles, fidgeting as he reaches for my hands, cupping them within his. "I need to tell you something, but you have to *promise* me, you'll hear me out... you *promise* not to lose your shit..."

Boom.

Boom.

Boom.

My heart thumps against my ribcage, the blood thumping in my ears as I wait with bated breath.

"I need you to promise me baby," his voice is strained, his eyes not moving from mine as his thumbs rub over the back of my hand.

"Promise," I mumble quietly through the whirlwind of

thoughts that seem to be spiralling out of control, my over thinking mind slowly drowning me.

"When we first met, the night I bumped into you..." he trails off, his hand tightening in mine and I nod, "the way Tryst treated you... the time I saw you in the coffee shop all those months ago with the marks on your skin that you tried to hide... I saw them all Connie. I knew what that monster was doing to you... just not to the extent that he was."

I swallow the thick lump down that's bobbing in my throat, my eyes stinging as the memories plague me.

"When I had you, and I knew you were away from him and safe with me, I didn't know what to do to help you... so I called in a favour with someone, someone who could help with *unwanted* situations." Kaleb stops as he licks lips, swallowing before continuing. He removes one of his hands from mine, rubbing it on the material of his pants.

"*Unwanted* situations?" I repeat, my voice low and flat.

He nods. "I arranged for somebody to take care of Tryst."

I furrow my brows, not quite sure what he means until suddenly it clicks, making everything fall into place.

"You killed him!" I shout, pulling my hand from his abruptly and scooting further back even though I had nowhere else to go.

"Shit, no, no baby, no," his eyes are wide and frantic as he shakes his head from side to side, "I didn't kill him, but I did arrange for *someone* to kill him." He swallows again and I see his Adams apple bob up and down his throat.

"What?" I whisper, shock blanketing me at his admissions.

"But when they got there, he was already dead... we've..." he stalls, "me, Titus, Nate and Keaton have been working on it ever since to try and work out who did this to him."

I can't speak, my throat burns, my eyes blurring everything else around me as the hot tears begin to cascade down my cheeks.

"You work in..." I stammer through my choked sobs and realisation hits me, "you don't work in insurance?"

He shakes his head before it falls forward and I scoff.

"Has anything you've told me been true, Kaleb?" my nose streams, my eyes stinging but the tears refuse to stop.

"Yes," his voice is quiet, "but we've never really sat and spoke about what I do, or who I am."

"Then who are you?" I sit a little taller, tears still rolling down my cheeks as I angrily palm them away. My gut twists and aches at what he told me, even if he was doing it to protect me, he was still willing to kill a man, a man I once loved. I do get his rationale behind it, he knew that Tryst wouldn't stop, so by doing this, he knew I would be safe but it still doesn't make the bitter pill any easier to swallow.

"My name is Kaleb Mills, that is true." I see a slither of a smile try to tease at his lips but he stops it when he sees the broken state I am in. "I work with Keaton my twin, Titus and Nate. We did all grow up together. I don't work in insurance; we have our own security firm so to speak..."

I narrow my eyes on him as I cross my arms across my chest.

"Titus is a bodyguard, Nate does the cyber side of things, Keaton does the accounts... and me?" he rubs his large hand across his chin, "I don't really know what I do anymore." I hear the crack in his voice, "ever since I lost Ruby, I sort of lost my way... until I found you."

"Ruby?" her name piques my interest, my breaths slowing as I shudder on my inhales from the sobs.

"Yeah, she was a client." Kaleb nods, his eyes averting from mine as he sighs, looking out the window.

"That you loved?" I couldn't help but ask, the sting in my tone apparent.

"No, no, nothing like that, darling." His eyes slice back to mine, "she was *just* a client."

"Did she find out you tried to murder her abusive ex too?" my snarky remark comes out a lot harsher than it sounded in my head.

"No," his voice was barely audible, and I could see the pain flash across his eyes as they darkened to almost black. His shoulders sagging as I watched the man I was so hopelessly in love with become a shell of himself, crumbling right before my eyes.

"What happened?" I whisper, too scared of what was about to come from his mouth.

"I couldn't save her; I convinced her to come with me. I promised I would keep her safe, until I couldn't. He got into her head, working his way back into her life." His jaw tightened as he grits his teeth, "I tried reaching out once she left, just to get the confirmation I so desperately craved of knowing she was okay. That she was safe, and he stuck to his promise of changing." His voice breaks, stopping abruptly and I see the glisten of tears that prick his eyes.

"He murdered her. Beat her black and blue..." he swallows, and I see the tears begin to fall. "It destroyed me, took me years to get over it, years for me to finally not let the image of her laying there trigger my emotions," he chokes, his fingers pulling at a piece of loose cotton thread on the bed spread that lay beneath him. "It took me *years*," he rasps, "then along came you," his eyes finally lift to mine, "and I vowed I was never letting you out of my sight, I wasn't going to let you succumb to the same fate as Ruby.

I would lay down my own life, sacrifice myself over and over before I let you go. And that's when it got complicated, baby," his trembling hands reach out for mine, scooping them inside his, and this time, I don't pull them away. "Because I fell so deeply in love with you, and the only way I thought I could keep you safe was to get rid of the monster that fed your demons," my tears begin to fall.

"I'm not asking for forgiveness, you may never forgive me, but I couldn't just assume you would always stay around, I knew there would be some point in time where you would want to leave, begin to spread your beautiful wings again like the butterfly you mentioned back at the Hamptons..." he smiles, a tear running off his face and dissolving into nothing. "I didn't want to clip your wings, but knowing Tryst was nowhere near to hurt you, it made my decision a little easier," he sniffs, "and I am sorry Connie, I never wanted to hurt you the way I just have. It was never my intention, but I will make it my job to find out who killed Tryst. Just to give you peace, to give you the freedom you deserve my love, because you really do deserve the world. I just hope you let me be the one to give it to you."

I sit, frozen and silent at his admission and numbness slowly smothers my body.

"I need some time," I nod, my throat thick, making my voice distort slightly.

"Okay," he whispers.

I stand slowly on shaky legs and walk to my wardrobe, grabbing a duffel bag and filling it with clothes.

"Connie," Kaleb appears in the doorway of the wardrobe, but I don't respond. Barging past him, I drop the bag on the bed as I go through my drawers and grab my toiletries. "Baby?"

I sigh, turning abruptly to face him, "I need some time," I repeat, and he stumbles back, the bed hitting the back of his knees as he sits.

"Where will you go?" he asks but I ignore him because the pain that is searing through me is too much for me to handle. "But this is your home," he says pained, the tremble in his voice is almost enough for me to forget his admissions, drop my bag and crawl into his lap. But I can't.

"Not anymore, Kaleb," and with that final word, I zip up my bag and walk out of the bedroom, not looking back.

CHAPTER FIFTY-THREE
CONNIE

IT HAD BEEN TWO WEEKS SINCE I WALKED OUT ON KALEB. TWO weeks of insufferable heartache. Two weeks of feeling as if a knife has twisted so deep into my gut, I fear the pain will never leave. Two weeks since I walked out on *him.*

He has reached out to me, but he doesn't know where I'm living. I kept quiet, and he honoured the space I asked for. I understand his reasons for doing what he did, I'm not even mad about that. I am mad that he kept it from me, that he thought he was helping me by not saying a word and keeping tight lipped. I resented him for it. I feel like a fool who had been blinded by him. But it doesn't mean I don't still love him. Because I do.

More than anyone I have ever loved before.

Reaching for my phone, disappointment surges through me that I don't see his name on my phone. Maybe he has given up on me.

No, he wouldn't.

"Shit," I grit as I lock my eyes on the time.

Running out the bedroom, I grab a banana on my way out and close the door to the penthouse behind me. I was not about to be late for my first day of looking after Celeste. Pressing the button continuously for the elevator, I was getting panicky. I hated being late.

It'll be fine, of course it will.

I am a hot, panting mess by the time I get on the sidewalk outside the apartment block, and I am so grateful for the ice cold air filling my lungs. Holding my hand out, a taxi pulls in almost immediately and I am hoping this is going to be the sign that me and Celeste are going to have the best day.

Throwing the driver my notes, I slip out the back of the taxi and run towards the steps of my dad and Reese's place and press the ringer. The door swings open and I see a flustered Reese. Her blonde hair looks slightly matted, her eyes red rimmed and Celeste is clinging onto her for dear life.

"You look about as good as me," I half laugh as I pass her.

"I'm having second thoughts," Reese blurts out and I turn to face her, she's bobbing from foot to foot and bouncing Celeste in her arms to try and calm her fussing whilst Celeste claws at her neck, grabbing her thin, silver necklace.

"It'll be okay. It's only for a few hours," I give her a soft smile as I drop my bag on the floor and edge towards Reese. "Just take it slow, go into the office for a couple of hours, it'll do you both the world of good," I nod slowly at her as I step closer and hold my hands out for Celeste who comes willingly. I smile, placing a kiss on Celeste's head. "See, we will be fine."

I have no idea the range of emotions that must be going through Reese's head. I want to reassure her and tell her I get it, but I don't get it. All I can do is *try* to understand. Reaching for her hand, I give it a gentle squeeze.

"Go and get in your car, do as much as you can and when you're ready, we will be here. I'm not going anywhere today with Celeste."

I see a glimmer of tears in Reese's opal eyes and my heart hurts.

"It's okay," I pull her in for a hug, Celeste patting her mom on the top of her head then leaning into her. "Now come on, we don't want our little princess getting upset."

Reese sniffles and nods, grabbing her keys off the side unit and her bag.

"I would just run a brush through your hair," I try and say as kindly and softly as possible, lifting my hand and pointing to my own hair. She sighs, turning quickly and looking in the mirror that sits above the side table. Pulling her golden blonde locks from her hair-tie, she runs the tips of her fingers through, smoothing it out before pulling it back into a high, tidy yet messy ponytail.

"Better?" she spins to face me, her eyes pinned to mine.

"Perfect," I beam, wrapping both my arms around a fussing Celeste, the longer Reese is taking, the more Celeste is picking up on the emotions that are slowly filling the room.

"Bye baby," Reese just about manages, "call me if any problems." I nod.

"Bye mommy," I hold Celeste's little arm up and wave as Reese slips out the door, I hear her held in sobs just before the door closes and as soon as Reese is out of sight, Celeste starts to cry.

"Oh angel," I soothe, running my hand over her head softly, wrapping her tufty curls round my fingers, "It's okay, we've got this," I chime, kissing her on the top of her head and walking down into the kitchen. "We've totally got this," I say to myself as she still screams in my arms.

I finally got her settled as we sat and played in the playroom, towering blocks and Celeste knocking them over. She giggled every, single, time. Her big, wide eyes find mine as she begins to rub them, a soft whinge leaving her.

"You tired baby?" I reach for her and pull her onto my lap, cuddling her for a little while and enjoying this moment as I sing a soft lullaby. I check the time; it's just gone eleven thirty. I stand up with her and go to look at the schedule that Reese left for me. "It's nap time for you little miss," I shuffle her in my arms and prop her up, so her head is on my shoulder, my arms wrapped round her little body.

"I love you so much," I whisper, turning my face to the side and kissing her on the side of her head.

Putting her down and placing her pacifier in her mouth, within minutes she has drifted off and I just stand at the side of her cot and watch her. Her long, brown lashes fanned out over her cheeks, her soft breaths comforting me. I slip her into her sleep bag, zipping her up and successfully not waking her. The house is slightly chilly so hopefully, her sleep bag will keep her warm. Closing the door softly, I walk quietly into Reese and my dad's room to grab the baby monitor.

Once downstairs, I fill the kettle with water and place it on the stove as I begin to boil it. Opening the cupboards, I grab some salted chips and find the lunch that Reese made for me. Salami and mustard on wholegrain. My stomach grumbles.

Flopping down on the sofa, I take a moment. I feel so grateful that Reese and my father have allowed me to do this, allowed me to spend one on one time with my little sister. I resent myself for missing out on so much, for being so selfish when I run away. It doesn't matter how many times people tell me I wasn't being selfish, I was. I knew I was. I was never in denial about it. I was a selfish bitch.

But not anymore. I sigh, taking a mouthful of my tea before placing it down on the coffee table just in front of me. I never drank tea before Reese, I never got the appeal. But now I would choose it over coffee, unless I'm in a little coffee shop. Something about barista made coffee just hits different.

Chewing on my lunch, I let my mind run wild with my consumed thoughts. I had been living in the penthouse for a little over two weeks. I didn't tell my dad why I needed the keys just that it was time for me to start a fresh and he was as happy as a pig in shit. Of course, he was. He had his little girl back. Part of me feels like I need to tell him about Kaleb, but at the minute, I'm not sure if I need to. Is there even a me and Kaleb anymore? My heart thrashes in my chest at the familiar ache that starts coursing through me, the lump growing in my throat as the threat of tears fill my eyes.

Maybe we were never meant to be together. Maybe he was the one who showed me that I needed to grow, to branch out and do this thing called life alone. But that thought plunges me into the darkest depths of my thoughts, because if he was only meant to be a lesson why do I feel like my life has ended and I am just existing but not living? He made me feel alive. I had never felt that way until him. I swipe away a stray tear, placing my half-eaten sandwich back on the plate. Suddenly, I've lost my appetite.

I hear the key in the front door and stand in a rush, placing my plate on the coffee table and pressing on my tip toes to look at myself in the mirror opposite. Running my ring finger under my eyes to discard of any smudged mascara.

"Connie?" Reese calls out, her head popping round the doorframe of the living room.

"You're back," I smile at her, my lips wanting to pull into a full smile, but I stop them.

"Yeah, three hours was enough," she smiles, placing her bag on the floor in the hallway then joining me in the living room.

"You have done so well, I'm proud of you," I step towards her, hugging her tightly. "She has been a *dream,* she really is such a special little girl."

"She really is," she sighs blissfully, as we break our hug, her eyes gliding over to the baby monitor.

"Sit down, I'll go make another tea and you can tell me all about your first day back at work."

Sitting crossed legged, Reese takes a sip of her tea and visibly relaxes into the armchair.

"So, Hernandez, what was it like being back?" I take my own sip of tea as she smiles.

"It was amazing, I felt like I could pick up where I left off if that made sense? It was nice seeing Julia and a few others and so much nicer knowing that bitch face isn't there anymore," she sniggers and my stomach twists, nodding in agreement. Reese sees my smile slip and her eyes widen slightly. "Connie," she stammers, and I wave my hand in front of my face, indicating for her not to worry about it.

"Sorry," she winces, taking another sip of her tea, "but it was good, I felt *good*. It was nice for human interaction," she laughed, "but my god, I forgot how persistent your dad is!"

I roll my eyes, "Bet he loved having you back."

"He did," her eyes drift to the baby monitor as it flashes and I shuffle forward, ready to put my tea on the table.

"No, finish your sandwich," Reese gives me a stern look. "I'll get her," she beams, placing her own cup down and rushing out the room.

My phone pings, my heart racing in my chest before sinking into the depths of my stomach. It would only be Kaleb.

Slipping it out my pocket, I see his name as I hover my finger over it. Letting my eyes close for a moment, I click it. Opening my eyes, I begin to read.

Baby,
These last two weeks have felt like eternity. I feel like I am walking along the crevice of a cliff, waiting to slip and fall into a never-ending loop of darkness.
That's what my life has been since you walked out; darkness.
You were the light I needed, and I know I was the light you had so desperately craved.
I can't, no, I don't want to do this thing called life without you.
You are my reason for breathing Connie, my reason for living.
I want it all with you.
You want me on my knees? Done, I'll stay on my knees for the rest of my life if that's what it would take for you to forgive me.
You want me to crawl over broken glass? Done, I'll happily bleed out for you, for as long as you want me to.
You want me to walk on burning coal? Done, I'll walk until I am nothing but ashes at your feet, if that's what it will take for you to forgive me.

I would give my last breath for you, darling.
Please...
I am lost without you, just half a man missing the other
half of his soul.
I am forever indebted to you, my love.
Kaleb.

I choke out, tears rolling down my cheeks as I re-read his message until my sight is completely blurred.

"Connie!?" I hear Reese's voice laced with concern, her sitting by my side as she cuddles a still sleepy Celeste. "What's happened?" her voice is a whisper as her arm wraps round my shoulders.

"It's Kaleb," I sob, palming my tears away as I let my phone slip out of my grasp.

"Is he okay?" I can hear the panic pricking at her voice and I instantly feel bad knowing exactly where her overthinking mind will take her. Placing my hand on her thigh I nod.

"He is fine."

"Okay, phew," she exhales heavily, her hand pressed against her chest to slow her racing heart. "What's happened? The fact you moved into the penthouse, well, I assumed something must have gone wrong."

"He planned to have Tryst killed," I swallow the thickness in my throat down, "and I'm not even mad about that, I mean I am, I *was* mad about it because it is fucking psycho but I get it. I get his rationale behind it. It's fucked up, I know," I continue to cry, humiliation flaming my cheeks. The more I had time to think about what he admitted, the more I do really understand why he did it. "But he didn't tell me, I only found out because a letter was dropped off at his apartment," I stop, sniffling as I intake a shudder of breath.

"Letter?" her brows pinch as Celeste dozes on her mum's chest.

"*The* letter," I nod, nibbling my bottom lip.

Her mouth forms the perfect 'o' at my words.

"Except, the letter wasn't written by Tryst..." I stall my words for a moment as my heart begins drumming in my chest. "I knew his hand writing... it wasn't his handwriting."

"May I see it?" Reese asks and I inhale sharply, nodding. I stand and walk into the hallway, grabbing the letter from my coat pocket and padding back into the living room. With shaky hands, I unfold it and begin reading aloud.

To whoever finds this first.

Connie. Sweetheart, I'm hoping it's you.

I know you're going to be shocked and mad, I mean, I had it all right? The fame, the fortune... everything in-between.

I never meant to hurt you the way I did. Once I did it once, I couldn't stop. It was like my new addiction. The first couple of times I hated myself for it, but the more I did it, the more I wanted to.

There was something about you, something about how you changed and grew as a person when you left your moms' and dad's place and it terrified me that one day you were going to leave me. So I suppose the only way I could explain it and make you maybe understand the thoughts that plagued me was that if me treating you the way I did... well it gave me some sort of hope that you would never leave.

But it seems my plan backfired and never worked out the way I planned.

Please know I didn't do this because of you. Or did I?

You will never know I suppose.

I did this because the voices in my head were too loud.

I was good at hiding my darkest thoughts, wasn't I?

I am hoping I'll find peace, but let's be honest, I'll be in hell.

But even in hell, I'm at peace. No longer fighting the constant demons.

No longer needing to fight.

I was free.

And now so are you.

Tryst

My throat burns as I ignore the lump that is choking me. My eyes pin to Reese as I fold the letter up carefully, running it through my fingers continuously. Reese says nothing, just sits with patience as she waits for me to find my voice.

"I took it to Kaleb at work, I just couldn't get my head

round it. Then fear crippled me that it had been *made* to look like a suicide, when in fact, it was not."

"No," Reese whispers, her eyes wide. "Even with what he said, you think it wasn't suicide?"

"It's not his writing Reese, and the fact it was delivered to me... whoever done it wanted me to find out." I protest, letting my head fall. "After I read it, I turned up at Kaleb's office a crying mess," I scoff, "that's all I have done lately, cry." I sigh heavily, shaking my head from side to side.

"I feel ya, I've been there hun. I love your dad, so, so much..." she smiles as if memories are playing over in her head, "but my god, the man reduced me to tears so many times." She pulls on her bottom lip with her teeth. "When it came round to the grovelling, I was too exhausted. He explained everything in his letter, and yeah, I could have held a grudge, I could have made him beg on his hands and knees for forgiveness. I'm stubborn and strong willed, but at that point... I just wanted him, we had been through *so much,*" she whispers now, her eyes falling to her daughter.

"It all worked out in the end," I smile through glassy eyes and Reese's eyes find mine, "shit sorry, I totally crashed your story," she looks at me apologetic and I laugh.

"It's okay."

"No, it's not. I'm sorry, please..." she reaches for my hand, giving it a squeeze.

I nod, looking down into my lap as I rub my palm up and down my jeans.

"I took the letter to Kaleb, I'm crying and hyperventilating, and I hold the letter up and I can see by the look on his face, he knows what it is. He knows why I'm there..." my bottom lip trembles and I try my hardest to not give in to any more fucking tears. Sinking my top teeth into it and biting down hard.

"It's okay, Connie." Reese's soft voice blankets me and all I can do is nod through the tears that I have no control over.

"He has known all along; he has known that Tryst didn't kill himself." I choke through sobs, and now, I'm a blubbering mess. "But he could have just told me, I grieved for my ex who lost to demons. None of it made sense, Tryst lived the rock 'n' roll life, but he never got down about it," I suck in a breath, "even when he was assaulting me, he was never phased. Nothing phased him. He was so high on it all, that he never hit the almighty low from his comedown."

"He assaulted you!?" Reese shrieks and my eyes widen.

"Shit, Reese," I stammer, my voice trembling as fear courses through my blood, "you can't tell dad, please, don't tell Killian," My whole body begins to shake, hot tears cascading down my cheeks.

"Fuck, Connie," she chokes, moving Celeste into her left arm as she stirs and pulling me in for a hug, her face against mine, her lips close to my ear, "I knew he'd treated you badly from when we talked when I visited you, but you shouldn't have gone through that alone," she whispers, and I can feel the wetness on her cheeks as her own tears fall.

"I had Kaleb," my voice is low, the admission lifting some of the heavy burden I have carried. All I have wanted to do was call Reese when shit hit the fan, but I couldn't. Because I was being too *selfish*. I resented the wrong people, and that was so fucking wrong of me. "He saved me Reese, if it wasn't for him..." I can't even finish the words that are sitting on my tongue.

"I know," is all she says, her arm still wrapped around my tiny frame.

"I just needed space, I don't want to lose him, I love

him," I shudder on my inhale of breath, the tears slowly dissolving.

"And you won't lose him, I promise."

We sit and talk a little more until exhaustion floors me, yawning and rubbing my eyes I finally push myself up from the sofa.

I needed to go home.

Then tomorrow, I needed to fix this with Kaleb. I didn't want to do this life without him. Reese is my proof that life is so God damn short.

Anything can happen and I didn't want to ever be without Kaleb.

CHAPTER FIFTY-FOUR
KALEB

I FEEL LIKE AN IDIOT. I'VE BEEN STANDING HERE IN HER PENTHOUSE for over an hour, candles lit, and vases of roses scattered from the front door to the living room where I am currently standing. Twisting my wrist towards me, I check the time. Reese assured me she would be home by now. My gut twists as perspiration beads on my forehead. Was she lying to me? Maybe Connie wasn't coming. I sigh, looking around at my surroundings and instantly missing her. I can smell her, see little pieces of her scattered around.

I hear the key in the front door and my heart is suddenly in my throat. I stand tall, my eyes pinned to where she will be walking round the corner any minute.

Three.

Two.

One.

Her eyes widen, her lips parting as she gasps before her hands cover her mouth.

"Surprise," I rasp, my voice thick as I struggle to speak.

"Kaleb," she whispers, not moving from the spot she seems to be anchored to.

"Hey baby," I croon and my heart gallops through my chest like a hundred racehorses beating down the track.

"How did..."

"I have my ways," I smirk, trying to make light of this weird situation.

"Does that way begin with an R?"

I laugh, dropping my head as I look at the floor for a moment and when I lift my head, my eyes land on her walking towards me. I bite my tongue, her eyes volleying back and forth between mine. I fall to my knees in front of her, my head falling forward as I press it against her stomach.

"Connie, I am so sorry," I whisper, my hands shakily skating up her side, my fingers wrapping round her waist as I hold her.

"Gramps," her soft voice swarms me with butterflies, "look at me." I let my head tip back, her beautiful green, doe eyes on mine. Her fingertips run along my strong jaw line before stopping at the base of my chin as she pushes softly. "I don't want you kneeling in front of me, I don't need you to stay on your knees, or to crawl across broken glass, I don't even want you to walk across burning coals and fall as ash at my feet," she whispers, not taking her eyes from mine. "I just want you."

My heartbeat slows, my eyes glassing as happy tears prick at them, relief washing over me. Rushing to my feet, I wrap my arms around her waist and pick her up effortlessly, her legs wrapping round me as I hover my lips over hers.

"Don't ever leave me again," I beg through a whisper, "I couldn't survive if you did."

"I won't," she smiles, edging closer so our lips touch and I feel the spark devour me whole, the current so strong swimming through my veins. I pull away, a whine leaving her as I do.

"As much as I don't want to stop... we need to talk," I swallow the lump away, I don't want to go back into this with secrets. I want to be honest with her, no more skeletons hiding in the closet, no more secrets lurking waiting to pounce at any moment.

We need to start this fresh.

Our new beginning starts today.

"Not tonight, Kaleb, please." She whines against my lips, "Tomorrow, tonight I just want to forget about everything and everyone else." Her hands clasp at my face, tilting my head back so I'm looking at her. "Please, Kaleb."

I nod reluctantly, my heart hammering in my chest, "I need to tell you, it's eating me alive," I practically beg.

Her soft, pink lips brush over mine, "Just for tonight, *please,*" she repeats and I'm hoping tomorrow is not going to be too late. Her lips are on mine, her hands still cupping my face as our kiss deepens, her tongue gliding over mine, our teeth clashing as the spark between us burns to desire. My fingers skim down her back, rounding her peachy ass as I let my fingers dig into her ass cheeks, pushing her closer to me.

"Make love to me Kaleb," her voice barely audible as she begs, "I need you," she whispers through kisses.

"Not as much as I need you, darling."

WE LAY IN HER BED, HER HEAD ON MY CHEST AS MY HEART BEATS steady beneath my skin, her fingers trailing up and down over my broad chest.

"I'm sorry," I whisper, my chin to my chest as I kiss the top of her head.

"Kaleb," I can hear the exasperation in her voice.

"I know, darling. Not tonight, I just needed to say that," I hum, slowly tipping my head back until its resting on the pillow again.

"I looked after Celeste today," she mutters softly as she shuffles her head back so her fingers can entwine in my dark dusting of chest hair.

"Yeah? How was that?" I ask, a hint of a smile gracing my face as I know how happy she would have been.

"It was amazing, albeit it was only a few hours, but to have that one-on-one time with her that I missed out on..." she sighs, "it was perfect." She lifts her head up to look at me, "I said I will do it so Reese can go back to work, I have nothing else to do and I can't just stay at home, I would go insane."

"Yeah, I get that, you need a little independence back in your life."

"I'm not getting any younger, at the grand old age of twenty two," her eyes slice to mine, and I let out a deep laugh.

"Oh, to be twenty-two again."

"What back in the olden days?" she leans up on her elbow and kisses me on the cheek, "Did you have colour televisions back then?" she snorts.

"You little minx," my head tips back as my laugh grows, I rise up over her and pull her on top of me.

"Steady now Gramps, don't want you to throw your back," she continues her smile so wide as she fights, her giggle escaping.

"I'll show you gramps," my voice is low as I clasp my

hand round the back of her head and bring her lips down to mine, kissing her with force.

"Show me," she whispers, her eyes dancing with mine. I would never tire of her. I feel sad to have never felt a love like this before, that I have never had a woman love me back as fiercely as I loved her and I intended on spending the rest of my life showing her just how much I did.

SAT UNDER THE BLANKET IN HER LIVING ROOM, SHE WAS SITTING all starry-eyed watching *Beauty and The Beast*.

I wasn't interested in the film; I was too busy watching her lose herself and show me every emotion that came oozed from her whilst watching. It was becoming something of a tradition for us; just like when we watched *Tangled*.

"I would love a library like that," she sighs blissfully as she watches the beast show Belle his library.

"You want it? Done."

"Really?"

"Of course, darling, anything to make you smile," my voice is low as I pull her into me.

"You make me smile baby, I only ever need you."

Anxiety ripples through me at the unspoken truths and hidden secrets that are lying between us.

"Can we talk?" I finally say, as she pulls her eyes from mine. "You said last night to wait till tomorrow, yet here we are, and I still haven't said what I need to."

Her glistening green eyes dart back and forth from mine, her body twisting to face me.

"I don't want this moment to be ruined, can we just have this weekend? I promise, tomorrow night we can sit and talk, you can tell me whatever it is that's eating you, but I've arranged to meet my moms for lunch tomorrow and I would love if you would come with me," her voice is small as her eyes filled with hope.

"Of course, I would love to," I nod, leaning forward and kissing her on the forehead, lingering for a little while.

"But," she whispers and it has be pulling back from her, "I do think we need to have a do-over." I nod

"And after tonight, we can talk about it all. All of it." My tone is a little harsher than intended and I sigh.

"I want to date you, Kaleb. I want to do dinners, days out, holidays…" she pauses, "I want it all with you, but I want everything in the right order. I want to be dated; we sort of just…"

"Fell into it with each other," my voice is hoarse as I swallow and she nods slowly.

"And I am so glad we did, but we lost the excitement and the buzz of a new relationship."

I can see the words that are spilling out of her are hard to say, I can see by the pained expression on her face.

"I get it baby, I do," I edge closer, cupping her cheek in my hand and my heart warming as she leans her face into it.

"So, I'll live here, you live at home and we will take each day as it comes," she swallows, her voice thick of emotion.

"Okay," I just about manage as I feel my own throat thicken. This isn't a bad thing, yet I feel like I've just taking an almighty blow to the stomach which has winded the air out of my lungs. But for her? I'll wait, I'll take it slow. It's not an unreasonable request… I'm just possessive over what is mine and I hate being without her.

CHAPTER FIFTY-FIVE
CONNIE

I was nervous. Constantly pacing back and forth in the lounge. I changed my outfit four times before settling back on my dark denim jeans, heeled black boots and a white blouse. Smart casual. I think. Looking at my watch, Kaleb should be here any minute. I asked him to leave last night and as much as it gutted me to do it, I needed to. We do need distance put between us for us to grow, I want to fall deeper in love with him and enjoy every minute with him. The buzzer goes suddenly, my head snapping up.

Rushing for the door, I swing it open and let my eyes drink in the handsome man in front of me. Dressed in a white, open collared shirt and jeans and all I can think about is jumping into his arms and letting him devour me.

"We're matching..." I blush as I continue to let my eyes roam over his body.

"Well, look at that, so we are," he winks at me, stepping slightly over the threshold. "You ready to go?" he smiles, holding his hand out for me to take which I do gladly before he pulls me into a kiss.

"Ready as I'll ever be," I mutter, pecking him on the lips again.

"Everything will be okay," he tries his best to reassure me, but the nerves that are tingling throughout my body suggest otherwise. His fingers lace through mine as we walk down the corridor to the elevator that serves my penthouse.

"It's so bittersweet being here," I look over my shoulder at the door of my home and smile.

"How come?"

"Well, Reese used to live a couple of floors down, and this penthouse was my dad's. She never knew he lived here but he knew where she lived. Thinking back, it was a little creepy how obsessed with her he was." I scoff a laugh as we step into the waiting elevator. "We had thanksgiving at the penthouse, and I remember Reese dropping her candied yams when my dad walked round the corner. I was so fucking naive."

"Why do you say that?"

"They had been seeing each other behind closed doors for a while, they were even married after one drunken night! It didn't matter how much they vowed to stay away from each other, they always gravitated back," I sigh, cocking my head to the side as the elevator descends, "like moths to a flame."

"Mmhmm," Kaleb hums in agreement, "some people are written in the stars, destined even, and it doesn't matter what you do, if you're both meant to end up together, you eventually will."

"I like that though, it's like the perfect happily ever after in the fairytales I watch, that's why I love them so much and the romance books I read. They're guaranteed happily ever after." I turn to look up at Kaleb who is watching me, "You're not always promised them in real life," I whisper as my heart bangs against my ribs.

"*You* are though," he squeezes my hand and I lean into him, "you deserve to get your happy ever after."

Silence falls between us as the lift doors open, Kaleb leading me into the main lobby of the apartment block and past Frank.

"Connie," he nods his head, his hat tilting slightly.

"Hi Frank," I breathe through a smile as Kaleb opens the passenger side door to his car for me. Slipping in, he leans across and straps me in as he makes sure it's secure. "I'm not a child," I roll my eyes at him as he stands back on the sidewalk.

"I know, love, but at least I know you're safe," his handsome face is smothered in smugness.

He slides in beside me and pushes the start button on his car, the engine rumbles.

"So, tell me more about what happened in that apartment block," Kaleb asks as he pulls into the flowing traffic.

"Hmm," I tap my finger to my chin, "what *didn't* happen in that apartment block," I wiggle my brows as his hand skates across the centre of the car and slips between my thighs, giving me a gentle squeeze as his brows raise, causing his forehead to crinkle. I laugh, "Nah, nothing like that," I shrug, "just found out that my best friend was sleeping with my dad, found her pregnancy leaflet and before she could tell me that she was pregnant my dad burst through the door rambling on, something along the lines of '*if you think for one minute I'm not going to be a part of my baby's life...*' blah blah blah, then I called my said best friend a gold digging whore, erm, I got over my tantrum... obviously," I smirk, placing my own hand over his, the warmth of his skin causing my skin to pebble. "Planned her baby shower, my dad didn't turn up, Reese was pissed so I went to see my dad to find out what this absolute horrid woman he worked with had over him. I found him in his office drinking himself into a deeper depression, so I did what any daughter would do and threw my sneaker at his head," I roll my lips and I hear Kaleb choke on a laugh.

"You did what?" he roars as he puts his blinker on to pull down a side road.

"Mmhm, he was being all dramatic and stubborn so... it worked anyway," I roll my eyes, "then in that same office, on the same day, he told me that said horrid woman was actually my birth mom." I simmer down quickly, going mute in an instant as I puff out my cheeks.

"What?" he turns to look at me as we roll to a stop at the lights.

"Have I not mentioned that before?" I pull my brows together, averting my gaze from him.

"Not that I recall."

"Yeah, it wasn't a great time for me... that's when I..." I stall, suddenly finding it hard to breathe as my chest tightens.

"Left with Tryst," he whispers, his grip tightening on my thigh. I screw my eyes shut, taking deep inhales of breath through my nose and letting them slip past my lips on their exhale. "Connie?" I ignore his voice but within seconds, he is round my side of the car, opening my door and unbuckling me.

He helps me out the car and holds me as I come apart in his arms. "It's okay baby, I've got you."

Car horns are going behind us, but he doesn't rush me.

He lets me breathe through my panic attack until I am ready to open my eyes.

His thumb pad wipes away a stray tear from my cheek before wrapping his arms round the top of my shoulders, holding me tight as he rests his lips on the top of my head.

"It's okay," he soothes, tightening his grip as I settle in his arms. "It's okay."

WALKING INTO SARA BETH'S, KALEB CLINGS ONTO MY HAND, HIS fingers locked through mine as we stop at the server station.

"Hi, table under Connie?" Kaleb asks, I haven't spoken since my panic attack. I have no idea why it came on as suddenly as it did, but I'm putting it down to the admissions of things that I had buried deep within myself. Kaleb seems to bring all of that out in me, which is good. It stops me harbouring onto things and people that hurt me.

"Ah, yes. Follow me, your guests are already here." The server nods, grabbing two menus and leading us towards the table where my moms are sitting. They stand as soon as they see me, slipping from the booth.

"Kaleb," my voice is trembling, "this is Lara," I point, "and this is Katie," I force a smile even though I feel like I am about to throw up through nerves.

"Baby," my mom, Lara cries as she pulls me from Kaleb, holding me tight before stepping back and examining me from head to toe. "You look so well," she gasps, looking behind at my second mom. "Doesn't she look well Katie?" She nods in agreement.

"Come, come, let's sit down," she holds her hand out for me to take my seat, Kaleb sliding in beside me.

His hand rests on my thigh, giving me a gentle squeeze as they both pin their eyes to him.

"Mom, Mom," my eyes move between both of them. "This is Kaleb."

"Kaleb?" my mom, Lara stammers, side eyeing Katie.

"Yeah," I smile, turning my head to look at him.

"It's so nice to finally meet you, Lara and Katie," Kaleb extends his arm across the table to shake their hands.

"And it's nice to meet you too," Katie smiles as Lara taps on her phone. Katie nudges her and she slips the phone back inside her bag.

"I can't wait to hear all about how you met, but first, I can't begin to explain how excited we were to receive your message."

I swallow and nod, my eyes pinned to Lara.

"I thought it was time, and what with Killian's—I mean dad's—accident I thought life is too short to hold grudges."

"Accident?" Katie pipes up, her eyes batting back and forth, "Is he okay?"

"Yeah, he is fine," I roll my eyes, "there was a car accident, but he luckily came away okay. You know what he is like, always a drama," a small laugh bubbles out of me.

"So, you reconciled with your dad before us?" Lara places her hand at her chest, visibly wounded at the words that left my mouth.

"It wasn't planned that way, Mom. I went to see Reese..."

"Oh," they both say in unison.

"Wanted to meet my baby sister," I exhale heavily, "I had no intention on seeing Killian, Reese swore to keep our meeting on the quiet until her phone rang and next thing I knew, we were on the way to the hospital."

"How did it go?" Katie asks.

"As well as it could have done, I suppose. The bridges are no longer burned between us."

"That makes me happy," Lara smiles.

"Look, things are not going to be just forgotten about, but I want to make a fresh start for everything. The last year of my life has been filled with grief, hate, love, entrapment and freedom. I have been through it all, but now it's time for me to leave it all behind me and start again. So, this is what I am doing. I am starting again. With you, with Dad and Reese and with Kaleb." I turn to look at him, giving him a small smile.

"And we back your decision, one hundred percent," Lara nods, "we have missed you so much," she chokes out, tears brimming in her eyes as my mom wraps her arms around her shoulders and comforts her. Guilt swarms me.

"I missed you both too, more than you would ever know. But what happened with..." I close my eyes and swallow the lump down, "I just couldn't bear to look or even be near any of you. I lived a lie for twenty-two years; my whole entire life was a lie. I just don't understand why you couldn't tell me. It wasn't as if I was a child who was finding out, I was an adult. I would have been sad but at least I wouldn't have been blindsided. I was like a horse with its blinkers on until that day. That day changed the chemicals that made me who I am. The resentment I felt for all of you, it made me sick to my stomach. I mean, how could I hate my three parents *that* much. But then it all sort of faded, I understood why you done it the way you did. You were protecting me, shielding me from a mother who never wanted me." I chew on the inside of my cheek, Kaleb's hand still on my thigh.

"I couldn't have wished for better parents. I'm just sad that it all happened the way it did, the thought of knowing that her blood courses through my veins makes me nauseous. I want *nothing* to do with her. Even when she is on her death bed, I have no interest in her at all." I reach for the glass of water that sits on the table and drink half of it.

"I can't change that, I can't change my DNA, but I can forgive. I don't want to go through this life without any of you. You're my make-up, my heart and my soul. Not her. She's the science, but I don't care about that, I care about *you*." I place my glass down and reach across the table, taking one hand from both of my moms into mine. "I love you both, so *so* much," I choke.

"And we love you," Katie sobs as we finally shed the tears that have been threatening since the moment I walked into this restaurant. The whole time, Kaleb's hand was on me, reminding me that he was here. That he would always be here. Through the good, the sad, the bad and the ugly. He was always here, and right where I needed him.

PUSHING MY PLATE AWAY, I RUBBED MY BELLY. I WAS STUFFED. WE all ordered the lobster rolls after Reese recommended it to me this morning. She came here with Harlen when she was trying to get him to sign with her and it quickly became a favourite of hers.

"So," Lara wipes the corners of her mouth then places the napkin on her empty plate. "How did you two meet?" I watch as her eyes lift from mine but slice over to Kaleb's before narrowing in on him. Uneasiness sinks deep inside of me.

I shuffle in my seat, my hand skimming up his back and wrapping my fingers over his shoulders.

"Want me to tell them, or you?" I smile at him, my eyes wide and full of love as I look at the handsome man sat next to me. I know he is *so* much older than me, but when we're together, I don't even think about the twenty years or so age gap. Because love is love, and when you know you've met your soulmate, you know.

"May I?" He turns to look down at me, his lips curling into a beautiful smile and my heart flutters in my chest.

"Of course," my smile is a permanent fixture as I listen.

"Our first meeting was in a coffee shop in London, your beautiful daughter came over and demanded I moved as I was in *her* seat," he laughs softly, shaking his head from side to side at the fond memory of our first meeting. My fingers reach up as I skim the tips of them through his thick, black hair that has a glossy shine to it, the fine grey hairs showing occasionally in certain lights.

"London?" my moms exchange glances, brows raising and lips twisting.

"Yeah, I was there for work, Connie was with Tryst," his voice tightens and his jaw ticks.

"I see," Lara remarks to him, her tone curt.

"She was very strong willed, held her own which I liked. And honestly, the moment I saw her, I thought she was the most beautiful woman in the world."

"I am glad to hear that," Katie pipes up, her hand covering Lara's.

"Then I bumped into her again back here, at one of Tryst's shows and somehow, we just kept finding each other, as if fate planned it for us."

"Fate?" Lara smirks, and my eyes narrow on her for a moment as I can't help but notice her condescending tone.

"Yes," Kaleb's tone is clipped. "*Fate*."

My eyes move between Kaleb and my moms, and I can't help but feel the tension brewing between the three of them.

"Call it what you want," Kaleb continues, his hand reaching for mine and placing them interlocked on the table for all to see. "I am obsessively, irrevocably, in love with your daughter."

"I think that went well, don't you?" Kaleb brushes the back of my hand against his lips as we weave between cars.

"Yeah," I smile, my heart still cartwheeling in my chest at his declaration of love, "it did go well."

"Hopefully I won their hearts over," he smiles goofily at me.

"Of course, you did," I sigh blissfully, as we pull into the underground parking lot of my apartment.

"Can I take you for dinner tonight?" Kaleb asks as he pulls into my allotted space.

"Like a date?" I say excitedly as I twist in my chair, Kaleb cutting the engine.

"Yes, like a date," his voice is low and sexy as he leans over the centre of the car and cups my face, his eyes volleying back and forth between mine before he slowly edges his lips towards mine. "I'll never tire of kissing you," he whispers before his soft, plump lips brush against mine, his eyes fluttering closed.

"Good, I never want you to stop kissing me," I just about manage as my hands move to his face, holding him tightly.

Our tongues move in slow, sensual strokes. Our lips finding their own rhythm as my heart sings along in my chest.

"I love you, Kaleb. I never want to lose you, to imagine a life without you."

"Baby, you will never lose me. You're it for me. You were made for me, I was made for you. We were destined, written in the stars above us. You're my reason for breathing, the reason my heart bangs in my chest, *you* are the reason for my existence."

"What did I do to deserve you?" I whisper against his lips, my eyes falling between us.

"You did nothing, my love. You are the most deserving woman of love; I am the one who should be asking what I've done to *deserve you*."

Silence falls between us, our heads pressed together, our steady breaths matching as we enjoy this moment.

It feels like hours have slipped past when we finally make our way inside the apartment, hand in hand, smiling from ear to ear like two lovesick puppy dogs. Kicking my sneakers off, I finally slip my fingers from Kaleb's and walk further into the apartment.

"Wine?" I call out as Kaleb rounds the corner to the kitchen where I am standing.

"Please," he smiles, curling his fingers round the edge of the worktop, his eyes raking up and down my body, his tongue darting out as he slowly runs it across his bottom lip.

"Why are you staring at me like you want to eat me?" I smirk, turning quickly to hide my blush as I reach for two wine glasses. My breath catches at the back of my throat when I feel his large hands skim round my body, pressing into my stomach.

"Because darling, that's exactly what I want to do," he kisses the shell of my ear as his whispers set my body on fire.

My heart skips its beat in my chest, causing it to rise and fall quicker. Turning me to face him, his eyes are hooded and deliciously dark. Lifting me onto the edge of the work surface, he grips the inside of my legs and pushes them apart, his eyes falling for a moment.

His fingers skim up my thighs, slowly against the material of my jeans until he gets to the button that is stopping him from getting to what he wants. His burning eyes flick up to mine, a hint of a smirk pulling at the corner of his lips. Fumbling with the cool, brass button, he pops it through the slit as I push up, lifting my ass from the surface as he tugs them down my legs and all the way off my feet, discarding them to the floor. He sucks in a breath as he focuses on my lace, hot pink panties.

"Can you just walk round in these all day?" he hums against my skin as his lips press against my neck, trailing them down and across to the other side.

"Maybe," I smirk, "I'll think about it."

His fingers skim across my bare thigh, drawing circles over my skin. His touch is hot, burning me softly as he continues his trail. A whimper leaves me as his callous fingers press against my clit through the thin material, before he steps back and hooks his fingers round the side of my panties and pulls them to the side. His hot fingers circling over my clit then gliding them down to my opening, swirling the tips in my arousal before dragging them through my folds and back over my clit. My soft moans fill the room, as Kaleb falls to his knees. Lifting his fingers from me, I instantly miss his touch as his hands wrap around my ass, his fingers digging into the skin as he pulls me forward and to the edge. I keep my eyes on him the whole time. Gliding his hands round and back on my thighs, he pushes them further apart as he edges his mouth closer to my sex, his hot breath on my sensitive skin before he swipes his tongue through my pussy lips, spreading them as he does.

"Oh," I whisper, my fingers wrapped tightly round the edge of the work surface.

The tip of his tongue flicks over my clit quickly, two of his fingers teasing at my opening as I watch him fill me. My eyes roll in the back of my head at the pleasure that overcomes me, pulling me from reality for just a moment. Kaleb flattens his tongue, stroking me harder and deeper as he devours me. His spare hand skims down my leg and wraps round my ankle as he pushes it up, bending my leg at the knee as I rest my foot on the edge of the work surface.

"Good girl," his voice is a low growl, my eyes focus on the glisten that marks his lips and my cheeks burn. I feel his tongue on me once more, my orgasm clawing her way out as he buries his tongue deep in my folds, his fingers pumping in and out of my pussy with ease.

"Oh, Kaleb," I moan, my chest rising and falling fast as I try and fill my lungs with air. I uncurl one of my hands from the work surface, ignoring the ache deep within my knuckles from where I had been gripping so tightly, causing them to go white. Entwining my fingers through his thick, dark hair, I tug at the root as his head moves from side to side, his tongue flicking over my clit as I feel the delicious burn radiating deep within me.

"I am so close," I moan, my head tipping forward as his eyes connect with mine as I watch his tongue push me to my orgasm. His fingers slow, pulling to the tip before slipping into me hard and fast, but his tongue stays the same. Slow and hard as he focuses on my swollen clit.

"Kaleb, don't stop. Please, just like that," I manage to squeak out as my body begins to tremble, a blanket of shivers covering me as my orgasm peaks, ripping through me. I cry out, and I hear Kaleb's animalistic growl vibrate against my core. My hips bucking as Kaleb treats my pussy as if it is his last meal, licking, sucking and savouring every ounce of me whilst I ride my orgasm. He gradually slows, his fingers slipping out of me as he pushes them past his lips, sucking on them and moaning in appreciation.

My cheeks pinch crimson and I try to hide my face with my hands.

"Nope," I hear his voice, his hands removing mine from my face, slowly pulling them down, "don't ever hide from me, my love," his hands clasp my face, tilting my head back as he lowers his lips over mine, "ever."

Just as he is about to kiss me, I jump when I hear banging on my front door.

"Shit," I grit out, shoving Kaleb away from me as I cover myself over and bend to pick my jeans up from the floor, tugging them up my legs as I jump around on the spot trying to pull them up.

Bang, bang, bang.

The noise is so loud, it's echoing around the large penthouse. Kaleb is close to me, but panic creeps up my throat.

"Connie!" I hear my dad bellow through the front door.

"Oh fuck," I swallow the lump down in my throat. I turn frantically to see Kaleb, my eyes widen. "Don't say anything, keep your mouth shut," my eyes bug out of my head, waiting for Kaleb to register. He nods, pretending to pull a zip across his mouth but he looks just as nervous as I do. His normal brazen facial expression is replaced with a lip chewing, eyes dancing nervous boy.

"Connie! Open this door, right now!" My dad shouts again, followed by three large bangs.

"I'm coming! Be patient!" I try to lace my voice with humor, but I'm not fooling anyone.

I rush forward towards to door, stopping as I look at myself in the mirror. My eyes are all hazy and glassed from my orgasm, my cheeks red and my chest scattered with red blemishes.

I inhale deeply, my heart jack hammering in my chest as I wrap my fingers round the doorknob and brace myself for what is hurricane Killian.

Three.

Two.

One.

Twisting the doorknob and pulling the door open I plaster a smile on my face as I welcome my dad.

"Dad, hey, so nice to..."

But he isn't here to see me. His eyes are wide and bloodshot, his jaw is wound tight, and his fists are balled by his side.

"Where the fuck is he?" he barges past me, knocking into me as he does but he doesn't even notice. He is in a blind rage.

"Dad!" I shout as I turn and watch him stalk towards Kaleb. Kaleb doesn't falter, just stands tall waiting for whatever is coming to him.

"You," Dad growls, shoving Kaleb hard, making him lose his footing for a moment. "You no good..." he grits out, shoving him again.

"I think you should stop," Kaleb says calmly but that only seems to enrage my dad more, like a matador waving a red cape in front of a bull.

"Cunt," Dad's voice is full of venom as he continues shoving Kaleb back. "Are you a pervert?" Killian asks, his brows furrowed.

"Are you?" Kaleb retorts back and I gasp, covering my hand over my mouth. "Aren't you engaged to a girl twenty years younger than you?" Kaleb smirks, him and my dad toe to toe. There isn't much in their height, I would say Kaleb is slightly taller.

"Dad, please," I rush over to them, pushing my way between them. I see the anger in my dad's eyes slowly slip away as he focuses on me. "Please don't do this," I whisper, placing my hands on his chest. "I love him."

My dad scoffs, rolling his eyes, "You're twenty-two, what do *you* know about love?" his harsh words slice through me like a knife, easily cutting into me and making me bleed. Silence fills the room, tension growing, and I feel sick to my stomach.

"This wasn't supposed to happen," Killian rasps, his frantic eyes moving from me and up to Kaleb. "This wasn't part of the plan," I watch as my dad's jaw tightens, his eyes widening once more as his eyes land back on Kaleb.

"What?" I snap, turning to look at Kaleb, whose eyes are burning into mine. Turning my face back round to look at my dad, panic claws at my insides, my throat thickening. "What do you mean?" I am surprised at how calm my reaction is, I feel like I am trembling.

"Oh," my dad grins, a low chuckle escaping him as he runs his hand through his thick, brown hair. "Kaleb, Kaleb, Kaleb," my dad tsks, shaking his head from side to side and rubbing his hand over his stubble, the scratching noise filling the deadly quiet room. My dad reaches for me, pulling me next to his side as he wraps his arms round my shoulder in a comforting way.

"Seeing as you haven't told my daughter, why don't you do it now? In front of me. I want to be here as you shatter my daughter's heart into pieces, at least that way I'll be here to pick the pieces up." My heart sinks into the depths of my chest, and suddenly, I forget how to breathe.

Kaleb says nothing, but his eyes tell me everything I need to. I have been lied to. *Again.*

I watch as his stormy grey eyes begin to glass over, the way his strong jaw tightens as he tries to fight whatever urge is brewing deep inside of him.

"Kaleb," I whisper, because honestly, that's all I can manage right about now.

"Tell her, or I will," my dad's tone is clipped, his grip on me tightening.

Kaleb runs his hand along the side of his head, grabbing a handful of hair at the nape of his neck before he lets out a deep exhale.

"Baby, please remember..." Kaleb takes a small step towards me but then stops. My eyes burn as I fight with the tears that are threatening to fall. "I wanted to speak to you yesterday, but you said you wanted to enjoy the weekend..." he trails off and I can hear my heartbeat in my ears, I give a small nod. "This is what I wanted to tell you..." he trails off, and I watch as his hard facial expression begins to slip, and I see just how much he is hurting. The vulnerability is written all over his face.

"Tell her!" Killian's voice booms round the penthouse making me jump in my skin.

"It wasn't fate that led me to you in London..." he swallows hard, his hands locked together in front of him.

"What was it? Or should I ask, *whom* was it?" My dad jibes, poking the bear.

I choke on my intake of breath, tears rolling down my cheeks and I don't even need Kaleb to tell me. Everything makes so much more sense now.

"Your dad hired me to find you, to bring you home to

him..." Kaleb struggles to get the words out, his own tears escaping and running down his cheeks. I watch as they run until they fall from his rounded chin and dissolve on the floor. "But I wasn't going to let you go that easy, I meant what I said earlier, Connie, you're my start, my middle and my end. You're my reason for breathing, the reason my heart bangs in my chest, *you* are the reason for my existence. That will never change, Connie. Ever. I don't care how long it'll take for you to forgive me, but I will never give up on us."

"I think you should leave," I whisper, not able to look at him anymore until I can get my feelings in check. Kaleb doesn't move. It's as if he is anchored to the ground, unable to move, even if he wanted to.

"You heard my daughter, she wants you to leave," my dad drops his arm from me and steps towards Kaleb.

"No, not just Kaleb." I shake my head from side to side, "I want you *both* to leave." I mumble, crossing my arms against my chest suddenly feeling incredibly small.

"What?" I hear the hiss in Killian's tone.

"You heard me, I want you both gone." And now I lift my head up and look Killian dead in the eyes. "Yes, Kaleb lied to me, but so did you. You had the chance to tell me everything in your '*dad of the year*' speech in hospital, but you didn't." I shake my head from side to side and disappointment surges through me. "So please, just go." I sigh, suddenly exhausted and on the verge of my legs buckling beneath me.

Neither of them says a word as I walk through the middle of them, ignoring the pull towards Kaleb as I head for the stairs, walking to my bedroom. I still as I get to the top of the stairs, "Oh," I turn to look at the two men I love most in my life, but right about now, I hate them both.

"Close the door on your way out," I spit, picking my heavy legs up and slamming my bedroom door.

I wait and listen, the front door suddenly closing and once I know they are gone, I slide down the door and fall apart as I finally give into the tears.

CHAPTER FIFTY-SIX
KALEB

THE ACHE IN MY SOUL IS A CONSTANT REMINDER THAT I HURT HER.
Again. The look on her face as the words spilled out of my
mouth was enough to haunt me for the rest of my life. The
way her deep, beautiful green eyes slowly lost their sparkle
as each word slipped past my lips. I had no idea how many
days it had been, each one passing in a blur. It was as if I
was sitting still, frozen in time, yet the rest of the world
continued around me and for some reason, that made me
feel bitter. But I had no right to feel bitter because I was the
one who caused it. I was the one that had her heart in my
hands, and all I done was watch it disintegrate in my grasp.

Sighing, I bring the bourbon to my lips and take a
mouthful, not even wincing as the oaky liquid coats my
tongue. I have become numb.

I sent Doris home, I had no need for her. I hear the
elevator ping and see Titus and Keaton strolling down the
hallway towards me.

"Go away," I groan, sitting in the dark living room. I had
pulled the curtains in every room and not opened them
since.

"Nope," Titus' deep voice rips through me as he enters the room, Keaton pacing over to the windows and ripping the curtains back. I turn my head quickly, the autumn sun bright and making me squeeze my eyes shut.

"Fuck you," I grit, slowly opening my eyes again but squinting as it takes them a moment to adjust to the now light room.

"Enough is enough," Titus stands in front of me, his hands fisted deep into his light grey suit pants.

"Leave me alone," I bring my glass to my lips to take another mouthful of the poison that is numbing me from feeling. From feeling the thousand shards that my heart has splintered into. The pain is excruciating but I have no one to blame but myself.

"We've let you have your moment, now it's time to man the fuck up and pull yourself together," Titus' voice booms round the room and I turn my head away from him, so I don't have to look at his punch-able face.

"We get that you're sad mate, you're allowed to be sad," Keaton kneels in front of me, his brows furrowed softly as if the concern is filling him as each second passes. If I didn't know Keaton, I would think he was about to give me some soft love, a little brotherly advice... but the problem is. I do know Keaton. And he isn't that kind of brother. "You need to stop acting like a pussy," he smiles at me, reaching forward and slapping me on the cheek three times.

"You're a cunt," snatching his hand away and pushing him a little harder than I intended, he loses his balance and tumbles back, but Titus stops him from falling. Titus doesn't lift his eyes from his phone, and for some reason it aggravates me.

"Who you texting?" I ask, pushing from the sofa and

stumbling. The copious amounts of alcohol hitting me like a freight train.

"You fucking stink," Titus grunts, locking his phone and slipping it in his back pocket, "and trying to sort out this stuff with Xavier's daughter."

I smirk, stepping forward slightly, "Oh yes, the job that I am *irrelevant* in."

"Oh my god, you're such a child," Titus rolls his fucking eyes at me and Keaton dips his head as he chuckles to himself.

"Am I?" I taunt, stepping to the side and trying to will my legs to carry me and not let me fall.

"Where are you going?" Titus calls out, but they're hot on my tail.

"To get another drink," I shout as I stumble towards the kitchen.

"I don't think so," Keaton grabs my shoulders, slowly turning me away from the kitchen and I let out a loud sigh, moaning as he does.

"You need a shower, I can smell the alcohol seeping through your pours," Titus says as he turns me towards the stairs.

"And? I like it. I've got no one to smell nice for now anyway," I shrug my shoulders up, my voice a little quiet when suddenly I hear the droning hum of a song. I spin a little too quickly, knocking myself off balance but of course, good old Titus is there to catch me. My eyes take a minute to focus but when they do, Keaton is rubbing his finger and thumb together as if he is playing a small violin. "I hate you," I grit, my jaw ticking.

"I love you too brother," he chimes, standing the other side of me and practically dragging me up the stairs to the bathroom.

. . .

Sitting in the kitchen, my fingers curled and wrapped round the hot mug of black coffee that Keaton had made. I could feel his eyes burning into me, all the unspoken questions bouncing round in his head that I am adamant he couldn't wait to ask me. But, he kept them to himself which was unusual for Keaton.

Titus re-appears, a heavy burdening sigh leaving him as he picks his own cup of coffee up.

"What's wrong with you?" I ask, my tone sharp as the words slip off my tongue.

"Just this bullshit with Xavier's daughter and the Knight brothers," he shakes his head from side to side as he looks inside his coffee cup.

"Are you no closer to getting her over here?" Bringing the cup to my lips I take another mouthful, grateful that I am starting to sober up.

"Nope, Xavier was meant to have her in the air by the weekend, but the way this is going I'm worried she won't make it."

"Well, shit." I grit, placing my cup on the work surface as my brows lift, my eyes not moving from Titus. Keaton's eyes bat back and forth between us, and I feel like there is something Titus isn't telling me.

"So, are you going to stop walking around like a stroppy teenager?"

"I'm not like a stroppy..." I rub my lips into a thin line, closing my eyes as I inhale deeply.

Keaton scoffs.

"She doesn't want to see me, I've fucked it," my voice is low, my jaw ticks as I grind my back teeth.

"I would stop grinding them pearly whites of yours if I

was you, you keep going at the rate you are and you'll have no teeth left to grind, your dentist will be rubbing his hands together whilst getting your implants ready." Keaton laughs as he walks round the work surface, patting me on the back a little hard and it feels like he has knocked the air out of my lungs which causes me to cough.

"You haven't fucked it," the voice of reason that is Titus fills the room, "you just need to tell her dad to go fuck himself. You've let him win. He got what he wanted, his daughter back in his life... and what did you get?"

"Fucked over," Keaton replies dryly.

I slowly turn my head to look at my brother, my eyes narrow on him and just as I am about to stand up in my blind rage, Titus' hand rests on my shoulder, giving it a gentle squeeze. I instantly cool off, facing Titus.

His head dips, his shoulders curling forward as he leans down so that his eyes are level with mine. "Go and get your girl back."

CHAPTER FIFTY-SEVEN
CONNIE

THE MINUTES TURNED TO HOURS, THE HOURS INTO DAYS, THE DAYS into... nothing. That's how it felt now. Everything that once filled me with joy was now empty. I was numb. I don't even know how long it had been since he told me that he was working for my dad. I knew there was something off, and if I had really thought about it back in the beginning, I would have worked it out, but I didn't. The whole time I was with Kaleb I was blindfolded. Navigating through life using every other sense but my sight. He blinded me, and it wasn't even in a bad way. No, he showed me what life should feel like, what *love* should feel like. I am upset with him, yes, but I am angrier with myself that I dismissed him all weekend when he tried to tell me.

"Here," Reese's soft voice pulls me from my thoughts as she hands me a cup of tea. "Tea makes everything better," she smiles sweetly as she sits next to me on the sofa.

"So, I've heard," I mutter, words barely audible. "I'm pissed at you, I don't want it to drag on because honestly I am over all of this. The secrets, the many skeletons in the closet but I just want you to know I am angry with you too."

I puff my cheeks out and ignore the anger that is trying to force its way out of me.

"I get it Connie, I would be shocked if you wasn't. I'm sorry, I was between a rock and a hard place and I knew what your dad was doing was for your own safety... but I get it. So be angry at me, I can take it," she gives me a small smile as the heavy silence fills the room. Moments pass before I hear her say, "Your dad has taken Celeste out for a few hours, so it's just me and you," she leans forward and clicks the button on the remote before scrolling and finding *The Vampire Diaries.*

I smile, but that smile quickly fades when I am reminded of my weekend in Covington with Kaleb. It feels like a distant memory now, so much has happened since then. Everything has changed. The sting in my eyes is back, the burn in my throat as the apple sized lump lodges itself there. I swallow it down, ignoring the chokehold that my emotions have on me.

"Kaleb took me here a few weeks back," the quietness of my voice has Reese facing me and reading my lips more than listening to my voice.

"You went to Mystic Falls!?" she screeches, the excitement evident in her voice and I nod.

"It was everything and more," I sigh, and I see her smile slip, her eyes that were just full of sparkle now fading into darkness.

"Shit, let me turn it off," she edges forward, reaching for the remote and I place my hand over hers, shaking my head from side to side. "Leave it on," my eyes burn into hers as the corners of her mouth lift. "Please."

SLIPPING UNDER THE WATER OF THE HOT BATH, I'M ALONE WITH my thoughts again.

How did I get here?

Kaleb is my happy ending, I know deep in my heart that he is the one for me, yet I feel like every obstacle has been put in our way to stop us from getting there.

I needed to stop moping, I bet he is fine. He is probably back at work, out drinking with his friends whilst fucking anything that moves. My stomach rolls as nausea crashes through me.

Squeezing my eyes shut, I slip further under till I am completely submerged. The quietness and stillness of this moment fills me with peace, and I let my eyes close. I could easily stay here until my last breath runs out, drowning myself to death seems a pretty good way to go.

The struggle begins, and everything in my body is screaming at me to give in, to slip to the surface and take in the air that my lungs are so desperate for, but the thought of doing it isn't enough to make me *want* to do it. I am reminded of an earlier thought that I had when I was in a low point months ago. *You can't always walk on water, sometimes you have to slip and fall. It's up to you whether you keep fighting to reach the surface or let yourself sink into the depths of the ocean.*

Opening my eyes one last time, I look at the blurred vision in front of me when images of Kaleb fill my mind. His gorgeous grey eyes fixed to mine, his smile growing as he tells me how much he loves me whilst his hand cups my face so I can lean into it. I have never loved a man so fiercely as I have Kaleb. Memories flash by quicker now, us back in the Hamptons, laying on the rug as we drew shapes into the carpet talking about our future together, the wine we snuck into the shed for Titus' daughter and her friends, the way he made love to me for the first time and letting *me* take control, to take everything I needed. He saved me, giving me a reason to *live*. And after everything Tryst done to me to make me feel broken and unlovable, Kaleb fixed me. Bit by bit. The fight was becoming easier to ignore now as my heartbeat slowed, my lids getting heavier as well as my chest, fear grips me and that's when my thoughts scream at me.

What the fuck was I doing?! I didn't want to do this! I reached up with all the strength I had and wrapped my fingers round the edge of the bath and pulled myself out of the water, just as Reese fell to her knees by the bath.

"Connie," she calls, wrapping her fingers round my wrist when suddenly, I gasp, choking on my own breath as the air fills my lungs. "Oh my god, Connie," her pained voice has my eyes filling with tears.

"I'm okay, I'm okay," I rasp as she reaches behind her and grabs the towel from the rail, placing it over me.

"What were you thinking?!" her voice moves up a pitch or two.

"I wasn't," I admit, shame blanketing me. "I was never going to do it, I just had a moment..."

"A moment? Connie, having a moment is stepping outside and taking a breather. Having a moment is turning your music up so loud your ears hurt just so you can scream it out. Having a moment is locking yourself in the bathroom and crying until you have no more left to cry," her brows are furrowed causing deep creases in her forehead to appear. "Having a moment is not trying to drown yourself," a tear escapes her opal eyes, rolling down her cheek and falling off her chin, dissolving into the towel. "Having a moment is not trying to kill yourself," she whispers as if saying the words out loud is too painful.

"I wasn't trying to kill myself, I just needed..." I sigh, "I wasn't trying to do it," I nod firmly, slowly sitting up, crossing my legs underneath me. "I'm sorry, I didn't mean to scare you."

Her face lifts to look at me, and I can see the pain in her bloodshot eyes. "I've already lost one person I love, I don't want to lose another," she chokes, tears streaming down her face now.

"I was being selfish," I reach for her, wrapping my arm around her neck and pulling her into me for a hug as her body trembles with her cries.

———

We both agreed not to tell my dad about what happened a few days ago. He didn't need to know. I sat in the living room waiting for Reese who had gone to get snacks when I heard her phone ring. Muting the TV, I sat still as I tried to listen to who she was talking to. I trusted Reese with every fibre in me and I wasn't worried she was telling my dad. I was worried she was going to tell Kaleb. Nerves crash through me, and I feel the panic beginning to claw up my throat. Pushing off the sofa quietly, I tip toe over to the door, popping my head round the door frame but she isn't there.

"She's fine," I hear her voice as she comes into view and I panic, tucking myself back round the door frame so I am out of her line of sight. "Kaleb, please." She pleads and my heart breaks at the thought of him being hurt. "I know you do and *trust* me when I say she needs to see you too, but she needs time to heal Kaleb." She sighs. "Emotionally, physically..." she stalls for a moment, "mentally, Kaleb."

There's a pause while she listens.

"No, no, nothing has happened. She just needs time to get her head round everything. Please Kaleb, I'm begging you. I'll get her to call you in a couple of days, if she wants to."

My heart drums in my chest and all I want to do is hold him and tell him how much I love him. "Thank you, I'll keep you updated." She ends the call and I hear her footsteps approaching. I panic, running onto the sofa and launching myself onto it all whilst trying to act cool.

"Why is the television muted?" Reese asks, her forehead creased, her eyes pinned to the screen.

"I have no idea, maybe I done it by accident?" I shrug my shoulders up and take the bag of candy from her. Her brows dive further. "You know, you keep frowning like that your forehead wrinkles are going to get *so* much worse."

Her eyes are wide like saucers before her lips pull into a smile. "Fuck you," she laughs, flopping down next to me. I reach for the remote and turn it off mute, she gives me the side eye and I give her a bigger shrug. Pulling on the bag to open it, my hand dives in to grab some candy.

"Crisp?" she asks holding the bag out towards me.

"Yes, I'll have some *chips*," I give her a wink, taking a handful with my spare hand, "you live in America darling, you really do need to keep up with the lingo."

Reese rolls her eyes in an over exaggerated way which makes me scoff a laugh.

"They're crisps," she counters, keeping her eyes peeled to the television.

I tsk and shake my head as we both settle down and continue watching *The Vampire Diaries.*

It had been a week since the bath incident.

It had been three weeks since I last saw Kaleb.

And every single day I went without speaking to him, my heart ached a little more each day.

Reese had convinced me to go out for the evening with her for dinner and drinks and as much as I wasn't feeling up to it, I think it will do me good. Pulling my phone out of my bedside cabinet, my finger rested on the power button. Before I could lift it, I had turned it on. I watched as the screen lit up, waiting with bated breath to see if he had messaged me. My heart sunk a little when nothing come through, but then I saw one notification. I felt my heart skip beats as it fluttered in my chest. Going onto my messages, I smiled when I saw his name.

> *Hey baby.*
> *This will be the only message I will send. I know you're going to need time to get your head around all of this. Let me start by saying how sorry I am, my intention was never to hurt you. Ever. You've had enough of that in your life, why would I want to bring you more?*
> *Yes, I should have told you from the start, but I was being selfish in wanting you all to myself because I knew as soon as I told you that I was hired by your dad, you would have upped and left. I couldn't not have you close to me. The thought of you running away had me in a chokehold. I couldn't breathe without you. My world was so bland before I met you, and now I see everything in such a vibrant and colourful way and it's all because of you. The last few months we have spent together have been the best of my life, and that's no exaggeration. You honestly were the reason my heart started beating again.*

This right here, the weird moment we're living in was what scared me about you knowing the truth. I hate that you're not with me, and I feel angry for feeling this way when it was me that caused it.

I promise to give you the time you need to heal, my love. I promise to be patient with you.

Just promise you will come back to me.

Because you are the air that I breathe, and without you Connie, none of this makes sense.

Take a week, a month, a year; just don't give up on us. I never meant to hurt you.

The thought that I am the one to have put you through this guts me to my core. I can't eat, I can't sleep.

I'll spend the rest of my life making it up to you.

I will be on my hands and knees and at your mercy if that's what you want.

Anything for you, my love.

I never wanted to be the one to clip your wings, I wanted to be your cocoon until you were strong enough to spread your wings and fly, my little butterfly.

I just wanted to be the one to make you smile, morning, noon and night and the thought that you're not smiling right now haunts me.

It's you and me, always. I love you Connie, no matter what happens between us, always hold onto that.

Because I do. I love you. I would always choose you, in this lifetime, in the next, I would choose you forever. You have given me more love than I ever deserve, you have given me a reason to smile, I forgot what being happy felt like until you.

But most importantly, Connie. You have given me a reason to live.

And it's all because of you.

I'm yours, always and forever.
Kaleb xx

I choke on my sobs, causing me to hiccup. My heart skips two beats to every one beat. A tear rolls off my nose and onto my screen and I wipe it away with my thumb pad. My eyes a blur so the screen that was once so clear was now hardly visible. I hear my bedroom door open and see Reese through my tears.

"Oh my god, what's happened?" she asks, rushing towards me. I would like to tell her she looks nice, but I can't see what she is wearing through the rush of tears.

"You smell nice," I sob, sniffing as she leads me to the bed as we both sit.

"Er, thanks," confusion fills her voice. She wipes my tears away with a soft tissue and holds my hand in hers. "Talk to me, what's happened?"

My mind floods back to when I walked in on her watching *The Notebook* and the sorry state she was in which causes me to scoff a laugh.

"Why are you laughing?" her brows furrow.

"Wrinkles," I sniff, palming a stray tear off my cheek.

"Piss off will you," she swats my arm, "what is wrong with you?"

"Well, I turned my phone on."

"Did you call Kaleb?" she asks, her voice soft and low.

"No, but a message come through and it just made me realise how much I love that man." Her hand rests over mine as she gives me a smile. "And then I remembered walking in on you whilst you were a crying mess because you chose to watch a film that quite literally ripped your heart out."

"It's a really sad film, okay?! And I had a real shitty day if I remember rightly."

I nod, "I know, and now I get it. I get how you were feeling. The pain I feel is minuscule to the pain that consumed you." I nod, tears threatening to fall once more, "and I am sorry if I was ever insensitive or come across as ignorant. That was never my intention," and I hear her gasp.

"Oh, Connie," she wraps her arms around me and pulls me into for a hug. "You saved me, if it wasn't for you, I would still be locked in that hotel room self-wallowing. You never were insensitive or ignorant. You had just never felt a pain like it, so it was hard for you to relate, but I wasn't going to hold that against you." She breaks away, tucking a strand of my long brown hair behind my ear, "I would have never wanted you to experience that kind of pain, no one deserves to know what it feels like to lose something you love so dearly, especially you."

I nod, sniffing and willing for the tears to stop.

"You're going to get your knight on a white horse to save you and ride you off into the sunset."

"Even though you shattered my dreams last year by telling me fairytales aren't true..." I smirk, giving her the side eye as she rolls hers.

"I don't think I said it *quite* like that, but I was a different person then. I was deep in grief, and don't get me wrong, the grief is still within me, but I just channel it differently now. I am healing and your dad is a big part of it."

I sniff, a shuddering sigh leaving me.

"Kaleb is your fairytale, you'll get your happily ever after."

I inhale a shaky breath and just take a moment to reflect on everything that was just said.

"You look nice," Reese breaks the silence and gives me a smile. I let my eyes fall to look at my black mini dress.

"Thanks, not sure the running and smudged mascara really goes but..." I lean into her as she wraps her arm round my shoulders. "You look really nice too, the colour red really suits you," I smile but she can't see it.

"Do you think my fiancé will think it's too short?" she asks as I sit up.

"Stand up." She does, giving me a twirl and I smirk knowing full well my dad is going to go bat shit crazy. "Nahhhh," I dismiss her with my hand whilst holding my smirk.

"I'm not changing."

"Good," my eyes roam over her and I smile when I see she is wearing her Louboutin high top sneakers. "Nice sneakers."

"I know, my best friend's dad got them for me," she winks before tipping her head forward and letting out a laugh.

"I still can't believe you slept with my dad," I shudder, turning my nose up.

"I know," she blushes as she walks towards the dressing table, pulling the chair out, "now, sit down, let's sort your make-up out."

CHAPTER FIFTY-EIGHT
KALEB

SITTING IN MY OFFICE, I KICK BACK ON MY CHAIR AND SIGH. IT HAS been the day from hell. Titus brought me up to scratch with what has been going on with Xavier and Amora. Amora has a target on her back, their issues are with Xavier, but they know going after her will hurt him more. He put a bullet between their father's eyes, and now, rightly so in their eyes, they want blood.

I have no idea why Xavier wants our help when he has his own business over in England, but I am assuming he doesn't want to mix his business with his family. Xavier has managed to keep her safe up until now and Titus and Xavier have decided to get her on the plane next week. I close my eyes for a moment, and as soon as they're closed, I see Connie. Her long, brown hair softly blowing in the sea breeze, she's smiling, and her eyes are sparkling like the opal ocean behind her. She had never looked more beautiful than she does right now.

I inhale sharply, rubbing my temple as I reach for my phone and open my messages. My heart skips a beat when I see that she's read the message I sent.

I debate sending another message but decide against it. She'll come to me when she's ready. When Titus and Keaton came to see me when I was at my lowest, they told me to go and get her and fuck, did I want to. But I knew if I did, I would only push her away. Connie is so head strong and stubborn and the last thing I wanted to do was put her or myself through any more heartache because I was trying to rush her. I know a simple *sorry* isn't going to do anything, and even sending roses wouldn't help. They would come back with their heads lopped off. I knew what I was going to do to apologise, it just wasn't the time. I didn't care that my heart felt like it had been ripped from my chest, torn and beaten until it hardly beat anymore before it was violently shoved back in my chest.

All I cared about was her.

She was my priority.

She will *always* be my priority.

CHAPTER FIFTY-NINE
CONNIE

We sat at the champagne bar in *The Plaza*, losing ourselves in easy conversation. It felt good being out, but at the same time I wanted nothing more than to be at home with Kaleb. I hadn't been back to the penthouse since the day my dad turned up and literally turned my world upside down. I packed a bag and headed to his home with Reese. My dad knew he had fucked up. I was beyond angry with him and haven't spoken to him since, despite being in his home. He needs to stew in what he did, the way he went about it was all wrong and honestly, it was a dick move.

"Do you want another glass here, or shall we move on?" Reese asks over the soft Jazz that is filling the bar.

"I'm easy, what time is dinner booked for?" I ask, looking at my watch.

"Eight fifteen, we have about an hour and twenty." She shrugs her shoulders up before wrapping her fingers round the stem of the glass and draining the contents.

"Come on, let's go to the restaurant and sit up the bar there," I smile, finishing my own drink before slipping off the barstool.

"Sounds like a plan, stan," Reese chimes as she jumps off the stool then links her arm through mine.

It felt weird being back in the plaza, this place was home for such a long time for me, but now, it felt like the *old* me, and as much as I craved for her to come back, I don't think we would work together anymore. So much has happened which has shaped me and made me grow in a way I never expected to and going back to how I was before would only feel like I was going back in life and not forward where I should be heading.

From here on out, I was only going forward. One step at a time.

Our dinner was delicious, and we spent the evening reminiscing, and it wasn't until I was sitting there with her that I realised how much I missed her and how we were back then. Carefree, young and living our best lives.

"Shall we go dancing?" Reese asks as we step out into the cool air of the city.

"Yeah, where do you have in mind?" I shiver, internally cursing myself for not bringing my big coat.

"I heard about a good little club in downtown Manhattan, you okay with that?" Her face turns to look at me and I smile.

"Yeah I am good with that," I pull her closer to me to try and keep the warmth between us. "As if you're getting married soon," I say with a deep exhale and I can see my breath in front of me, that's how cold it is.

"I know," she sighs blissfully, "and that reminds me," she stops in her tracks, taking my hands in hers as she waits in front of me.

My eyes bounce back and forth between hers as a smile graces her face.

"We need to get your dress fitted, can't have my maid of honour in an un-fitted dress now, can we?" her smile widens as her eyes light up with glee.

"Maid of honour?" I stutter, my heart racing in my chest.

"Of course, you do want to be maid of honour, right?" I can see the worry flash across her eyes.

"Oh my god, of course I do! I just wanted to make sure you did want me," I feel my eyes well as I pull her in for a hug, "thank you for asking me, I would love to be part of yours and my dad's big day."

"I've added Kaleb to the list, but I can take him off," Reese rushes out as we break away from each other.

I shake my head from side to side, "Keep him on there for the minute... I haven't made my mind up yet," I smile, linking my arm through hers as we continue walking.

"Love it, make him sweat a little bit," she nudges into me and laughs.

"Yeah, something like that," I feel my stomach knot, my heart constricted at the thought of hurting him. As much as I have loved being back with Reese and our friendship picking straight up as if no time at all had passed between us, I missed being with Kaleb. I missed everything about him. His gorgeous grey eyes that showed me exactly what he was feeling before he told me, his beautiful smile that only seemed to come out around me, I don't think I have ever really seen him smile at anyone like the way he does with me. His scent, oh, his intoxicating scent. Tobacco with a hint of suede and laced with a sweet vanilla. I still have no idea where the tobacco comes from, I have never seen him smoke but his scent has me addicted alone. I miss the way he makes my heart stutter in my chest, making it skip beats which causes my breath to catch at the back of my throat. I miss all of him.

I listen to Reese chat away about her plans for the wedding, my head moves up and down in agreement with what she says, and I make the odd humming noise, but I wasn't really paying attention. My thoughts were with Kaleb. All I could think about was what he was doing now? Was he missing me like I was him? My heart ached heavily in my chest, I hated that we were apart, but I do think the time between us will do us good. I hoped.

Swallowing the bitter taste down, Reese pulls me into the warmth of a club, giving the doorman a knowing nod as she passes. I feel my shoulders drop as the heat cuddles me. I didn't want to move from this spot. She checks our little jackets into the cloak room then places her hand over mine as she drags me up the stairs towards the loud, thumping music.

"You okay?" she shouts over the noise and I nod.

"Yeah I'm fine!"

But the truth was, I wasn't fine. I didn't want to be here, yet I agreed to it for her, because deep down I feel like I owe her this for being a shitty friend over the last year or so. I know if I told her how I was feeling, she would leave here in a heartbeat. But I didn't want her to leave. I didn't want to ruin her night because I was a heartbroken fool. I hadn't realised it until earlier just how deep and fast I had fallen for Kaleb, and it scared me to my core. It didn't scare me in bad way, it scared me in the best way possible. The kind of scared you feel when you're about to jump from a plane and free fall through the sky just to get that buzz.

That's how he made me feel. As if I was free falling and on a constant high.

"What do you want to drink?" Reese asks me as her body begins to move to the rhythm of the music.

"Vodka cranberry!" I shout and she gives me the thumbs up, shuffling into the heaving crowds. I look around, constantly seeking her out. Why did I stay here? I should have gone with her. This was a mistake, being here in these crowds is freaking me out. Fear strikes through me like lightning when someone accidently knocks into me. He apologises profoundly but I ignore him, frozen to the spot. My palms begin to prick with perspiration, my heart galloping in my chest.

"You're fine," I remind myself, pulling at the elastic hair tie that's on my wrist and letting it hit my skin. I do it again. "Totally fine," I swallow down the thickness that's in my throat, my eyes not moving from the area I saw Reese disappear into. We should have stayed together. What if something happens to her? What if something happens to me? I gasp for air, suddenly feeling as if I am unable to breathe when I see her, smiling and rocking her hips from side to side as she stops in front of me.

"Connie," I hear the worry in her voice, her eyes moving back and forth between mine.

"Yeah," I just about manage but my voice is inaudible over this booming music.

She passes me my drink before leading me out to the quieter corridor near the rest rooms.

"Are you okay?" she asks, her hand resting on the top of my arm and giving me a gentle, reassuring squeeze.

"I just," I stutter, struggling to get my words out as my eyes scan the heaving club.

"It's okay, just take a breather," Reese reassures me, smiling as she begins to inhale deeply and exhaling slowly.

I nod at her, closing my eyes as I inhale deeply, mirroring her and as soon as my eyes are closed all I see is him, my soulmate.

After a moment or two, I slowly let my eyes open and Reese is there smiling, her head dipping slightly as she looks at me.

"Better?" her voice is soft and soothing.

"Yeah," I roll my lips, stepping forward. It wasn't a lie, but it also wasn't the truth.

"Come on, let's dance it out. You'll feel much better," she wraps her arms around my shoulders and walks me back towards the crowded dance floor. I down my vodka and cranberry and place my empty glass down on a table as we pass.

"Thirsty?" Reese smirks, taking a big mouthful of her own drink.

"Yeah, or more like a bit of Dutch courage," a nervous laugh bubbles out of me, "let's get another one, come," I tug her hand towards the bar, I wasn't going alone.

We stand at the bar and Reese is bopping and jumping around to the song that is playing and I can't help but smile.

"What can I get ya?" the barman grasps my attention and I turn to face him, giving him a smile as my eyes roam over him in a quick sweep. He is tall, broad with dark hair, dark eyes and covered from head to toe in tattoos.

"Two vodka cranberries please," I shout, leaning over the bar. I know alcohol isn't going to help my flutters of panic attacks, but I need it to get through the evening.

"Got it," he grunts, grabbing two glasses and filling with ice before adding the vodka.

"Make them doubles!" Reese shouts, throwing him a wide smile. He rolls his eyes, shaking his head from side to side as he adds another measure. Topping up with cranberry, he slides them across the bar, and I fumble in my bag for my credit card.

"It's on the house," the barman grunts, wiping down the side then moving along the line to serve more customers. I turn to look at Reese who just gives me a wink and a lift of one of her shoulders.

"Thanks!" I shout on deaf ears, smiling as I reach for the drinks and hand one to Reese.

Her eyes widen as a familiar beat blasts through the speakers *Machine Gun Kelly – Maybe* begins filling the room and the dance floor erupts. Lifting the glass to my lips, I take a large mouthful and begin to dance. I can't remember the last time I felt so carefree and just danced. Reese is jumping up and down, singing along to the lyrics. She reaches for my hand, spinning me round and I laugh as we jump up and down, the whole floor doing the same thing.

"I feel like I'm letting everything go!" I shout over the music and Reese beams at me.

"Good! It'll make you feel so better," she slows for a moment, "whenever it gets too much, just remember this moment and dance it out."

I smile, wrapping my arm round her neck and pulling her close to me, "I love you!"

"I love you more," squeezing me, "I am so grateful for you."

The music begins to die down before another song begins to play, we break away and I let my arm lift in the air as I rock my hips from side to side with the beat when suddenly I feel a hand move round my hip, splaying across my stomach before I am pulled back into a hard body. My eyes widen and I freeze, Reese lifts her face to look at me and her own eyes widen.

I grab the hand and pull it off, spinning round but stepping back as I do only to have relief wash over me when I see who it is.

Callaghan.

"Cal!?" my mouth agape, my eyes bugging out of my head as they roam over him. He looks good.

"Hey sweetheart! How are you doing babe?" he asks, before stepping towards me and giving me a hug.

"I'm getting there," I give him a slow nod, letting my eyes fall to my feet for a moment when I feel his hand on my shoulder.

"It's been tough, I'm not going to lie..." he runs his hands round the back of his head, tilting it to the side. "It really rocked through Rox and me."

My stomach knots as flashbacks of how him and Rox watched as Tryst done what he did. My eyes dodge to the side and I see Rox approaching with a large smile on his face.

"Sweetness," his eyes rake up and down my body before pulling me in for a hug.

"Hey," I hold my hand up, then take a little step back so I was closer to Reese. I had no idea why, but something felt off. I felt it deep in my gut. Reese must've picked up on my body language because her fingers linked through mine.

"Can we get you a drink? Then we will let you have your evening," Callaghan's eyes move between me and Reese as his smile grows slowly.

I turn my head to face Reese, unsure on what to do and as the seconds tick by, I rush out, "Yeah, sure."

"Cool! We're in the booth at the back, go sit down and

I'll meet you over there," Cal winks and I feel nausea roll in my stomach. "What are you drinking?"

"Cranberry juice," I smile, the lie slipping easily off my tongue.

"Two cranberry juices coming right up," he gives me a little nod, saluting me with his two fingers.

We walk slowly over to the area, Rox behind us. We stop as we approach the red roped area, Rox stepping past us and opening it.

"Thanks," I mutter, stepping up onto the raised VIP area, Reese close behind me. We sit together, Rox sitting over the other side of the table, his eyes moving between me and Reese.

"You both look petrified," he lets out a deep laugh and I shrug my shoulders up.

"Maybe it's because I don't trust you," I lick my lips, the spite apparent in my tone.

"What have I done?" he asks, pressing his hand to his chest to indicate he is wounded by my words.

"If you don't know, then that's even more of a problem, isn't it."

His head turns to see Cal holding our drinks, holding them out for us to take. Reese takes hers then passes me mine.

"Thanks," I mutter, my eyes falling to my drink and uneasiness swarms me.

Silence falls across the table and I watch as Reese downs her drink in one.

"Drink up love, I need the loo," she smiles at me, but I know that's her way of telling me we need out.

I take a sip of mine, then place it on the table.

"As much as this was lovely, I'm not ready to talk to either of you. You let him do what he wanted with me, you could have stopped him, but you never did. You're both a constant reminder of the worst days of my life and I don't want to be reminded of that. The only reminder I will allow is the grief from losing my boyfriend. I don't care who he was before he died, I didn't know that Tryst. I'm grieving the Tryst from years ago, the one that would never, *ever* make me feel the way that he did." And with that, I stand, Reese standing with me. "Sorry I can't stay to talk more with you, I just don't want to," I shrug my shoulders up as Reese steps down out of the area and I follow. "Take care of yourselves," I nibble the inside of my bottom lip, nerves crashing through me like a constant loop of waves. I turn, not looking back and ignoring the hammering of my heart in my chest as it soon fades and blends in with the heavy beat of the music.

Pushing through the restroom doors, relief rushes over me. Once inside, I walk over to the basins, wrapping my fingers round the edge.

"Something felt off, or was that just me?" I ask, lifting my head and finding Reese pacing back and forth in the mirror behind me.

"No, no, something definitely felt off," she nods, stopping in her tracks as she moves aside to let two girls walk out of the restroom so now it was just us.

"I don't trust Cal; Rox I think I could, if I needed to… but something about Cal threw me off. He tried to kiss me the night I caught Tryst fucking some girl," I shake my head from side to side as I spin, tipping my head back. "He tried to do more, but Kaleb turned up," I scoff a laugh as the memory floods me, "of course he did," I let my head tip forward as I focus on Reese. "Let me use the restroom, then I think we should leave, do you?" I place my bag next to Reese's on the countertop.

"Yes, one hundred percent. We can chill at home and watch a film? End the evening with a bottle of champagne in your room? We can have a sleepover," she laughs as she tops her lipstick up in the mirror.

"Now, that sounds like a plan," I smile, throwing her a wink as I slip into the bathroom, locking the door behind me.

"I think we need to watch a Rom-Com, how about you?" she asks, I can see her trainers under the door.

"Yes! *Did you hear about the Morgans?*" I ask, standing from the toilet.

"No! Who are they? What happened to them?" Reese responds and I burst into laughter, flushing the toilet.

"It's a film you idiot! With *Sarah Jessica Parker and Hugh Grant,*" laughter ripples through me as I unlock the restroom door and swing it open, the colour draining from my face when I see Reese laying on the floor.

"Shit!" I rush to her, rolling her on her back. Her eyes are closed, holding my fingers under her nose I can feel her soft breath, pressing my fingers to her neck I feel her racing pulse. "Reese," I shake her softly, tears pricking my eyes as I try and ignore them. "Reese," my panicked pleas are getting louder when I hear footsteps behind me and turn my upper half to see Callaghan.

"What did you do?" Tears are streaming down my cheeks.

"Sorry baby, I had to remove her from the situation, because sweetness, she was going to be a problem," he smirks, his eyes moving to a lifeless Reese on the floor, "and she was so easy to get out of the way, she sunk that drink like it was water," I see a darkness in his eyes that truly petrifies me. "But you..." he steps towards me, and I freeze.

"Don't come near me," I shout, stumbling to my feet. I

slowly look over to my bag to try and run for it, but I don't stand a chance. He lurches forward, grabbing me as I scream but he covers my mouth with his hand. I go to open my mouth so I can sink my teeth into his skin but as soon as the thought enters my head, his fingers knot a fistful of my hair and smashes my face into the basin with force. The pain sears through me, but it soon fades when the room goes black.

CHAPTER SIXTY

KILLIAN

Sitting on the sofa with a cup of tea, I turn my wrist towards me and look at the time. It had just gone eleven. Reaching for my phone, I check my app to show me Reese and Connie's location. They're still at the club. I smile, even though Connie is pissed with me, I am glad that she and Reese are re-building their friendship. Reese was so miserable and lonely without her. We have an amazing relationship, but sometimes a girl needs her best friend.

My eyes slice to the monitor, and I see Celeste sleeping soundly and my heart thumps against my chest. The feelings of love that consume me from that little girl are too hard to even try to comprehend into words. I loved Connie with all my heart, but I missed out on so much and that was no one's fault but my own. I rub my palm over my chest, trying to relieve a little of the ache that was prominent, to think I told Reese I didn't want kids. The way her little face broke into sadness in front of me, and now, all I can think about is getting her pregnant again.

I am pulled from my thoughts when my phone begins

to ring, Duncan's name flashes up. My brows furrow and my heart begins to skip beats.

"Duncan," my voice is low as I push to my feet, placing my cup of tea on the coffee table without a coaster, knowing full well if there is a ring mark when Reese gets home, I'll be dead. I quickly grab one, then place the cup on it, smiling. It's the little wins.

"Killian, fuck," he is out of breath, the panic evident in his voice.

"What's happened?" Suddenly, I am frantic as I run my hand through my hair, my fingers grasping at a handful of hair, tugging it at the root.

"I saw your girl come in earlier, we had reports of a girl passed out in the restroom... it's Reese, man."

"The fuck!" I scream down the phone.

"She's awake, but she's crying for you. How quick can you get here?" he asks, my jaw is wound tight, my teeth aching from the constant clenching.

I look at my watch, "Give me fifteen. Get her water, call a fucking ambulance. Where is Connie?"

The line falls silent, and I can hear his breathless rasps down the phone.

"The girl she was with, she's my daughter."

"I have no idea, there was no other girl," and my heart plummets through my chest, my eyes widening at the words that are replaying in my head.

"I'll be there as soon as I can," I cut the phone off and dial Reese's mom's number, Liz.

"Killian, darling is everything okay?" her mom asks, the sleep evident in her voice.

"Yeah fine, I just need you and Mateo here to watch Celeste. There has been an issue at the club the girls are at."

"Are they okay?"

"Yea," I grunt, I hate lying to her, but I didn't want to cause any panic.

"We will be there in ten." I cut the phone off as I storm into the kitchen, fetching my keys and pacing up and down the hallway.

I had no idea what to do. Connie's phone was still showing at the club and suddenly, I feel bile crawling up my throat. Closing my eyes, I swallow it down, trying to ignore the nausea that is constantly swirling deep in my stomach.

Liz and Mateo burst through the door ten minutes later; I give them a small smile, but my eyes tell them everything they didn't want to know.

"I'll be back soon," slipping them a gentle nod, I rush past them and leap the steps. Running down the sidewalk, my feet beating the pavement as I reach my car and climb in. My mind is in overdrive, the adrenaline has soon replaced the fear that was coursing through me. Pushing the stick into drive, I pull out, not even looking over my shoulder as I press the pedal to the metal and drive towards the club. The unwanted thoughts invade me, but it doesn't matter how much I push them out my head, they're still there haunting me.

The drive is short and fast, fuck knows how many red lights I skipped. I am just grateful that I didn't get pulled over. Someone must be looking over me tonight and I know exactly who it is.

"Thank you," I whisper as I pull onto the sidewalk, abandoning the car and slamming the door shut.

"Hey, you can't park there!" someone shouts at me, but I just flip them off as I walk with heavy footsteps into the club.

Duncan is there ready to greet me, "Boss," he nods his head.

"Where is she?" I ignore him, I'm not here for work. I am here for Reese.

"Second floor office," I nod, running up the stairs and taking them two at a time, I could hear the blood thumping in my ears, my heart jackhammering in my chest as I reach the second floor, pushing the door open with force so it hits the wall.

My eyes land on Reese who is a trembling mess, her eyes red raw as the tears continue to cascade down her cheeks.

"Oh, baby," I rush towards her, falling to my knees as I cup her beautiful, tearstained face in my hands. I swipe my thumb across her cheeks, trying to catch a few of the tears.

Suddenly, rage consumes me with force when my eyes catch the flickering image of the club's CCTV video and I see my daughter's lifeless body being carried out of the club by some man I don't know.

"Who the fuck did this?" I ask, my eyes bouncing round the security team that work here. I stand slowly, worried that my legs are going to buckle beneath me. "WHO DID THIS?!" I shout so loud, my veins distended from my neck, my forehead creased from the constant frown I am wearing. Reese sobs in front of me and my rage slowly slips away.

"I want to know how the fuck that cunt managed to get into this club, drug my fiancée and *my* daughter and slip out the fucking door without anyone realising!"

"We don't know," one of the useless sacks of shits pipes up.

"Fuck off," I grunt as I focus on Reese, "baby, do you remember who did this?"

She nods.

"It was Callaghan. Tryst's band mate, she told me earlier that he tried stuff with her before, back in New York at one of Chord's concerts, but Kaleb showed up and stopped him." She trembles as I hold her, "Killian, I'm scared," I lean in, placing a soft, lingering kiss on her forehead.

"We will find her," I mutter against her skin before my lips press against her forehead once more, "I promise."

Slipping my phone out my back pocket, I find his name. Slowly bringing my phone to my ear, he answers on the first ring.

"What?" Kaleb's gruff tone instantly gets my back up.

"I don't like you, not even remotely..." I inhale deeply as I comfort Reese, my eyes pinned to the screen as I watch it on loop as my daughter's lifeless body is carried out into the busy New York streets. My eyes filling with tears as I try to ignore the emotions that are trying to suffocate me. "But I need your help."

CHAPTER SIXTY-ONE
KALEB

"Slow the fuck down," I urge, my own panic coursing through me at the words that I'm hearing. Surely, I didn't hear him right. "Tell me again, what's happened?" praying that my mind was playing tricks on me as I sit in my office. We had been working late every night trying to work out a plan to get Amora here as soon as possible.

"Someone drugged and took Connie," I can hear how frantic he is, my heart exploding in my chest before shattering into a thousand pieces of devastation. Rage burns through my veins like poison, flares of red misting my eyes as the phone slips from my hand, falling to the floor in slow motion before I hear it smash on the tiles. High pitched ringing fills my ears and the voices round me slowly blur. I can't breathe, my lungs tighten and burn as if a knife has been plunged deep into my chest, twisting in as far as it can go and winding me as I choke on my own breath.

"Kaleb," I hear a distant voice, but I can't move. I am anchored to the spot, my legs heavy. Swaying on the spot, the voices in my head are screaming at me to snap out of whatever fucking head fuck space I am in.

"Mate," the voice becomes clearer, and I know whose voice it is. Keaton.

"Brother," I gasp, my eyes focusing on who is in front of me, "fuck, it's Connie."

I watch as he looks to Titus and Nate before his eyes are back on mine.

"What's happened?" Keaton's eyes bug out his head and the fear is evident on his face.

"Reese said someone called Callaghan took her," I struggle to get the words out, stuttering like a fool as I stumble over my words.

"Nate!" Keaton snaps, turning away from me as his own rage consumes him. His strides are long as he walks towards where Nate is sitting with his earphones in, in his own little world, blissfully unaware of the devastating chaos that is unfolding in the room. Keaton yanks his headphones off his head and throws them on the desk with force.

"What the fuck?" Nate fumes, his brows pinched as he pushes his glasses up his nose, pushing his hair away from his forehead.

"Get up Connie's phone," Keaton snaps as I close the gap between us, Titus' hand on my shoulder, gripping it tightly in a reassuring manner.

Nate taps away on his computer and as soon as I see her location, I rush out of the office with Keaton and Titus hot on my tail.

"Stay here," I grit out, turning and pointing at the both of them as I unlock my car.

"No chance, you're not doing this alone."

Pushing my hand through my hair, I feel my frustration creeping over me.

"One of you need to stay with Nate, I need someone here with him," my voice cracks and suddenly I feel a wave of emotion hit me. Bringing my fist to my lips, I close my eyes trying to compose myself when I feel hands clasp round my face, holding me.

I let my tear-filled eyes land on Keaton, his own eyes red rimmed.

"I'll stay," Titus' deep voice booms through the large underground parking lot and I nod. Sniffing, I swallow the lump that is lodged in my throat and turn on my heel, Keaton's arm wrapped round my shoulder as we walk to the car when I hear Titus call out.

"Kaleb!" I stall, looking over my shoulder at him. "Bring our girl home," he gives a nod, and I nod back.

"Let's go get our girl," I hear Keaton growl and I feel the fire in my belly erupt.

"Let's go get her."

I DRIVE AS FAST AS I CAN TOWARDS THE CLUB WHERE CONNIE'S phone is showing, my heart sinks as I pull up behind what I am assuming is the complete abandonment of Killan's car and cut the engine.

"Nice parking," Keaton scoffs, rolling his eyes as he slams the car door shut.

"Mate, his wife was knocked out and his daughter got taken," even saying the last words makes the bile rise from my stomach and burn my throat. Keaton stays tight lipped as he follows me into the still busy club. I see a broad doorman who eyes me up and down.

"I'm looking for Killian."

"And you are?" he looks away from me as he speaks into a mic, "yeah boss I've got someone here to see you..." I watch as he nods, his eyes meeting mine and a small smirk pulls at his lips. "He said to send up the guy who was fucking his daughter whilst he was paying him."

"Tell him he's a cunt," I snort, barging past him as he calls out after me.

"Second floor office, daughter fucker," his loud and low rumble of a chuckle echoes.

I growl, flipping him off and running the stairs two at a time to get to where Killian is.

Panting when I reach the top, I walk into the office to see Reese sitting there in tears whilst Killian comforts her.

"Took you long enough," Killian rolls his eyes at me.

"Don't fucking start with me, where the fuck is she?" I snap as I storm into the room, my eyes fixing on the screen as I watch Connie's limp body being carried out. "Callaghan the cunt," I ball my fists by my side as I feel Keaton grab my shoulder.

"Breathe," he says lowly so only I can hear.

I squeeze my eyes shut for a moment as I inhale slowly.

"Where is she?" I grit, my jaw clenched as I turn to face Killian. I watch as his hard face expression slowly beings to slip and he shows just how vulnerable he is feeling.

"I have no idea," he finally admits, "I can't seem to get a lead on him, it's like he just vanished."

I shake my head from side to side, "I'm not having it," I shove forward, pulling the useless piece of shit security guard from his seat and sit down rewinding and replaying the same clip over and over.

"Where are the other cameras?" I ask, when I see Cal slips to the left of the club. Turning in my seat to face the other useless pricks. They just look at each other. "Well!?" I shout, my voice bouncing off the walls and making them jump, I twist in my seat as my eyes land on Killian, "Do yourself a favor mate, once this is all over get yourself some new security. Waste of fucking time, useless cunts," I spin on my chair and click through the computer.

"Fucking tell him," Killian snaps, his voice booming round the room.

"Killian!" Reese calls out, as if scolding him.

"Check the computer drive for the alley cam, they might have picked something up," one of the scrawny guards finally says.

"Thank you," I say calmly.

Clicking through the folders, I land on the camera that points down the alley.

I scoff, "What a sloppy, useless cunt." I growl, my back teeth grinding as I pull out my phone and snap a photo of the screen then push Titus' name, sending him the image before I call him. The phone doesn't even ring and he answers.

"Titus, get Nate to run the number plate in that picture I just sent. This guy is either really fucking stupid, or really clever. Either way, he wants to be found," I cut the phone off and push away from the desk.

I watch as paramedics rush in to check Reese over and as much as I want to stay and make sure she is okay, for Connie's sake, I also need to leave.

"I'm going," I say to the room, avoiding eye contact with Killian.

"Not without me you're not, she's my *daughter*."

"And she's *mine*," I growl, running my hand through my hair in frustration. Clicking my neck from side to side I steady my sights on Killian. "Get your shit, let's go."

I watch as he looks at Reese and she nods, tears

brimming in her opal eyes. "Be safe," she whispers as he kneels in front of her, kissing her softly.

"I love you."

"I love you," she repeats back as he stands, and strides towards the office door. I follow and just as I get to the door, I still for a moment and turn.

"Keaton, stay with Reese."

"But," he stammers, his eyes wide as my words hit him

"No buts, stay with Reese." I give him a curt nod and I am surprised that I didn't get a snarky response from him. "Thank you," my voice is low as I take a deep breath before me and Killian walk out of the office together and down to the street beneath us.

"I need to make a quick stop," I say to Killian as he unlocks his car, climbing in, I slam the door.

"Just tell me where we need to go," he says, starting the engine of his Range Rover before pulling off the sidewalk.

Giving him a curt nod, I push the address into his sat nav as he swings the car round in the road and heads towards our destination.

My heart is in my throat, adrenaline pumping through my veins. I don't care what I need to do or who I need to do it to. I would burn the world to ashes to ensure I got to her safely and I didn't give a shit who I had to set on fire to do it.

CHAPTER SIXTY-TWO

CONNIE

Light slowly creeps in as my bruised and heavy lids flutter open, my vision blurry as I try to focus on something. My head feels like it's trapped in a vice, searing a crushing pain through me causing me to wince.

"Hello," I croak, as my eyes begin to focus on the poorly lit room. I try to move my aching arms but it's not until I slowly tip my head back, I notice my wrists are bound together and I whine as my body feels heavy and sluggish. Slowly looking down, I am still dressed in my dress, my white trainers stained with my blood, my legs cuffed and wide. My stomach rolls.

Panic sets in as I get flashbacks of Reese lying on the floor, completely lifeless.

"Reese!" I scream, my voice hoarse but all I hear is my pathetic voice echoing round this large, empty room.

I try and pull on the restraints but all that does is make them tighter, cutting into my skin.

"Shit," I hiss, as I try and work out where I am. My head is hazy, and I struggle to fill in the gaps. "Help!!!" I scream again, my voice cracking. I am thirsty, my mouth and throat dry. My heart thumps under my skin when I see the door handle lower slightly, my skin prickling with fear when I see Callaghan enter the room with a sickly grin and suddenly, the memories from the club sink in, making my stomach knot.

"You're an asshole," I scream as he closes the door quietly then walks slowly towards me.

"I am, thank you," he nods his head as if I am paying a compliment before he stops in front of me, his finger trailing down my cheek which makes my skin crawl and I spit in his face. His hand drops from my skin as he slowly wipes away my saliva from his cheek, smirking before his eyes are back on me.

"They'll be here soon," I choke, trying to hold off on showing him any of the emotion that is currently vibrating through me. He drops his finger from me and lets his head fall forward as he lets out a soft, evil chuckle.

"Oh, sweetness," he sticks out his bottom lip trying to imitate a sad, pouty bottom lip. My eyes flicker back and forth from his as I feel the sickening fear swirling deep in my stomach. "They're not coming..." he snickers, his hand reaching forward so quick I don't even see it until I'm feeling his fingers digging into my cheeks, hard. My eyes begin to water, my breaths through my nose harsh and ragged as I can't hide the panic that is clearly seeping from me.

"You've been here *days* and they haven't even tried. I've kept you drugged until now. I think they've all grown a little tired of the drama you cause. First you run away from Daddy dearest because you find out you're the spawn of a slut, that saying is true... the apple don't fall far from the tree," he smirks, "then you try and become some whore groupie and mewl until Tryst gives you all the attention," his face edges closer to mine and the staleness of his breath mixed with the strong alcohol that laces his tongue makes my eyes water. "I got him hooked on the drugs, I started the whole ball rolling," he licks his lips looking proud with a sickening grin on his face "Tryst told us you were a frigid little bitch, a cock tease, but I knew once I got you, you would do anything I wanted you to. You're my obsession, I have tracked your *every single move*." He stumbles back slightly, but his fingers dig deeper into my skin, bruising instantly. "And then Tryst..." he licks his bottom lip, his dark, menacing eyes bounce round the room, "tragic, Tryst," and I watch as the sickening smile widens on his face which makes my blood run cold.

"He was another easy target. Of course, no one would have thought any different. Tragic story of a broken boy. But I wanted you to know that it was me, I mean, why would I let him get all the attention?" his admission makes my stomach roll, but I wasn't surprised. "I used to watch as he fucked you, used to beat myself off as I watched. And then he gave us the live show, Rox begged me to stop him, but why would I?"

I writhe under his grip, the restraints pinching my skin, my eyes filling with tears as he squeezes tighter, my teeth biting into the soft flesh inside my mouth and I taste metal, telling me I've made myself bleed.

"And now here you are, I have you, fuck it was so easy." His lips press to the shell of my ear, and I feel them brush against the skin, making me shudder, "And between you and I," I feel the smile curl his lips, "I fucked every inch of you, you were so fucking wet and the way you taste," he pulls his mouth from my ear, and I hadn't even realised but I had tears rolling down my cheeks. His grip loosens on my cheeks before he holds the back of my head, licking away my tears. "Fucking delectable," he breathes, his eyes flickering with darkness.

He steps away from me and my bottom lip trembles, my breaths stuttering in my chest as I try and hold off the chokehold of sobs, I am holding in.

"Have a drink sweetness," he bends and reaches for the glass of water. Lifting it to my lips, I rub my lips into a tight line, pulling my head back trying my hardest not to have to take a mouthful.

"Fucking drink," his bloodshot eyes widen as he pushes the rim of the glass into my lips and I feel a small scratch, my lips automatically parting as my tongue tries to run along them, but the liquid is on my tongue before I even had a chance.

"Now look what you done you silly little girl, you've made yourself bleed," he shakes his head from side to side as I see the chip on the rim of the glass. His thumb runs across my closed lips, and I see the blood on his thumb pad before he puts it past his own lips and sucks it clean, his eyes rolling in the back of his head.

I feel my legs begin to give way, my head rolling forward as my eyes roll back. Panic claws at my throat, my racing heart beginning to slow.

"Don't panic sweetness, you're just going to sleep for a little while." I hear the sound of his belt buckle undo and I try to scream but it's no use. "I just want to fill you with all of me, now sleep my sweet one, sleep."

And before I can even try to fight, it's pointless. I am completely paralysed before being plunged into a never-ending darkness filled with an infinity of nothingness.

CHAPTER SIXTY-THREE
KALEB

Killian boots it down the freeway, I hold onto the handle above my head. Not because I am scared, but because my fingers are bit to shit. The ache is evident in my fingers where I am holding so tight, my knuckles white.

My phone rings and it connects to Killian's Bluetooth.

"Nate," my voice raspy as I try and keep hold of my emotions.

"We have his location, you weren't lying when you said he was sloppy," I can hear him tapping on his keys. "But he isn't stupid, I bet he has been planning this for a while," I chew the inside of my bottom lip, my heart pounding against my ribcage.

"Can we not?" Killian grits, I slice my eyes over to him as he tightens his fingers round the steering wheel.

"Sorry," I hear Nate mumble as he still taps away, silence crackles round the car as we wait.

"Are you both okay?" Titus asks.

Me and Killian exchange looks and give each other a tight nod, "We will be," we say in unison.

"Right, Kaleb, it's on your phone," Nate's timid voice fills the car and I'm already opening his message.

"Got it, keep eyes on us," my voice is tight as I cut the phone off and punch the location into the sat nav as I watch it calculate the route.

"Fucking Brooklyn," I smash my palm down on the dash, "of course, that's where Tryst was from..." I pale, swallowing, "shit..." I whisper as I open my phone and scroll through the messages until I land on Xavier's name and open his message.

"What?" Killian asks my eyes scanning the texts as I continue to scroll, "What the fuck is it!?" his voice louder now.

"It's Tryst's apartment." I swallow, my eyes looking at the address I sent Xavier when I first contacted him, "how the fuck did I not even think to go there?"

"Because that would have been too easy, this kid isn't dumb. He is a fucking mastermind," Killian's voice is tight as he swerves along one of the lanes and swings the car round so we're heading back towards the bridge.

My feet nudge the black bag by my feet, my heart ricocheting in my chest.

"I cannot wait to get my hands on that cunt, I swear to god, if there is a single hair missing from her head, I am going to fucking gut him."

"You'll have to beat me to it," Killian growls, his fingers wrapping round the steering wheel as his knuckles turn white and we speed towards our final destination.

The tyres crunch over the gravel as Killian skids into a parking spot, putting the car into park and he's out of the car in a flash. Reaching for the bag between my feet, I jump out and reach for his shoulder.

He turns quickly, his face etched with worry.

"You need to calm down..." I whisper, "I get you want to get to her, so do I, but we have no idea what he is capable of." I swallow as the bile threatens to rise.

I hear the sigh escape Killian, my eyes watching as he crumbles in front of me. He has aged in the last few hours we have been together. I can see all of the emotions that he is feeling, guilt, remorse, resentment and fear. The fear is the most prominent.

I give him a tight smile, walking towards the side of the apartment block and drop my bag to the floor before kneeling and unzipping it. I grab a pair of leather gloves and throw them to Killian before putting my own on. Reaching back into the bag, I pull the two Glock 19s out and load them.

Standing, I put the lock on both of them before sliding mine inside my suit pocket, Killian slips his down the back of his jeans, pulling his jumper down and over the evident bulge.

Bending, I pick the bag up and place it back in Killian's car.

My heart is drumming in my chest, black spots blur my vision as I we take each step closer to where she should be.

Killian stays close behind me as we enter through the communal door. He is expecting us.

Walking slowly up the stairs, my heart is thumping in my ears. I have never been more nervous than I am now, the woman I love is a few meters away with some fucked up psychopath. My mind is showing me every scenario and it's scaring me. I don't think I could even explain to you what I am willing to do for Connie. I will rip him limb by limb if there is a single scratch on her.

Setting off on the second flight of stairs, my flight or fight response is in full swing but there is no fucking way I am going to let flight take over. I would happily lay down my life if it meant saving her. Always.

She was my life, my reason for existence.

Nearing the top of the stairs, I look over my shoulder and place my finger over my lips. Killian nods, his eyes closing for a moment as he flexes out his fingers. I slowly slip my hand inside my suit jacket just to feel the gun.

I stand outside the door, pulling my phone out and checking the apartment number one last time. I close my eyes, just for a moment and I see her. A small smile plays across my lips as I draw in a deep breath then exhale it slowly.

Stepping back, I lift my leg and kick the door in, it smashes against the wall and I wince. Pulling my gun out, Killian mirroring me as we step over the threshold.

"Connie!" I shout, my voice cracking as I do, my fear so etched into me at what we could possibly find. Cold perspiration beads on my brow as we walk through the apartment.

"Connie!" Killian calls out after me as we move forward, all the doors open apart from one.

I cock my head towards the door, Killian nodding as we approach. I still, trying to silence my rasps, they sound loud in my head. Pressing my ear against the door I can hear soft sobs and the sound of his voice, my skin pricking.

"Don't panic sweetness, you're just going to sleep for a little while."

My jaw ticks as the anger bubbles deep inside of me, I push the handle down and push it open and what I see in front of me makes my blood run cold. My beautiful love, bound up by her wrists, lifeless as she just hangs there and all I want in this moment is to see those beautiful, emerald green eyes. The sick little cunt is unbuckling his pants and all I can do is stand there, watching my worst nightmare playing out in front of me. My eyes scan over her limp body and I see the marks on her skin from him, the blood stains on her sneakers, bloody hand marks wrapped round her thighs, and I feel the angry tears begin to fill my eyes as I take a moment to just let the horror show in front of me burn into my core memories.

"I just want to fill you with all of me, now sleep my sweet one, sleep." His fucking seedy voice fills the room and I feel a rage I never knew I had inside of me. Turning my head slowly to lock my eyes on Killian, I see his jaw lax, his eyes wide and bugging out of his head as tears roll down his cheeks. My heart shreds at seeing him break into pieces in front of me, in front of his daughter. My eyes slip down to his hands, panic searing through me as I watch his fingers loosen round the handle of his gun and I watch as the gun tumbles through the air. And that's when the fight response kicks in.

He is so in his fucking disgusting head; he hasn't even heard us. My lips curl in disgust as I unlock the gun which makes him jump, and just as he turns round to see where it come from, he lunges himself towards me. I pull the trigger and watch as the bullet whizzes out of the barrel, the bang filling the room and all I can do is watch in slow motion as the bullet penetrates through the front of his head before he drops to the floor in front of me. And once he is down, my legs buckle beneath me as I fall to the floor and let out a heartbreakingly pained scream that scares me to my deepest depths.

CHAPTER SIXTY-FOUR
KALEB

I CRAWL, LIKE A FUCKING DOG ON MY HANDS AND KNEES OVER TO her lifeless body. Killian is sat on the floor, head in his hands trembling. No one should have to see their child this way. Every fibre in my body burns with a rage that is so consuming I'm terrified it will never leave. This moment right here is burned into my retinas, I will never un-see this. I'll be haunted for the rest of my life, and I'm scared to close my eyes because every time I do, this is what I'll see. I ignore the blood that is pooling all around me, ignoring the urge to take my rage out on the corpse of Cal. No, I am too focused on her.

"Connie," my voice cracks as I kneel in front of her, "baby," I choke.

I have no idea what he has given her, but my heart stutters in my chest as I watch her chest rise and fall slowly.

I jump when my phone buzzes in my pocket, I drop my head as I stuff my hand in my suit pants and grab my phone. Keaton.

"Hey," my voice is low as I turn to look over my shoulder at Killian who hasn't moved.

455

"Did you get her?" Keaton's panicked voice makes my chest ache.

I nod as if he can see me, "Yeah, we got her," I sigh, turning to face forward, my eyes slowly lifting to her.

"And Callaghan?" He asks and I can hear the rasp down the phone line, the tightness in his voice telling me that he is clenching his own jaw as I tighten my own.

"Dealt with," I grit, ignoring the bile that is burning the back of my throat. I cut him off and dial Titus' number. I hear some muffled voices, before I hear Titus.

"Yeah?" the gruffness in his voice comforting somehow in this moment.

"Call your mate Xavier, get someone over here sharpish. I need a clean-up," I struggle to even get the words out, the harsh reality of what has not long taken place in this room choking me. If we were a minute or two later, we would have been dealing with something else entirely.

"Not a problem, I know he has a team out in Aspen, but he sent someone to Tryst's apartment didn't he so I'm hoping he has a team close by."

"Thanks, just get it sorted. Sooner this cunt is gone the better." I sigh, letting the phone fall from my ear as it slips from my grasp, softly hitting the floor and I can still hear Titus' voice through the speaker but I ignore it.

"I need to get her down," I mumble as my eyes pin to her, "Killian, help me," I plead as I stand, looking behind me but Killian is nowhere to be seen. I pace back to where he was, my brows pinch as I spin to face her when suddenly, the air is knocked out of my lungs, winding me in an instant as I feel a burning sensation radiating through my chest. I stumble forward slightly, my hand pressing to where I feel the pain. Slowly dropping my head to look down, I see blood covering my hand rapidly. Falling to my knees, all I care about is getting to Connie. If I could get to her, everything would be okay. Dragging myself along the cold, damp floor, each movement gets harder as ragged pants leave me.

"Connie," pained sobs leave me, my arm reaching for her sneaker, my bloody hand marking the leather before I feel another burning sensation rip through me. All I want to do is cry out, but even that is too much. "Love..." I just about manage when I hear a loud bang before everything goes black and that's when I finally see her.

My darling, Connie.

CONNIE

I wake slowly, the bright lights hurting my eyes, the low and steady beep ringing in my ears. It takes me a moment to realise that I am lying in a hospital bed. Panic courses through me as I sit up quickly, looking round the room to see it empty.

"What the fuck?" I whisper to myself, before the pain rips through me that I am here, alone. No dad, no Reese and most importantly, no Kaleb. My lips feel bruised and swollen and so do my eyes. Slowly bringing my fingers to my lips, I gasp as I feel them and instantly remove my fingertips. Reaching for the call button, I press it repeatedly as I wait for the nurse. A young nurse walks in, instantly smiling as she enters the room.

"You're awake," she pulls my chart from the end of the bed and places it on the table that sits over my bed.

"I hope so," I grumble, rubbing my lips together and

instantly regretting it as I wince. She shakes her head softly side to side, her smile still evident.

"How long have I been here?" I ask, panic creeping through me, my chest tight suddenly.

"Since about two a.m. this morning," she looks down at her watch that is clipped to the pocket of her scrubs, "it's now just gone one p.m."

"Oh," I nod, swallowing the lump in my throat.

"I'll get the doctor; he will want to sit and have a chat with you. Also, your friend will be back shortly, they went to get a coffee," and before I can ask her anything more, she walks out of the room pulling the door shut slightly.

My heart skips a beat, a silly smile pulling at the corners of my lips at the thought of it being Kaleb.

A loose bit of hair falls onto my face, I push it back and wince when I feel a plastic splint on the bridge of my nose. Panic settles deep inside of me when I get a flashback of the evening in the club. My blood runs cold and suddenly, fear prickles my skin causing goosebumps to erupt. What if it's Callaghan here? What if he bought me here as a ploy? Oh my god, what if he done something to Reese, Kaleb or my dad?

I don't lift my finger from the buzzer, because if it is Cal who walks through the door, at least I can call for help. My pulse quickens underneath my skin as I see a figure walk past the blind, I see the door move slightly, my eyes don't move from the door when I see Reese walk in, my pulse slowing instantly before I burst into relieved tears.

"Oh my god, Connie, you're awake! Are you okay?" she rushes over to me, the bed dipping as she sits on the edge of it and pulls me in for a cuddle whilst being gentle with me the whole time.

"I thought you were Cal," I hiccup and stutter through

the ridiculous number of tears that roll down my cheeks. "My mind is fuzzy, I have certain bits flashing back but they don't make sense. I remember hearing Kaleb's voice, but I don't know if I dreamt it and my Dad's too? Were they there?" I ask, my heavy eyes lifting.

I see her face fall as she breaks away from me, her hand clasping over mine.

"You have nothing to worry about with Oal, he won't be bothering you anymore," she whispers, swiping her own tear away.

"Did Kaleb come to visit?" I manage, my voice cracking and by the look on her face, I already know my answer. Tears prick at the back of my eyes, my bottom lip trembling. Sinking my teeth into it then wincing as the soreness reminds me that I am wounded.

"It's not that he didn't want to..." Reese stammers out, her hand squeezing mine a little tighter. "They rescued you, your dad and Kaleb," she smiles softly but that smile soon slips as if she has just remembered something that pains her.

"Then why are they not here?" I whisper, my vision blurred by the pooling of tears in my eyes.

"Oh honey," she chokes, I can hear the pain in her voice as she sniffles, her eyes streaming. Her soft thumb pad rubs back and forth over the back of my hand, but the comforting motion begins to get sore.

"What is it?" my voice tight as my throat swells, my eyes burning with the build-up of tears that I refuse to let fall.

"Kaleb," her head falls forward and I see the tears roll off her cheek and dissolve into my hospital sheets.

"No," my voice is barely audible as the whisper escapes

me, my eyes narrowing on Reese as I wait with bated breath for confirmation of my worst fears.

"He is in surgery," and a little swarm of relief sweeps through me that he is alive. "He is in critical condition, the doctors were surprised he was still holding on when your dad brought him in," I shake my head from side to side in complete shock of the words that were leaving her lips.

I drop my head into my hand and jump as the pain slices through me, throwing my body back towards the pillows as my head falls back. My heart aches in my chest as the tears continue to roll.

"Your face is really swollen," she whispers, standing from the bed and that's when I realise, she is still in her dress.

"Why are you still in your dress?" my brows knit.

"Because I haven't been home since," she looks down at her body then back up to mine.

"You've been searching for me all this time? You've not once gone home?"

"Sweetie," I freeze as the name rolls off her lips and her steps falter.

"Don't call me that," my teeth clench and I ignore the painful, burning ache that radiates through me.

"This all happened in under twelve hours, as soon as your dad got to me, he called Kaleb. They left me at the club with Keaton to find you," she edges closer to me, pushing my hair from my face gently.

"Cal told me it had been days," pained sobs leave me as my chest rises and falls quickly.

"Cal was playing tricks with you," and I see the sorry look in her eyes at the torment.

"Everything hurts, my head is fuzzy, and nothing makes sense," I admit. My chest tightens as the last few minutes of conversation play back on repeat and I find myself gasping for air. "Reese," I panic as she runs for the door, shouting for help as I clutch at my chest through the thin material of the hospital gown.

The nurse from earlier rushes in and pulls my hand from my chest, holding my hand in her cool grasp.

"Breathe," her voice is low, her clear blue eyes steady on mine, "just breathe, Connie."

I nod, sucking in as much air as I can to fill my burning lungs.

"In," she says slowly, and I inhale through my nose. "Out," smiling at me, I let the breath out of my lips. "Again," she nods and I repeat the steps until I lose the panicked fear that cripples me. "You're okay," she lets go of my hand, patting it gently before stepping back and checking my monitor.

I hear a commotion outside and before I can ask what is going on, I see my moms bursting through the door, their hands moving to their mouths when they take in the sight of me.

"Oh, my baby," my mom, Lara calls out as she rushes over to me, throwing her arms around me and holding me tightly but I wince as pain rocks through me.

"She's in a lot of pain," the nurse pipes up, looking down her nose at my mom, "can you let her go a little?" smirking she walks and leaves the room.

"I'm so sorry darling," she gasps, tears rolling down her cheeks when my other mom, Katie stands next to my bed.

"It's okay," my voice is a squeak when I see Reese hovering by the door, a smile slowly creeping onto her face when I see arms wrap round her.

"Dad," I rasp, my voice is hoarse.

"Baby," he steps into the room, his fingers linked through Reese's as he moves closer to the bed.

"Dad," my bottom lip trembles when my eyes glance over him, blood stained into his shirt, and a wail escapes my lungs that I have no control over when it hits me that it's Kaleb's blood.

Letting my head fall forward I can't hold onto anymore of the pain that is harvesting deep in my chest, the last few hours have hit me like a tidal wave, and I have no control over the emotions that are escaping me. My whole body shudders as the screams pass my lips, burning my throat as it mixes with the bile that is threatening to leave me.

No one moves closer to me, no one tries to comfort me. They just watch as every ounce of my pent-up feelings pour out of me.

"I can't do this without him," I finally manage, my voice cracking. Slowly lifting my head to look round the room at them all standing there, their pained expressions clearly written all over their faces. "I don't *want* to do this without him," my voice is a little stronger this time.

"And you won't have to, he is in good hands," my dad tries to reassure me but until I hear it from the doctors mouth I won't rest.

"What happened to him? Please tell me," I beg.

"He got shot, lost a lot of blood. I carried him to the ambulance and that's all I can tell you," my dad's voice is tight and thick.

A knock on the door pulls all the attention from me and I grateful. I hear the sound of footsteps beat across the floor when I see an older male doctor appear at the foot of my bed.

"Hey Connie," he smiles at me as he holds my files in his

hand. I roll my lips, inhaling deeply and ignoring the soreness, my eyes squeezing shut for the moment.

"I'm doctor Nico, how are you feeling?" he asks, and I let my eyes sweep over him. He must be around my dad's age, his hair short and black, his deep hazel brown eyes locked to mine.

"Numb," I nod, picking the skin round my nail bed.

"It's been a lot, I can imagine," his voice is soft and low, and I feel a rage burning deep in my belly.

"Can you imagine?" I snap, my fingers curling so both of my hands are balled into fists. "Can you imagine being strung up and drugged? Can you imagine what it was like to have such a blow to the face that most of your face swells up? Can you imagine what it was like…" and I stammer over my words, a suffocated choke of sobs trembling out of me.

I can hear the low rumble of my dad's growl filling the room, my moms now either side of my bed as they grasp their small hands over mine.

"I didn't mean it like that," I watch as he retracts over his words and steps closer to me, "Connie, what you went through was horrific. No one, and I mean *no one,* especially *you* should have to go through something like that," he takes another step closer. "From what I can work out," his eyes move from mine as he looks round the room with caution before they land back on me, "Would you like to have this chat in private?" and I know why he is asking me.

I shake my head from side to side.

"Okay," he smiles and perches himself on the end of the bed before clearing his throat. "Firstly," he swallows, "we had to reset your nose, obviously I don't know for certain how your nose broke but from looking at the damage, it would seem your face was…" he stalls, fidgeting and I can feel the burn in my throat, a large lump forming. "Hit into a hard object with force. One of your eye sockets is broken, as well as one of your cheek bones,"

I can hear the tension brewing in the room, and I am terrified to slice my eyes to my dad.

"You have rope burns on your wrists and ankles," I watch as the doctor takes a moment to compose himself and amongst the chaos of the last hour, I hadn't even seen that my wrists were bandaged up. "Now, without further tests... we won't be able to see if you were..." he stops, and I can see the remorse in his eyes at the words that are about to leave his lips.

"Raped," I say deadpan, "you won't be able to see if I was raped," I ignore the bile that is burning my throat as it slowly rises.

I hear the cries from my moms, Reese sobs into dad's chest and I can feel the rage that is burning into the side of my head from my dad's heated gaze.

Doctor Nico opens his mouth, but I beat him to it.

"Do the tests, do whatever you need to do." And that's when I shut down, the pain suddenly numbing completely and the tears that were threatening to fall dry up.

CHAPTER SIXTY-FIVE
KILLIAN

PACING UP AND DOWN THE HALLWAY, I CAN'T SIT. MY MIND IS racing at one hundred miles per hour, playing on repeat seeing her hung there and lifeless, the marks that the little cunt left on her skin and just as we nearly had her, Kaleb got shot down, but he didn't give up until every bit of strength he had left inside of him had faded, and that's when the second shot hit him, ripping through his skin. It all happened so quickly; I was sorting the shit show that was Cal out with Xavier when I heard the first shot. Xavier told me to go, and he would get the clean-up sorted. The flashbacks of my fumbling for my gun plague me and it felt like everything moved in slow motion, I couldn't move quickly enough even if I wanted to.

My Glock is loaded, my legs heavy as I drag them towards the room where Kaleb and Connie are, the sheer panic of knowing that whoever was in there could have shot her filling me. She was my priority and I know Kaleb would have understood. He would have told me to save her before saving him and that's what I done.

I saved her before I saved him.

My trembling hands shake as the gun vibrated between my clasped fingers. Steadying my shaky breath, I round the corner and see a larger guy, red spikey hair hovering over Kaleb's body, my heart thumping hard when I see his bloody hand gripping onto her sneaker. Adrenaline spikes through me and I feel a strength I never have as I slowly lift the gun and begin walking forward and just as he shoots again, my finger wraps round the trigger and the bullet glides through the air, hitting him in the back of the head and all I do is watch as he falls to the ground. As soon as I hear the slump of him hitting the ground, the gun slips out of my hand before I run towards where Kaleb and Connie are. Reaching for her first, I untie her from the rope, and let her collapse into my arms as I fall to my knees, kissing her forehead as I hold her limp but warm body in my embrace. Pulling her into me, my head tips back as the tears roll down my cheeks.

"The ambulance is on its way, I'll help you move them," Titus' voice rocks me through to my shaken core. I shake my head from side to side not wanting to let go of Connie.

"Let Nate take her, we need to get Kaleb up," Titus kneels down in front of me and I see the kindness in his eyes, and I know I can trust him. I slowly nod, kissing Connie on the forehead again as a skinny, tall guy appears at my side and I can see how hard he is trying to hold off his emotions at the sight that is laid out in my arms. He pushes his glasses up his nose before he bends down and pulls her from my arms, holding her tightly he turns and begins to walk out the room.

"Take care of her," my voice breaks as I stumble to my feet, Titus gripping me to stop me from losing my balance as I watch Nate walk out the room with my first baby, my daughter.

As soon as Connie is out the room, Titus' whole character changes, his demeanour shifting. He grabs Rox's body and pulls him off of Cal. I knew it was Rox as soon as I saw him, I had never met him but knew he was part of the band.

"No good pieces of shit," he spits on him before focusing on Cal. "Kaleb fought so hard to keep her away from Tryst, he didn't even think about this cunt. After finding Cal trying to force her into something she didn't want at one of Tryst's concerts, he knew what he was dealing with but after Tryst died, everything mellowed out. His worst fear came true," Titus' shoulders sag as he reaches for Kaleb, rolling him over and slapping him on his face a little hard.

"Stay with me mate, the ambulance is on its way," Titus' gruff voice slows and falls into a soft hum. He rips Kaleb's shirt open, taking it from his bleeding torso as he tears it into shreds, tying and trying to put pressure onto the wounds.

I snap out of whatever trance I am in and place my fingers at his pulse in his neck.

"He isn't going to last much longer," I keep my voice low as I whisper to Titus.

"He won't give up on her that easy..." Titus smirks when he hears Kaleb groan and my heart sinks in relief.

"I know I don't like you," I smirk as I crane my neck, so my eyes are level with his closed ones, "but I don't want you to die," and I hear a low scoff leave him. A trickle of blood runs out the side of his mouth and I know I need to act quickly. Standing back, I inhale deeply before bending back down and picking Kaleb up as gently as I can and roll him over my shoulder.

"You don't get to die," I grunt, the weight of him on my shoulders heavy, a burden I don't want to be carrying for the rest of my life.

"Take him to the street, I'll start sorting this whilst we wait for Xavier's guy," Titus gives me a tight nod before I begin to move, willing for my buckling legs not to give out on me. Not just yet.

"Did you hear me?" I grit through my clenched teeth, "you don't get to die; she needs you as much as you need her." I pant

as I get to the front of the apartment, my eyes move from the stairs to the elevator when I see the out of order sign pinned to it. "Fuck it,"

I wrap one arm over Kaleb's body and ignore the wetness that seeps through the thin material of my shirt knowing full well where it's coming from.

"I know I don't agree with your relationship," I continue talking to Kaleb, but I have no idea if he is even still conscious. "But I have no right to judge when I married her best friend drunk one night in Vegas. Then I became utterly obsessed with her that I wouldn't let her move on from me. And like a cunt, I made her go through the annulment by herself because I couldn't bear to be present when the only woman I have ever loved chose to walk away..." I stop midway down the steps, inhaling deeply and readjusting Kaleb slightly. "I broke both Connie and Reese, but I knew I couldn't let Reese go. She was made for me; she was my soulmate, and I was hers. I won't watch my daughter go through the heartbreak of losing you, so you will not die. Keep fucking breathing and don't go into the light..." I stop as I reach the first level landing, "or whatever shit they say," I puff, "one more flight mate," I begin walking again. "You don't get to die Kaleb. She loves you and I know, begrudgingly, how much you love her. And you won't hear me say this again, so you better be listening..." I stumble off the bottom step and see the paramedics rushing towards me, "you have my blessing," and my legs give out under me, my muscles going into spasm under my trembling skin as the paramedics pull Kaleb from me. All I can do is watch from the floor as they lay him down on the stretcher that is waiting for him on the sidewalk when I hear them shout that they've just lost his pulse.

CHAPTER SIXTY-SIX
CONNIE

I SIT ALONE WITH MY THOUGHTS, MY EYES PINNED TO THE TICKING clock on the wall as the seconds slip past like hours. Doctor Nico returned an hour or so ago telling me that no trauma or bodily fluids were found when they carried out the tests and I have never felt so relieved. He has been gone ever since, he told me he would go and get me an update and here I am, sitting in the bed staring at the clock.

Tick, tock.

Tick, tock.

Tick, tock.

I am disturbed when I see Keaton in the doorway with a huge bear, balloons and flowers and a small smile graces my lips.

"Hey, you, you look pretty," he winks before he is shoved through the door, Titus smiling at me as he barges past Keaton and leans in, placing a kiss on my cheek.

"How are you?" Titus asks as he sits in the high back chair next to my bed, Keaton following and placing the flowers on the table that sits over my bed along with the large teddy.

"I don't care about me," I smile, "but once I know Kaleb is okay, I'll start thinking about me."

"He will be okay," Keaton smiles, "I can feel it, it's a twin thing," he gives me a little wink.

"What happened in there, if Kaleb shot Cal," I keep my voice low, "who shot Kaleb?"

"Rox."

My blood runs cold and just as I am about to cry, I see a doctor wrapped in dark blue scrubs walk into the room. My heart races in my chest, skipping beats as my breath catches at the back of my throat. I feel Titus' hand clasp over mine, Keaton holding the other one. The young female doctor pulls her mask down, her eyes bouncing between the three of us.

"Kaleb is in intensive care, the surgery went well, we had a few minor complications but nothing that will affect his recovery or his way of living," she gives me a small nod and I see a hint of a smile grace her lips before she steps back. "I'll have a nurse come down and take you to him shortly," and I nod, constantly nod as the tears roll down my cheeks.

"He's okay," I whisper to Titus and Keaton. "He's okay." I repeat.

THREE MONTHS LATER

My fingers trace over the two bullet hole scars, my heart breaking in my chest at the memories that still haunt me. I wish I could say we were over it, but the truth was, we aren't. The trauma is buried deep inside of us, instilled and imprinted on us for life, but we know with time and healing we will get there, *together*.

I pout, my eyes stinging with tears as I circle each of the imperfect scars and sigh. His fingers grip my chin and tilt my face up so I have no option but to look at him.

"Baby, don't be sad. I'm here. You're here. We're alive and together and that's all that matters, sure, I have a couple of scars but they only make me look a little more macho, don't you think?" he smirks, his breath on my face as his lips hover over mine and just when I think he is going to kiss me, his lips trail to my forehead as he places a soft kiss in the centre of my head, lingering for a second or two.

"It just makes me sad," I admit, willing for his lips to close over mine.

"I know it does," he whispers, "things about that moment haunt me too…" he trails off for a moment, his spare hand gliding down the side of my naked body as he traces shapes on my pebbled skin with his fingertips. "But let me make you forget, just for a while…" he smiles, his eyes hooded as he pulls on his bottom lip softly with his teeth before they connect with mine, he tongue pushing past my lips, gliding across my tongue and his fingers continuing their trail until he meets the apex of my thighs.

My eyes flutter shut as I feel his fingers drag across my skin and over my round ass, slipping between my thighs from behind and pushing two of his fingers inside of me, curling them at the tips as he pumps them in and out of me in a slow and teasing manner. Kaleb breaks away from me, rolling behind me his lips brushing against the shell of my ear. My head tips back as wetness pools between my legs, soaking his hand. He groans, and my legs part for him. His thumb brushes against my swollen and sensitive clit and my breaths are snatched from me as pleasure blankets me.

I watch through hazy eyes as he slips his fingers from me and kneels between my legs, pushing them wider.

"Sit up against the headboard," he orders, his voice like silk as it dances across my skin.

Shuffling back like he asks; I sit and wait for him.

Leaning over me, his lips hover over mine once more.

"I am going to eat your pussy, and then I am going to fuck you so fucking hard," his voice is low as his pleasurable threats make my stomach flip and heat blossom between my thighs.

Swirling his fingers back in my arousal, they slip in with ease now as I watch intently as he lowers his top half down until his mouth is where he wants it to be. Turning his head to the side, he places soft and wet kisses on my inner thighs whilst fucking me with his fingers. Moans mewl from me, filling the room as the pleasure deep within me intensifies. Dragging his lips back over my skin, he parts my lips and kisses along my pussy until he reaches my opening. Lifting his lips from me for just a second, his tongue flattens and swipes through my folds causing me to gasp and arch my back. His hand skims up my body, splaying against my stomach as he holds me in place, his tongue continuing his assault against my clit.

"Shit," I whisper, my head tipped back as my eyes close. His tongue slows, my hand moving to his hair as I grip, "stay like that," I moan, "please," I beg.

Flattening his tongue against my clit, gliding down to my opening, his fingers thrusting deeper into me. My hips grind against his fingers, and I hear him groan as his tongue finds my clit again.

"I'm getting close," my head falls forward as I watch how his tongue works me up and I feel my stomach flip, my pussy tightening round his fingers. He growls, slipping his fingers out of me as he falls back onto his knees grinning at me, a shimmer of my arousal on his lips.

My chest rises and falls, my skin tingling with my orgasm teasing to explode through me.

"Why did you stop?" I pout, now totally aware that I am naked and still sitting with my thighs parted.

"Because I want you coming on my cock, baby." He winks, falling forward and crawling over me. I shuffle down slightly, resting my weight on my elbows as he lays between my parted thighs, his erection pressed against his toned stomach. He grips my knee, pushing it up so it's bent, and the other stays pressed to the bed. Rearing up, he fists his cock slowly, pumping his hand up and down his girthy length.

His fingers rub over my clit, and I can feel my nerve endings tingling as my orgasm teeters.

"I'm not going to last long," I whimper, my breath shaky as he continues rubbing slowly over my sensitive nub.

He edges closer to me, his lips hovering over mine. "You're so fucking beautiful," he murmurs in a soft tone before he swipes his tongue past my lips, our tongue connecting as I moan into his open mouth, his fingers still swirling over my clit.

"Please," I whisper against his mouth.

"Please what?" he taunts, and I feel the smirk against my lips.

"Please..." I stammer as pleasure burns deep inside of me, "please fuck me."

"You're such a good girl," he smiles and without giving me any indication, his cock slips into my soaked pussy, my head falling back as he fills me to the hilt. Pulling his hips back, the tip of his cock sits at my entrance as he teases me.

My eyes fall between where our bodies are connected as I watch him slowly push his beautiful dick into me.

My body begins to tremble, his fingers digging into the skin on my thighs as he adjusts his pace, so his cock is pounding in and out of me. Lifting his eyes to meet mine, he lowers his hot mouth over my pert and hardened nipples, flicking his tongue across them and sucking them into his mouth which causes a shot of pleasure to ripple through me.

"I'm so close," I moan out.

"Good," he grunts, lifting his own head and letting it fall back as he loses himself in immeasurable pleasure.

Pressing his thumb back against my clit and pressing a little harder, I tilt my pelvis up to meet each of his hard thrusts into me. A shiver dances up my spine, my legs trembling and my toes curl as I come, my orgasm shattering through me as I ride it out.

"Fuck, yes, fuck," he moans, as he continues to fuck me hard and fast before his own orgasm crashes through him. His lips press against the tip of my nose softly then he collapses on top of me, making me fall back into the pile of pillows. His head is on my chest as my heart dances in my chest. No words are exchanged. We just lay here in the silent bliss in our post orgasmic state. My fingers trail over his shoulders as I crane my neck so my lips purse on the top of his head.

"I'm so in love with you," I mutter into his thick, black hair.

"I love you forever," his voice is slow and low before I feel him getting heavier, then, within minutes soft snores escape him and I smile.

CHAPTER SIXTY-SEVEN
KALEB

THE LAST FEW MONTHS HAD FLOWN PAST, CONNIE AND I WERE struggling to find ourselves again after what had happened. Between therapy, long conversations, and a lot of healing we were slowly getting back to what we once were. We had gone through a trauma that neither of us deserved, but we do honestly believe it has made us stronger than ever.

As soon as I was out of hospital, I didn't let her out of my sight. I moved her back in with me and I honestly thought she was going to put up a bit of a fight, but she didn't. I think after nearly dying, my whole outlook on life had changed, and so had hers. My mind flashes back to the scariest day of my life, and my heart drums underneath my skin.

When I finally come round, I think she is a hallucination sitting next to my bed, my very own guardian angel. I have so much I want to say, the words laying heavy on my tongue, but she presses her finger against my lips. She just shakes her head from side to side as the tears flow out of her beautiful green eyes, rolling down her cheeks and dissolving into her lap.

"Kaleb," she chokes, reaching for my hand and holding it tightly.

"Your face, oh baby," my voice cracked as my eyes sweep over her face, her eyes black and swollen, her check grazed and mixed with a blue and yellowish bruise. Her nose is covered by a plastic splint, dried blood round her nostrils and her beautiful plump lips are split and swollen.

"Don't worry about my face, Kaleb... you could have died," she angrily swipes a tear away and I can clearly see the frustration that seeps from her. She couldn't hide it even if she wanted to.

"But I didn't, a lot of things could have happened my love, but they didn't. I am here and alive..." I smirk, "barely," I try and make a light-hearted joke of the situation, but she doesn't even smile.

"Let me apologise, if I could have just apologised and explained what had happened... then..." I begin to stammer, wincing as pain burns through me and I see the panic in her eyes, the pure fear flashing through them.

"I don't want you to apologise. Fuck, Kaleb, it should be me apologising to you! I should have let you tell me your side but I didn't. I shut you down. Every single time and for that I am sorry. So, so sorry. You nearly died!" her voice raises slightly, and I somehow love her a little more fiercely.

"I just want us to draw a line in the sand, I want us to have our new beginning, our happily ever after. Yes, it's going to take some work and fuck this is not going to be an easy journey, but I just want you. You." Her voice is strained as she cracks, her trembling hand reaching for my chest as her fingers splay against my heart. "I would give all of this up to just be with you," and it fucking kills me that I can't sit up to wipe her tears away. "Promise me Kaleb, promise me that none of this matters anymore. Just promise me that from this moment *on, we don't look back, promise me that we only move forward."*

My eyes feel heavy, and I give her a tight smile, "I promise baby," I squeeze her hand, bringing the back of it to my lips as I kiss her skin softly. "We're just two souls, with two hearts beating as one. You're the other half of me darling, I never felt complete until I met you."

She chokes out sobs, her whole body trembling as the tears leave her.

"Fuck, darling all I want to do is scoop you up and hold you until your tears dry."

"I am just so obsessively in love with you Kaleb, the thought that I nearly lost you killed me."

"I'm irrevocably in love with you, baby. I was never going to leave you; it wasn't my time. We are only just getting started darling."

I AM PULLED FROM MY THOUGHTS WHEN I HEAR HER VOICE, calling me. Turning round as I clasp my cuff link into my shirt sleeve. My eyes are wide like saucers as I take in the beauty that saunters towards me, and now she is in front of me, I feel the silly and giddy smile that lights up my face. My greedy eyes sweep over her, and I feel my cock stir in my pants. The gold one shouldered dress clung to her body in all the right places, and I see a little of her glorious, tanned skin tone through the thigh high slit. Her outfit is finished off with gold, strappy heeled sandals and all I can think about is fucking her against the wall.

"Fuck, you look stunning," I sink my teeth into my bottom lip and it's hard for me to pull my eyes from her rare beauty.

"Well, my handsome *Gramps,* you look very beautiful

too," she places her hand against my chest, pressing onto her tiptoes as she places a soft kiss on my lips. Her long, chocolate dark hair is pulled round to the side and over her bare shoulder in a loose plait and weaved with ivory flowers. A few strands round her face fall, framing her face.

Wrapping my arm around her waist, I pulled her into me, so our bodies were flush and I see the heat flame across her cheeks.

"We'll be late," she whispers as my lips connect with her neck, her head tipping to the side and giving me more access. Brushing my lips across and pursing them against her pulse, her fingers wrap round the breast of my black tuxedo suit jacket.

"I don't need long princess, especially with the way you look in that dress."

Gripping her chin, I tilt her head back slightly as I trail kisses along her jawbone. My free hand grips onto her bare thigh, digging my fingers in slightly harder than before I trail my fingertips over her skin. I rasp as her scent intoxicates me. Walking her back towards the wall, she smiles as her back hits the hard surface. Placing my hands either side of her face, I kiss her with hunger, and I feel I am too far gone to be gentle. I need her like an addict needs drugs.

Her fingers fumble with my pants, tugging them down in a swift move before she wraps her arms around my neck, her eyes alight with fire. Skimming my hands down the side of her body and pushing her dress skirt up around her waist, her greedy little hands wrap round my thick cock as she pumps slowly up and down my length. I slip her panties to the side before digging my fingers into her bare ass and lift her in the air, her legs automatically wrapping around my waist as I line my throbbing cock at her dripping wet pussy. Edging the tip in slowly, her eyes roll in the back of her head as I thrust myself into her hard and fast, her pussy tightening round me as I begin fucking her like I hate her, her loud moans filling the bedroom as her back hits against the wall. My pounds are relentless, her fingers scratching up the back of my head which makes my skin explode in goosebumps and sends shivers up and down my spine as my cock slips in and out of her fast, my orgasm teetering on the edge of the cliff as she clenches around me, her hips rotating as she gyrates over me.

"Fuck darling," I grit, digging my fingers into her skin harder.

"Keep fucking me hard Kaleb, I am going to come," she screams, driving me on to keep up the harsh and pounding rhythm.

"Yes, oh, oh," her eyes roll in the back of her head, and I smile as I pound into her one last time before I fill her to the hilt and my orgasm rocks through me, my whole body going rigid as I empty inside of her, riding my orgasm until we're both panting. My forehead presses against hers, my smile grows and suddenly, soft laughs escape us.

CHAPTER SIXTY-EIGHT
CONNIE

WALKING OUT OF OUR BEDROOM, OUR FINGERS ARE LACED together as we head down the hallway of *The Plaza* towards the bridal suite.

"I know I have already said it," Kaleb's voice is low as we stop outside the room Reese is currently in, I turn my face to look at him, but we're interrupted when Liz opens the bedroom door all flustered, reaching for my arm.

"Thank goodness you're here! Reese needs her friend, she thinks she doesn't look *bride* enough," she rolls her eyes in an over exaggerated manner and now I know where Reese gets it from.

I look over my shoulder and give an apologetic shrug of my shoulders.

"I'll see you soon," he nods, his voice a whisper as it dances over my skin and I reluctantly pull my hand out of his, his fingers digging into my skin as he tries to keep hold of me and laughing when I finally pull away. I push up slightly, kissing him on his lips.

"I'll see you soon, then," I nod softly, my lips curling into a smile as I step into the bridal suite, but Kaleb doesn't leave immediately, which makes me turn my body to face him once more. He steps forward, his shiny brogue hanging just over the threshold of the room and he leans against the door frame, his arms crossing against his broad chest as his eyes roam up and down my body and I watch a crooked smile play against his lips.

"What?" I stop, my cheeks heating under his intense gaze.

"I didn't get to finish what I was going to say earlier," he shakes his head from side to side before letting his head drop, his eyes batting to the floor for just a moment before his grey eyes are back on mine, baring me his soul. My heart skips in my chest as I await the words to leave his lips.

"You really are the most beautiful woman I have ever laid eyes on; I count my lucky stars every day since meeting you. I'm in awe of you."

I feel the happy tears prick in my eyes as I turn away for a moment, swiping my ring finger under my eyes but when I turn to face him, he has gone.

"I love you," I whisper to the empty doorway before I turn and walk to where Reese is waiting.

"Wow," is the only word my brain can seem to muster when I take in the beauty that is my best friend.

"Yeah?" she smiles, her eyes flicking down to look at her dress before they land back on mine.

"Yes!" I rush over to her and wrap my arms round her shoulders, "Reese, you look like a dream, my dad is going to fall over his tongue," a soft laugh bubbles out of me as I run my fingers down her arms and hold her hands before I take a step back so I can just admire her one last time. Thin, ivory spaghetti straps sit over her shoulders with a simple round neck cut. Her dress fits to her body like a glove, and fans out slightly from her knees. I spin her round to appreciate the cowls back that ripples before small buttons trail down past her buttocks.

Tears prick in my eyes as I turn her back round. Her honey blonde hair is styled in classic beach waves that tumble down her back and is finished off with a pretty veil slipped into the back of her head.

Lifting the skirt of her dress, she shows me the white, sparkly *Louboutin* sneakers that I bought her. Pain sears through me, trauma raising its ugly head as flashbacks plague me of my matching pair, bloodied in Kaleb's handprint.

"My something old," she smiles, letting go of her dress and all I can do is smile as she pulls me from my morbid thoughts. My eyes scan to her neck to see a beautiful gold chain with a rainbow and an infinity symbol. I see her watching me before she says, "Your dad had it made for me, he was my rainbow after the storm, plus it incorporates Celeste..." her fingers grasp the delicate rainbow as she continues, "and the infinity symbol because..." she scoffs as she looks up at the ceiling to stop the wave of tears that threaten to fall, "*infinity.*"

"I am so happy for you Reese, after everything you have been through you deserve this and so *so* much more." And it doesn't matter how much I try; I can't stop the tears that are rolling down my cheeks.

"Oh, Connie," she sobs, stepping forward and wrapping her arms around me tightly. "But I'm going to say now, I'm not going to start calling you *mom*," I tease, my smile growing as the seconds slip past.

"You twat," she laughs as she pulls back when we see Liz walk round the corner with Celeste who is wearing an ivory dress with a netted tulle skirt that has specs of gold laced through to match my dress. Her brown hair is finished off with a flowered headband and my heart bursts.

"Oh, my angel," I choke, reaching for her and taking her out of Liz's arms. Celeste smiles, reaching for my face and I kiss her delicate little hands. I am so lost in Celeste, that I didn't even hear Mateo come in, and the photographer follows behind snapping away.

"Mi amor," Mateo sobs, pulling out a handkerchief when he sees just how beautiful his daughter looks.

"Daddy," she chokes, as he wraps her up in a loving embrace and holds her close.

"Are you ready mi amor? Are you ready for your forever?"

She nods, her eyes slicing to mine as she blows me a kiss.

"Is it our time to go?" I ask as nervous flutters swarm me.

"It is," Liz says as she hands Reese her ivory peony bouquet that is wrapped with a champagne silk ribbon, then she steps closer to me and hands me mine that matches, just on a smaller scale.

"Then let's go and get you married," I whisper, waiting for her to pass with her dad, her mom scoops Celeste from my arms before following behind them.

Excitement courses through me and all I can think about is seeing Kaleb standing at the end of the aisle with my dad. Their relationship has grown over the last few months to the point my father asked him to be his best man and invited Titus, Keaton and Nate to be part of his groom's party.

Inhaling deeply, I follow behind Liz and close the bridal suite door behind me.

. . .

Standing outside the closed double doors, I stand behind Reese. Bending slightly, I pull out the train on her dress one last time. Inhaling deeply, nerves begin to drum through me. The wedding co-ordinator gives Reese a tight nod and a wink and that's my cue to move in front of her. I quickly get into place, Liz slipping in behind me and that's when the creak of the heavy double doors echoes round the airy room, goosebumps prickle my skin when I hear *Rewrite the stars – The Piano Guys* filling the room and my eyes begin to fill with tears.

Taking one last deep breath, I step forward as everyone stands but everything else blurs out around me when my eyes find him. My heart sings along to the soft beat of the music, his eyes fixed to mine, a slow smile gracing his face as I step closer to him. I dip my head when I reach the top of the aisle, branching off to the left as I stand tall and wait for my best friend. My dad has tears streaming down his face as he stands proud, his chest puffed out and his hands locked in front, one clasped over the other and my heart swarms in my chest. I watch as Mateo kisses his daughter on the cheek, his pride shining from him as he places her hand into Killian's, and I am so blessed to be witnessing the beginning of their forever.

CHAPTER SIXTY-NINE
KALEB

WATCHING THE WOMAN I LOVE WALKING DOWN THE AISLE, HER eyes stayed pinned to mine as I watched the stars shining in her emerald depths, I swear a fell a little harder for her then. It got me excited about what was to come between us. This was just the beginning of our story; we were nowhere near the end just yet.

"Hey handsome," she smiles, distracting me from my thoughts of earlier in the day.

"Don't say that to me in front of your boyfriend," Keaton whispers loudly, elbowing me in the ribs and I laugh.

"In your dreams," she scoffs, placing her small hands on my chest as she rests her head on me.

"You know it," Keaton winks, taking a mouthful of his whiskey before he disappears onto the dance floor.

Titus scoffs, shaking his head from side to side at my brother's stupid comebacks.

"You okay mate?" I ask, knowing full well Titus is beyond stressed.

"I have been better," he side-eyes me, lifting his glass to his lips and taking a mouthful of his own whiskey.

"We will get her back, me, you, Keaton, Nate…" I inhale sharply, "and Xavier," I place my hand round Connie, resting it on her lower back. "There is no way he will stop until she is safe, and neither will we," I give him a firm nod and he just grunts. One thing with Titus, he hates not doing the job right, but the job was never *just* a job. It got personal, it got complicated and now he is beating himself black and blue over it. But it doesn't matter how much we tell him we will fix it, he is too fixated on self-sabotaging himself. I sigh when he drains his glass and turns away from me and moves towards the bar.

"There is nothing more you can do, baby."

"I know darling, I know," I mutter, wrapping both my arms around her now and placing my lips to the top of her head.

She looks up at me, her eyes wide and full of them glistening stars that I always see when I look at her, her lips parted. "Dance with me," she whispers and my lips brush against hers.

"Always, my love, I will always dance with you."

Skimming her delicate fingers down my body until she reaches my hand, she laces them through mine and leads me out onto the dance floor. I don't see anyone else but her, since the moment I met her, I've had tunnel vision. It's always been her.

The soft country intro starts as *Beautiful Crazy – Luke Combes* begins to play. Her arms reach up and lock round my neck, my hands resting on her waist as we slow dance, forgetting every person around us.

"I can't wait to dance every dance with you," she smiles as her lips brush against mine.

"I look forward to it," I mumble before I press my lips over hers, losing myself in her completely.

"You're free my little butterfly, are you ready to spread your wings?" I ask as the song begins to fade.

"Only if you fly with me," her green eyes bounce back and forth between mine.

"Always baby, always..." letting one arm fall from around her back, I reach inside my tux pocket and pull out a set of keys, holding them up and I see the confusion mask her pretty face.

"Now, it's not a proposal, but it is a sorry..." she goes to answer back but I shake my head from side to side, "it's a sorry for all the times I have hurt you, it's a sorry for all the times I made you cry and most importantly, it's a sorry for not being there for when you needed me," her eyes glisten under the dance floor lights showing me the tears that are pooling. "It's a sorry I haven't taken you back to '*The Love Lodge*' like you asked..."

"Kaleb," she whispers her hands slipping from my neck as she clasps my face in her hands.

"Welcome home, baby," I just manage to slip out before her lips cover mine, my arm wrapping back round her body as I lift her feet from the ground. "The start of our forever," I whisper against the shell of her ear as I break away and hold her that little bit tighter, "the first chapter of our happily ever after."

EPILOGUE
TITUS

I STAND IN THE WARM SPRING AIR, INHALING DEEPLY AS I TIP MY head back and look at the clear night sky. This should have been an easy job; this should have been a straight swap over as such. But the Knight brothers got to Amora before I even had a chance to. They blindsided us and took her right from our grasps. Xavier is hunting them down and has promised that she will be on the next flight to America, but I'm not holding my breath, because if I do, I'll be dead.

I've told him he has a week.

A week to get her on that plane or the job is off.

I have my own shit to deal with, I don't need to be babysitting a twenty-one-year-old brat.

"Hey," I hear Nate's voice behind me, and I inhale deeply, "you coming back inside? They're doing the cake."

"Yeah, yeah, I'm coming," I grunt, turning round and walking back into the reception, I wrap my arm round Nate's shoulder as I plaster a smile onto my face. That's enough wallowing over Amora Archibald for one day.

I'll pick it back up again tomorrow.

AMORA ARCHIBALD

I knew the day was coming, it had been planned since my father took some nasty people down and bought them to justice. He knew he fucked up. He knew he messed with the wrong people.

But it was too late.

What's done is done.

All I had to do now was keep my head down and focus on my studies.

That was all I needed to do.

But yet, I didn't do what I was asked. No.

I was targeted, hunted and found myself the new obsession of the Knight brothers.

That's when my whole world came tumbling down.

I'm now being sent some asshole from America, named Titus, to watch over me twenty-four-seven, my freedom gone in a snap of the fingers, and my father is on a rampage because of what they're threatening to do.

Are you ready?

Are you sure?

Yes?

Then buckle the fuck up.

My father might be Xavier Archibald the third, but I am the spawn of him.

The Daughter of Satan.

I'm Amora Archibald, and this is my story.

Connie and Kaleb will return in The Loathing along with Nate, Keaton, Killian and Reese.

The Illicit Love Series is four books of interconnected standalones.

ACKNOWLEDGMENTS

My readers, thank you for reading The Resentment. I hope you loved Connie and Kaleb's story and enjoyed seeing a few familiar faces.

To my book bloggers, thank you for everything you do. Sharing my cover reveals, making and sharing edits and teasers for my stories, the recommendations of my books, the Reels, the TikTok videos and edits. You will never know how much your support means to me. It means the world to me. Thank you, thank you. I am forever grateful.

My BETA's, thank you for reading my first draft of The Resentment, you will never know how much you helped shape this story and how much I appreciated your feedback.

Ellie, thank you for everything.

Robyn, my PA. My friend. My dark and twisted sister. My otter. Thank you for putting up with me and not leaving me. I love you. Please don't leave me.
    Ever.

Lea, my editor. Thank you so much for doing such an amazing job like always, so grateful for you.

Leanne, once again you smashed this cover out of the park. I am so grateful that I messaged you back in 2018, and thank you for sticking with me, and for putting up with my indecisiveness.

My posies, Sophie and Harriet, thank you for joining my team and doing everything you do. I would be lost with out you. I know I have made friends for life.

Lastly, my husband. I wouldn't have started this journey if it wasn't for you. Thank you for believing in me and more importantly pushing me to not give up and to take the leap. None of this would have been possible without you.

If you enjoyed The Resentment, please tell your friends and share on your social media platforms, and please, if you can, be sure to leave a review.

Love you all x

Printed in Great Britain
by Amazon